W Th

CU00926679

The War Nurses

Lizzie Page

BASED ON A TRUE STORY

bookouture

Published by Bookouture in 2018

An imprint of StoryFire Ltd.

Carmelite House
50 Victoria Embankment
London EC4Y 0DZ

www.bookouture.com

The song 'Gilbert the Filbert' comes from the 1914 tune composed
by Herman Finck and Arthur Wimperis. Finck, Herman and
Wimperis, Arthur, 1874-1953 Gilbert the filbert. Allan & Co,
Melbourne, 1914. While every reasonable attempt has been made
to obtain permission, it has not been possible to trace or contact the
respective copyright holders.

ISBN: 978-1-78681-373-2
eBook ISBN: 978-1-78681-372-5

To all the War Nurses, everywhere.

Elsie Knocker – 'Gypsy', motorcyclist nurse, dare-devil mother – one of only two women on the Western Front and the best friend I ever had.

PROLOGUE

It was a perfect racecourse. The ground was firm and the weather conditions were fine, at least they were to start with. I was towards the middle of the pack, enjoying myself, biding my time, until suddenly the heavens opened and everything was blown wide apart.

I had guessed it might rain. My brother Uilleam said, 'It will be a catastrophe if it does,' but I love riding through a downpour. The earth churns beneath you as you fight just to stay upright. The bends become slippery and take your breath away. My more cautious rivals fell behind as I tore on.

The rain wasn't cold like it is in the Highlands, where I had gone to school. It felt good on my cheeks and trickling down my neck. I was on my Douglas motorbike, two years old and a beauty to behold, and he was puttering along beautifully. The gap between me and everyone else was growing.

And then, I don't know how it happened – maybe it was my goggles misting up like a January sky, maybe it was a message from God telling me to slow down – but somehow, I got lost. I had followed the signs fastidiously but what I didn't realise was that the signs weren't just for our race: that '2km' carved into a tree-trunk could have meant to anywhere.

So, I went one way, through brambles and rushes, low-hanging branches, and the pack went another. I was oblivious at first, enjoying the storm. It was only when I stopped completely, turned off the engine, looked around and could hear nothing except for the sound of one solitary bird chirruping that I realised: I had gone wrong.

Retracing my tracks, I got back to the course as fast as I could. Naturally the others were a good way ahead now.

I patted Douglas – we had lost a light in the undergrowth – and sped up. I thought of how Uilleam would laugh if I failed to finish, my father would be unsurprised and my mother would be pleased: 'Maybe it's best you stick to horses, Mairi?' and it drove me forward.

So I pressed on for I had nothing to lose. My thighs ached and the small of my back was pulsing but my reckless riding paid off… I found the pack again, beaten by the rain and moving at a sick snail's pace. First they were twenty yards ahead, then ten, then five, but they were either too timid or too tightly bunched to make a break for it. No one was going to box me in. I swerved clean on the outside. I was alone again, tearing up the open road with Douglas roaring underneath me.

Two more hairpin bends were accomplished, just the straight, smooth promise of the finishing line to go. I heard the crowd before I saw them. I thought I could make out Uilleam waving. He had assured me he would be at the end, with a slice of fruit cake.

I was ecstatic, but just as I pulled forward for the last triumphant few yards, someone came out of nowhere, like a burst of unexpected sunshine, and shot past me. She went by at a most *ridiculous* odds-defying speed. She was creating merry hell. She was lucky she didn't kill herself. I was left spluttering in the backdraught of black smoke.

It was Gypsy.

I knew Gypsy only by reputation back then: I had heard she was fast but not furious, a devil in a race. A hero on a bike. And off one.

After I got to know her I realised that, if anything, her reputation didn't do her justice: she was more magnificent, more extraordinary, more *everything* than anyone else. She would always be one step ahead of me.

There are people you come across in life who you feel like you have known forever. You sense their fears; you can read their dreams. That's how it eventually became with Gypsy and me. It felt like we were destined to be together. I used to think it was written in the stars that I would follow her to the ends of the earth.

And that, I suppose, is what I did.

For as long as I could.

CHAPTER ONE

Dr Munro came to my home in Chedington, Dorset, in the last week of August 1914.

'Is this the house of Mairi Chisholm – and her parents? Good, I have something I would like to talk about with you all.'

My mother rang the bell for tea, eyeing me uneasily. My father marched down from his study – he disliked an unexpected guest – but he shook hands with the stranger, greeting him warmly. This allowed my mother time to furiously mouth questions behind their rigid backs.

'What trouble are you in now?'

'I'm not!'

'How long has this been going on for?'

'Nothing's been going on!'

'Why didn't you tell us?'

It took me a good few moments before I realised that my mother thought the man had come to our house to propose to me!

I cringed and shrugged at her, hoping my raised shoulders conveyed, *Mother, I have never seen this man before in my life.*

Dr Munro was a tall, no-nonsense fella with a thick ginger moustache and a narrow build. Despite his height, he didn't take up much room. You wouldn't notice him in a crowd, so maybe I *had* seen him before and missed him? Perhaps he *had* seen me walking to the post office or maybe he had observed me in church. I often fancied I made a pretty picture, on my knees at the altar. And maybe without my having the faintest inkling, he had fallen in love with me? He might have knocked on doors around the village – it wouldn't be difficult to find my name and address, how many pious young redheads were living in Chedington? – then decided to make his approach.

That would require some nerve, a quality I did generally admire, but even so, it seemed… impulsive. Foolhardy even.

The idea of a secret admirer was unexpected, yet flattering. I had not experienced a lot of male interest, truth be told, although I had not been seeking it either. My brother Uilleam's friends had, on occasion, set my heart a-flutter but more because they were different to what I was used to, rather than because they had any particular appeal.

However, if I wanted an engagement – which I was not sure I did – then I would have preferred the gentleman to be at least thirty years younger than Dr Munro appeared. And perhaps someone who trimmed their facial hair more than occasionally. Would it be wrong to ask for broader shoulders too?

I knew that one of my mother's darkest fears was that I was 'unmarriageable'. In spite of my feelings, or rather lack of feelings, towards this doctor, it occurred to me how pleasant it would be to prove her wrong for once (not that she would admit it).

Yet Dr Munro seemed in no hurry to get to the question of why he was here. We drank tea in the drawing room and talked of the weather. Which was, as my mother was fond of saying, unusually *kind* for this time of year.

Inevitably, our conversation turned to the recent outbreak of war. Although I tried to keep up with the news on the wireless, most of what I knew about it came from my father, who was fervently in favour of military solutions to just about *anything*. I had never heard my father's opinions on the Belgians in particular before, but now he agreed with Dr Munro that they were a plucky people who must not be crushed. As for the Germans, I had in the past heard my father admire their manufacturing, but now they were 'methodical' and 'desperate'. Dr Munro disagreed here, saying it was 'six of one and half a dozen of the other', and my father, who instinctively knew when he had an audience, reined himself back. Now the Germans were not so much 'methodical' and 'desperate', but 'efficient' and 'dutiful'. Dr Munro added that he had spent many happy summers in Berlin, a centre of intellectual thinking and technological advance. Surprisingly, Father agreed. A shame to make enemies of such people.

Dr Munro thought, optimistically, that the war would be over by Christmas. My father, determined to out-do him even in positive thinking, said he would lay good money that it would be done and dusted before October's end.

As their conversation turned to Lord Kitchener – 'a superb commander' according to Dr Munro, 'The Kaiser underestimates him,' opined my father – I tried to imagine the wedding. I had always thought I'd marry in the Highlands – and since it appeared that Dr Munro may have some Scottish in him, there was no need to rethink the location. Certainly, my father would be wearing his military kilt and he would insist we listen to the meow of bagpipes. He might even have a go at playing himself. There would be a rare blue sky and sunshine. Rice would be thrown and nestle in my veil, Mother might cry into Father's handkerchiefs and Uilleam would tease us.

I liked the way Dr Munro talked. Perhaps not *quite* enough to marry the man and to listen to him talk all day long, but he had a compassionate and intelligent way about him. Shooting him side-ways glances, I imagined our wedding night. Me in a new nightdress with more – no, *fewer* – ribbons than usual, he in his… bedtime finery? Surely, he wouldn't want to do *it* at his age.

I was tempted by the vanilla macaroons, but I did not want to be proposed to with crumbs in my mouth, so I held off. However, I could have had ten vanilla macaroons by the time things came to a head. Father and Dr Munro discussed Russia – my father: 'The average Russian wants war no more than the average lamb wants to be slaughtered', Dr Munro: 'The average Russian has no more *say* in what he wants than the average lamb'; the French – my father:

'self-interested, self-serving', Dr Munro: 'It can appear that way'; even the Japs – my father: 'The Orientals are untrustworthy', Dr Munro: 'The Orientals are an unknown quantity'. We circled and circled the most important question, as though too timid to get into a cold bath, until finally, Dr Munro announced that he may as well get to the crux of it: he had something of sensitivity to ask of me and indeed of my parents.

Everything seemed to slow down. My father put his cup and saucer on the table with a loud clunk. I watched the rise and fall of my mother's chest and the flush on her throat, which crept up to her cheeks. I had no idea what to say. Perhaps I would ask if he would be opposed to a long engagement – wouldn't it be sensible to get to know each other properly? I couldn't imagine how my mother would respond to that. Nor him, in fact – he was old enough already. Might he not die if he had to wait very long?

Dr Munro did not get down on one knee, but he did walk the long expanse of the room to take the vacant leather armchair to my right.

'Mairi,' he said and I nodded resolutely. I had a feeling this was a once in a lifetime event for me and I was determined to treat the moment with respect. I might let down my poor suitor, yes, but I would let him down gently. Dr Munro was clearly a good man. The last thing I would want to do was humiliate him.

'Would you do us the honour of joining our war effort?'

It turned out that Dr Munro *did* indeed want my hand, but not in marriage. He had heard of my riding ability. The hairpin bends I negotiated so well. The competitions I won.

My courage.

This was what had piqued his interest.

I let out a breath. I didn't know if I was happy or sad. *Happy*, I thought. Disappointed, a little. Curious, a lot.

Dr Munro explained that he was setting up a 'Flying Ambulance Corps' to travel to Belgium and join the war effort over there.

'Flying?' I spluttered, still trying to catch up with the change in proposal.

'Well, not *exactly* flying.' He gave me a toothy smile. 'By that we mean... very fast motorised vehicles.'

'We had horse-drawn wagons in my day,' my father said nostalgically.

'Very good they were too,' agreed Dr Munro. 'But this is the future.'

Dr Munro made the undertaking sound relatively simple: retrieve soldiers in difficulty. Maybe give a hand on the ground.

'But I'm not a nurse,' I told him.

'You'll soon learn. It's only dressing wounds, that kind of thing. Most treatment will take place at the hospital.'

I explained that I had just started volunteering in London for the Women's Emergency Corps and I wasn't exactly available for... I didn't know what to call it. I decided on 'a trip'.

'Have you seen much action there?'

'In the city? Not yet, but—'

'Your driving – your bravery – is what we are looking for, Mairi.'

'Her brother Uilleam taught her to ride,' my mother said abruptly, as though aggrieved on behalf of her neglected son. 'He's very talented too—'

But Dr Munro interrupted with a list of my motorcycling achievements as though she hadn't spoken at all. 'First at Chichester, first in Bournemouth. And second at the Dorset... I heard it was an utter mudbath—'

'I may well have come first,' I said stubbornly, 'but for the signs.'

He smiled. My father smiled. My mother did not. She had never held with my riding motorbikes, and it was only after many hysterical threats (her) and desperate promises (me) that I had been allowed to join a club and to race at all.

'Would you like to go out to Flanders, Mairi? To do your bit?'

I imagined rescuing soldiers from the methodical and desperate but also intellectual and technologically advanced Germans. I imagined the gratitude on plucky Belgian faces. Dressing the occasional wound, driving up and down rough terrain – *were there any hills in the lowlands?* – Uilleam gruffly explaining to his friends, 'My sister is as tough as any fella.'

This was a far superior picture of the future than the one of me with rice in my veil and Dr Munro in his best pyjamas.

'What do you think?'

Everyone looked at me.

I didn't have to think. 'I'd love to,' I said.

*

'Impossible,' my mother said that evening. 'You are too young.' She would have much preferred a proposal even if I had turned it down. At least then there would have been a clean vote of confidence in my eligibility.

'I won't stop you travelling,' she said, 'but if you must have excitement, what is wrong with the Caribbean?' I knew she wanted me to go out to the Chisholm family plantation to watch over Uilleam, who would be heading there to manage it soon. Uillleam had been delaying his departure for years, but the outbreak of war had given him a much-needed shove. My mother pretended that she wanted me to go because it would be an interesting experience for me, and not because Uilleam couldn't be trusted not to burn the place down or get in a fight with the natives.

'The heat doesn't agree with me. Think of my freckles!' It was true, I was a proper Scottish-looking girl, with a mongrel cross of gold-and-red hair and white skin that demanded shade. I once overheard my mother tell her friend that my looks were an 'acquired taste'.

But my father, a Scottish-looking man if ever there were one, became my strange ally in this. For once, he took the position that if going to Flanders was what I wanted, then that was what I must do. As soon as he said this, my resolve hardened. I could feel the new sensation of his approval raining down on me. My mother was not going to get in its way.

*

We ate a light supper, the three of us still at odds. Uilleam was out with his local friends who I was not allowed to meet nor to mention. It was still warm and summery, but the sun was low in the sky and you knew autumn was snapping at its heels.

My father talked about opportunities to serve, dedication, a call to duty, a responsibility. He was only sixteen when he first went to fight in South Africa so I suppose, for him, at eighteen I was positively ancient.

As he was warming to his theme, it occurred to me, not for the first time, that my mother did not like him much.

What my father did not say was: *Thank goodness, one of the children takes after me. Pity it wasn't the boy but you make do with what you get.* But it was evident to me, and probably to my mother, that he was thinking this.

I basked in it. I demolished all the food in front of me, like a champion.

My mother fought back by not saying a word. Her bowed head sank lower, her parting down the middle so firm that it looked like a white thread of cotton. I was wondering if she would save her face from going into her soup, when finally, she rose from her chair with great dignity and walked out the room hissing, 'Mairi is *not* going anywhere.'

'Oh yes, she is,' said my father, and that, as they say, was that.

CHAPTER TWO

My mother refused me a single suitcase. I called her petty and accused her of wanting me to be a coward – the worst thing a Chisholm could be – but she would not bend. We were similar in that way. I could have persuaded the housekeeper to tell me where they were kept and taken one – but my mother would have been furious. She did not want to be complicit in my going and as a kindness to her I did not make her so.

In the end, I wrapped my supplies in a bedsheet and tied it to myself like I had seen native women do with their babies in Uilleam's secret copies of the *National Geographic*. My mother also refused to give me any money, but I had some savings – from winning races funnily enough – and Dr Munro had explained that I would receive a small service stipend. That would do me. I'd never been a big spender.

The only trouble I had packing was deciding which books to take. I had two Bibles: one well-thumbed edition passed down from my grandfather, and another, more ornate, that I had won at school for an essay on forgiveness. Although I feared it might get ruined, I decided to take the school one. The other could await my return by my bedside like the faithful friend it was. In addition, I took another old favourite, *Alice's Adventures in Wonderland*. I rather felt like Alice, following the white rabbit (or Dr Munro!) on a curious adventure.

The morning I departed, my mother refused to come out of her bedroom or say a word to me. Even my father was nowhere to be found but that was normal – well, normal for him. Once away, I resolved, I would write to let my mother know I had forgiven her. And that I was managing very well without her silly suitcase, thank you.

Later that day, I pushed Douglas up the gravelly front of the West Cliffe Hotel in Harwich on the east coast of England and found a shed in which to park him. Groups of people were milling around, some in civilian clothes, many, or maybe even most, in uniform. It seemed we weren't the only ones using the West Cliffe as a last stop before heading to the continent. Everyone seemed caught up with one another. Everyone appeared to be in the middle of some fascinating conversation.

I was hot and trembling. It had been a wonderful ride and I had enjoyed two picnics in the sunshine en route. Douglas was in peak condition. Both times I stopped, passers-by had come over to compliment him. Here though, no one gave me so much as a second glance.

A solidly built soldier was embracing a blond woman wearing a long red dress right in front of me. He kissed her fiercely and his hands travelled up her scarlet hem. A friend had once shown me blurry photographs she had found in her father's room of a naked woman with her lover, but I hadn't seen this behaviour in real life before. Throughout my journey to the coast I had felt grown-up, but seeing this reminded me that, in some areas, I was still inexperienced.

You can still turn back, I told myself. But I couldn't – if only because I wouldn't be able to stand the glee on my mother's face and the disappointment on my father's if I returned home.

Walking quickly past the fornicators, I haughtily said, 'Excuse me,' and the man replied, 'Excused!' The woman he was pawing laughed loudly.

In the large, dimly lit foyer of the hotel, staff at a mahogany reception desk were dealing with queues of animated people. On the wall behind them, there were rows of keys that they plucked at every few minutes before moving on to someone else. I stood nearby for some time, the staff skilfully ignoring me. I didn't know what I should do. Somehow, I felt bemused that I was there: that I had agreed to this.

Dr Munro eventually found me, thank goodness, as I was still tempted to turn homeward. He rubbed his hands when he saw me. The way he said, 'Well, well… here you are!' made me think he had doubted that I would turn up.

He was flanked by a couple, who he introduced as Helen and Arthur. 'From America,' Dr Munro explained.

As we shook hands, I found myself saying, 'I'm from Dorset, and Scotland, and from all over the place really!'

Dr Munro patted my shoulder and said, 'You must need a drink after all the goings-on…'

I nodded in agreement, although I wasn't sure which goings-on he meant.

Helen was stern-faced with tiny round glasses, and Arthur was too but the severe look suited him better. Two blinking owls, they were one of those couples who had grown to look like each other, like my late grandfather and Betty his pug. But while Helen's hair was wispy and tied away in a messy bun, Arthur's was thick and slightly too luxurious. They looked exhausted, especially Helen, and I thought –rather unfairly – *we haven't even begun.*

Straight away, Arthur told me he worked for the *New York Times.* I didn't know about that kind of thing so I asked what it was. He didn't titter but I could tell he thought my question was ignorant. *I* was ignorant.

'It's the largest newspaper in America,' he said. 'And probably in the world.'

'I see,' I said, vowing not to ask him anything of substance again. 'What do you do, Helen?'

'Me?' Helen seemed surprised to be spoken to. She pushed her glasses up her nose dreamily. 'I'll do anything.'

'Really, Helen?' Arthur laughed. 'Must you show your hand so soon?'

I had no idea what they were talking about. Helen took pity on me and added, 'I play piano. I love to read. I enjoy both poetry and plays.'

'She also sews.'

'Yes, Arthur,' she said, as though this was a private joke between them. 'I sew very well.'

I gazed at her, mystified. Had Dr Munro perhaps recruited me to the American Needlework Society by mistake?

She went on, 'I *have* done first aid, don't look worried, Mairi. But I dare say, my strengths may have more to do with morale.'

'Oh! Do you envisage a problem with… morale?'

Arthur put his arm around Helen, and for a horrible moment I worried that they too were going to engage in the open-mouthed kissing I had seen outside.

'Helen envisages a problem with *everything*, don't you, darling?'

Fortunately, Dr Munro was smoothly making his way over to us, although when I saw the tray of drinks my heart dropped further. I was not practised in drinking alcohol – for some reason people always assumed us motorcyclists were as good at downing spirits as we were with revolving wheels.

'Helen fears we're going to serve as undertakers rather than drivers and nurses.'

'It's just what I read in *your* paper, darling—'

'Absolute nonsense,' Dr Munro said firmly as he passed around the sherry. 'Cheers everybody. To Belgium.'

'To Belgium…'

I was to share a room that night with another member of our party, a woman yet to arrive: Mrs Elsie Knocker. Her name called to mind a bosomy housemistress. I hoped she would not tell me off *too* much. At school, I could sometimes win over the matronly types but I hoped I wouldn't have to here. I heard that she was thirty – a good deal older than me – and I hoped she would not see through my pretence of acting mature. Arthur had started calling me 'young Mairi,' which grated, but I didn't know how to correct him without confirming it.

After our drinks and with tiny droplets still perched on his moustache – *thank goodness we were not engaged!* – Dr Munro handed me my room key. Clutching it tightly, I made my way through the maze of corridors across carpets the colour of baked apples. Loud laughter came from some of the rooms, silence from others. In one, someone was whistling a song I knew from school: 'Give my Regards to Broadway'. It was strange to hear it here.

The hotel bedroom was small and sparse. Although I was initially disappointed, it felt appropriate. Luxury on my last night in England wouldn't have been right. I needed to prepare for the austerity of the future, though in truth who knew what to expect? I used to eavesdrop when my father told Uilleam wartime anecdotes, but he had a parent's way of making even the most interesting things sound boring, so I usually drifted off, preferring my own imaginings.

I put away my things neatly and tried to decide between the two single beds. I wanted to choose the worst one so I couldn't be accused of selfishly snagging the best, but there was little between them.

After about an hour, I went down to dinner where I met another member of our party, the charming Lady Dorothy. Pink-cheeked and smiley, 'Lady D', as we quickly came to call her, was easy to talk to and so reassuring that – despite her incongruous hat with cherries on the top – after five minutes in her company I grew assured that everything was going to be *utterly marvellous*.

When I quietly turned down Dr Munro's offer of whiskey, Lady D confided that she too was not a great drinker and thought it a pity liquor was so fashionable. She also couldn't believe I was only eighteen, which I decided, coming from her, was a compliment. We didn't talk about the war – a relief, for I kept forgetting whose side everybody was on or indeed where everything in Europe was on the map – but instead discussed our respective journeys to Harwich. She thought trains were 'marvellous' and added quietly that she had taken the opportunity to leave 'Votes for Women' leaflets on each of the seats.

'You didn't,' I said, uncertain if this was a joke. I had never – to my knowledge – met anyone who would do anything like that before.

'I most certainly did,' she said, pleased with herself. 'I may leave some here too!'

Fortunately, Dr Munro joined in, urging us to explore the gardens later. 'The azalea japonica is exquisite!'

I nodded obediently and Lady D murmured, 'Very good, Hector.'

I wondered if I too should call him Hector but decided against it. My mother would say I was being 'presumptuous', although I doubt she would have said the same about Lady D, suffragette or not.

I was eating bread and butter pudding – which, frankly, could have done with a good ten more minutes in the oven – when I noticed a woman in the doorway of the dining room waving – *at us?* I wasn't quite sure. She weaved her way between the tables towards our group. She was wearing a brown leather coat buttoned all the way down over a forest-green skirt or dress, and was clearly hot off her bike. Nearer our table she removed her helmet, goggles and the coat. (It *was* a dress underneath, a gorgeous one.) I had never seen anyone so cavalier about disrobing in a restaurant. I decided she must be either very posh or not posh at all – those of us in the middle wouldn't dream of making such an exhibition of ourselves.

The waiters with their knuckles of pork, the waitresses with their fish knives, even the soldiers who had been pawing at their wives' hems watched her. She was taller than most – longer, rangier somehow – and not *pretty* as such, but definitely compelling. She had dark wavy hair, and eyes the colour of khaki. It gave me a thrill to see that we were wearing the same type of boot.

'This is Elsie Knocker. This is Mairi Chisholm. You will be sharing.'

The prodigal room-mate was nothing like a housemistress or indeed anyone I had met at school. She was impossibly glamorous, especially for a thirty-year-old!

She looked at me and said, 'Please say you don't snore.' And with a shock I realised – more from her languid voice and her calm, self-confident expression than her actual looks – who she was.

'Gypsy?'

'Ye-es?'

'Oh gosh, we've actually met before—'

'Have we?' she said. 'I don't…'

I blushed. It seemed unfair that she had made such an impression on me that day and I had left none on her. She couldn't even recollect the first thing about me! *Maybe*, I thought leniently, *it was because I looked so different now*. I had a far more fashionable hairstyle than that day in the downpour. No more mud-splattered cheeks. I had tried to make an effort for the journey – maybe I had succeeded.

'The motor track. Women's stiff reliability trial? Dorset?'

Elsie narrowed her eyes. 'Did I beat you?'

'Only just.'

Elsie smiled. 'Good.'

*

We *had* actually chatted that day, though. It wasn't like we were complete strangers. Uilleam had been eager to meet the lady who handled her motorcycle like a dream *and* had the extraordinary looks.

'They call her Gypsy,' he said, awed.

'I know,' I told him. 'Calm down, you look like Bessie when she's discovered a bone.'

We found her in the tea tent. The canvas roof was sagging under the weight of the rain and from each corner a steady stream of water sluiced down. Elsie was sheltering next to a table, surveying the diminished spread. More unexpectedly, she was hand in hand with a small, earnest-faced boy. Dark-haired, dark-eyed, he barely came up to her belted waist.

'Well done,' I said.

'Thank you.'

She eyed me kindly. I realised she probably thought I was a mere slip of a thing. People always did.

'Do you race?'

'Yes and… I was only five seconds behind you.' *Hadn't she seen?*

'No prizes for coming second,' she said, but her face was still friendly enough.

'Well,' I said uncertainly, 'I got two shillings.'

She laughed so I did too. I liked her.

The boy tugged her hand and she knelt for him to whisper in her ear. Then she looked him in the eyes as though they were talking through issues of national importance. 'One more, but it's the last. Understand?'

He made his way joyfully over to the depleted cake stand.

'Boys have such appetites.'

And then some other people came over wanting to take Elsie to be photographed. I expected her to refuse or at least to say 'How dreary!', but she grinned at me and raised her dark eyebrows at Uilleam: 'Let me just do my hair.'

There were no photos for coming second.

As we walked away, Uilleam whispered that it was a pity she was married, and I teased him: 'If she weren't, do you think she would consider *you*?' He just laughed. My handsome brother – he takes after our mother in looks – is the Chisholm clan's only son. He did not lack confidence with ladies or in life, but surely he must have known even he wouldn't stand a chance with a woman like Gypsy?

*

Coffees were served. Arthur and Helen whispered throughout. I believe they didn't think much of us. I concentrated on my coffee. At home, I wasn't allowed it – at least, I was never offered it. I decided that coffee would, in future, be 'my drink'. After that we had wonderful mouth-burning mints, then I offered to take Elsie to our room. It was strange leading her down the corridors as though I were in charge. Elsie surveyed the room while I waited for her verdict. 'It's fine,' she said, and I replied, 'I thought so too!' a little overenthusiastically.

Elsie didn't express an opinion on the sleeping arrangements so I felt I hadn't made a faux pas. She unpacked briskly, lit a cigarette, then stood staring out the window. Our room was at the back of the hotel overlooking the manicured lawn and presumably the Japanese azaleas. For a short moment, it was as though she had forgotten I was there. Then abruptly, she turned, shooting me her winner's smile.

'Smoke?'

I shivered. 'I'm too young.'

'Not too young to volunteer?'

'My father always said I was the most pig-headed child.'

Elsie didn't say anything but blew circles of smoke. I wished I hadn't said the word 'child'. It seemed to reverberate around the walls and bounce on the beds. I tried again. 'I have a lot to offer the war effort.'

Elsie smiled to herself. 'I'm sure you do…'

'You were with a little boy; I remember, at Dorset?'

'Kenneth? Yes.'

'Charming.' She wasn't forthcoming on the details but I continued. 'He's your son?'

'Of course.'

'How old is he?'

'Six.'

'Aah,' I said. *What should I say to that?* 'That's a lovely age.'

She smiled. Her cigarette was stained with lipstick.

I ploughed on. 'Your husband didn't mind you joining the effort then?'

I expected her to say 'We'll only be in Belgium for two or three months,' which is what everyone (apart from Mother) had been saying, but instead she replied flatly, 'I don't have a husband.'

That took me by surprise. A young widow was a rarity. 'Oh?'

'We lost him. In Java.'

I thought of the *New York Times*, unbeknown to me, one of the World's Largest Newspapers, and decided, *I am not going to show myself up again by asking what Java is.* Instead I said, 'Oh. I'm so sorry.'

*

The others were taking a walk but we decided not to join them. As Elsie said pointedly, 'We will see plenty of them soon enough!' Instead, she suggested she go and get some drinks to have in our room and even though I didn't want any more alcohol, I agreed.

While I was waiting, I wrote a letter to my mother, beginning, dramatically: '*My last day on English soil*'. I explained that the group were spiffing. '*You would like them,*' I wrote, feeling she'd like Lady D if not the others. I didn't mention the suitcase – foolish to hold a grudge when I was on the precipice of a great adventure.

Even after I had finished, Elsie still hadn't come back, so I dashed off a letter to Uilleam too, gloating that I was sharing a room with none other than the infamous motorcycling dare-devil 'Gypsy'. I could just imagine his face on reading it! He always hated to be left out of the fun.

Some time later Elsie still hadn't returned, so I decided to go and check that everything was fine.

Retracing our steps through the shadowy passages of the hotel, I felt brave, as though I were already on a rescue mission. It was after eleven at night – I rarely stayed up so late – and all the rooms were quiet now.

There were still a few people milling around downstairs, but I picked her out right away, talking with a man in uniform. He held his arm up against the wall, right over her. I couldn't tell if it was protective or menacing or both.

'Elsie?'

The soldier straightened when he saw me. Elsie flattened her hair.

'Mairi, goodness, have I been gone an age?'

'Is this your sister?' demanded the soldier. His accent was somehow not as handsome as he was.

She replied, 'Kind of, right, Mairi?'

I didn't know what to make of her. All this smoking, drinking and telling lies to strange men would have made my father's hair stand on end. I hesitated but she said, 'I'm coming now.'

I returned to our room and moments later she was there too, with a bottle and two glasses on a sopping tray. What I had seen was much on my mind, but I figured, *the Bible doesn't address this directly. It's not as if there are commandments about smoking and drinking and telling lies to strange men.* And maybe, hers wasn't a *real* lie, maybe we were *kind* of sisters…

As we drank, Elsie asked what I thought of the other members of our group.

'Arthur seems nice.' What I was actually thinking was, *he's good-looking*, but I didn't like to say.

'He's an intellectual.' The way she said it made it seem like that wasn't a good thing.

'Helen is clever.'

'A writer,' she said dismissively. 'Fiction.'

'Lady D is…' I was going to say 'a suffragette', but decided on 'lovely' instead.

'Too lovely for us. I give her six weeks at most.'

'Dr Munro is… kind?'

'But mad. Completely mad as a…'

I felt this was a step too far and was just about to tell her so when I heard a yelp from outside. I froze. *Had the war come to England?*

Elsie got to the window first, then beckoned me to have a look. There I saw Dr Munro – the same Dr Munro who promised my father duty and decorum above all else – wearing only his long johns and standing with legs wide apart, reaching forward to his toes. I wondered if he was stuck, but then he moved – arching from one side to the other while letting out more whoops.

'I believe that's... saluting the moon. Or is it downward dog? Either way, we're lucky he's dressed; he usually likes to do his exercises *sans* clothes.'

'Mad as... a box of frogs?'

Elsie took my hand, and I let her, surprised. No one had held my hand for a long time. My family did not do touching. For a moment, we stood together like that at the window and I remembered her standing the same way with her son.

'You and I are going to have such a time,' she murmured. She turned back to the tray. 'Another drink?'

Later in bed, I had to put my foot down on the floor to stop the world from spinning. Alcohol was good. Adventures were great. And I kept thinking about what Elsie had said about us being *sisters*. To think previously Uilleam had been enough for me! What a fool I was. How I had missed out by only having one silly brother. I couldn't believe I had not only acquired a sister today, but such a splendid one at that.

I wanted to ask Elsie something, but the harder I tried to make my words sound normal, the more wobbly and out of control they came out.

'Gypsy, no, Elsie...'

She was standing by the window, still smoking. 'What?'

'No-oo, I can't say it...' I slurred.

'Sisters can tell each other everything!' Elsie said, and I thought, *I'm going to remember that forever.*

'So… can it be true… our flying ambulance corps is… *gulp*… made up of a… *burp*… naturist, a pianist, a journalist, a lady and a… widowed mother?'

We both giggled. I couldn't stop giggling. What a funny place this world was! Even if it did whirl somewhat.

'And a non-smoking schoolgirl, yes.'

'I'm not a schoolgirl any more!' Laughing, I sat bolt upright. Bad idea. The churning got faster and faster. I kept thinking of the plump cherries on Lady D's hat.

'Watch out Germans! We're on our way!' Elsie said sarcastically.

'We are sooo ridiculous…' I continued.

'We're not though, Mairi. Who do you think the soldiers are but farm-boys, postmen and train drivers?'

That seemed incredible to me. That we weren't real nurses, I could just about accept, but the idea that soldiers weren't *real* soldiers I could not.

'Won't we be a laughing stock out there?'

'I don't mind being a laughing stock,' retorted Elsie drily. 'I just don't fancy coming back as chicken stock.'

'I dare say, Kenneth would rather his mother stayed alive too…' I added, feeling that was a profound thing to say. The fact that Elsie was an actual mother was incredible to me. She wasn't like *my* mother and she wasn't like the mothers of the girls I knew. I had so many questions but for now the ones that pushed themselves to the forefront of my mind were: *Why did I drink that last one? Am I squiffy? Or am I, perhaps, not squiffy, but dying?*

'Maybe I'll find a rich and plucky Belgian to be a father for him,' Elsie said, then snorted. 'Although the sight of Munro just now might have put me off men forever.'

'Gypsy,' I murmured, and I was about to ask how she had acquired her exotic nickname when I realised I had something more urgent to contend with.

I couldn't keep it in any more. I ran out the room, down the corridor and thumped on the door of the lav at the end. Thank goodness, no one was in there, else I don't know what I would have done. I pushed through and knelt at the bowl as though I were about to pray. The floor was cold and damp but I wouldn't let myself think about that. I made it just in time. The drinks, the coffee, the dinner, the dessert, the stupidly wonderful mints, all sprayed out of me.

When I woke up some time later, I was in the hotel bed, wearing my nightdress (fewer ribbons) tucked up under smooth unfamiliar blankets, with no recollection of how I had got there. There was a glass of water on top of my Bible on the bedside table, which I gulped down thirstily. *How could she have known how much I needed that?* I thought, wondrously. I looked over to the other bed to whisper my appreciation.

Elsie was not there.

CHAPTER THREE

The SS *Princess Clementine* looked magnificent, a white hulk gleaming in the autumn sunshine. I had never seen a ship so big before: it was about three times the size of my old school building (which was by no means small). As we drew closer, I could just make out uniformed men hanging off her railings, waving at the people gathered behind the barriers on the port. Some people on land were shouting up to them.

'Love you, Ernie!'

'You'll be back soon, Bernard!'

Dr Munro had given us Red Cross armbands and as we pushed our motorcycles up the gangplanks, some of the watching people clapped us. I was already emotional and these gestures of support made me more so. I was torn between feeling a fraud – I had done nothing yet – and feeling proud of myself. My grey overcoat felt heavy for the time of year but that too added to my air of *person with responsibility*. And then some of the men already on board whistled at us. I couldn't believe it when Elsie put her fingers in her mouth and gave a full-bodied whistle back. My mother would have been horrified.

'What are you doing?'

She shrugged. 'How do *they* like being called like a dog?'

Elsie's motorcycle was a powerful Chater-Lea, complete with a sidecar. Elsewhere, Arthur and Helen were driving our two ambulances onboard: a converted Daimler and a Fiat. I was looking forward to having a go at driving them both, especially the Daimler, which had a much bigger engine than I was used to.

'You're looking rather green around the gills,' Dr Munro commented.

'She's seasick,' said Elsie.

Squinting at me, he said, 'We haven't gone anywhere yet.'

'I'm a real landlubber,' I muttered, not daring to look at either of them. *I will never drink alcohol again.*

When I had asked Elsie where she had gone during the night, she said, 'Out for some air,' but also 'I'm afraid I sleep badly.' I knew from Uilleam that giving two reasons for *anything* was as good as an admission of guilt but she just smiled at me. She was as bonny and blithe that morning as if she had had a full night's sleep. *That smile isn't cricket*, I thought. It gave her an unfair advantage.

We sat in the middle deck because Dr Munro thought it best we stayed out of the wind. 'We don't want to catch colds,' he warned firmly. I wouldn't dare. The sea was smooth though and thankfully, my fears that I would be rocked or thrown around proved unfounded. Groups of soldiers were talking and laughing, some had their feet up on the tables and although it was before ten, some were drinking beer.

Dr Munro was telling us about the actual Princess Clementine for whom the ship was named. She was the third daughter of King Leopold of Belgium; her father gave her independence to travel but without her mother's approval. She later wrote, thanking him, saying '*Thanks to you, I have been able to find happiness.*'

I wondered if Dr Munro was retelling this for my benefit? He must have known how my mother would react to this whole escapade of ours. But he didn't meet my eye, and had soon moved on to an equally long-winded history of the HMS *Ulysses*.

Still slightly nauseous, I went for a walk. Arthur and Helen had grabbed chairs some way away on a lower deck. As he saw me, I'm sure Arthur buried his face in the newspaper so I wouldn't notice him. Nevertheless, I had nowhere else to go and so I approached them; Helen at least gave me a welcoming smile. On the front page of Arthur's paper, the headline read that sugar prices were rising. This was grand news for plantation owners in the Caribbean. I was about to say that my father would be delighted, but I hesitated. Much as it was a conversation-starter, I had a feeling that Arthur already had me down as a 'spoilt thing'.

Helen, as ever, was writing in her notepad. Her swirly notes were so messy that I wondered how she could ever read them back.

'May I look?'

Reluctantly, she passed it over. I could just make out '*A dark, stormy night on the SS* Clementine.'

'Stormy?' I looked at her, mystified.

'Well.' She shrugged. 'I do exaggerate sometimes.'

*

The more time I spent with the group, the more worried I became about how we would manage in Belgium. We just seemed so ill-prepared. At breakfast back in the hotel, Arthur, bad-tempered and yawning, had made a fuss over the eggs. They had not been poached to his taste. Lady D had taken some bread that was not meant for our table and the waiter had come to ask for it back. There was an altercation. Dr Munro was late for breakfast, because he had been doing exercises in the hotel garden again. Helen seemed apart from everything, as though she was an observer not a participant – in this way she reminded me of my mother. Elsie ate a single rasher of bacon, then pushed the greasy plate away. She seemed to live on cigarettes. Although I thought she was adorable, I admit that I was especially unconvinced by what Elsie might be bringing to the corps. If she had been at home with Kenneth for the last six years, then of course she might be good with children, and she was *definitely* good with men, and at consuming cigarettes and alcohol, and at racing motorcycles she was probably unparalleled, of course, but apart from that…

Twenty minutes or so later, I climbed to the upper deck to where I could look out at the vastness of the English Channel. I was moving further away from home, and although I was apprehensive, it felt right. I had felt stifled living with my parents; even excursions with Uilleam or motorcycle races couldn't allay that. The London war-work hadn't been busy enough; I needed stimulation. The sun made dappled patterns on the water, which was a soothing blue-grey. My headache had tapered off. I was beginning to feel like myself again.

I spotted Elsie chatting to a soldier with oily hair and the sort of pencil-thin moustache that was popular now. Would I always find her enjoying some flirtation or another? She waved to me but I didn't go over to them, so she left the fella and came to me, which I thought was nice. She didn't have to.

She had run out of cigarettes earlier, but now she had a handful. 'That man just gave you them?'

'Oh Mairi, Mairi, Mairi, I'm going to have such fun with you.'

She didn't make sense sometimes, but then, I supposed, not everything had to. Together we looked out to sea and agreed it was a beautiful day for a sail.

Lady D had brought wrapped corned-beef sandwiches from the hotel and although it was early for lunch, I tucked in royally. She also gave me some of the mints she knew I'd liked from the night before. 'Save them, Mairi,' she said, 'there might not be mints where we're going…' She looked at me with sympathetic eyes. I looked away. I hate it when people feel sorry for me. I wanted to say that I already knew about deprivation – after all, I had been at boarding school from the age of nine – but she had already gone to stand by the steamed-up windows, a melancholy expression on her pretty face.

Dr Munro was launching into the life story of another ship when Helen appeared, full of self-importance, her arm around a shaking young soldier. He had tufty white-blond hair, tears spilling down

his freckly cheeks and a nose so large that I initially assumed that
was where his problem lay. But it wasn't that. He had fallen down
the ship's stairs and hurt his arm.

'Should we do something?' I nudged Elsie.

'Helen's got it under control,' she replied, which I guessed meant
she hadn't a clue what to do.

'That's a break,' Helen confirmed as she rummaged among our
first-aid boxes before opening one. The boy was crying harder. Tears
stuck to his eyelashes, giving the impression of a frightened calf. It
was probably his first time away from his mum. Helen gave him
some medicine, then tied up his arm with a splint and bandages.
She did a surprisingly neat job and I could see she was pleased with
it herself. I was also impressed by how gentle she was with him.
She asked him questions about himself: his name was Jim – Jim
Mason – he was eighteen, he had never been on a ship before. I
didn't realise at first that the questioning was not mere prying, but
was designed to distract him from the issue at hand – or rather
of his painful arm. When I did realise, I thought it was clever of
Helen. In fact, she had done everything far better than I could have.
I had a sinking feeling that maybe Elsie and I would be the weaker
members of the corps.

There wasn't much I could do, but I passed him a mint. Briefly, his
sad eyes lit up, but even better, Lady D nodded approvingly at me.

Helen took off with poor old Jim back to his troop. Arthur raised
his eyebrows at us. Each time he turned a page in his paper, he licked
his finger first. His pink tongue, peeping out every few minutes,
made me feel sick again.

'What a disaster: sent back home to his mum and dad while
everyone else has a most spiffing adventure,' I said cheerily.

'Hmm,' said Dr Munro, pouring more whiskey. 'Not everyone
likes to get… *stuck in.*'

'How do you mean?'

'I've seen cases like that before.'

He didn't say any more and I didn't like to press him. Later, I went and looked at the stairs where Helen said he had fallen. They were pretty steep and the surface was slippery.

Land was ahoy! And there were loads of small fishing boats and larger cargo boats and all sorts of vessels nose-to-nose in Ostend harbour.

'I want to speak to you all before we disembark,' Dr Munro said. I groaned inwardly. I wanted to check that Douglas had weathered the journey. *Who knew there would be so much waiting around?* Still, it was easier to trust Dr Munro when he was in his uniform with its shiny buttons. It gave him a certain authority. His cheeks were pink and his hair windswept like a golden scarf.

'The important thing is that we work as a group, a tight-knit group. In a way, it's like a marriage. Consideration and respect for each other are a must.'

Elsie whispered. 'Do you think *he* ever married?'

I wanted to laugh. I thought of his ungainly cat-stretching on the lawn. 'I doubt it.'

Then I remembered how I had not only imagined that Dr Munro had come to propose to me, but I had considered asking for a long engagement! I felt my face flush. I couldn't imagine Elsie making that kind of vain mistake.

'Inevitably, things can cause bad feeling within the group. Money, for instance, can cause discord.' He paused and surveyed us as though he were seeking out a dissenter. 'Well, we don't have much, so that shouldn't be an issue.'

Lady D sighed. Arthur and Helen raised eyebrows – and consequently matching spectacles – at each other.

'And hanky-panky.' He paused.

I dared not look at Elsie's expression. I wondered what she would make of *that* phrasing.

'Finally, as Dr Freud would say, "Ego".'

'Dr Freud' and 'Ego' joined the growing list of things I had never heard of before. I squinted, trying to guess what it meant. *Ego – go – I go – Egg?*

'Please leave your egos at home. Forget what is best for us as individuals and think firstly of the group. In a few minutes, we shall disembark in Belgium. May God be with us.'

'May God be with us,' Lady D and I repeated enthusiastically. *I knew what that meant!* It wasn't until later that I realised that the others had stayed silent.

*

I hadn't anticipated the sheer number of people going the other way. It was only three weeks since the war had started; how could this many people be on the move? There were motorcars and wagons, there were carthorses and yappy dogs, bicycles and tricycles, massive trunks like treasure chests, old men with medals on their blazers, pregnant women and babies in wobbly prams, all waiting to be loaded onto boats. I even saw what I fancied to be a rare Henderson Four motorcycle. Uilleam would be annoyed to have missed that!

'They want to get to England,' Lady D said knowledgeably.

'They're Belgian?'

'Yes.' She paused. 'I hope they receive a good welcome.'

The waiting children ran back and forth on the sand in wooden clogs, enjoying the sprays of salty water. The adults looked at them without smiling or even talking, although sometimes they called a child back, admonishing them, perhaps, for going too far. It was strange to think that we were going to wherever it was that they were running from.

'War is terrible,' said Lady D.

Perhaps, I thought, crunching another mint and thinking of the Henderson Four, *though if it's like this, it won't be too bad.*

*

It transpired we didn't have enough petrol for the ambulances, which I found disturbing: I had thought we were better prepared than that. At the port, Dr Munro and Arthur ran around looking for someone who could help. Dr Munro's French was excellent, Arthur's not so much. I had only learned French at school, but I was hopeful that I would be able to make myself understood – rather more than Arthur – *le pauvre*!

Eventually, Elsie grew fed up with her task of 'guarding the vehicles' and left to approach a corpulent Belgian colonel. I'm not sure what happened, but he agreed to give us enough fuel, he estimated, to get our vehicles clear to Ghent. From there, we would be on our own.

'What did he say?' I asked as Elsie walked victoriously over with a can in each hand.

'He said, "Oh, if only I wasn't a married man!"' She was still laughing as she filled up the tanks. Dr Munro and Arthur didn't say anything.

Dr Munro took the Daimler, Lady D took her turn at the wheel of the Fiat, but Arthur looked longingly at Douglas and asked for a go. I didn't like to refuse. I was realising that all the vehicles were now regarded as communal, and what had been a glorious present to myself in July had now been subsumed into the war effort. Helen went with Lady D. I could have gone with Dr Munro, of course, but Elsie proposed I go in her sidecar, which was a relief. Dr Munro was a master of many things but he was a stranger to small talk.

'Do you think we'll be able to cope once we get there?' I asked Elsie as we pulled on helmets and goggles.

'We'll do fine,' answered Elsie airily. She looked down at me. 'Blasted lock doesn't work.'

I resolved to fix it for her as soon as I had the chance. I would always leap at any opportunity to do something for her.

'I just wish we had some training before we left, don't you?'

Elsie looked surprised. 'How do you mean?'

'We don't know the first thing about nursing!' I gave a hollow laugh.

Elsie paused. 'I don't know the first thing about *war* nursing, no,' she said, chosing her words carefully, 'but I trained at the children's hospital in Sevenoaks and served as a midwife at Queen Charlotte's.'

'Oh,' I said, tugging at the door handle. 'I may know a way to fix this lock.'

So it was just me.

We drove away in our queer convoy. I kept an eye on Arthur but I needn't have worried. He was a proficient rider. Belgium was an incredibly flat country, with tidy fields and tree-lined roads. I felt increasingly excited now I was here, not only on foreign soil but also travelling towards a war zone!

At first there was little evidence that the Germans had invaded the country – indeed, had managed to occupy most of it. However, after we had been on the move for about an hour, we spied a huge crater by the side of the road. We pulled over to examine it. It was about three metres wide and two metres deep.

Dr Munro shook his head sadly. 'The shell that did this must have been very large. Imagine if you were nearby, how the ground must have shaken beneath your feet!'

I was not upset to see it. Until now our existence as the flying ambulance corps had felt like a fairy story. The mass exodus at the port may have been an over-reaction – *perhaps everyone was just making a to-do about nothing.*

This shell hole revealed they were not.

We continued with our journey, although we did not swap drivers as I had hoped. I carried on, remarking excitedly about the sounds and sights – 'Wasn't the landscape rather like England?'– until Elsie turned to me, shouting over the engine:

'You know I can't hear a word you are saying!'

*

An hour later, I was keen for a wash and regretting having lunched so early. Dr Munro had mentioned the possibility of a meat stew for supper and I was hoping it would be that. With potatoes, cabbage and cauliflower, please. Back home, my mother would be tucking into venison, pork or chicken in a rich gravy. She would be picking at the vegetables. (Mother had an aversion to food that wasn't meat or pudding.) Father might be brandishing his fork, ranting about politics or praising Lord Kitchener. I wondered if Mother and Father would be speaking to each other now. Mother had sent Father to Coventry for less than this in the past. Or Uilleam might be up in his room, looking at his reflection in the mirror – I always teased my brother that nothing fascinated him so much as his own hand-some face. I supposed he would be preparing for his own imminent voyage – across the Atlantic Ocean in an even bigger ship than the *Clementine* – although, knowing my brother, he would be leaving his preparations to someone else!

I thought we would settle directly into quarters in Ghent, but as we travelled down another pretty road with evenly pruned hedges, I suddenly noticed that it was unusually quiet. There were hardly any carriages, there were hardly any cars, there were hardly any people, and I wondered if we had taken a wrong turn. The last sign I had seen read 'Nazareth' and it had given me pleasure to see a biblically named town in Belgium. A reminder that God was with us. Just as I was going to shout this to Elsie, a woman ran out into the road in front of us. She may have heard our noisy convoy coming past, or maybe it was coincidence. She was wearing nurse's overalls. She stood dead in the exact path of the Daimler, the same way I have seen panicked foxes with piercing yellow eyes do at sunrise.

Dr Munro had the presence of mind both to forcefully brake and to swing the car away from this sudden obstruction. Elsie swerved similarly with the Chater-Lea and I felt myself lift up into the air before the sidecar bumped smack, back into the ground.

'Heavens!' she cried. 'Are you all right, Mairi?'

I said I was super. It was quite a thrill. Elsie jumped off her bike. I was still fiddling with the stubborn lock of the sidecar when Elsie reached the woman, then ran past her towards a small low-roofed building. I decided to leave the lock and, proud of my ingenuity, hopped over the top of the sidecar instead.

As I drew closer, I saw that the woman's nursing uniform was covered in so much blood it looked like a butcher's apron.

Everyone was already in the hall. I was the last in. I couldn't believe my eyes.

We were in a makeshift hospital, if you could call it that. All around were rows of men laid out on the floor. Some dead, some dying, men with their jaws blown off, arms and legs mutilated. Some were in uniform, most were not. Some hadn't only been shot at, but stripped or stabbed too.

Everyone else set to doing something. Arthur and Helen must have slipped back out to the cars, because they reappeared loaded up with our first-aid boxes. Dr Munro was kneeling by someone's side unravelling bandages. Lady D was down on the floor tending to a blasted eye. Elsie was covering another wounded soldier with one of our towels. Everyone was doing something, except me. I just froze. I didn't know what to do, and even if I had, I didn't know what to do it with.

'What's *Mairi* doing?' someone – Arthur? – asked and I heard Elsie, 'She'll buck up soon.' I wanted to say something, but I had lost the ability to speak. Strange thoughts swirled in my head. My father talking about the line of poplar trees by the Modder River. How the men had failed to spy the Boers and had to lie prone on the veld – if they moved they would be fired upon.

'What did you do, Father?'

'I smoked my pipe.'

I saw a tin bucket, grabbed it and ran out the back door. I vomited copiously, the second time in two days. My breakfast, the sandwiches, the mints, everything.

How did I think I could do this? I, who had only practised slings at school on Katherine McDonald (and only got a B+ at that)?

I retched and retched again, wiping my mouth on my sleeve. Pouring my guts out.

My father: '*What would you have done at Belmont, Uilleam?*'

'*I'm not sure…*'

'*I fixed my bayonets, and just saw their heels…*'

I suddenly saw long, shiny boots in the mud. Elsie was standing over me. I breathed in and out, steadying myself. I didn't want to make myself look even more of a fool than I already had.

'They've been massacred,' I said and puked again.

Why didn't my father warn me that there were such things as a face without a nose? How could that be?

'I want to go home…' I continued. Tears filled my eyes, my throat. I sounded like the feeble child I had so desperately been trying not to be, but I didn't care. I had never felt so powerless. They had chosen the wrong person for the job.

'There's not a safe passage out any more, Mairi.'

'But it's… hopeless.'

Spots of blood were on the ground. I eyed the splattered trail to a chestnut horse that stared steadily ahead. Clipped to it was a wooden carriage. There were still two men in the carriage, leaning together, heads close. Did anyone know about them?

'Just do your best.'

I don't have a best. I don't even have a worst.

'I've never done anything like this before.'

'Munro wouldn't have selected you if he didn't think you would be up to the task.'

I lifted my head up from the bucket, averting my eyes from the staring horse.

'How do you mean?'

'He said: "Despite her youth and quiet manner Mairi is as cool as a cucumber".'

'Dr Munro said that?'

'He said you've always been a trooper. And a damn loyal friend.'

The horse swished its tail. *Flies*, I thought. *Black hungry flies.* The men in the carriage hadn't moved a jot. Men alive a few hours ago, worrying about their dinner, their uniforms, their girlfriends… and now they weren't.

'But I don't know Dr Munro! I only met him the one time when he asked me to join. How would he possibly know this about me?'

I had caught her out. Elsie squatted next to me. She didn't recoil from the smell in the pail, which I continued to grip on to for dear life.

'You ride, don't you?' she said. 'They say you are fearless.'

'That's different,' I whimpered.

'You were educated in the Highlands?'

'So?'

'You'll be stronger than most and with a darn sight more common sense.'

I didn't know about that. I only knew that whatever I had just said, I couldn't go back home now. Not like the broken boy on the ship – I couldn't face my parents, their battles over me. I coughed. Of course, I was going to have to go back into that terrible place. I was going to do the right thing. Put others first. And I *would* find the strength. From the place that always gave me strength. *How had I forgotten that?*

Elsie stood up. She looked composed: *No doubt the sort of woman a Belgian colonel would be delighted to fornicate with*, I thought wildly. I dared take one hand from the bucket to grab her slender wrist.

'Would you pray with me, Elsie?'

'No,' she said. 'Thank you.'

I thought in that polite *thank you,* there was still hope, so I pushed on. 'Let's ask God to keep us safe…'

When people didn't believe, it worried me. God might not deign to perform goodness if only a few people had faith in him. I suppose it was silly insecurity, but I doubted Lady D and I would be enough to keep God interested by ourselves. We needed Elsie.

She shook her head. '*I'll* keep us safe, Mairi.'

'I am going to pray now.'

This is not just any town, this is *Nazareth*, I thought. I should have remembered.

'Very well.'

Yea, though I walk through the valley of the shadow of death; I will fear no evil: for thou art with me…

Elsie didn't move away, so maybe she wanted me to pray for her even if she wouldn't pray herself.

'Gypsy, I mean Elsie?'

She stroked my hair. 'I'm sorry Mairi, but we need that bucket.'

CHAPTER FOUR

After the resident nurses declared the situation under control, we continued on to the military hospital in Ghent. It was a beautiful old building with large, rectangular windows and everything was industrious and orderly. It was an enormous relief to arrive there after the horrendous experience at Nazareth.

Our team were ready to roll up our sleeves and jump in, but now we faced a new obstacle. We were not authorised to get involved with anything. *We could spread disease.* And there were plenty of Belgian doctors and nurses here anyway. There were plenty of injured soldiers too, but they were comfortably housed in the efficiently run wards. Everything ran like clockwork. It looked like Belgium did not require a flying ambulance corps from Britain after all.

Even so, according to Dr Munro, the situation could rapidly change and we must stay prepared, ready to spring into action at any given moment. So, the day after we arrived, he went to deal with tiresome bureaucratic formalities while we were put to work in the hospital kitchens or fields. After a few days of peeling and scrubbing great sacks of potatoes and turnips, I felt bored with life. I couldn't get the mud out from under my fingernails. Uilleam thought it was hilarious. He wrote *'If that is all war entails then I might change my mind about the Bahamas.'* It wasn't funny though. *If I had wanted to get this familiar with turnips*, I thought resentfully, *I could have just helped in the kitchen at home.*

On the fourth day I asked Dr Munro if, *please*, I could get some hands-on medical experience and he agreed. From then on, if a new load of patients were brought in *and* if the Belgian nurses were particularly busy, I was invited to the wards to help with the less serious cases.

'At last, patients not potatoes!' I said to Lady D, who always could be relied on to smile at a silly observation.

Dr Munro showed me how to open iodine phials and how to change dressings. We had to keep scrupulously clean. He showed me how to apply sticking tape to pads, sighing unpatriotically as he did so, 'Our tape isn't half as good as the Germans'.' He explained how to make tourniquets and ligatures. 'Our enemy is blood loss,' he said. 'Keep that in mind at all times.'

'I will!' I agreed eagerly.

'Modern weapons are going to cause more damage than we anticipated,' he added, but though I nodded sincerely, I didn't understand what he meant. I hadn't anticipated much.

But there were so many medical staff in Ghent that, mostly, all our corps had to do was keep the patients company and make sure they were warm, comfortable and had plenty to drink. That was another thing: Lady D had brought boxes of Bovril from England. The Belgians didn't know it at first. And then, once they tasted it, they didn't like it much!

I happily mispronounced the Belgian men's names and listened to tales of their families and their pets. I was relieved my French was not too wanting. I told the soldiers whether '*il pleut* or '*il y a soleil*', and asked them if they felt '*froid*' or '*chaud*'.

In return, they taught me swear words, in both French and Flemish, and all the body parts – and I mean *all*, even the ones I expressly asked them not to!

At first, I thought the soldiers must feel robbed: only a few days in and already demobbed, what bad luck! But the men didn't seem aggrieved. I imagine most were only grateful to be alive.

On those special days, when I could practise on, or wash or shave the patients, play cards, spoon-feed them, it gave me a great sense of purpose, but with all the turnips that needed peeling it didn't happen often enough.

*

In the evenings, we sat in our small, shared kitchen. Arthur was usually engrossed in the *New York Times*, Helen would be staring into space and scribbling, while Lady D might chat about the women's movement and discuss her leaflets. 'I'll make a suffragette out of you yet,' she said.

'You already have!' I admitted. My father always complained that I was easily swayed. It was probably true, but that didn't mean the things I was swayed towards were wrong.

Tonight, Lady D was sewing. A pair of Dr Munro's trousers had already split around his privates and Lady D was determined to make them 'shell-proof'. I switched between reading *Alice's Adventures in Wonderland* and studying the Bible. I was particularly interested in any references to Nazareth – I found a section where Jesus studies at the temple in Jerusalem without his parents knowing and then returns home to Nazareth, and another where Jesus goes to the synagogue in Nazareth and is rejected. I tried to work out what it meant.

I couldn't write about what had happened in Nazareth to Uilleam or Mother. I didn't want to worry them and they would have worried. We had been plunged like a vegetable – like a turnip! – into boiling water and pulled out just as quickly. It was disorientating. I tried to talk about it with the others but they weren't particularily forthcoming.

'It's done now, young Mairi,' Arthur said to me, and Helen nodded. Elsie said little beyond murmuring 'terrible, terrible'. Dr Munro didn't say much either. Everyone seemed to have put it to the back of their minds. Perhaps it was best I put it there too? I suppose I was also invested in not remembering because I felt so ashamed of my poor show. Oh, I did 'get stuck in' eventually, but I had done the worst possible thing: I had frozen. I had surprised myself, and not in a pleasant way. Determined never to repeat that experience, I decided that if ever there was something even slightly risky then I would raise my hand the highest for it.

Unfortunately, the biggest risk in Ghent appeared to be choking on a turnip.

*

Elsie had told me that she slept badly, but she hadn't warned me that she cried out in her sleep. At first, I found her fragmented calls disturbing, but then I became used to them: they reminded me that I was not alone. In the morning, despite the tossing and turning of the night, Elsie invariably appeared refreshed or, as she said, 'like a daisy.' I didn't know how she did it.

One evening, her cries were so feverish that I worried she would disturb the others so I woke her. She got up and we sat smoking cigarettes at the window, looking out at Orion and the Big Dipper. Elsie knew the names of all the stars. She seemed in a relaxed mood so I decided to ask her a question: 'Why were you known as Gypsy?'

She smiled. 'Is it because of my blazing eyes, my wild hair and my independent spirit?'

I didn't know what to say. I felt quite awestruck. 'Well, is it?'

'Maybe,' she said. 'It's more likely that since I was the only woman at the Gypsy Motorcycle Club I was the one who got stuck with it.'

*

While the rest of us toiled in the kitchens, waiting for Dr Munro to find us a new base, Elsie found herself a more glamorous job: driving a major about on his rounds. The car was a four-cylindered shiny black Imperia and had us all gaping. I imagine she nagged the major about her need to be closer to the action because one day, she came back with the windscreen riddled with bullets. They had got caught in enemy lines. She was, typically, blasé about it. Horrified, Dr Munro insisted she stop. She did, but not until she had served three days 'notice' first.

Elsie knew that I was a bit apprehensive about driving the Daimler, so she suggested that I practise. I did clumsy figures of eight around the hospital grounds. I enjoyed being back behind the wheel and the patterns the tyres made in the shingles. I was even daring enough to give the car a longer stretch to town and back – a twenty-minute joyride – but that evening , Dr Munro requested to speak to me. I'm not sure if he had been tipped off – by Arthur or Helen maybe – or if he had spied me speeding away.

I was anxious at having been caught. At home, a transgression like that would have my father bellowing so loudly that the neighbours' dogs would be howling.

Dr Munro wasn't *angry* with me, but disappointed at my waste of petrol. 'Profligate,' he repeated as I stood, head bowed, in front of him, trying to remember what exactly profligate meant.

'What made you do it, Mairi?' he asked, shaking his head. Then he narrowed his eyes. 'Look here – was this Elsie's idea?'

'No!' I responded quickly. In the same way I protected Uilleam from my father at home, my instinct here was to keep Elsie out of trouble. 'The stupidity was all mine.'

Elsewhere, the poor Belgians were trying to defend themselves from the invaders. The newspapers were calling it 'The Rape of Belgium'. Although I had started out on this adventure with very little opinion on Germans – apart from the fact that my German teacher Herr Hausmann had issued *far* too much homework and Frau Lehrner was pretty (she would have been the perfect match for Mr Saunders the unmarried art teacher) – I increasingly felt a loathing in my belly at the thought of them. Even the word 'German' made me cringe. They were the monsters who'd done what we'd seen at Nazareth and, in my head, they had done that *because* they were German.

Two hundred and fifty thousand Belgian refugees had left for Britain. Over one million had journeyed to Holland. Everyone left was engaged in the war effort. Building rows of trenches and tunnels, front lines, lines further back, erecting communications and installing signals. Everywhere, barbed-wire walls were being erected and sandbag mountains built. But for us, during those few days in the kind October sunshine of 1914, all we had was turnips and all we could do was wait and peel. Wait and peel.

CHAPTER FIVE

Everyone at the hospital noticed Elsie flying around in her long leather coat. When she told people that she was a widow (admittedly, she did so only when asked), they loved her all the more. A woman with a tragic past? *Allow me to comfort you.* The appeal of a woman who has suffered is universal. Sometimes, I longed for a more romantic past. All my stories involved school: sports days, egg-and-spoon races, French lessons. Or school holidays: Uilleam and me hiding in an oak tree or shrieking, 'Geronimo!' while jumping off cliffs into the sea. Most people weren't interested in my childish tales so I was learning to keep my mouth shut about it. The range of subjects adults enjoyed talking about was surprisingly narrow.

One evening, Elsie appeared in our shared kitchen in the green dress from the hotel in Harwich. Although she often wore it, it always looked fresh. As she grabbed my hand, the skirt made a swishing noise. I had grown used to her pawing me – I liked it.

'Won't you come dancing, Mairi? A handsome Gilbert is taking me out.'

'Gilbert the Filbert' was a song from back home that we had discovered we both loved. It reminded Elsie of being at nursing college in London, and it reminded me of secretly dancing with Uilleam (secretly because my father hated to see the way Uilleam moved).

> *I'm Gilbert the Filbert the Knut with a K*
> *The pride of Piccadilly the blasé roué*
> *Oh Hades, the ladies, who leave their wooden huts*
> *For Gilbert the Filbert the Colonel of the Knuts.*

I am known round Town as a fearful blood
For I come straight down from the dear old flood
And I know who's who, and I know what's what
And between the two I'm a trifle hot

When a fella actually named Gilbert came calling for Elsie, the nickname stuck and after that all her beaus – and there were quite a few – became 'Gilberts'.

'Who is it this time?'

'Johannes? Or was it Jonty? You never know, he might have an attractive friend…'

'Where can they possibly take you?' Arthur asked, grimly.

Elsie grinned. 'Locals have their ways.' She looked at me. 'Well, little sister? No point sitting in all night, pining for home.'

I demurred. Peeling vegetables was exhausting and demoralising and left me in no mood for socialising, plus I didn't want to get on the wrong side of Dr Munro again. Anyway, I didn't know what to do with an attractive friend. I wondered if Elsie got up to the open-mouthed kissing that some couples were demonstrating at the Harwich hotel. I didn't like to ask.

Not long after Elsie had departed for her date, Helen returned. She had been out with a turnip-gathering contingent when they heard that the Germans were advancing.

This would once have been terrifying, but we had heard it so many times over the last few weeks that it went in one ear and out the other.

Helen was looking more tired than ever. She was attached to her notebook and had tucked her pen behind her ear. She sat down heavily, then looked at us as though hoping we might entertain her. Lady D was immersed in her sewing – pyjamas now – and Dr Munro was out, trying to get petrol or doing his exercises, I wasn't sure. I had noticed that Arthur wasn't very attentive to Helen and decided I didn't want a bookworm for a husband.

Finally, Helen spoke up. 'Where's Elsie gone now?'

Arthur didn't mind talking about Elsie though. 'Out with another Gilbert the Filbert.'

'Another one? Goodness.'

'I think the last one may have died.'

'How long 'til Elsie notices?'

I didn't like the way they talked about Elsie. It reminded me of a woman in the village who shouted 'Trollop!' at the post-office mistress. I had tentatively said it once to Arthur but he had insisted they were joking and I was oversensitive. Maybe Americans were different? I tried to concentrate on passages from my Bible, but Helen seemed keener than usual to engage me in conversation.

'I've decided to write a romance.'

'Oh?' I said. I wasn't sure what reaction Helen was looking for.

'I'll be sure to put you in it, you brave young thing.'

'Me? No.'

I found that hard to believe. It must have been clear to her, to all of them, that I hadn't done anything special. Quite the reverse. I was a liability in an emergency. I was sure that if there was a way the flying ambulance corps could go on and leave me with the turnips, then they would. I sometimes wondered if they'd only taken me on for my motorcycle (although at that moment poor Douglas was covered in cobwebs at the back of the hospital grounds).

'Yes, you!'

'But I was rubbish.'

'You were splendid in the end, Mairi,' Helen said kindly.

Lady D looked up from her sewing, nodding in agreement. 'Don't doubt yourself, girl.'

No one had ever put me in a book before. This was something else I knew would make Uilleam jealous.

'And Elsie?' I considered. 'Elsie will be in it?' I had been aware of Elsie throughout that terrible day in Nazareth: the way she snipped the bloody clothes off agonised men, her attentiveness, her fearless-ness, her warmth. It wouldn't be too much to suggest that she came alive in the horror of it all.

Arthur laid down his paper for once.

'Of course *Mrs Knocker* will be in it. They say she brought a man back to life downstairs yesterday. A proper resurrection.'

Helen sighed. 'That was due to the volunteer nurse who called it wrong, Arthur, and not entirely down to our Elsie—'

'If you were dying in a muddy ditch, who would you want to see leaning over you?'

Not me, I thought glumly. *You'd probably try to hide from me.*

But Arthur was asking a rhetorical question. 'Elsie, that's who! She's your main character, right there.'

Helen looked unconvinced. 'How does the story end, though?'

'How do all romances end? A marriage and a happy ever after.'

*

For a while, I nursed a secret fancy that Elsie might marry my brother – that way we could be *proper* sisters. Uilleam had certainly found her attractive – well, who wouldn't? I might once have thought it preposterous that Elsie would give him a second glance, but Uilleam was as handsome as any of her Gilberts – maybe it wasn't as crazy an idea as I had first thought. So I indulged myself with fantasies of Uilleam and me showing Elsie our favourite places – climbing trees, prancing around the village, tinkering about in the garage or racing our bikes all the way to Saunton Sands. I might even win this time.

I pictured the three of us in the drawing room after dinner, entertaining Mother's circle of friends with our modern ways. Father would be standing at the fireplace, judging. Usually, Uilleam and I were found wanting, but Elsie would impress him. She had the war service that Uilleam would never have. She would be the child my father yearned for: the one who was both beautiful *and* brave; and he would be grateful that we – *that I* – had brought her to the family.

But I knew deep down that the personalities of both Elsie and Uilleam meant it was unlikely. A marriage can't be built on good looks or spiky witticisms, can it? Possibly without any real basis, I secretly doubted either had what my father would call *staying power*. And while perhaps you could have a marriage with one reckless character, I doubted that you could have one with two.

Arthur got up, lit a cigarette, then handed it to me. That was one thing I was getting good at: smoking. I was certain it put years on me.

Elsie arrived back earlier and noisier than usual. I noticed Arthur and Helen look at each other with knowing glances. I think Elsie must have been drinking stronger rum than she was used to, for she virtually twirled into our quarters as though she were still listening to music.

'*Bonsoir, mes amis*. For the benefit of our American companions, that means "Good evening friends".'

'Here she goes again,' mumbled Arthur.

'Was this Gilbert nice?' I asked timidly.

Helen laughed. 'They're all nice, aren't they?'

'To be frank, I'm not sure he was.' Elsie smirked. 'They look so handsome in their uniforms, but I fear my standards may be slipping due to lack of sleep.'

'You have standards, Elsie?' Arthur could never miss an opportunity to make a dig.

'*Touch*é,' she snapped back. 'That means—'

He interrupted, 'I know what it means.'

I didn't know what annoyed him so much about her. She was only joking – at least, I hoped that was all it was. But Arthur didn't like Elsie's jokes.

*

The Germans were advancing day by day. The Belgians weren't expecting this – *who could have expected this?* Compared to the organised grey military machine of the Hun the Belgian army was an altogether more ramshackle affair. I saw old men, ex-servicemen, crying in the streets, desperate to help, but *how?* Young men were scooped up into troops, but a week's training counted for little against dastardly German soldiers with twenty years' experience.

We lost villages and villages as the Germans marched onwards.

And still the flying ambulance corps waited and peeled turnips. If only a war were decided by who peeled the most turnips, we would have been victorious in a matter of days.

Finally in mid-October, Dr Munro found us a base of our own. It was in a town called Furnes, in an old school building that had been converted into a military hospital. A Belgian medical team was already established there, but a flying ambulance corps was needed.

We were provided with three rooms in which to live, and the use of the school kitchen. These lodgings were less comfortable than those in more organised Ghent – but perfectly adequate for our motley crew. On the day we moved in, Lady D produced six old teacups, a tablecloth, a small vase and even a bunch of freshly cut tulips. She found a kettle and made us English tea. She apologised profusely for the lack of saucers and spoons as though it somehow reflected on her, but we thought it was lovely.

The only thing *we* lacked now was action. 'To our wonderful group,' said Dr Munro, raising his teacup and looking proudly at each of us. In a low voice, he obliquely addressed, for the first time, the horrors of our time in Nazareth. 'I hope we never again encounter what we experienced on our way here.'

'Hear, hear…'

'But if we do, I have faith in *all* of you, in all of *us*.'

Was it my imagination or was he looking mostly at me? I blushed. Even my neck grew hot. Elsie put her cool, reassuring hand on mine.

'We are a team. Consideration and respect for each other—'

'Are a must!' Elsie and I chorused, finishing Dr Munro's sentence.

He laughed, abashed. 'By Jove, you *have* been listening!' He raised his cup again. 'Everyone – to new beginnings…'

We clinked cups excitedly, until Lady D said, 'Careful, they can't withstand too much!' and we laughed again.

We were about twenty miles from the front line, where Belgian, French and British soldiers were facing off the German enemy. Sometimes, you could hear the rumbling of shells like distant thunder.

*

At Furnes, from the outset, I was encouraged to observe the more experienced nurses and allowed to treat some patients. Even just a few days of this did my confidence the world of good.

One overcast afternoon about ten days after our arrival, news came that there were wounded men in a field some thirty minutes' drive away. Dr Munro and the others weren't at the base; they were once again on the hunt for food and petrol, but even if they had been there, Elsie and I would have immediately volunteered to go. Me because I still wanted to make up for my previous performance, Elsie because she was Elsie. We grabbed our helmets and ran for the ambulance. My heart was racing. I was determined not to let anyone down.

Elsie, behind the wheel, set off at a lunatic's pace. We hadn't gone far before we saw a soldier driving a horse and cart pulling wounded or dead men towards the hospital. Sobered, Elsie slowed to pass them, but once they were out of sight we quickly picked up speed again.

Twenty minutes later, we were parked under a copse of trees and moving smartly towards the field with our stretcher. It was an oat field, I think, and the stalks were tall and brownish, ready to harvest. It was hard to see anything through them.

As we pushed on, I realised with a start that this was *the most* stupid idea. We could be fired at – fired *on* – like this. Anything could happen. And how would we find anyone in here?

Elsie told me to wait with the stretcher as she waded out further into the oats.

I stood still, shivering.

'Get down!' she hissed back at me and I dropped to my knees. I held my breath, waiting for someone to shoot me, and then I saw them ahead. First I thought they were scattered rocks, but they were sprawled grey-uniformed Germans, virtually indistinguishable from the sky, from heaven, where it appeared that most were on their sweet way.

Elsie whispered my name. I crawled over. We were in a mud churn. *Didn't I used to love mud?* It seemed inconceivable now.

If I am to die, make it quick, make it decisive, none of this hanging-on-by-a-thread stuff, please.

I said, 'They're all dead.'

But Elsie hissed back, pointing. 'There's one over there who isn't!'

The only way you could tell was by the twitching of his knee.

'But he's German anyway,' I whispered.

Our eyes met, and I felt like a fool.

The not-dead soldier opened his eyes and raised his hand palm upwards almost as though he was asking, *What can I do?* Elsie crawled on her hands and knees over to him. Her bag scraped across the mud.

'We are going to help you,' she told him. She looked over her shoulder back at me. 'What's the German for "We'll take care of you"?'

'*Wir kümmern uns um Sie…?*'

But just then, there was a terrific rain of bullets overhead.

'They're firing on us!' I said incredulously. 'The Germans are firing on us!'

Elsie made up her mind quickly. 'We'll leave him for now… tell him we'll come back.'

But I didn't say anything because I was too busy scrambling for dear life, focused on the trees in the distance, willing them closer, before finally taking shelter in the protective canopy of branches. Shells whizzed past, there was a humming sound, a pause, and then the brutal thud of explosion.

I kept telling myself, *Each grey lump out there is a German soldier.* I wasn't sure that even in their death throes they mightn't try to kill me.

Eventually the shelling stopped. It was early evening. The sky had turned pink with red streaks, some orange, and now it was fading to a darker blue. *How could the sky still have beauty? Hadn't it seen what we had?* Elsie wouldn't even let me smoke because the light would draw the snipers' attention.

She nudged me. 'I thought you were a non-smoking schoolgirl anyway?' Despite myself, I smiled.

We decided we – *he* – could wait no longer. Crouching low, we re-entered that terrible field. Fat wild pigs were snuffling among the bodies. *They aren't bodies, they're rocks*, I told myself. I retched and spat out bile. We stooped as low as possible, still exposed. We found him again, still twitching with life. We dragged him out of the field. It was agony to be stooped so low but it was not quite low enough if they wanted to kill us. Our tin hats would not protect us if anyone fired. As we struggled out of the field, I was thinking to myself, *this is the first time I've come so near to death.* My own death. And I accepted it. I was not frightened. I was faithful and open to all possibilities ahead. I caught sight of Elsie's face, drained of colour; her eyes had never looked wider, but we nodded at each other. We were of the same mind: we would rather die trying. I had my faith, I don't know what Elsie had. A death wish, maybe? No, I don't think so. A lust for life, perhaps.

*

We somehow made it back to the Fiat. As we unceremoniously parcelled the soldier into the back, I thought of the Guy Fawkes procession through Chedington that Uilleam and I used to love. The effigy of the guy pulled around, then dumped on the wood ready to burn. *Remember, remember.* This poor boy was also falling apart at the seams.

I drove so Elsie could work on the boy in the back. Of course, this didn't inhibit her from barking out instructions at me.

'Faster, Mairi!'

'I'm going as fast as I—'

'Watch out for craters!'

Not only were Belgian roads more fit for horses than motor vehicles, they were also mostly shaped in a kind of hump: perfectly appropriate in a country liable to flood. Less appropriate for driving a breakneck mercy mission, possibly while under fire.

As I slammed our way through that bleak countryside, I recited the prayer that came most easily to me. '*Our Father who art in heaven. Hallowed be thy name—*'

'What was it again, Mairi? *Wir kümmen un sid?*'

'No, it's *Wir kümmern uns um Sie.*'

'For goodness' sake. *Wie Kümmern—*'

'*For thine is the kingdom, the power and the glory—*'

'Try *that* in German.'

I ignored her. '*In Earth as it is in Heaven—*'

'If there is a God, then… what kind of monster is he?'

I couldn't understand how it wasn't obvious. 'It's not God who does this, Elsie,' I explained patiently, as I would explain many times to come. 'It's humans.'

'How can you want any part of it? A God who would let this go on? And turn a blind eye?'

Finally, we arrived at the hospital and dragged in our poor grey lamb.

CHAPTER SIX

Elsie was wrapped right around the German boy when I tiptoed back to the ward later that evening. For a few seconds, I watched her slumped over him. They fitted perfectly around each other, reminding me of Helen's glasses locked away in their case. I patted Elsie's shoulder. Her hair was like liquorice and I had a peculiar yearning to stroke it.

'Elsie,' I whispered. 'Your Gilbert is waiting.'

A uniformed man had arrived holding a wilting tulip and asking for 'Miss Ilsa'. Elsie had told me it irked her when the Gilberts brought gifts that weren't useful, so I decided not to mention the flower. Fish or soap might have swayed her tonight; a tulip would not. This Gilbert was handsome, dazzling even. Clean-shaven and smelling of spice, perhaps in another life he would have been on the stage.

Elsie looked puzzled and then she seemed to come to. 'I'm not leaving.'

I didn't know what to say. I had only known her a few weeks, but I had not seen Elsie become attached to anyone in particular. I suppose, given her gleeful chopping and changing of Gilberts, I'd doubted that she could. She reminded me of our old cat, Barney. Barney came for food and it was then that he allowed you to pet him. It was always Bessie the dog who seemed to have deeper feelings. I began to feel bad for Barney. Maybe I had underestimated him.

'You've been looking forward to it—'

The boy groaned and his eyelids fluttered. Elsie raised up slightly on one elbow.

'He is "*funfzehn*". That means fifteen, right?'

'He can't be.'

'He must have lied about his age to the recruiters.'

I didn't know what to say.

'He just wants his "*mutter*". Imagine if it were Kenneth. Kenneth in nine years' time.' Her face was contorted with anguish. 'Perhaps I should have left him with his friends…'

'He'll be fine, Elsie,' I said, although *what did I know?*

She turned back and laid her head gently by him.

'*Wir kümmern uns um Sie…* shhh… *wir k*ümmern uns um Sie…*'

Back at the door of our lodgings, I explained to the gentleman caller, the handsome Gilbert, that Elsie was 'unavoidably occupied'. I was as sympathetic as I felt the situation required. His smirk lost its sparkle for a moment before he gathered himself and then the charm was switched back on: 'So, Miss, what is your name?'

'Mairi Chisholm.'

'Like *marry*?' he asked, showing me his even teeth. I gave the dutiful smile that was expected. How many times had I heard that in the last two months? It was as though my name served as a kind of gentleman's prompt.

'And you, are you unavoidably occupied too?'

Why would he think I would want to go out with him, just because Elsie couldn't? Inviting me as his second choice: how could anyone think that was kind?

After politely declining the handsome Gilbert's request, I joined the others playing cards in the kitchen. Helen dealt. She was the most efficient at it, so we had stopped taking turns and left it to her. I liked the noise the cards made in her hands as she shuffled. I usually favoured queens, had a mistrust of jacks and preferred clubs above all other suits: this set of playing cards was no different.

While she dealt, I kept picturing that grey field of horror and thinking: *I could have died today – and here I am about to play pontoon.* I couldn't find logic or meaning in it, no matter how much I repeated it in my head.

Lady D had moved on from mending pyjamas and was knitting gloves from a pattern she had found in a housekeeping magazine (she kept all manner of things in her room). She looked up with a smile. 'The men will need these soon.' Dr Munro was studying his crinkled map. He liked to predict where the Germans would advance next. Sometimes he put little coin armies out in a pattern on the table. Drawing closer I saw they were in the shape of an 'S'. He was worried that the Germans would take the higher land and we would be stuck in the lowlands around the Ypres Salient.

'Why does it matter?' I asked tentatively. I wouldn't make a great war general. 'Because,' Dr Munro explained patiently, 'living conditions for our men will be far worse.'

I was still vexed.

He slid the coins across the table. As I watched, I realised that the coppers were the Allieds: the rest were the Germans. And there were a lot more Germans. He picked up a jug of water as if to pour it over the coins.

'The rainwater will gather here, don't you see? Their men will be high and dry while ours will not.'

In that case, I doubted the practicality of Lady D's gloves.

Helen dealt me an eight of clubs and a six of spades.

'Twist.'

'You *always* twist, Mairi,' Helen said with mock disapproval, before dealing me a three of hearts.

A wind was up. Outside our quarters, the trees rattled as though they were trying to get in.

'Is Elsie out with another Gilbert tonight?' asked Arthur casually as he surveyed his hand.

I was tempted to say, *What's it got to do with you?* But I was glad of the chance to respond with something complimentary to Elsie for once. 'She is with a patient.'

Arthur raised his eyebrows. 'Some… playboy?' The word 'playboy' sluiced around his mouth.

'No.' My vehemence surprised me. 'This one is very young,' I added shyly. 'A German.'

I was glad they didn't remark on that.

'Not good to get attached.' Arthur's voice was gruff.

Lady D smiled gently with her sympathetic eyes. 'But unavoidable sometimes.'

'Mairi?' prompted Helen.

'Twist again.'

Tsking, she dealt me a jack. Diamond.

'Bust.'

Arthur excused himself. Helen watched him move across the room, her face unreadable.

In the early hours of the morning, Elsie came in, waking me up. In the candlelight, her eyes looked huge and wild.

'Awful, awful…'

I tried not to think of him with his palms raised so helplessly. He could have been my teacher Herr Hausmann's son. Didn't Herr Hausmann have a son, Stephan, in Hamburg?

A person could go crazy thinking like this. God wouldn't want us to think like this.

'If we could have got to him sooner, if we could have treated him earlier—'

'I know,' I said soothingly. I hated to see Elsie distressed.

'It's not on,' she said darkly as she pulled off her boots. And I knew she was cooking something up.

*

The next day, I was doing a bit of routine car maintenance – a job that I was always happy to get stuck into – when I was sent on an important errand: petrol and meat supplies. Everywhere we went, we had to bring our passports to show that we were not infiltrators. How many times would I pat the pocket I had hidden mine in, checking it was still there?

A young fella with dark, collar-length hair and a bright-blue school jumper filled one can of fuel for me. He had forgotten to ask to see my passport, which gave me hope that he wasn't too much of a stickler for the rules. Tentatively, I asked for more petrol, but he said there were strict limits on how much he could give. I explained, 'We are with the hospital,' then, when he didn't respond, I added quietly, 'No one need know if you gave us extra.'

He shook his head.

'Just a little…?'

'No.'

Two grubby children peeped out at us from behind a thin kitchen door. When I looked over at them, they shot back inside giggling but I wasn't in the mood to play games.

'Is there anyone else here?' I asked him. Elsie always came back with loads of fuel. 'Mum or Dad maybe?'

'I'm almost fourteen,' he said fiercely. Only four years younger than me, one year younger than the German boy. He made his fingers into the shape of a gun. Pow pow. 'You can't have more.'

'I understand.'

'I'm going to tell someone you asked.'

'It's fine,' I said, quickly filling up the car. This was awful. 'Thank you.'

I continued into town. Near the station, I gave some money to a little girl begging. I probably shouldn't have, but I couldn't just walk past. The butcher's was at the end of a parade of abandoned shops; I knew it from the queue of cooks, nurses and servicemen outside. I joined them, listening to their conversations about where everyone had gone or was going. Meat dangled from hooks. Blood-red, pink speckles, ribs and bones. I tried not to think of Nazareth. Or dead German schoolboys. *Deep breaths.* That distinctive smell of death.

I was *not* going to be sick. I was over all that. Dr Munro had taken me aside to advise me that whenever I next felt *nauseous*, I should replace my bad thoughts with happy memories. I should block out the trigger, whether it was a nasty smell, sound or whatever, and think of happy things. So I did that now. I imagined racing my Douglas along open roads with Uilleam next to me on his Royal Enfield, the air on my face. *See the daffodils grow in the hedgerows, Mairi. Let the sun warm our cheeks. Think of the apple crumble waiting for us at home…*

It was my turn at the counter. *Don't fail this task, Mairi*, I told myself. *We've got to eat.*

The butcher had an aggrieved face with a squashed nose like he'd recently taken a thumping. His neck was pale and spotty and the skin on his round cheeks was so stretched and scarlet it looked painful. He served me and we even managed some banter – *in French!* – which I felt was more like it. He told me that my red hair was unusual. *It's not that unusual*, I thought, but I said 'Thank you.' Elsie had told me I needed to accept compliments gracefully.

He asked where I was from, and I said, 'England *and* Scotland,' then added, 'I'm here to help the war effort.'

He was delighted. 'Come back after the war and we will have a feast!' I promised I would – 'What's more, I will bring my whole family too!' How his face softened when he grinned. The nose was no longer a problem. I was aware the whole queue was listening approvingly to us.

He said 'I'm staying put. German advance or no.'

'That's the spirit!'

'Too right!'

'Here's to plucky Belgium!' I felt quite fired up with the fighting talk! A spontaneous burst of applause wouldn't have been out of place.

'We won't let the filthy baby-eating Boche get the better of us. I'll take them on with my bare hands. Rip them from ear to ear.' He smiled at me as he mimed his plans.

'Oh, absolutely,' I agreed, feeling sick again.

I explained that we were six adults after enough meat to last us the week. He packed some up. It was remiss of me, but it wasn't until I had passed over the notes that Dr Munro had given me that I asked what kind of meat it was. The exuberant butcher told me.

'Horse!?' I echoed incredulously. This was clearly one of those ridiculous language issues. Could I be confusing horse with *cheveux* – hair? 'Hare' was like rabbit and I was partial to rabbit pie. 'You don't mean—' I imitated riding a horse, with a weak 'neigh'. As one, the queue looked at me mystified. It felt like charades at Christmas, and my futile attempts to get Father to guess 'O Little Town of Bethlehem'.

'Neigh?' said the butcher, now playing to the crowd. The crowd chortled.

I thought, anxiously, *maybe Belgian horses don't neigh.*

'Ee-aw?' I tried, feeling ludicrous.

The butcher moved on to the next customer, a square-faced young woman I recognised from the hospital. She too averted her eyes from me.

'*Excusez moi, Monsieur,*' I interrupted. 'Is there… nothing else?'

The butcher blinked. 'Very fine horsemeat.'

'Oh, I see. Thank you.'

I walked out of that shop with a horse in my bag, a jagged tightness in my stomach and a sour mouth. Exchanging negative memories with positive ones didn't work. I recited a prayer:

Calm me, O Lord, as you stilled the storm
Still me, O Lord, keep me from harm.

Let all the tumult within me cease.
Enfold me, Lord, in your peace. Amen.

I was nervous at the thought of telling the others about my strange purchase. I decided I would take their lead: if *they* thought horsemeat was fine, then I would hold my nose and tuck in; if not – if they were as appalled as I was – I would throw the package in the canal and work out how to make up the lost money for Dr Munro. I wished there was just one thing that I could do without a hitch or complication. Elsie would have done it in five minutes flat *and* got the extra petrol *and* a date with some handsome Gilbert she would have won over in the queue.

When I got back, Arthur, Helen and Elsie were arranged around the kitchen table. They looked as though they were gathered for an ordinary family supper and I was about to make my horse announcement when I realised that they were in the middle of a terrific row. It seemed, incredibly, to be over the way the table had been laid.

Elsie was speaking passionately. 'Poppycock, Arthur! I'm saying, look where the rules get us – this urge to have the cutlery in its place, it lands us in trenches. It lands us in No Man's Land.'

'It's not about cutlery, Elsie,' Arthur was saying through gritted teeth.

'Yes, it is. The wrong knife for fish, the wrong spoon. Oh my! Why not just eat?'

'Good manners are vital.'

Helen was staring at her reflection in the spoon. 'Consideration and kindness are vital. The rest is just artifice.'

'It's about standards!' hissed Arthur.

'Oh, and *you* always maintain high standards, do you?' Elsie laughed bitterly. His face changed. It was like she had shot him through the heart.

They both rose, their chairs scraped on the floor and I was scared they were going to fight – I mean, brawl like drunk men in the street on May Day. I thought Arthur would never forgive himself if he hit Elsie – if he hit a woman – but the anger he had towards her then was something dreadful, and she seemed to hate him right back. Helen placed down the spoon and looked up at them, her mouth open.

It was at that moment that Dr Munro raced in, pulling on his shirt over his vest. I was momentarily spellbound by his gingery-white chest hairs. 'We're needed!'

Forgetting the argument, we grabbed our helmets and dashed out to the two cars. The frail November sun had all but disappeared and the sky was a smudge of purple. Feeling the rush of adrenaline, I squeezed into the Fiat with Dr Munro and Elsie. As Elsie drove, Dr Munro explained that Dixmude, a village about twenty miles away, was falling. The Germans were advancing fast.

The rain had started up again. The car was running tickety-boo, thanks to me, and we had petrol.

'It's driving well, isn't it?' I said proudly.

They didn't reply. I retreated into myself, worrying about what lay ahead. *Please don't let it be another Nazareth.* I thought about my father and realised that I hadn't thought about him, or my mother, or even home for a few days. I felt this showed I was adjusting to my new life.

It took a good while to get there, fifty minutes or so, and by the time we did, the sky was black. It was a particularly starless night.

Even when we arrived, I didn't feel ready for whatever lay ahead. My knees knocked together and against Elsie's thigh. Dr Munro reminded Elsie to back the car in in case a fast escape was necessary. Then he told us to wait, before finally giving us the go-ahead to creep forward to the house at the top of the hill.

Everything was in darkness. The only light was the half-moon. It requires a special kind of faith to run into a pitch-black house when guns may be firing outside. Elsie was right in front of me and she whispered to me to hold on to her. I did so obediently, tugging at the back of her coat like Kenneth might have done. And then we found ourselves in a shadowy side room – perhaps what was once a sitting room – ready to deal with casualties.

At first, none were too bad, thank goodness, then word got around that we were there and more injured men began arriving, apparently from all directions.

Someone brought us in a table so we treated them on that. Dr Munro and Lady D were working in an adjoining room. Arthur and Helen took another.

'We're going to run out of medicine at this rate,' Elsie said.

'I'll go back,' I offered. I thought that was what she meant for me to say.

'Don't be mad,' she whispered.

A cacophony of noise started outside. Guns firing. We stood in the dark as men were brought to us. Some came in on stretchers, some were just dragged by their friends. At one point, Elsie was feeling her way around a man with a bloody leg wound. 'Light, Mairi!' she ordered.

I lit a match, creating a fleeting illumination. Just long enough for us to see, hopefully not long enough for any enemies to know that we were there. I gulped loudly. *I would not be sick.*

Elsie told the friend who had brought this man up, 'There's nothing we can do, I'm sorry.'

'There must be!' the friend said hotly. 'His wife is having a baby.'

Elsie repeated 'I'm sorry,' and when he didn't say anything, she added, 'I really am sorry,' and the poor friend finally got the hint and dragged the dying man off the table and out of our way. I squeezed the friend's shoulder as he went by and heard him let out a sob.

Elsie whispered to me, 'Good thing we checked. I nearly wasted a shot of morphine.'

I wondered how the others were getting on. Perhaps they were having an easier time of it? But then I heard Arthur yell, 'We're running out of kit, here!'

Dr Munro shouted back, 'Just do what you can, Arthur!', which even *I* knew meant nothing.

The rattle of guns and the crashing of shells went on outside. Flashes of unhelpful light. Rainwater noisily pouring down drains. Some men we could deal with on the spot. We filled them up with painkillers or applied clumsy splints. The man who had lost his thumb, the fella whose bottom had been grazed by a bullet. Some, particularly the ones who'd got it in the chest or the abdomen, needed surgery. And fast. Elsie and Dr Munro violently pumped one man back to life. For now.

*

One afternoon back in Ghent, side by side over a tin bucket, peeling turnips, Dr Munro had explained the procedure of 'triage' to me. It came, he said, from the French word 'to sort' and it heralded a revolutionary new way of nursing. The patients with the most life-threatening injuries should be delivered to the hospital first. This seemed logical, even to a nincompoop like me, so I couldn't get my head around what they might possibly have done instead of this in the past. Dr Munro had sighed, thrown away a particularly rotten-looking turnip and explained, 'When I was a young man, it would have been the most senior men who were dealt with first, regardless of urgency.'

*

It was decided that Elsie and I would take some of the most injured men back to Furnes at once. Dr Munro and Lady D would bring the next transport later. Arthur and Helen would continue as they were and wait for the return of the car.

Lots of people were involved with carrying the allotted four casualties to the car. Pour souls. It was a bumpy, dangerous descent from the house to the vehicle. As we raced them into the car, we were fired on – *sniper!* – and one of our helpers – the friend of the dead father-to-be – took two bullets to the stomach. We ducked down, in panicky chaos, then Elsie decided, 'Put him in with the others, now.'

'There's no room!' someone else said. The ambulance could only carry four.

'He'll go on the floor,' she barked. 'Hurry.'

Elsie insisted on driving. I was relieved, for I hadn't driven in a night this wet or black yet. She needed me to navigate. 'We'll be fine, darling.'

'I know.'

The roads were saturated. Rain slammed down, bounced off the surface. The wipers couldn't keep up and we had to continually hand-wipe the windscreen. It was the wrong side of midnight. Elsie drove with her typical contempt for caution. I imagined this was what flying might feel like as we hurtled through the dark. Elsie's foot was jammed on the accelerator. She could drive anything they put her in but she knew the Fiat like the back of her hand.

The racket the men were making took me back to visiting a cattle market with my father. I swallowed the thought away. I could smell blood. I tried not to think of the horsemeat I had carried earlier that day. I felt sick. *Dead men in Nazareth.* Cherries on a hat. Blood spots.

'Talk to me,' Elsie said. 'Tell me something nice.'

I told Elsie about the best beach in England, Saunton Sands. Uilleam and I would take her there when all this was over. We would build castles out of sand and watch the tide fill up the moats.

There was a howl from the back of the car. I thought of the jellyfish that Uilleam and I used to splat with our spades before burying them in mass unmarked graves.

I screamed. Something dark and terrible was in the road. Elsie braked and we flew forward hard. The men in the back cried out in pain. I jumped down from the car to investigate. I was terrified and as I ran forward, I realised I wasn't wearing my helmet. It could be a German roadblock; I might have walked straight into a trap. My last thought would be: *such a foolish mistake.*

It was a dead horse. Long-tailed rats were running over its eyes, exploring its face (sometimes, even I wondered what God was thinking when he created rats). It was in our way. A massive obscenity of a roadblock. First, I tried to shift the beast. I thought that if two or three of the five men in the back had been fit enough to assist, we might have been able to do it, but those fellows were in no state to move their own legs, never mind lift a dead weight like this.

Only a minute in the open and I was drenched to the bone.

I prayed for strength. Elsie sidled down from the driving seat and joined me in trying too. They say you get superhuman strength in an emergency but this beast did not budge. We measured the space between it and the side of the road with our hands. This space was ten hands wide; how long was our car?

'Let me try,' I said. There was not an inch to spare but we could give it a go.

Elsie said if we were going to try, she wanted to be the one to do it.

If we went too close to the edge, we would tip up into the ditch. The ambulance would be lost – and as for its passengers…

Elsie, full of gumption, cranked up the engine.

Once again, I told her to stop. How about we take out the men, carry them to the other side of the horse, drive through and *then* pick them up? That way, if we collapsed into the ditch then they, at least, would be free.

'But if we collapse, they'll just be stuck on this perishing road until goodness knows when,' Elsie pointed out through gritted teeth. I was wasting time.

There was no alternative but to edge forwards. I held my breath, as though that would give the car the extra lightness it needed. Slowly, Elsie made our vehicle creep around the fallen horse. Our ambulance had never seemed so fragile. The human condition had never seemed so frail. I guess we both had on our minds the poor German boy killed by our delays.

Inch by inch, we proceeded. Shivering, I prayed – but only to myself, because I didn't want to set Elsie off on an anti-God tirade.

Whoever dwells in the shelter of the Most High will rest in the shadow of the Almighty.

I will say of the Lord, 'He is my refuge and my fortress, my God in whom I trust'—

'Elsie, we're too close!'

Inch by inch, we got past without toppling.

We were off again, in the driving lane. It took me a few moments to realise that the groaning in the back had quietened down. While the sounds of their suffering had been horrible, the silence was even worse.

After we had been driving for another twenty minutes or so, I saw another black shadow ahead. I screamed at Elsie to stop, although she saw it at the same time as me. This time it was what we had originally feared, a gaping crater in the road. If we hadn't spied it, it would have swallowed our ambulance up whole. I remembered how curiously I had looked at that first hole in the road I had seen on arriving in Belgium: what an alien sight it was. Now there was nothing so distressingly familiar as these scabs in the land, like a wound in Mother Earth's skin. Again, we had to do the measurements, the calculation and then drive the car in a similar side shuffle on the road to get past without falling.

This was how I imagined God treated the Egyptians who kept the Jews in slavery. Were there going to be flying frogs next? A plague? What had the Belgians done to deserve this? What had we all done?

I wasn't sure how much further Furnes was, but I kept telling Elsie, 'Nearly there!' and 'You can do it!' We were both nearly broken with exhaustion. Every part of me was chilled. My feet felt like ice. Elsie had driven for miles in this darkness: this was after a day's work in the kitchens, then those long hours of looking after men in the dark house on the hill.

To get into the Furnes hospital, you had to take a sharp left turn at the old school gates. Elsie attempted it three times, knocked off the wing mirror, failed again, then threw her hands in the air, admitting defeat for the first time since I'd known her.

'You do it, Mairi! I can't.'

We swapped seats. The steering wheel was clammy to the touch. I got us through the gates on first attempt, and once we were in, we both shouted for assistance.

As soon as we opened the back door of the ambulance, it was overwhelmingly obvious: we had taken too long. Of our five precious cargo, three had expired, including the Good Samaritan who had helped carry the others down.

Please God, let me understand your reasons for this. I know you are wise and I know there will be some explanation…

There was no time for tears. We dragged out the stretchers and ran the surviving two men inside. Twenty minutes later, we were driving back to the village for the next load and I was praying that the petrol would see us out the night.

CHAPTER SEVEN

'We need to make a radical change, Munro.'

A few days later, we were at breakfast in the old school kitchen. I liked plain porridge, had always eaten it, but I knew Arthur and Helen were growing desperate for some 'goddamn flavouring'. 'If only there was cinnamon, or honey,' they whispered. There were sometimes fried potatoes for breakfast too but mostly these were saved for meals later in the day. Occasionally, I'd catch myself thinking fondly of the breakfast I had eaten in the Harwich hotel. The adequately poached eggs. I would not allow myself to think of the wonderful breakfasts Cook had made us at home. I would *not* dwell on golden smoked kippers.

The two survivors from the fallen village were being expertly cared for by the Belgian doctors and nurses. 'They should make it,' one of the nurses told me, nodding fiercely. 'They're grateful to you ladies.'

The nurse knew one of the men who hadn't survived – Belgium was a small world back then, and it felt like everyone knew everyone. He was a local man who had worked at the bank in Furnes. 'Always had time for us,' she said. 'Patient with the old people.' This nurse was a volunteer and young – as young as I was – she was struggling not to cry.

'Munro? I *said* we need to make a change.'

At Elsie's words, Dr Munro placed down his English paper (which was full of talk about the king's engagements and next to nothing about what poor Belgium suffered!) and blew on his pipe. Something in his stern demeanour said that he had been waiting for this. I thought he might say he 'wasn't angry but was disappointed', but he didn't.

Elsie continued. 'A *radical* change.'

At this, Dr Munro snapped: 'Just get on with driving and nursing, instead of looking for complications.'

'I'm looking for a solution!'

Elsie had never looked more handsome than she did that morning. She stood, fierce as a bull, ready to charge at Dr Munro, who was the matador... no, he was the red rag.

'If you have time for navel-gazing then something is wrong.'

'Shock is killing them. Not wounds. Three mothers lost their sons yesterday. Unnecessarily.'

'Unavoidably—'

'Half the time when we drive the poor souls from the battlefield to the hospital, they die in our ambulances or near enough.'

'I know that, Elsie,' he said.

'It's not good enough.'

'What is the alternative?'

I was thinking the same, *What is the alternative, Elsie?* It's all very well to criticise – '*it's all too easy to be negative,*' as my father would say – '*but what is the answer?*'

But Elsie was a step ahead of us, as usual.

'If they will not survive the journey to the hospital... then the hospital must go to them.'

'Oh no. Absolutely not.'

Arthur joined in. 'Elsie, enough acting the hero. You put us all to shame.'

Elsie ignored him. She spoke only to Dr Munro.

'We *have* to get closer to the battlefield. Otherwise, much of what we do when they are in hospital is in vain.'

Arthur seemed to take this as a personal attack. His spoon clattered into his flavourless porridge. 'This is so typical of Elsie,' he addressed the rest of us, 'she sees a rule and wants to stamp over it.'

'Oh, but—' Helen said.

'Elsie doesn't know the meaning of the word "team"!' Arthur barked in his wife's direction. Helen blinked at him, taking it all in, no doubt ready to regurgitate it in her 'romance'.

'It's too much of a risk,' Arthur went on. 'We'll be shelled to kingdom come.'

I was surprised when Helen then spoke up for Elsie. 'She *has* got a point. You've said similar things yourself, Arthur.'

Elsie continued, with a grateful glance at Helen. 'Everything I've seen, everything I've done tells me it *has* to be that way. We have to get nearer to the boys.'

She grabbed a bowl of porridge to demonstrate her theory in much the same incomprehensible way as Munro did with his coin armies. 'If the fighting is here, what use is a hospital over there?'

She pulled at the tablecloth as though determined to tip everything over. However, Dr Munro anticipated her, slamming down his fists so that nothing could move.

'What is this tomfoolery? Change for the sake of change is ridiculous.'

'It's not for the sake of change!' Elsie roared back. 'It's for the sake of the boys!'

I could see she was struggling not to swear.

Dr Munro lowered his voice. 'Elsie, you are a thrill-seeker and this makes you dangerous.'

She laughed. 'It's not me who does their evening exercises in their smalls.'

Munro's face was red with fury now. 'And who will pay for this ridiculous caper?'

'We will save on petrol… All this toing and froing is expensive.' She was smirking slightly. 'Some would say "profligate"!'

'The British Army won't fund it. The Red Cross won't… they're desperate as it is.'

'We can raise money. How difficult can it be?'

'No. We began as a group. A group is how we stay. No egos, remember?' He looked at me. 'Don't even *think* about it, Mairi. I have a responsibility to your parents—'

'I know,' I began. I felt terrible. I liked Dr Munro enormously. I would be eternally grateful we weren't engaged, but he *was* a marvellous leader. He, more than anyone else – more even than Elsie – explained things properly to me. I knew his heart ached for the lost men: he only wanted the best for everyone. We all did.

'I promised them "no unnecessary risks".'

I didn't know that…

'No unnecessary risks?' Elsie was shouting now. 'You brought a child to a war zone, for God's sake!'

This was unfair. Hadn't I proved myself?

I butted in. 'I'm not a—'

Too late. Dr Munro stomped out the hall. His footsteps down the passageway made a dramatic echo.

'Oh, brave naturist!' Elsie called after him in her mocking voice.

'Come on, Helen. I want nothing to do with these, these…' Arthur was searching for the right word. Eventually he decided on 'Herberts,' which made Elsie's lip curl even more.

'Herberts?' she repeated. 'Is that the best you can do?'

At that, Arthur got up, threw down the handkerchief that doubled as a napkin and walked off. Helen followed him but reluctantly, giving us a resigned grimace. Elsie lit a cigarette, shrugging as though all this bad atmosphere had nothing to do with her. I didn't know what to do. I couldn't help dithering. *What was the right thing to do?*

Lady D arrived bright, bushy-tailed and, as usual, completely unaware.

'Shall we pick some turnips today, girls?'

I went back to our room, feeling upset at the beastly altercation. I *liked* our team. I had had my initial doubts, yes, but it hadn't taken me too long to realise that *I* was the chink in the armour, not them. *They* were all exceptional. I had more than an inkling that my father wouldn't like this latest development – Elsie's plan – but I pushed it away. He was miles away now. I had to make my own decisions.

After we had returned from the fallen village the second time, I had crept into the kitchen and thrown out the horsemeat. I couldn't bring myself to cook it or even cut it. It crossed a line. Dr Munro asked where the meat was and I considered saying it was stolen or lost, but in the end, I just said it was inedible. He didn't mention it again, preoccupied as he was with saving the lives of the Dixmude fallen. As soon as I could, I teamed up with Lady D and we went hunting, with some success, for rabbit, which I turned into a stew to much (undeserved) acclaim.

I was settled in Furnes and had thought I might stay until Christmas or until the war ended, whichever was first. To leave now seemed ludicrous. *But how could Elsie think we could set up a clearing station just yards from the firing line?*

She had not directly asked me to join her, but I knew she wanted me to go.

Would I be able to manage the work? I wondered. *Yes. I was learning fast.* So many things that would have been alien to me just eight weeks ago as I mooched around Dorset were normal to me now: the importance of keeping the injured warm with hot drinks, but not if the patient is suffering an abdominal wound; even the most badly hurt soldier likes a cigarette; everyone likes morphine but – *please* – mark the patient's forehead with an 'M' to avoid an overdose; being too free with the antiseptics could sometimes (often) make things worse; a broken bone, especially a femur, could prove fatal; a Liston Splint was hardly worth the bother; the quicker we got to them the better…

Back in our room, I noticed a postcard on Elsie's bed, which I couldn't resist picking up. On one side there was a delightful picture of two bonny children – twins maybe – ice skating in Dutch national dress. It was entitled 'Double Dutch'. On the blank side, Elsie had written in her urgent black scrawl:

My darling Kenneth,

How the devil are you? I hope you are as wonderful as ever. Have I told you I have a best friend? I have never had a best friend before. I often watched enviously as you and little Clive played your games together. Her name is Mairi and she is strong as an ox and as pretty as a picture. She has bright orange hair, a sweet turned-up nose and is formidable. You will meet her one day!

Ta ta for now, my sweetest, bestest boy.

All my love,

Mama

How could I resist that? No one had ever so much as *remarked* on my nose before. Until that moment, I had thought my nose was entirely unremarkable! Not any longer. *Pretty as a picture*, that was me. And I had a best friend. I had someone who respected me, who trusted me. And hadn't she promised to take care of me? I felt like Alice falling down the rabbit hole, presented with a bottle: *Drink Me!*

Yes, Father, I am easily swayed. So what?

CHAPTER EIGHT

It had once been a beautiful three-storey house. Now, it was a house with a fallen-in roof, missing windows and floors and only two out of its four outside walls standing upright. It was not safe. It was a hazard. It looked as though it might collapse at any moment. But it you looked closely you'd find a trapdoor that led down to a secret underground world – a cellar. Elsie had found it with the help of a Gilbert – a Dr Gus Van Hint. He was attached to a Belgian army battalion that, unlike the English authorities, seemed keen to help our new project.

I followed Elsie down six uneven stone steps into the cellar. It was a small space, probably about half the size of a classroom. It was dank, dark and dirty. The grates in the ceiling let in little air and less sunlight. The dust got stuck in your throat. Coughing wouldn't clear it.

I knew instantly, as Elsie had known before me, that it was perfect.

The most important thing was its location. It was in the abandoned village of Pervyse. Unlike Ghent or Furnes, everyone had gone from Pervyse. No petrol boy or patriotic butcher remained here. There were no women picking turnips in the fields. There were no civilians left. We were north of Ypres, south of Ostend, about five miles from the hospital at Furnes. One hundred yards from the front line. The mere run of a rugby pitch. One try and we would be at the heart of the Western Front. Or to put it another way, the Germans would be at our throats. The Belgian Army was building trenches only a few metres from us. The British Army was not much further away.

Elsie's idea was that we would be an interim measure for the wounded – an interim measure before the other interim measures kicked in. We would pull the injured out of the trenches and carry them to the safety of our dressing station. Then, underground and therefore out of both the shells' and snipers' way, we could assess their condition, bandage them, administer pain relief, warm them by the stove or with a hot-water bottle, make them comfortable or sew them up before we sent them back to the trenches or off to the hospital…

Alternatively, we could send them off to the morgue.

We would be the go-betweens. If our men weren't strong enough for the journey, they'd go when they were. And if they were ready, off they could pop.

'Find them, fix them, ferry them, forget them!' said Elsie with a reassuring wink.

Of course, it didn't work *exactly* like that.

*

From the glassless windows of the house above, we hung a triad of flags: Belgian, French and English. I didn't think we would find the Scottish flag for love nor money, but a few days later, Dr Van Hint had tracked one down. I could rest easy. The Saltire made an excellent fourth addition.

My mother had always said that a house without windows is like a face without a soul, but I doubt my mother had seen many a face without a soul. It was nothing like that: the cellar house, with its quartet of flags, represented something wonderful to the soldiers fighting nearby. It was a beacon of light and comfort. The Belgians called us '*Poste de Secours Anglaise*' – British First-Aid Station – and word quickly spread that we were there.

Elsie and I went hunting in nearby abandoned houses for furniture and we found a strong low table and some invaluable lanterns. There was no room for beds, so instead we picked up straw. I thought of Jesus born in a stable in Bethlehem. I liked the humility of it.

Carrying armfuls of the stuff to the car, Elsie laughed. 'Straw brings to mind the three piggies, doesn't it? Kenneth used to enjoy that.'

I smiled at her. 'We all know how *that* turned out!'

Elsie laughed, picking up a second load. '*These* little piggies will be fine.'

I couldn't stop grinning. I had made the right decision.

We had left behind anything that wasn't immediately useful. There was no room for excess or luxury – I left Alice to her fate in Wonderland and the playing cards I bequeathed to Arthur – although I kept my Bible, of course. Elsie loaned Lady D her favourite green dress. We took one ambulance – I hadn't known that the Fiat was Elsie's own – and we also had the Chater-Lea with its temperamental sidecar and my Douglas.

The Belgians lent us a chef, Martin, who had recently lost a leg up to his knee (and along with it his good temper) and a reckless driver, Paul. Elsie said, 'All the best ambulance drivers are mad.' She always excused Paul, even though he had a habit of disappearing at the worst possible times.

Martin and Paul spoke Flemish and very little English or French. We managed to communicate though, with grunts, sign language and routine. They would, when necessary, spend the night on our straw, at the far end of the cellar. Nobody else seemed to raise their eyebrows at this, so, although it took some effort, I kept my eyebrows low too.

*

The evening we moved in – 12 November 1914 – Elsie instructed me to chop off all her hair. At first I thought she was making a joke, but she handed me some scissors, sat on the floor and refused to get up until I did it. I didn't want to. That liquorice-glow hair! She wouldn't be Elsie without her stunning brunette frame. I held her hair away from her head, and felt a nervous sadness as the blades wrenched it free.

I needn't have worried though. With no distractions, her face looked even more beautiful. I think Elsie knew it too!

Elsie said I didn't have to cut mine. I had enough self-awareness to know that whatever Elsie thought about my upturned nose, I didn't have the symmetrical features required to carry off such a short style. But I also knew the shorter style wasn't just practical, it was symbolic too. Our new life warranted seriousness. Hair was a frivolity and those days were behind us.

So I surrendered to the determined snip of the scissors.

'I look terrible, don't I?' I whispered.

'Fiddlesticks,' said Elsie. 'You look like a beautiful young warrior.'

'Elsie?' I asked uncertainly, when I wasn't looking at her face, 'What happens if the Germans break through the lines?'

'Can you run fast, Mairi?'

'Twelfth in county cross-country, 1911.'

'Good,' she said. We didn't discuss it after that.

After my cut was done Elsie held up my locks to the candlelight, where they looked more beautiful than they had on my head.

Then Elsie entwined my ginger locks with hers. 'Forget blood brothers, we are scalped sisters,' she said and I felt like I would burst with pride.

That first night, as I lay on our straw bed, my 'scalped sister' asleep next to me, I wondered about the family whose blessed cellar we were occupying. I imagined a pink-faced sporty boy, and a bright-eyed academic girl with pigtails. I had a feeling that they were a good, hard-working family: I wouldn't have been surprised if the father was a doctor. I felt they would be lucky for us.

Was this why God had taken the men from the house on the hill? To bring Elsie and me to this place? Was this my mission?

Next to me, Elsie moaned, 'Not now, not now.'

I put my hand out to touch her cropped head. It was as prickly as the lawn of a tennis court. She opened her eyes, took one look at me, then drifted back to sleep.

CHAPTER NINE

Each day we woke at five and made our way to the cold zig-zag of the trenches – corrugated iron, barbed wire, wet shell holes. We distributed soup or sweet hot chocolate. We said comforting things and looked after the minor injuries. Helped the stretcher-bearers with anything more major. Sometimes, when the shells were incoming, we had to sprint for it.

The men were so grateful, so pleased to see us: it made utter sense to be there. To do anything else would have been an affront to humanity. I might not have entered this new mission for the most selfless of reasons, yet I was not a *truly* awful person for it was for selfless reasons that I stayed committed to it.

Before they got used to us, some of the men said 'Stay away,' or 'This is no place for you!' But, as Elsie put it, their trembling hands reaching for the handles of the mugs told a different story. Their tear-brimmed eyes did too – their eyes said *thank you, thank you for being here.*

Dr Munro, Arthur and Helen refused to view our new home. Dr Munro was furious with Mrs Knocker and 'her dangerous scheme', though he didn't attempt to stop us (I believe he could have if he put his mind to it.) I sympathised with him. The war wasn't what he'd been sold. We continued to see him most days when we deposited injured souls at the hospital, or when he had something to deliver to us, but he treated us with barely any more warmth or familiarity than he did Paul or Martin. After a while, I ceased to find it hurtful, although in the early days I sometimes found myself rushing back to the cellar in tears.

Unlike the others, Lady D visited whenever she could. She stuck a 'Votes for Women' leaflet on our cellar wall, and when it disappeared (I blamed Paul), promised to replace it. Unfailingly helpful, she was a great believer in 'four o'clocks' and it was she who implemented our afternoon-tea ritual at that time of day. If the Belgians had thought the two British ladies in their midst were crazy, then they probably found our approach to teatime even crazier. However, if any soldier was in our cellar at that time, they soon joined in.

I wrote to my parents explaining our move. Perhaps they didn't understand the implications, because they weren't worried. My mother wrote about her rows with Cook over vegetables and the behaviour of friends who she seemed to dislike more than her enemies. She also devoted paragraphs to Uilleam, who had finally left home for our family plantation. Mother had paid extra for a cabin above sea level, but should she have got him a double cabin? She hadn't realised that was a possibility! Ship breakfast was served between 7.00 a.m. and 10.00 a.m. – if Uilleam didn't manage to get up for breakfast, would he be allowed to go to the ship's kitchen for a sandwich? She didn't display much curiosity about my life, although she had heard that Belgian waffles were tasty if fattening – '*watch your waistline, Mairi!*' Every time I wrote, I mentioned that we would be grateful for supplies – nothing major, just old towels, blankets, tin cups etc – but she ignored my requests. She mentioned more than once that Father couldn't for the life of him understand why Dr Munro had split the group between two separate locations – but she never directly asked why this was, so I didn't tell.

If the noise had been bad at Furnes, here it was five times worse: the constant rhyme of shells whizzing over, the roar of the machine guns in chorus. You could set your clock by it.

And the smell, the dynamite, the petrol: the unnatural scent of unnatural things.

*

Elsie and I lived like an old married couple, the big difference being that outside our front door were the battlefields of Western Europe, and instead of going off to the factory, the farm or the market, we retrieved the injured, the dying and the dead.

We learned each other's strengths and overlooked each other's weaknesses. Elsie was steely in a crisis – she didn't suffer from shaking hands, she let no quiver of indecision be shown. She always knew exactly what needed to be done. All I had to do was to follow her orders, and this I did willingly. It soon became apparent that Elsie didn't have the patience for administration, book-keeping, records or any 'dull things' like that, so I was charged with overseeing the logbooks. This was more time-consuming than you would have thought; however, I was naturally adept at organisation. Perhaps it was because I was in charge of the books that I felt our lack of resources more keenly than Elsie did. It was another growing worry. Elsie had financed us so far with her savings – but we had nearly cleared them out.

'Can I ask you something, Elsie?'

'Yes?' Her voice was wary. She didn't like personal questions. That was another thing I had learned.

'How on earth are we going to keep this going?' I remembered Dr Munro's assertion that no one would pay for this ridiculous caper and Elsie's glib response.

'Something will turn up,' Elsie said.

'But we are running out of everything.'

She ignored me. 'It always does.'

*

Obviously, we couldn't allow the men in the trenches just to drop by, otherwise we'd have been inundated. They had to get permission from their superiors. We dealt with all manner of problems from shakes and barbed-wire wounds to gangrene – one time, we even had to pull out a soldier's tooth. The men carried their own first-aid kits and plenty of them had tried to mend themselves, only to make it worse. Then there were the larger problems: like when the men were hit by incoming shells, or, of course, when they were ordered over the top.

If Elsie was out, and I was in the cellar with our companions – lice, spiders, mice and perhaps a poorly fella with a broken kneecap or a nasty wound – I liked to sing. I didn't have much of a voice, but it helped. Elsie suggested hiring me out to the Belgian Army.

'You could be their secret weapon! The Germans would give up if they were subjected to that for long!'

Uilleam used to say that kind of thing so I didn't mind. Anyway, I was a better helper than I was a singer and that was the important thing. After my initial freeze in Nazareth, I never failed to get involved in *anything*. I snipped, I cleaned, I comforted, I prayed. I reassured. I didn't let *ugliness* put me off anything and there was a lot of ugliness. I nursed our vehicles too (and even managed to fix the door of the sidecar). Elsie often told me that I was a trooper. I knew my limitations: I lacked experience and education and I was poor on innovation and taking risks; but I hoped my strengths – I was strong, reliable, cautious and gentle – more than compensated.

I made sure I didn't complain either. That gnawing space in my belly – I didn't complain. The terrible noise of shells like a constant earwig – I didn't complain. The dust sticking in your throat – I didn't complain.

Actually, there was one thing I did occasionally grumble about: the lack of toilet facilities. The ablution-run from cellar to woods with a spade was precarious, at night it was horrible and when menstruating it was even worse.

Despite never changing her clothes, rarely washing and her boyish cropped hair, Elsie's company was still sought after, especially among the engineers who occupied an abandoned house nearby. And Elsie still loved socialising. She was excellent at poker. Reputedly, she had the best po-face in Belgium. She always had cigarettes to share. There were even the occasional Gilberts – yes, even here in Pervyse there were admirers, there were dates, perhaps there was even canoodling.

I didn't know how Elsie, or indeed anyone, had the energy for it. Elsie always asked if I wanted to come out with her. I never did. I tried not to let her gallivanting hurt me, but I was jealous. *Wasn't I enough?*

But then, I was consoled, for she always came back.

One night, after we had been in the cellar for about three weeks, Elsie clattered down the stairs late, red-cheeked and full of rum. Usually, I pretended I was asleep, but that night we started chatting and I couldn't stop laughing. She kept repeating 'Plump up the pillows, Mairi!' like we were in a fancy hotel.

Pillows? I had almost forgotten what they were.

She was in talkative mood. 'Did you ever read *Villette*?' she asked.

I hadn't, and I was surprised Elsie was a fan of Charlotte Brontë. I would have thought she was more in the Emily Brontë camp.

'What's it about?'

'The main character – it's Charlotte Brontë really – falls in love with a Belgian, Monsieur Héger.'

My heart beat faster. *Why was she asking this, why now?*

'Have you fallen in love with a Belgian, Elsie?'

'In love? No, never,' she said. 'I wouldn't mind a little magic though.'

I wasn't sure what she meant. I cursed the fact that I wasn't as well read as I should have been.

'Do you ever wish you had gone to the Caribbean with your brother – for the quiet life?'

I laughed. 'Only every hour of every day.'

'Really?'

I paused.

It was dreadful here, cold and brutal, but at least I was doing *something*. I wasn't sitting on some sugar plantation, growing fat off the land. That winter, for the first time in my life, I felt wanted, I felt important, I felt needed. Elsie was a big part of that.

I would have told her, but she had fallen fast asleep.

∗

One of the better times of the day was after the morning trench visit but before the afternoon visit, when the post-boy wobbled towards us, fearless (or foolish!) on his pushbike. He was a handsome, curly-haired lad who liked to playfully read the front of our letters before slowly handing them over:

'Mrs Knockers?'

'It's Mrs *Knocker*, thank you, cheeky.' Elsie grabbed at the envelopes.

'Miss… Mmm… Cheese-ham?'

'Thank you!' I snipped the mail from his outstretched hands.

Neither of us did badly letters-wise. Though for no particular reason, I decided that where I did well in volume, I probably did less well than Elsie on content.

∗

We had been in the cellar house for about a month when I was tested in a new way. I was coming back from Furnes late one afternoon. I don't know if 'enjoy' was the right word, but I was not unhappy riding the Chater-Lea on the country roads adjacent to the Western Front. The sidecar was so laden down with much-needed supplies picked up from Furnes that the bike was slower than usual, but still it managed a pace. I felt that empowerment – oneness – that I sometimes got when I rode, like a small clenched fist of freedom.

Then, in the approaching dusk, I saw something in a nearby ditch. I thought it was an injured horse or fox, until I had nearly gone past, when I realised it was a man. I parked up and ran over. He was in a uniform, too dark to make out the colour, and he was soaking wet, covered in water or blood. I hauled him out of the ditch and hoisted him back onto the road. How strong I had grown! My arm muscles stuck out like cricket balls. Uilleam would have laughed at my manliness.

I tried to lift him up but he slumped back onto me. I couldn't work out where the blood was coming from but there was so much, it was like he had been bathing in it. He was barely conscious. I told him to wait, rummaged through the supplies, then gave him a shot of morphine as quick as I could.

This was my first emergency without Elsie by my side, talking me through it, but I knew what I had to do.

One of his arms was nearly falling off. He was trying in vain to keep it in place. As I examined him, I could see that he had already attempted a tourniquet to stem the flow of blood. It wasn't tight enough. There was a similar attempt at his knee. I re-did it. And there were wounds in his chest too.

'I've heard about you, Mrs Elsie Knocker!' His breath came fast.

'I'm not Elsie,' I told him. I couldn't tell if this brought him disappointment or not.

'You're the other one then?'

'Mairi Chisholm, at your service.'

'Why! You're just as good as Elsie,' he muttered.

'Thank you,' I said. In different circumstances, that would have made me chuckle. 'What happened?'

'I was… sheltering in a shell hole,' he said. 'Some shelter!'

I got him in front of me, told him to hang on to the handlebars. I don't know why I thought that would work. Elsie would have known better. He wobbled straight off the bike and it took all my might to stop him smacking onto the ground. I realised with some horror that I might have caused him further injury, but he managed to half-grin, half-grimace up at me. My heart went out to him.

'Just leave me,' he panted.

'Don't be daft.' I started emptying the sidecar as fast as I could. It took a while because it had been so densely loaded. I had to tug at things that had been jammed right in. I stood all the supplies on the slope down to the ditch, trying not to think of Dr Munro's exasperated comments: 'This is the last lot, Mairi. We're running low as well. Tell Elsie she has to order her own stuff and pay for it directly.' And of what Elsie would say if I lost it all.

Somehow, I managed to flop him in. There were still stray items rattling around by his feet. He whispered that his name was Sandy. By a wonderful coincidence, he was half-Scottish, on his father's side, and had spent two summers in the Highlands. 'I love the wild,' he said. I don't know why, but I was powerfully reminded of Uilleam. 'Shh, conserve your energy,' I told him.

'Yes, Miss Chisholm,' he said. No one ever called me that and it gave me a warm feeling.

When we arrived at the cellar house, I tooted the horn urgently and Elsie came out, prompt as a cuckoo in a cuckoo clock. I felt proud of her and proud of me – for hadn't I just managed this brilliantly all by myself? Together we hauled Sandy in and gave him more pain relief. He was shaking violently. The morphine wasn't even touching the sides. His eyes were already glazing over and the last thing he said to me was how cold his feet were. I covered them with a second blanket and told him to rest.

I said, 'I'll drive him up to Furnes first thing.'

'We'll see,' Elsie replied.

She was in no rush to treat his falling-off arm either.

'He's really not well,' Elsie said.

'He's a trooper,' I pointed out. I exaggerated: 'He was joking all the way here.' She nodded thoughtfully.

'I'll just pop back for the supplies, shall I?'

'Good idea.'

I went over to Sandy, touched his pale freckly cheek as he slept. 'Won't be long.'

*

I was only out twenty minutes at most. It was even darker now, but I recognised the bend of the branches and the curve in the road and I found the supplies all right. Everything was in the ditch, just as I'd left it. Damp, battered, but nothing that wouldn't dry out.

By the time I got back, he was gone. I cried in Elsie's arms most of the night. I didn't know if he had a sister, a mother or a father. I didn't know anything. Elsie had known Sandy's next destination was the morgue. But I hadn't even considered the possibility.

*

The next morning, I apologised. I had let myself down. Elsie said, 'It's the nature of this place, the nature of this job.' It helped to hear it but she never reacted as I did. I supposed it had something to do with being widowed young. Except for the young German lad, Elsie kept her emotions packed tightly away. I had a lot to learn.

Later that day, I decided to ride to the spot where I had found him. Elsie argued, 'Look, not only is it dangerous, it's pointless.' For once, I didn't listen. I was determined to see if Sandy had left anything behind that we could send to his family. We often went through the men's overcoats, looking for memorabilia, photos, letters, pictures, anything to make it easier for those left behind. If, God forbid, it was Uilleam, that's what I would have wanted. Perhaps I had missed something in the darkness of the ditch that I would find now? Anyway, when I went back I couldn't find anything of Sandy, but what I did find, on my return, was a notebook deep in a bush right outside the cellar house. I pulled at it gently, remembering that everything could be a trap or set off a trap. Opening the notebook, I saw there was writing on the front page: *Anglaise Devoirs' Madeleine* – 'Madeleine's English Schoolwork'. I waited until I was back in the cellar before reading further, but I was so intrigued that even those thirty extra seconds felt long.

Young Madeleine was learning the verbs and adverbs: *have, do, make, run*. She had neat curly writing, the way you'd imagine a young girl would write. *Quietly, Quickly*. She also made spelling mistakes, some of which had not been marked wrong, probably not to discourage her too much. Madeleine was not a natural English scholar. Maybe she was better at Maths?

I slipped her homework book inside my Bible. Madeleine was derived from the name Magdalene; it seemed appropriate for the little girl who once lived here. Her bookish failings only made me love her more. I put her next to John 20:18. 'I have seen the Lord.'

Over the next few days I found more clues to the cellar house's previous inhabitants: a small wooden car with no wheels that must have belonged to Madeleine's brother. A cracked half-saucer. *That* was a find because it had English engraving on the back. This, combined with the notebook, made me feel that the family must have escaped to England. They may have gone to Holland, or to France, but I put the notebook, the saucer and the car together and made London.

So. We were in the cellar belonging to Madeleine and her Britain-bound family. Somehow, this cheered me immensely. I connected it with Sandy too. If half-Scottish Sandy *hadn't* gone, I might never have found it. Everything happened for a reason.

After all this was over – *surely it wouldn't be long now?* – we would thank Madeleine and her family for letting us stay, and they would be grateful to us for keeping their home nice.

*

Not long after the Sandy incident, Lady D suggested that if the mountain wasn't going to Muhammad, then Muhammad should go to the mountain, which meant we were invited to Furnes for a party. Dr Munro apparently 'didn't mind if we came.' This was as good an olive branch as we could expect to get. I was delighted, and

Elsie, because she hated to stay alone anywhere, said she might as well come too.

We drove over on the evening of 25 December.

Christmas.

The war was supposed to be over, and we were meant to be home by now.

We hadn't brought anything with us. The prospect of arriving empty-handed made me anxious, but Elsie laughed. 'We're not miracle workers,' she said. 'There are no shops within twenty miles, they won't have any presents for us either!'

Their quarters looked cosy and inviting. We sat in the kitchen around the table amid the candles and lanterns: there was a pot of stew on the go that smelled wonderful.

But they *did* have presents! Not only had Lady D knitted us both long, winding scarves the shade of raspberries, but she'd made pots of plum jam too.

Dr Munro had somehow got a book of picture postcards for Elsie (to send to Kenneth, maybe) and a copy of *Through the Looking Glass* for me. I had no idea he had noticed my reading tastes. 'Keep it here if there's no room in the cellar,' he said gruffly. It was the first time he'd acknowledged our cellar life and it was a gracious thing to do.

His card read, '*God bless, Mairi.*' As Elsie read her card, she wiped her eyes with her sleeve, but she didn't show me what it said.

When we had quietened down, Helen stood, pressing the frame of her glasses into the bridge of her nose, awkward as ever. 'I wrote a limerick for you, Mairi,' she said, clearing her throat.

> There was a young lady from the Highland
> Who was very, very kind and
> She loved to sing songs
> That went on and on
> To her friends she was a real diamond.

I flushed. I had never heard such nice things. School reports dwelled on shortcomings – *Would it hurt Mairi to contribute to a class discussion? Mairi's performance has been little more than average this year.* As for my parents, saying nice things was not something they did, certainly not to my face (although I doubted they did it behind my back either).

Everyone clapped, then Arthur said, 'Helen, are you seriously rhyming "Highland" with "diamond"?'

Sitting down, Helen grinned at him. 'It's called artistic licence. *You* may not have heard of it.'

Peacemaker Lady D said, 'It's a perfectly legitimate rhyme!'

Arthur added, 'Well, I don't think Jessie Pope need worry yet.'

'I don't want to be *anything* like Jessie Pope,' said Helen loftily. 'That woman is a propagandist.'

'Her poems are highly acclaimed—'

'What did you think, Mairi?' Helen turned to me with her searching eyes.

'It's just… far too lovely!' I said.

'But it's all true, my dear!' she exclaimed.

I was unsure how to handle this. 'Does Elsie have one?' I muttered. I wanted to know if Elsie was a diamond too.

'Oh, yes!' cried Helen, rising again. She shuffled her papers, then curtseyed. She was more confident now. 'For Elsie…'

> There was a young lady from Devon
>
> Who liked to smoke cigarettes, seven,
>
> She smoked and she smoked,
>
> Until everybody choked,
>
> But they all said mm, she smells like heaven.

Everyone clapped and Lady D cheered. 'Another triumph!'

I couldn't help thinking my poem was more complimentary than Elsie's was. 'To her friends she was a real diamond' was superior to choking everyone with your cigarettes – impossible to interpret otherwise. I hoped Elsie had not been hurt. She was laughing as though she had not a care in the world.

'I may *once* have smelled like heaven, but those days are long gone!'

'Cigarettes seven?' said Arthur. 'I've seen Elsie smoke more than that of an evening!'

'But not at once,' said Elsie drily. 'I've only managed three at any one time.'

'I think the poems capture both their spirits very well,' said Lady D with finality. Dr Munro jokingly asked where *his* limerick was and Helen, looking flustered, promised she would work on it. I secretly wondered if she was struggling to find something that rhymed with *naked yoga* or *breathing exercises!*

Arthur said, 'I have something special for you as well!' I thought, *No more, this is overwhelming* but, smirking, he produced a turnip from his jacket. 'I know how you love these, young Mairi!' So that was a relief.

Lady D and I drank English tea, while the rest drank whatever alcohol Dr Munro had managed to get his mitts on. Helen read some more poetry – not her own, nor Jessie Pope's, but Keats. She had a lovely reading voice, and her American accent made it sound exotic. I closed my eyes to listen, and felt myself transported to somewhere peaceful and sane. Once she had stopped, we were quickly brought back to earth by Arthur, keen to talk politics. He was particularly interested in the Russian front. 'The cold will wipe them out!' he kept saying.

Helen looked at him sternly. 'Not tonight, Arthur, please.'

I was wondering when we would say prayers – it was Christmas after all – but no one mentioned them. However, towards the end of the evening, Lady D said, 'I suppose we should sing a carol or two!' so we lustily sang, 'Silent Night', 'Away in a Manger' and 'O Come All Ye Faithful,' and I thought *this is just as good a Christmas as any I've had before.*

I noticed Elsie didn't join in the songs. How many Christmases had it been since her husband died now? How painful it must be to be without him. I looked over at her and she caught my eye. I mouthed 'Merry Christmas,' and she did the same back.

Dr Munro and Arthur insisted we took their beds for the night – they would sleep in the kitchen. I acted grateful, but I was suddenly so exhausted that it made little difference to me what I slept on. Still, it was nice to be shown such kindness even if it served as another reminder that we should have done something for them.

When we drove back bleary-eyed at five o'clock on Boxing Day morning – so our boys hadn't had to miss a single trench visit – it felt like we had been on holiday. 'That was wonderful,' I said to Elsie. She didn't reply, but later I heard her tell Paul about the exceptional time we had had.

CHAPTER TEN

Dreary day in. Dreary day out. The freezing temperatures created a new set of problems.

'Like we didn't have hardship enough,' sniffed Elsie.

It wasn't just machine guns and shells that made the boys suffer so that January; their bodies were icing up. Crunch. Frostbite. The tip of the ear. The big toe got it. And then how it spread! I could never have imagined anything like it.

I don't know if we became hardened to horror, or if horror was normalised that winter. We were still compassionate, I hope, we were still gentle… but a man with no nose, a man whose jaw had been blown off, wouldn't *surprise* us any more.

Every morning and every evening, we crunched out on frost. Elsie and me, never getting warm, laughing, bickering, teasing, down the cold lanes of the trenches. Blue lips, fists clenched. Trying to bring good cheer, but sometimes the coffee froze over in the two minutes it took to get there. Sometimes, there was no time to eat or drink. If stretcher-bearers were there, they would pull the injured out; otherwise the task fell to us. Speed and safety was vital. You could dredge out a man only to have him shot in the chest if you dilly-dallied (this happened once). And strength, we had to be strong too. Every day was a test of endurance.

Driving a few miles up the road to Furnes was more dangerous now the roads were icy, so sometimes men stayed with us in the cellar for days and weeks instead of hours. Black ice caught me out a few times, but I managed to avoid falling into the roadside ditches.

But what improvements we saw when the boys were with us for even a day or two longer! A hot-water bottle, a blanket, a warm stove and some understanding could be transformative. Sometimes it would be enough.

It was a terrible time. To see humanity reduced in this way broke my heart. I hated what war did to us all. I cleaved ever tighter to the things I knew were good and pure: to God, to family and to Elsie.

*

Towards the end of January 1915, we heard that there was a new law. Women were no longer allowed on the Western Front. A new law passed and yet, an honourable exception had been made in our names. No women allowed on the Western Front, except for two: a Mrs Elsie Knocker and a Miss Mairi Chisholm! Elsie was speechless when she heard. Tears swam in her eyes.

'They know about us!' she kept saying. 'They know what we do. They care.'

I wasn't sure how to react. How absurd: *no women allowed?* Yet how wonderful to be considered an exception! It was such an honour that I didn't feel big enough to fill it. What if they discovered I wasn't good enough? I knew that Elsie was, but me? I bet everyone thought that I was just riding on her leather coat-tails.

I was proud that I would be able to write to my parents with the information about our exception, although I was certain my mother would treat it with less excitement than the time when their neighbour Mrs Barton had fallen off her horse and tumbled into Mr Harris's pond. At least my father would understand that this was an honour even if he wouldn't react as I would like him to.

The Belgian doctor, Gus Van Hint, brought us the fine news accompanied by a bag crammed with three-day-old bread. He spoke heartily between mouthfuls. 'Well, this is good news, except perhaps it's bad news.'

'Why?'

'Because… it sounds like we're settling in for the long haul.'

'I imagine we'll still be here by Easter,' Elsie said.

'That's if we've got enough money…' I replied. I hated to be negative at a rare moment of good news, but we were still in dire straits. A fact Elsie always seemed reluctant to acknowledge.

Elsie squinted at me. 'I may have an idea…'

'What?' I asked, but she said it was early days and when she had something of import to relate I would be the first to know.

Dr Van Hint shrugged. 'I think we'll be here until next Christmas.'

'No,' I said flatly. I couldn't imagine how the men could endure so long in the trenches.

He looked at me. 'Thing is, both sides still believe they can win it.'

'We *can* win it, though, can't we?' I asked optimistically.

He shrugged again, offering me some more bread. I picked out the mould and tucked in.

Things appeared to be going better for my brother in the Caribbean, at any rate. My mother wrote that he had met a nice girl from a good family (the good family was clearly more important than the nice girl). Everyone was frightfully hopeful. *Hopeful* seemed a cautious word but that was my mother all over.

In his letters Uilleam didn't mention *anything* about a nice girl or a good family. Instead, he ranted on about the oppressive heat and the sticky rum, the lack of interesting motor vehicles and the strange pungent herbs he was smoking. He also wrote a lot about when we were younger. I had never known him to be so nostalgic. It was out of character. '*Do you remember Christmas at Grandfather's? The time Bessie threw up on the tree?*' Or '*Do you remember the first time we went to Saunton Sands? Did Father step on a weaver fish or did I imagine it?*' He hadn't imagined it but I had no idea he looked back on those times with such affection.

He signed off with his flamboyant signature, and a postscript that made me smile: '*What's Gypsy doing now? What I'd do for five minutes with her!*'

*

In February 1915, Elsie found a little dog limping forlornly around the woods near the cellar. She removed the thorn stuck in his front paw and tweezered away the other splinters the poor mite had acquired. Then she warmed him by the stove on a blanket. Initially, I wondered (hopefully!) if the dog had once belonged to the house – if he was Madeleine's dog maybe – but he didn't seem to know where he was and often bashed into things. *Maybe he has poor eyesight?*

'What do you think he is?'

'He's a dog, Mairi,' said Elsie, grinning.

'I meant, a terrier cross or—'

'Whatever he is, he's sweet,' admitted Elsie.

He had a long brown nose and short white whiskers. His eyes were greeny-brown. He was small – he only came up to my knee – and good-natured. He was so confident, he must have been loved once.

We earnestly said goodbye, explaining that he should go and find his friends.

Elsie said, 'I bet after all that, he runs straight in front of the first truck he sees.'

But the little dog didn't run out. He point-blank refused to leave us. He *wouldn't* go. Even when we set him at the top of the stairs, pointing, *that way,* to the forests, even when we tried in French and German – nothing. So after about ten minutes of useless cajoling and persuading, I spoke up: 'Couldn't he stay with us, Elsie?'

Elsie looked doubtful. 'It'll mean more work—'

'I'm not afraid of hard work, Elsie, you know that.'

Elsie screwed up her face. 'We would have to agree on a name…'

'Is that a yes?'

'Do I have a choice?' Elsie smiled.

Suddenly I felt like I was six years old and I'd been given the best present. *We were keeping the dog!* I snuggled him in my arms and brought him back into the cellar. 'You're home now, fella!'

I was still wondering if he was house-trained and what he would eat and all those practical things, but just this once, I was determined to put the practicalities to one side.

'How about Gilbert?' I teased.

'No!'

'Hector? No, I know, Munro!'

Elsie mused, laughing. 'Arthur would get jealous if we did that.'

'Arthur then!'

'No!'

I considered. 'What was your husband's name? Perhaps—'

Elsie shook her head. 'Not suitable I'm afraid.'

I felt annoyed at myself. What an awful, *shameful* idea! To think of naming a *dog* after her late husband! And to actually say it out loud!

But Elsie didn't seem bothered. 'How about Bones?' she said. 'Or Bruno? Spotty?'

I picked him up and just then there was the sound of heavy gunfire overhead. Things were heating up. I cuddled him closely to me. 'There, there, shh…'

But his eyes barely flickered at the cacophony. He was as docile as anything.

'We could call him Shot?'

Elsie smiled. 'If you like.'

What a dog Shot was! He would climb onto your lap and sit as still as anything; at other times he might give himself a fright and chase his own tail. He would lick the men on their battered fingers or nuzzle under their arms. How they would respond to him! Nothing would cheer up a man with his foot blown off like a little beastie with a wagging tail. Nothing would cheer *me* up like the sight of Shot stretched out contentedly over the straw. When the war ended, or if we ran out of money and had to leave, I decided Shot would come home with me. Barney the cat would just have to get used to him.

Even Paul and Martin perked up in Shot's presence. Martin gruffly communicated that he used to have a Labrador, Noble. It was more than he'd told us in our months together and he didn't say much again after that, but he stroked Shot in the evenings and ensured he had food at least as good as any of us.

CHAPTER ELEVEN

After the evening run to the trenches, when both sides of the lines would be readying to sleep, you could usually count on it staying quiet. Still, it was a rare occasion when it was only Elsie, Shot and me in the soft light of that gloomy cellar. Perhaps we should have caught up on sleep, but sometimes, you must savour your moments awake to remind yourself that there's something worth living for.

It was March and the freeze was thawing. You'd expect to see flowers but nothing blossomed in or near No Man's Land.

There was a scuffling sound above us. If Shot hadn't been curled up, a little heavy weight in my arms, I would have thought it was him sniffing around outside, or a particularly intrepid fox.

Then came a friendly rat-a-tat on the cellar door. Shot pricked up his ears. I rose reluctantly.

'Perhaps it's a new Gilbert for you, Elsie.'

'I certainly hope so… I need some diversion.'

At the door was Tommy, a young lad with the British regiment nearby. He was wearing casual clothes – a tight vest top, baggy trousers and braces. The two lines went taut up his muscular chest like a railtrack. As he entered, I primly averted my eyes.

'Ah, Tommy! Mairi and I were just talking about you.'

'All good I hope?' He told us that he and the boys had clubbed together to get us a treat.

'A present? For me?' Elsie's voice was sensual – a contrast to the straw sticking out from her hair.

Tommy glanced at me. 'Well, both of you.'

'Oh.'

'You can't have *all* the attention, Elsie,' I teased her. She shrugged.

'Come see, ladies!' Tommy called enthusiastically. 'It's quite special.'

We followed him to the top of the stairs. My expectations were not high, and from the look on her face, neither were Elsie's. Food would be welcome; we were desperate for something that wasn't Maconochie. Maconochie was stew originally from my Scottish homeland but that was its only redeeming feature. A thin, wilting broth of carrots, potatoes and the blasted ubiquitous turnips, it had begun to turn up as the villain in my nightmares.

'Ta-daaaaaa!'

It wasn't turnip stew, thank the Lord, but I didn't think it was much to write home about: it was an antique chair, but not a chair anyone would have chosen. Its arms were long and scratched, its back heavy and old.

'Is this a joke?' I whispered to Elsie, but her eyes were shining.

'The fellas noticed you having to creep out after dark,' Tommy began hesitantly. 'And it's not bleedy safe…'

I wasn't sure what he meant.

'My darling. The romance!' squealed Elsie. I thought she was being sarcastic until, staring at the chair, I finally got it. *Ohhh…*

I don't know why, but the boys' thoughtfulness reduced me to tears. I covered my face with my hands and sobbed.

Elsie grinned. 'Of all the things… it's a ruddy *commode* that makes her weep!'

Tommy looked like he wanted to beat a fast retreat. The men didn't like to see us upset any more than we liked to see them sad. 'We appreciate all you do, ladies.'

We staggered down with it, hung some blankets around it and *voila* – our own private WC. No more running out to the trees in the middle of the night. No more cold calls of nature. Shot examined it with an approving sniff.

I didn't think I had ever been so pleased with a gift before, and Helen's limerick took some topping!

Tommy turned to go, revealing the taut, attractive Y of the braces stretched across his back. There was something mesmerising about his good looks. Two peas in a pod, he and Elsie were. Both tall, dark and delicious. They both knew it too.

Elsie followed Tommy to the top of the cellar steps. I could hear them chatting.

'Won't you marry me, Elsie?'

'That's the twenty-third time you've asked.'

'What's your twenty-third answer?'

I saw Elsie kiss Tommy, passionately. It was a lingering, outside-the-hotel-in-Harwich type of smooch. I didn't know what to do with myself. I examined the commode. Still they kissed. Then she pushed him away.

'Not a chance!'

She gave him five cigarettes though and he said, 'Blimey Elsie, where d'you get these?'

'I have ways.'

'I bloody know you do!'

Tommy was still laughing as he left. I didn't know what this kissing business meant. Surely Elsie wasn't *in love* with him? I said what I had heard Helen and Arthur once say about her – 'You are such an infant-snatcher!' It was, of course, water off this duck's back.

'If it weren't for my Gilberts, I wouldn't get through this.' She scratched behind her ears madly. 'I hope I haven't given him nits! Can you imagine?'

'He should still be playing in a playground.'

'So should you!'

At the low table, Elsie dashed off some messages to people whose names I didn't recognise: May Turner in the Somme, Bridgit Burns in Exeter, Philippa Bridlington in London. Elsie had friends every-where. It used to be a source of hilarity to me and Lady D that if we said, 'Cardiff', she would say she had a friend there; 'Manchester', she had a friend there; 'Sarajevo', a friend there also!

Elsie said, 'That's what happens when you get to the ripe old age of thirty-one.'

I couldn't imagine it myself and Lady D replied, 'I'm older than that, and I don't know *anyone*!'

I would have liked to have seen what Elsie wrote in her cards, but she only ever showed me the ones to Kenneth.

It was surprising how jolly those letters to her son were; it was as though Elsie completely separated herself from anything else she did. Elsie and I had dragged two young men squashed by a shell from a frozen trench that very morning, but would you have guessed from her postcard to Kenneth?

> *Darling boy,*
> *Today I saw a cat that reminded me of our neighbour's cat, Tiny. 'Cat' was one of your first words. I'm proud to say, 'Mama' was the other! I'd love to hear all your words now!*
> *Mairi sends big kisses, and I send all the love in the world, no, not just the world, there is not enough love here, all the love EVERYWHERE.*
> *Love Mama! (and Mairi and Shot the dog!)*
> *Xxx*

We had a play-fight over who was going to christen the commode first. It would not be me – Elsie would never let me forget it! Joking aside, Tommy's gift would make a big difference to our day-to-day lives and we were hugely touched. Perhaps we were on the up.

As we lay in the straw that evening, I thought again of Elsie's letter to Kenneth. There was no mention of his father, as usual. I didn't know what kind of a mention I was looking for, but there was never a '*Daddy would be proud of you*' or '*Daddy is watching from heaven*'. Yes, I know *she* didn't believe, but surely she wanted Kenneth to? As for the rest of her family, I knew only that she was adopted young after her mother and father tragically died. The family that adopted her now took care of Kenneth.

She was still awake so I asked, 'What was Kenneth's dad like, Elsie?'

'How do you mean?'

'You never talk about him. Was he fun? Sporty? Handsome?'

'Umm. He liked rugby, cricket, horses, the usual, you know.'

'How did he die, Elsie?'

'I… don't exactly know… like most deaths, it went slow, slow, and then quick, quick… slow.'

I took that in. Then asked, 'Was it unexpected?'

'Well, we had four weeks or so to prepare.'

'Did *he* know?' I said, gripped at the thought of having the answers to the questions that had been dogging me. She rustled the blanket and I was afraid she was going to get out of our cocoon. Talking about him was still so painful for her; I should have realised. I wished I could quote some passage from the Bible to comfort her, but it never did and she always liked me less when I tried.

She didn't move away though. She spoke softly, 'I don't think so…'

'Were you with him at the end?'

'Not quite,' she said shortly.

'You know how they say sometimes people prefer to be alone or with a stranger rather than their loved ones at the moment of passing?' I wanted to offer Elsie a small bone of comfort.

'I have heard that,' she said.

'Did it make sense to you?' I persisted. I shouldn't have kept on, but I had never felt closer to her. For a long time, I had needed her to open her heart to me, and I loved that she had this evening.

'Yes, he probably waited until I was out of the room… that would be just like him.'

'I'm sorry,' I said.

'Why are *you* sorry?'

Suddenly there was a banging on the cellar door, the kind that you can't ignore. Shot leapt to his feet, barking loudly. Elsie got up too, shouting fiercely: 'Who's there?'

She had just leapt to the top of the stairs when the door flew open by itself and Tommy fell in, onto her, his brilliant white T-shirt now covered in blood.

'Sniper,' he whispered. 'I lit… cigarette…'

'Tommy, I've got you,' Elsie said firmly. From the steel in her voice, you'd have absolutely no indication of the stricken expression on her face.

'Sorry to be of trouble, ladies.'

'Hang on, Tommy. We're here.' Elsie guided him down. I couldn't speak for shock.

'Tell Mum—'

'Oh Tommy, my darling boy, I will,' promised Elsie as she held him against her.

The next morning, out near the road, I was confused to find what at first looked like hair lodged between some bricks. It was fur, the fur of a darling brown teddy bear. Madeleine's bear? It felt like another miracle. Every time something truly awful happened, some sign would be sent to me.

I decided it was only because of what happened with our dear Tommy that I had found it.

'Is this to sell?' Elsie said when she spied it.

'No!' I felt quite offended. 'I… I… found it.'

'We don't have room.' Elsie looked shocked.

'It doesn't take up much space. Anyway, I can sleep on top of it.'

'Don't let Shot at it.'

'I won't.' I'd already had an undignified tussle with Shot and was determined that he wouldn't get near it again.

Coming closer, Elsie peered through the gloom at my stash.

'What the devil is it all anyway?'

'Madeleine's things.'

She looked at me the way we had started to look at some of the soldiers who'd been in the trenches too long. *You're not making sense.*

'Who is Madeleine?'

'The little girl who lived here before, look.'

I showed Elsie all the things – not only the bear, but the book, a ribbon, a half-deflated ball.

Elsie didn't even want to look at them. She was the least senti-mental person I had ever met. I said, 'There's no harm in it, Elsie.'

She paused. 'I suppose not.' She was about to say something else but changed her mind. 'Don't put it on my side, the last thing I want is to wake up to those frightful button eyes staring at me!'

I explained I was storing it away for when the family returned. Whenever she complained after that, I told her the same story. 'It's for Madeleine, Elsie, remember?'

She never took much interest.

Perhaps those things reminded Elsie too much of Kenneth. Over time, in my imagination, Madeleine had become my secret little girl who just happened to be far away. I saw her as mine, much in the same way as Kenneth was Elsie's son.

CHAPTER TWELVE

Later that month, while Elsie was out driving some injured men up to Ghent with Paul, a soldier dragged himself into the cellar. He had been shot in the leg and he was almost delirious with pain. Somehow, he managed to open the trapdoor before collapsing on the stairs.

The first thing I noticed about him was his enormous black beard. English soldiers tended to be fastidious about shaving; even if they'd just narrowly cheated death, many were frantic about getting rid of the five o'clock shadow. Not the French or the Belgians though. This man looked like a great big bear. His beard was dark and curly. A bird's nest. Young chicks could get lost in it.

I bandaged his wound and made him comfortable with a blanket in front of the stove. He was hardly aware of anything. His leg was a mess, I told him cheerfully, but I doubted they would have to amputate.

He startled at that. 'Amputate?'

'No, I mean I *doubt* they will. They won't. You *will* recover.'

He finally permitted himself a laugh. 'I understand.'

His English was good, he just hadn't heard clearly. His name was Harold and he explained he had been shot just as he got back from a scouting mission.

Harold seemed most annoyed that it happened when he was back, supposedly 'safe', not when he was in the danger zone. I had heard this before and knew there was a mixture of pride and humiliation in it.

He knew you had to keep your wound wet for fear of infection and in panic he had poured his own coffee all over it.

'Wasn't boiling hot, was it?'

'It's *never* boiling hot, is it?' he said, 'but it was a damn waste of coffee.' Then he promptly fell asleep.

Harold was one of the few wounded soldiers who came to us unaided. Most we picked up and carried, dragged or tipped down to the cellar. Maybe that was what made everything feel different about him…

Still, chores had to be done. Most mornings, after the trench visits, I did the logbooks: this soldier was the 387th we'd seen. The number seemed impossibly high – I could never have imagined we'd be so in demand.

I checked, logged and reorganised our supplies. I did some washing. I didn't mind menial tasks. When I was peeling turnips in Ghent I had railed against them, but here, there was something uncomplicated about the repetitive jobs. Sometimes, I could almost forget what was going on outside.

Our latest patient slept so quietly that for a few moments, I forgot myself. I began to sing. I must have been singing for about ten minutes and was building up to quite the crescendo when Harold rose up on one elbow and cried out, 'Love you forever!' before promptly falling back asleep.

I stared at his beardy face. It was the strangest thing. He must have meant those words for someone else, a wife or a girlfriend perhaps, but still…

It wasn't until Elsie had warmed herself by the stove for some time that she realised we had acquired a new patient. She peered at Harold – or the brown bear, as I regarded him.

'You've done a good job with the leg, Mairi, but couldn't you have sorted out his facial hair?'

I smiled weakly. For once, I couldn't help wishing she hadn't returned so quickly. *What other things might Harold say in his sleep?*

'What's he like?'

I told her what he had said about the coffee and she chortled as I thought she might. 'He sounds like fun.'

He wasn't as much fun as Elsie hoped though, because he slept all that day and all that night and he didn't call out again. The next morning he was asleep as we went out to do our trench visit and he was *still* asleep when we came back.

Paul was doing the weekly drive to Dunkirk that afternoon to pick up supplies. We decided that if Harold was strong enough for the journey, Paul could drop him off at the hospital on the way. *They* could operate on his leg if they deemed it necessary.

'I'll load him up,' Elsie said. 'Would you wake him, Mairi? I don't want to give him a fright.'

'My pleasure.' I wasn't just being polite.

I gently tried but Harold slept on, snoring peacefully.

'Goodness, so this is the sleep of an untroubled man!' Elsie laughed. 'Look at Sleeping Beauty.'

I continued trying to get him to stir, but Elsie decided I was taking too long and shook him to. *Why ask me to do it, if you're just going to take over?* Usually those woken abruptly, especially with an injury, come to in a cloud of complaining and groaning, but Harold woke smiling, his arms outstretched like a pope performing a blessing.

'I had heard about the nurses doing battlefield rescue. I didn't know you were actual angels.'

'We've heard that one before.' Elsie winked at me.

He pulled himself up and looked around him as though he were seeing the cellar for the first time. He was so amazed his mouth fell open.

'I thought I was in heaven.'

Elsie snorted. 'You are at Pervyse. A *Poste de Secours Anglaise*.'

'I know,' he said. 'I saw the flags in the distance and kept on walking. I'm glad I made it.'

How *we* must have looked to him, with our short hair, gaunt faces and our old dirty clothes, I couldn't imagine!

'How long have I—'

'Been asleep? About one day and one night.'

Harold hauled himself to his large feet, refusing our help and wincing only slightly. He smiled at Elsie.

'I thought I heard singing.'

'That was her.' Elsie pushed me forwards. I stumbled but corrected myself.

He bowed at me. 'A sweet tune and an even sweeter voice.'

Perhaps that was the moment we both noticed that despite his injury, his beast-like hairiness and his blood-stained clothes, there was something of good quality or breeding about Harold.

Elsie smirked. I was embarrassed.

'I thought you were fast asleep. I wouldn't have sung otherwise.'

'I wouldn't have mentioned it if I thought it would embarrass you.'

Elsie looked at the two of us. She slid her fingers along the table.

'Mairi sings nicely,' she said, for the first time ever. I looked at her, checking whether she was teasing or not. She continued, 'Sadly, singing is one of the few things I don't excel at.'

'And maybe German?' I retorted. Elsie could still make neither head nor tail of that language.

'Oh, but even that's improving nicely, *nein*?'

Elsie explained to Harold that we had arranged transport to a hospital for him. He looked relieved, then mystified.

'But where will *you* go?'

'We stay here.'

'Here?!' The word bounced off the cellar walls. Elsie and I both laughed at his astonishment. 'This is no place for you!'

We shrugged. Elsie was touching her lips contemplatively.

'Don't you get shelled?'

'Yes.'

'Sniped at?'

'Yes.'

'What if the Hun break through the line?'

'Indeed.'

'But… but…'

Not many of our patients were interested in what we were doing here, beyond saving them. It was unusual to have someone be curious about our lives, but Harold seemed instantly at home with us.

'How do you afford to run this place?' he asked.

'We manage,' Elsie retorted. In my head, I added *just.*

'You are always here?'

'Yes,' I intervened. 'At least one of us is.'

'In that case, I'll know where to come back to thank you ladies properly.'

Elsie helped him sit down, for he had begun to wobble. 'There's no need. We don't do *properly* here.'

Harold grinned at her. 'How about if I bring boxed sweets?'

'Oh, in that case… Mairi would sell her brother into slavery for a sniff of a *marron glacé.*'

'Elsie!' Categorically, this wasn't true.

'Then Mairi' – he bowed and for a moment, we could have been in a ballroom celebrating some duke's birthday – 'I will hunt the whole of Belgium for a *marron glacé* for you.'

I blushed. I couldn't forget what he had said when I was singing: *was it the morphine? Did he not remember at all?*

Harold smiled, then turned to Elsie. 'And you? What do you like?'

'I'm afraid that I abhor most sweet things.'

'What a pity,' he said. He looked closely at her. Their faces were only inches apart. I thought, *was this like the first meeting between Charlotte Brontë and the handsome tutor Mr Héger?*

'You… have remarkably pretty eyes: like sunflowers.'

*

When Elsie came back from helping Harold out to the car – they 'didn't need my assistance' – she was much cheered.

'He's a baron, don't you know!' She imitated his voice, 'You sing so beautifully. I thought I was in Tipperary.'

I imitated him too, although mimicry was not a talent of mine as it was Elsie's. 'You have very pretty yellow eyes!'

Elsie laughed. 'He's lucky he's got a leg to stand on.'

Something stuck in my throat as I asked, 'Another Gilbert for you, Elsie?'

The more I thought about his voice, and his curly black beard, the more peculiar I felt.

'He's more your type, I would have thought,' Elsie said, scratching her head frantically.

Of course Elsie would notice. I wasn't sure what to do. I looked at the indentation on the blanket where he had been.

'Don't be daft,' I said finally.

She shrugged. 'You'd make a fine couple.'

I had to say something. 'Do you want me to brush your hair, Elsie?'

'Please…'

*

A few days after Harold's visit, I went out to hunt. There were rabbit holes every three feet or so but I didn't see a single inhabitant. Perhaps the war had frightened the rabbits off too. I damn near sprained my ankle as well. It was my poorest shoot in memory until I turned my attention skyward and picked five sparrows out of an unguarded nest. I felt absurdly elated at the flutter of the feathers and the panic I caused. But who knew small birds had so little meat on them? It turned out to be a most pointless exercise, although Martin admitted they gave his stock an 'earthy' flavour. I said that was odd, because they weren't of the earth, more of the air. He blinked at me.

Food wasn't even our biggest priority. We needed medicine, petrol and blankets. I didn't know where we would get the money from, and I was certain that Elsie, for all her talk, didn't know either. We had got by so far on a wing (Elsie's) and a prayer (mine).

'Shouldn't we ask the Red Cross or the army for help?' I asked Elsie over sparrow soup.

'They'd only send us away from the front,' she replied spiritedly. 'We don't want to see out the war in some blessed hospital while everyone else is in the thick of it, do we?'

'I suppose not.'

*

Approximately one week later, my mother wrote that Uilleam's marriage was not going to go ahead after all. I couldn't make head nor tail of the convoluted story told over six pages (a record for my mother, who usually had some urgent flower arranging to oversee), but reading between the lines, the fiancée had called off the engagement, due to some '*ridiculous rumours*' about '*Uilleam's suitability*'. '*What these have to do with her, I don't know!*' wrote my mother, mystifyingly.

Mother's parting lines were clearer:

We need you to go to Uilleam in Trinidad and to patch things up between them for the sake of the Chisholm name.

I wrote straight back explaining that Uilleam *always* had my support but things were decidedly *tricky* out here. Perhaps Mother had read in the newspapers what we were up against? Didn't she understand that I was living in a cellar only one hundred yards from the Western Front? That we were doing our best to cope with hundreds of injured and dead soldiers? From these small seeds, my resentment flowered.

So when the post-boy brought me my mother's next missive three weeks later, I took it from him as though I were receiving something not at all to my taste.

'Miss M?' He smirked.

'Thank you.'

This time, Mother had written:

He's your brother, Mairi. A good marriage would benefit us all. It's all very well helping foreigners on the Continent, but your duty is to the Chisholms. You have to sort this out. For once in your life, don't be so selfish.

I couldn't bring myself to write back.

'Nothing to go out, Miss Mairi?' asked the post-boy when he next came.

'Not today.' I tossed him a silver coin anyway. Elsie had taught me to always treat those who helped us as best we could.

'Shame!' He winked at me. I felt a rising redness and was annoyed at myself.

Eagle-eyed Elsie also noticed I wasn't writing home as usual. I didn't want to reveal anything at first – I didn't criticise my parents to anyone (not even Uilleam) – but I couldn't hide anything from her. Tears in my eyelashes, I told Elsie that my mother expected me to abandon my work in order to go halfway around the world to arrange my brother's love life!

I added that she seemed most agitated that we were helping *Belgians* of all people.

Elsie laughed, which made me feel slightly better. It *was* a little funny, I supposed.

'You're not going anywhere, are you, Mairi?'

'No!' *This was my vocation. If we could just ease the poor boys' suffering by so much as an inch it was worth it.*

'Good,' she joked, 'because I need you to sort out *my* love life! There has been a distinct shortage of Gilberts lately.'

I wondered if she included Harold in that.

'I am disappointed that my mother...' I began. I couldn't say how much it hurt to be called selfish. Elsie stopped joking and put her hand on mine as I continued speaking, '...thinks so little of me.'

Elsie said, 'Sometimes people don't do what we want them to do or think what we want them to. *Especially* family, I have found!'

'So... how... how do you cope with that?'

'Accept that sometimes even good people get it wrong.'

I scowled. I felt terrible for thinking it, but I wasn't sure my mother should even be included in the category of 'good people'.

'But, they make me feel so...' I paused, unable to find the word at first, '...alone. I wish I belonged somewhere.'

'In that case find a family of people who *do* understand you,' Elsie advised. 'There are plenty who think a lot of you, Mairi.'

Did she mean she thought a lot of me?

'Is that what you had to do after your husband passed?'

'Well—' she paused, 'When I was widowed... I had to start again. It was painful, it wasn't what I expected, no one does, but it can be done, I promise.'

I sniffed. 'Can I still be your sister?'

'Scalped sisters?'

'Couldn't we be something a bit more poetic?'

'Shell sisters? Sniper sisters? Shrapnel—'

'Just sister will do.'

'Just sister it is.'

I looked up at her. 'We're nearly out of money.'

She took my hand, 'I know, sister, I'll think of something.'

*

Eventually my father wrote. It was only the second letter I'd ever had from him. The first was when I was at boarding school and I had the temerity to complain about one of the teachers who was overly fond of the belt. My father wrote that if I ever received a belting at school, I would receive double at home (I made sure I never did!).

He got straight to the point in this letter too:

Your mother is worried sick. She had a fainting episode so I took her to see Dr Barret in Exeter.

I pictured Father sitting at his mahogany desk, furiously dipping his pen into the ink. Great black blots like angry blood clots on the paper next to him. The pulse in his forehead blue and throbbing. Periodically, he would look out the window at our neatly mown lawn and the even more neatly trimmed hedges and he would frown.

All this business with you and Uilleam (what business?) *is not good for her head. Family comes first. I appreciate you are enjoying yourself* (enjoying!) *too much to leave Europe, but your mother deserves some respect.*
Father.

I guessed that this was his way of saying they accepted that I was staying put but that I had better bloody write soon, and of course, stickler for the rules that I am, I did.

*

Wire and mud, bandages and buckets. Life expectancies quartered. Boys born in 1896 or 1897 – like me – waiting for their number to be up. We stopped asking why, we stopped asking anything. There was never a satisfactory answer. *Just work, monotony helps you not think.* I put Harold and his love-you-forever to the back of my mind too. He would recover, we would never see him again and that was how it should be.

*

One morning down in the trenches, a soldier cleaning his gun called out, 'Hey! Remember me?'

I didn't. In their helmets, if the sun cast a shadow over their faces, the men were hard to distinguish. This man had the happy air of an escaped convict.

'Really? You don't?'

I smiled guardedly and bowed my head. I was thinking, *how quickly can I walk away?*

'It's Mairi, isn't it?'

'It is.' *Where was Elsie? She was great with the odd ones.*

'You saved my life.'

'Me?'

'The fall of Dixmude? You and Elsie got me to the hospital. They packaged me up and sent me out here.'

'Gosh,' I said, still uncertain. I would have thought those who survived that terrible night would be too injured to ever soldier again.

Elsie encouraged me to remember our successes, but it was the failures that stuck in my head: the slaughtered at Nazareth, the horse on the road, the dead Samaritan, Sandy, Tommy.

'And the other man?' I asked tentatively.

'Alive, thanks to you!' he chuckled. He wasn't crazy – it was just his way. I was filled with such relief I would have hugged him if his gun weren't between us. 'He's recovering in the Netherlands. I will write and say the lovely redhead is still saving lives.'

'Send my best wishes. And stay safe.'

'Don't worry about me.' Spitting on his cloth, he continued polishing. His weapon shone so brightly that, for a brief moment, I was taken back to the drinking glasses our housekeeper made sparkle every Friday. 'I'm a fortunate man.'

His words stayed with me a long time. Whenever I doubted myself, whenever I thought of my mother scolding me for being selfish, whenever I thought *we're going to run out of money soon*, the memory of him gave me a much-needed glow.

*

Occassionally, we went to Furnes for the evening. We went for Arthur's birthday in February and once again in March when Lady D had received a delivery of whiskey. We took Shot one time, but he made Helen sneeze. Elsie was never too keen to go. She preferred socialising with the engineers – there was one, Robin, who was disgustingly sweet on her – or she'd drive to France to meet friends there. I was also less enthusiastic about leaving the cellar than I used to be. It was silly, but I didn't like the idea that Harold might come back while no one was there.

I always enjoyed it when we did go though. It was an escape. We visited for Easter Sunday and sang 'It's a Long Way to Tipperary' and 'For He's a Jolly Good Fellow'. We discussed Churchill's campaigns: ambitious – the prospect of using aeroplanes in war – unlikely; the chance of American involvement – nil; and then Lady D gave her usual impassioned speech about women's right to vote while I clapped. I had been reading her pamphlets and I was fully onboard. Even Arthur supported Lady D's polemics, which surprised me.

Elsie didn't join in with the political talk. She wasn't interested in theories or philosophies: by nature, she was practical; her instinct was to mop up the mess that the politicians and generals got us into. She was, however, unbeknownst to me, passionately interested in the fates of the current polar expeditions. 'Such ingenuity, such courage!' she burst out when the conversation turned to the explorers. She looked desperate when Helen quietly explained that Shackleton and his crew were all missing, their ship had been abandoned and they were presumed dead.

And then we drove back home to the cellar. Going away and coming back made the cellar feel more like home than ever.

*

Despite Elsie's assurances, our finances were still a worry. A Belgian officer who had for some time been admiring my Douglas offered me money for it. I dithered at first, but I knew that one bike between Elsie and me was enough and hers was the better one, so I agreed a sale. I was unsentimental throughout the transaction, though I hid in the cellar rather than see Douglas go. I had loved that bike dearly.

As I ordered the things we needed and paid Martin and Paul some money we owed them – and asked them, please, to source us some beef as an overdue treat – I felt I had made the right decision. We could breathe easily for another month or so.

The imaginary conversation I had with Harold where I impressed him with my sacrifices also went some way to compensate.

At last, in May 1915, something did turn up. One of the friends Elsie wrote to in London, Mrs Philippa Bridlington, had been taking Elsie's letters to the newspaper office that just happened to be at the end of her street. Bish, bash, bosh: we were the front-page news of *The Times of London* and causing quite the stir.

'Didn't you know,' Elsie looked at me shyly, as though debating whether to continue or not, 'the newspapers are calling us "The Madonnas of Pervyse"?'

'Goodness!'

'Mairi!' Elsie laughed.

'What?'

'Don't pull that face.'

'What face?'

'Your face says, *Elsie! A Madonna? She's more like a Mary Mag-dalene!*'

I laughed. In truth, *neither* of us deserved to be called Madonnas. We were just hard-working women doing our best. Why couldn't they just say *that* instead of giving us these sensational nicknames? 'I suppose today's news will be tomorrow's chip paper.'

'No doubt.'

'I just don't see the point,' I insisted.

'You'll see,' she said.

*

A few days later, I did see. Elsie plonked a stack of money on the table for me to log.

I examined the bundle of notes and thought, *God has heard my prayers.* 'What is this?'

Elsie shrugged.

'Is it from your family?'

Elsie's family had never sent money before, but it seemed to be the most likely answer. She shook her head. Fleetingly, I wondered if Harold had something to do with it.

Elsie explained. It was from people, complete strangers, who had read about our efforts in the newspapers and now wanted to contribute to our cause.

'Well, I never.' I picked up the accompanying letter:

I saw your story in the Daily Telegraph *and felt compelled to put pen to paper… Never have there been two such noble heroines who have made such sacrifices risking—*

'Oh, just put it with the others,' Elsie interrupted, pointing to a pile of letters stuffed under the table. *How had I not noticed them before?*

'What? Really?'

'Fan mail,' Elsie said with little emotion. You think she'd be delighted, but she wasn't. This was business. 'People love to romanticise a war and try to get involved.' She shrugged. 'If it helps us buy what we need to continue, then let them.'

Our fame created more work for our friendly post-boy. Fortunately, he seemed to be growing and filling out as much as his post bags.

'Madonnas of Pervyse?' he read out slowly, then squinted at us with his lop-sided grin. 'That's not you ladies, is it?'

'It's not what we would call ourselves, no.'

'Then who's this? The "two stunning girls on the Western Front"? That you as well?'

I held out my hand. '*Thank* you.'

My mother also wrote that her circle had read about us in the *Dorset Sun* and were determined to '*… do their bit for the Madonnas of Pervyse. (But couldn't you live somewhere easier to pronounce?)*'. I was to send her a list of necessities immediately.

Since I had been asking Mother for supplies for the last six months, this grated more than a little. Only now, with the validation of the newspapers, did she want to get involved. She had evidently forgiven me for my interest in helping *foreigners*.

Still, I couldn't fault her efficiency. Mother and her circle burst into action knitting lavish scarves and gloves and acquiring blankets, belts and braces from goodness knows where. I wrote effusive letters – under Elsie's direction – saying how grateful we were:

'*Our appreciation knows no bounds.* Is that too much?'

'No.' I wrote it down. 'She'll love it.'

'*The boys will be forever in your debt.*'

'That's perfect.'

It made a welcome change from her worrying about Uilleam every line. And she didn't call me selfish again.

Now that we were in the papers, my mother had acquired a new passion for Mrs Knocker. '*Is she really as beautiful as everyone says*?' (My mother had a keen nose for a woman's appearance.) '*How does her little boy cope without her? What a darling he must be!*' I replied to these questions without Elsie's help because Elsie would only sigh: 'There's a reason a private life is called a private life, Mairi!'

So much was sent to us that we had to leave some supplies at Furnes with Dr Munro *and* some in the engineers' house. Robin stacked up our boxes heroically with his lovelorn eyes on Elsie.

'You're so good to us, Robin,' Elsie said, one hand on his wrist, the other fluttering over her heart.

'I'd do anything for you, ladies,' he said, red as sunset.

I was uncomfortably sure he would have done too – for one of us anyway! Oh, I *was* learning a lot!

We were also sent two hundred copies of the New Testament. There was a rumour going around among the soldiers that if you had this New Testament on your person when going into battle, you would survive. It looked like the people back home had also heard this. The trenches were a breeding ground for superstitions.

Elsie couldn't have looked at the books with more disdain. 'And they're in English!' she said, appalled. 'What Belgian boy will want to read the Bible in English?' She shook her head incredulously at the never-ceasing stupidity of people back home. 'Never mind, we're always running out of paper for the toilet.'

Delighted with our financial successes, in June Elsie proposed expanding the cellar house upwards. The ground floor would be converted into a clinic. We would be safe enough in daylight – though no guarantees of course – and then at night, we and any patients would retreat underground to sleep. We would learn from nocturnal creatures, bats and rats.

It only took an afternoon to build. We created sandbag walls where walls were missing. The engineers provided us with a tin roof. It had jagged edges that we had to take care not to bang into. It was remarkable to see it being constructed.

What a relief it would be to nurse in the light, in the air, where we could breathe more freely! We had always tried to do our best, but it felt like our best was about to become better. I thought if Harold ever came back to see us, he would be impressed.

And how nice to put Madeleine's old home to use again! What stories we would tell her one day! To think we were experiencing just a few moments in the long history of this house, of her family. Madeleine would grow up and one day, she might talk about us at dinner parties as she poured sweet wine and handed out warm bread. 'And this room was where Mairi and Elsie used to bandage the soldiers before sending them on.'

Martin made pea soup 'to celebrate'. We sat drinking it out of tin cups, searching out the odd prodigal pea.

I couldn't help feeling that the war would be over soon. It *had* to be, didn't it? Of course, I had no evidence for that. Quite the contrary: the trenches looked more permanent; wooden planks were nailed up, more barbed wire was set down, whole pavements were laid. These were sandbag villages, or even underground cities.

How could people go on killing each other when nature was once again bursting into life? Summer was determinedly on its way. They couldn't stop that. Nor the larks who never ceased piping, not even when the bombardments were at their worst. I saw ladybirds and counted their spots. Each spot represented a single day. A ladybird didn't have many days.

*

One sunny morning, I took Shot with us to the trenches. As expected, he proved as popular with the men out there as he was with everybody who came into the cellar. He nose-butted the soldiers, eyeing them curiously. They crowded around and stroked him. Although our Shot was not easily shaken by loud noises, and would even sleep through the whistle of shells, he became unsettled by so much attention at once.

'He smells fear,' I said. It was something my father used to say about animals.

'He'll be happy here then,' a soldier said. 'Fear's all you can smell.'

That wasn't *quite* true, unfortunately.

Shot was a delight: the men passed him around as if he were a chocolate bar, each taking turns in the pleasure. His little tail wagged and he made affectionate snuffles into their chests. Some of the men were more familiar with dogs than others, but they all had a go. A young soldier, Jake, held him close to his freckled face.

'Nan had a dog,' he told me. 'Hulking thing, big as a pony.'

The stories Shot would elicit never ceased to amaze me. It was as though everyone had an old dog's tale.

'She used to meet me after school, at the garden gate. I didn't appreciate her 'til she was gone.'

He was burying his face in Shot's furry back when there was the whizz, hiss and boom of a shell. It must have landed extremely close. Shocked, Jake dropped Shot to the ground and suddenly, before our stricken eyes, Shot panicked like he never had before. He clambered up the trench walls, and ran for it. There must have been a rip in the barbed wire, or a burrow or something. He was streaking up and away, towards the vast space of No Man's land.

I can't tell you the horror I felt to see our little dog making for that desolate landscape.

Shot was trapped between us and the Germans. Elsie was further along the trenches treating someone's eye. She wouldn't know what was happening.

He was still heading away from us. I waited for the sniper's bullet. I couldn't even scream for him.

Silence. The Germans must have seen him frolicking about, if only through their binoculars, but perhaps he pleased them too? Perhaps we were all in need of some entertainment.

He stopped, looked back at us.

Realising that using his name wasn't a good idea, I called, 'Here doggy!' instead. No response. Shot sank onto his hind legs.

I was going to have to go for him. I started to climb up the ladder, but they pulled me back.

Jake was weeping. 'I didn't mean to let go, Mairi.'

Shaking off the soldiers, I bolted my way up to the top and went over to him, crawling through the mud. One foot, two foot, three… waiting for one or both of us to die.

He came towards me. Thank God. I scooped him up, praying for safety, wincing at the prospect of the fire, the explosion, the bullet to the head. It didn't come. We backed off, Shot squeezed between my belly and the ground.

'I've got you, Shot,' I whispered. I felt the life pulsing through him in my arms. His racing heart. His silky ears.

I half jumped and was half pulled into the trench. I felt elated. What joy it was to be alive. We had been saved.

Elsie was striding towards me, her leather coat swishing from side to side. She stood over me, a giantess, hands on hips, fury in her eyes.

'Don't you ever, EVER do anything like that again, Mairi Chisholm.'

Elsie pummelled me: she actually punched my shoulders with her clenched fist, first one side and then another, not violently, not viciously, but certainly enough to hurt. I thought of my father hitting Uilleam – how he would not make a sound. How everyone conspired to pretend it never happened.

I stared at her, waiting for it to stop. 'Don't do anything to provoke him,' I used to whisper to Uilleam. '*Everything* about me provokes him,' he used to reply.

'I couldn't bear it!' she shouted, and pushed me again.

'It's fine,' I muttered. 'We're fine.'

'If anything happened to you, I would die.'

Elsie pulled me up from the trench floor. She hugged me, squeezing the whimpering Shot between us. She caught my chin between her hands, gazing at me like she was seeing right through me. Tears were falling down her face, making white tracks through her mud-stained cheeks. I stared at her in astonishment. Then she thumped my back again: 'You idiot!' I think she must have remembered that all the startled men were watching her because she straightened up and began playing to the crowd. 'Did you see what this crazy girl did?' Then she was off, checking wounds and telling boys they'd be back home with their sweethearts soon enough without once looking back at me.

CHAPTER THIRTEEN

The summer of 1915 dragged on. After the bitter winter, now the intolerable heat. The upstairs part of the cellar house was a great success, although like many great successes it brought with it an increased workload. We now had four army cots, two up, two down, and the men enjoyed being up top where they could feel the sun on their wounds and watch the clouds pass in the sky. Our lives took on a new rhythm. We were quiet for a few days, and then we were overwhelmed. Before an advance it was mostly calm… and then there were the storms.

We were invited up to Furnes for a party to celebrate Dr Munro's birthday in July. He wouldn't tell us his age although Elsie and I guessed it was somewhere between fifty-six and sixty-three.

Lady D had cobbled together a fruit cake. We made jokes about how if we fired it over the enemy lines, we could take down the Bosch, which she took in her usual good spirits.

Arthur and Helen had given our last set of playing cards to a young soldier.

'What could I do?' Arthur asked, raising his palms upwards. 'His friend had exploded in front of him. I wanted to keep his mind off it.'

Arthur had started making his own pack but said he got stuck on the picture cards. He shyly showed us his efforts. Elsie laughed, saying, 'What is this pornography?' about his queen. Arthur, who was in an unusually fine mood, grinned.

'I'll be looking for a new career after the war…'

'Well, there you are!'

Lady D entered the room with more tea.

'What think you of this?' Arthur showed her a wizened fella he had drawn, with a clumsy crown and sceptre.

Lady D examined it. 'It's a good likeness of Dr Munro.' She looked up at us helplessly. 'No?'

We fell about laughing.

I asked Helen how the limerick for Dr Munro was going. She wrinkled up her nose. 'I'm concentrating on my novel, so I haven't had a moment to spare.' I was going to ask more questions about the novel, mainly: *was I still in it*? but right then Lady D clapped her hands and proposed a game of 'Truth or Consequence'. It was a childish game we had played after lights-out at school, so I was surprised and a little alarmed when everyone agreed.

'Right-ho, so we need a question.'

'Nothing too…' Dr Munro advised.

'Too what?'

Dr Munro sighed. 'Too controversial, Lady D.'

'Scaredy-cat!' she said, but with affection, I think.

My heart started beating faster.

'All right, what was the best day of your life?' Lady D said.

Helen went first. She blinked at Arthur through her owl-glasses. 'The day I married you, stupid.' She looked at him, waiting for something. We all waited. I felt so awkward for her. Elsie was staring at the whiskey in her glass.

Arthur eventually responded. 'Let's set the scene. New York City Hall. This lady in a long pink dress—'

'I went through a salmon-pink phase,' said Helen, apologetically.

'Me in my only suit. Then to the party. The best in town. Your mother, my father… dancing in the ballroom at the Hotel Astor.'

'Kissing in the rooftop garden—'

'Arguing about your parents in the gallery—'

'Yes but—'

'And making up in the themed buffet room.'

Helen looked delighted, and I felt relieved. Arthur did *love* her after all. He just didn't show it.

Lady D began. 'Shall I? I have many great memories.'

'Let me guess, yours involves afternoon tea?' Dr Munro said, laughing.

'How dare you!' she retorted. ''So… last summer, I went on a march for the suffrage movement—'

'We should have guessed,' interrupted Arthur. Lady D carried on.

'The police arrested us, and I spent three nights in jail.'

We stared at her.

'But it was wonderful!' she said. 'I was *so* proud. And then after we got out, we met Mrs Pankhurst, who served us the most wonderful strawberries and cream. Oh, dear, I always mention food, don't I?!'

'I knew it.' Dr Munro chuckled. 'That's a shilling you owe me, Arthur.'

The best moment of my life? Was it when Harold lifted himself up and called out that he loved me forever? I flushed. My God, how easily swayed was I? He was delirious and besides, he hardly knew me! I couldn't imagine what everyone would say about this non-event. I garbled something about Uilleam teaching me to drive.

'I cranked up, held on to the wheel and off we stuttered. We went at high speed, around the town… I was only seven!' I added, delighted at their shocked faces. 'He did the foot pedals, I couldn't reach.'

'Well, that explains why you're such a good driver, you've been driving for longer than all of us!' cried out Lady D. I blushed. I didn't realise that anyone had noticed my competence on the road. But Arthur was still eyeing me closely. 'Really? I would have thought yours would have been a love story, Mairi.'

'Elsie?'

Elsie was playing with her glass, not paying attention to us. She wiped her mouth and looked up, startled.

'What was one of your best days?' I had secretly pictured her wedding day many times. Elsie would have been magnificent in a white gown to the floor, some ancient country church, some handsome groom. A vicar with a twinkle in his eyes. Timid flower girls with posy baskets. What a shame I hadn't known her back then!

'A best day? Huh! How about the day I beat you at the Dorset?!' Elsie laughed. The liquid in her glass swirled.

'What?' I was flabbergasted. 'You don't remember that!'

'Don't I?' Elsie laughed coquettishly.

'You *said* you didn't.'

'Did I? But no, it was a very special day.'

Everyone was looking mystified.

'How about another good time you've had?' Arthur cut in rather insistently. Maybe he too was aching to hear about Elsie's wedding day. Or surely she'd tell us about the day Kenneth was born? But Elsie shrugged.

'I haven't had so many best days… someone else have a go.'

If anyone else had said this I would have found it sad, but the smile on her face was so broad, *so Elsie*, that I still couldn't tell if she was being serious or not.

The next question was 'What has been your worst experience?'

Lady D immediately clarified, 'Absolutely nothing to do with *this* stinking war is allowed.'

Arthur began. 'Ah, easy. I arrived in New York in 1908. It was a hot summer. You know summers in New York!'

'We don't!' interjected Lady D.

'Well, humid, muggy, sultry, whatever you like. And I had got this job – so excited, you can't imagine. Then I got there, this office in one of the new skyscrapers, only to find there was no job. They denied ever having heard of me.'

'What had happened?' I asked.

Arthur shrugged. 'Maybe some junior thought it would be funny. Maybe they saw me and changed their minds. Who knows? I left there like a… like the small-town boy I was.'

I gave him a sympathetic look. It was unusual for Arthur to be candid, especially concerning himself.

'A few weeks later, I got a job at the *New York Times*.'

'Brilliant!'

'Post-boy!' he explained. 'I had thought I was going to be this big-shot writer, but my role was passing on messages.'

'How long for?'

'Three years,' he said, 'then I met Helen, married her, and my luck turned around.'

'Dad works for the *NYT*,' Helen explained. 'He's their lawyer.'

Arthur stared into his drink.

'I see,' I said, my mouth slightly open. I stared at them both. *I see.*

Lady D's tale of woe was about having her horse put down after he fell in a race. 'I was only a young thing,' she said. 'They had to fight to keep me away from him. First love can be very powerful.'

We were all silent for a moment.

I was dreading Helen's story. I imagined that she was going to say she was bullied at school. They would have made mincemeat of her at mine! But she said 'Pass', and instead of us pressing her, she was made to take the consequence, which was drinking a foul-tasting drink.

'It can't taste worse than Macanochie, can it?' she asked helplessly. Then after she sipped it, she spluttered, 'Oh, it does. It's terrible!'

When it was my turn, I said, 'Compared to yours, mine are far too trivial even to say out loud.'

New Year's Day, skipping into the library. Behind the bookshelves, Uilleam was bent over Father's knee and Father was spanking something rotten out of him. Uilleam was too old to be spanked. I didn't know what to do so I just backed away, went for a ride probably.

I didn't want to tell anyone this, so I too asked for a consequence.

I gulped the drink down dutifully.

'What is this revolting stuff?'

'I don't want to know,' said Helen wryly.

I coughed and suddenly the drink came up, landing neatly in my cup.

'Disgusting!'

'The next person who bows out can drink *that*,' said Arthur cruelly, but no one took him seriously.

I wanted to know how it came about that Elsie had been adopted. It struck me again that I didn't know much about her family; but Elsie wouldn't say what her worst experience was.

She would have to take a consequence too.

'Drink that,' Arthur said.

'No!' I said protectively.

'You can't bend the rules for her!' said Arthur.

I thought, *My, things have changed if I'm regarded as the rule-breaker!*

'Was it perhaps when Mr Knocker died, Elsie?' I persisted.

'Yes, I didn't accept it for a long time. I denied it until I no longer could.' Elsie was struggling to speak. 'Can't we play something else?'

Lady D triumphantly produced some jigsaws she had found in the old school cupboards but no one wanted to do those either. There were three: a wooden map of the world, a bucolic countryside scene and the Eiffel Tower in Paris. Lady D insisted we take them back to the cellar when we went back the next morning. Elsie resisted – 'There's no room to swing a cat.'

Lady D laughed. 'That's not what Shot told me.'

A few days earlier, we had carried a lovely boy, Vincent, in from the trench. He was bent in two, rigid as an old man. I doubted if his body would ever unfurl. His muscles seemed locked. Yet he had nothing wrong with him that we could see. It was shock, we decided.

When we returned from Furnes, Vincent and I sat together, working on the map of the world. There were five hundred pieces and between us, it took us about two hours. For much of the last hour,

I found myself praying *Please don't let there be any missing pieces* and then apologising: *Sorry God, for such a trivial request, but it would be helpful for this lad to achieve something.*

As he placed in the last piece, I whooped but deep sobs racked Vincent's broken body. He told me it reminded him of home.

Once he was able, we sent him back to the front line. I admitted to Elsie that I doubted he would last long. Somehow, I managed to say it without weeping. I was growing a hard shell around me: there was no escaping that.

Madeleine would love the jigsaws, I was sure. While her brother remained vague to me (although I had given him the temporary name of Felix), I was growing to understand more about my beautiful Belgian girl. Madeleine liked plain white socks pulled up to her knees. She wore her hair up in one long plait, in defiance of her mother preferring two. I imagined her playing dot-to-dot or noughts-and-crosses.

There would have been a piano here, I decided, and one day, there would be a piano upstairs again. Madeleine was already able to play 'Twinkle Twinkle', and one day, I would teach her to play 'It's a Long Way to Tipperary'.

So what if she struggled with English? We would get there in the end. Adverbs: *Quickly. Quietly. Slowly*. Verbs: *Do. Make. Run. Hide. Kill. Nurse.*

I had my puzzles and Elsie had her own entertainment: new Gilberts, the engineers whose place she loved to skip off to. I was more sympathetic to her 'hobby' as time went on. Now that Harold had failed to return, I understood the fear of getting too attached. It was rational to protect oneself. To lose someone you love, as Elsie had, yet still to be able to put one foot in front of the other, was remarkable.

Very occasionally, Elsie would take out her motorbike for a longer stretch. Sometimes, she rode into France to see friends there.

Of course, she shouldn't have. There was the worry of shelling and snipers and we agreed it was 'profligate' but Elsie said, 'Sometimes, you just need to ride and be free again.' I knew that feeling.

One time, that summer, she went out for over six hours. I prayed that she would return safe. She came back with her pockets and bag stuffed with fat, squidgy tomatoes.

'Ready to have the finest tomato salad in the land, Mairi?'

We gorged ourselves on them. We had two poorly men in cots and Paul and Martin were there, so they ate with us too. We didn't bother with cutlery, we just used our fingers and before long those little pips had got into everything. And then Elsie and I were both sick. Groaning, clutching our bellies, we had to take turns using the bucket and the loo. But most of the time we were laughing.

Elsie was the most wonderful friend. I didn't think we'd ever see each other in a corner without giving everything we could to help.

'Thank goodness for short hair!' Elsie moaned, leaning over the pot. She looked up at me deliriously, sweat dripping down her forehead, sick speckles around her mouth.

'Wasn't it worth it though, Mairi? Those tomatoes were delicious!'

CHAPTER FOURTEEN

I was outside reattaching the Chater-Lea's sidecar when a visitor arrived on horseback. He dismounted gravely, tied his horse, a white mare, then removed his helmet. His boots crunched rhythmically on the gravel. He had the air of an official or someone 'on important business'. I walked over nervously to see who had come to evict us. It was only as I drew closer that I realised with a racing heart: it was my brown bear, Harold the Baron.

I hardly recognised him without a beard. Shaving had taken years off him. I saw now that he was somewhere in the hinterland between my age and Elsie's. He had a smooth, square jaw, and you could see the shape of his lips.

Although upstairs was brighter and cooler, the noise was horrendous, so I led Harold self-consciously to the trapdoor. Harold swung his bag as he walked, and I realised, with a start, that it contained a bloodied rabbit.

I looked a mess as usual – I probably smelled of iodine, petrol or worse. Elsie had gone on an emergency visit to the trenches with Dr Gus Van Hint and I couldn't help feeling pleased. Elsie tended to dominate any conversation – it wasn't her fault, she was more interesting than me.

As Harold awkwardly descended, I complimented him on the recovery of his leg.

He said, 'I'll never be a long jumper but the three-legged race might yet be mine.'

I laughed, then out popped the words, 'You would need a strong partner!'

'Hmm, do I know any strong women?' he said mockingly, his finger resting on his smooth cheek. *Who was talking about women?* I thought. My heart had never beaten so fast. I swallowed, searching for the right answer.

'Elsie?' I said, my voice sounding thick and furry. 'Or me?'

I hurriedly lit the lanterns and candles so we could see. Even underground, there were judders where shells were landing not far from us. *Our poor boys…*

Harold told me that he was working with a colonel only twenty miles from here, it was his first day off in weeks and, as soon as he had the go-ahead, he had jumped on Doris, his horse, and set off at a gallop.

'And here I am!'

And here you are! I thought delightedly.

Harold noticed one of the jigsaws on the table. I hadn't made much progress since Vincent had left, but you could just make out a windmill.

'You have a long way to go,' Harold said earnestly. 'You must be patient.'

'I'm more patient than I used to be.' I smiled. His eyes locked on to mine. Somehow, I couldn't bear it so I looked away. Shot was there too, oblivious, lying on the straw.

'And who's this little fellow?' he asked tenderly.

Harold's an animal-lover, I thought approvingly.

'That's our Shot.' I explained how we came about him and Harold stroked his head and played with his ears.

'Quite the home from home,' he said approvingly. 'So where is Elsie?'

Well, at least he didn't ask straight away, I thought. *He must be patient too.*

I told him and he said, 'Ah, yes, I hear she is *always* in the trenches.'

I felt like saying, *I am too* but I didn't want to show him how petty I could be.

I had found a red ribbon out in the bricks some days earlier and knotted it around my wrist. I was certain it was Madeleine's or at least one of her dolls'.

Harold smiled at it. 'That's pretty.'

'Thank you.'

There was something romantic, something sensitive, in Harold that made me feel that he would have understood my yearning for the family who used to live here. I didn't think he would laugh if I said that thoughts of Madeleine helped keep me both grounded and strong. But I didn't tell Harold the story behind the ribbon, because he was unceremoniously pulling off his coat, sitting himself by the stove and, with a happy sigh, loosening his boots. I didn't want to spoil the moment.

'They call you "The Madonnas of Pervyse"?' he asked.

'You heard. Isn't it ridiculous?'

'No. It's entirely appropriate, Mairi.'

I flushed as red as the Queen of Hearts.

'I told my family about you,' he said, leaving me wondering which 'you' he meant. He continued. 'They send thanks and prayers.'

I felt tearful. *Prayers?* None of the others would indulge me any more. Lady D sang hymns loudly with her eyes to the sky but she wouldn't recite prayers. Dr Munro kept hinting that it was *belief* that was the crucial thing, not belief in *God* – a view I struggled to understand. Helen and Arthur certainly didn't have faith in Jesus. Arthur was a self-proclaimed atheist and a communist and blamed religion for the war. I told him that was ridiculous – surely nationalism, greed and ignorance deserved a greater portion of blame? But he would only reply, 'Young Mairi, you'll learn.' This was especially infuriating considering our respective positions: he still went to bed every night anticipating his newspaper and egg in the morning, whereas I slept in straw, half-expecting to be overrun by the Hun and strangled in my sleep.

As for Elsie – well, God was the biggest thing we disagreed on. We had to mutinously 'agree to disagree'.

'It's been a long time since I've heard prayers,' I whispered.

Harold's voice was gentle. 'I'm a Roman Catholic, Mairi. Would you like to pray with me now?'

I would have loved to have talked to the chaplains who visited the boys in the trenches – but it would have been wrong to divert their attention away from boys in need. But now Harold was offering me his prayers and I couldn't help but be moved to tears.

'I would like nothing more.'

Harold began. His voice was tremulous and deep.

You will not fear the terror of night,
Nor the arrow that flied by day,
Nor the pestilence that stalks in the darkness
Nor the plague that destroys at midday.

He stopped. It seemed that he too had a lump in his throat.

'Would you prefer it if I—' I whispered.

'No, let me go on.' Harold coughed dust, violently.

I closed my eyes again.

A thousand may fall at your side,
Ten thousand at your right hand,
But it will not come near you.
You will only observe with your eyes and see the
punishment of the wicked.

I felt cleansed, I felt safe. I had believed in God since before I could remember. He was always there. Jesus suffered. Our men suffer. But we will rise again. We will prove our love. We will not shy away from our burdens. If this was what God wanted, then I would do it without complaint.

To share prayers with Harold was like being part of a congregation again. It was like being in my bedroom at home. It was like being in school assembly. Together, we could move mountains. I imagined him leading prayers at my church in Dorset. How I would sit in the front row, gazing upon him admiringly. I would know how that leg had looked once and how he endured pain as though it was a mere splinter. He would sit next to me, take my hand, rest it on his uniformed thigh.

I felt a euphoria I hadn't experienced in a long time. Sublime, as his voice caressed the words...

> *I will be with him in trouble,*
> *I will deliver him and honour him.*
> *With long life, I will satisfy him and show him my salvation—*

'Well, well. It's like a chapel in here.' Daylight suddenly shafted through the cellar, then disappeared just as quickly as Elsie pulled the trapdoor behind her.

Harold raised himself to his feet. He clutched Elsie's hand and then they cheek-kissed like great friends. One, two, three, four times! I wondered if they would ever stop.

'Better a temple than a morgue,' Harold said smartly.

I couldn't help but be surprised at the speed at which Harold was able to change gear. When I've been praying, it feels like I'm in a different place, a higher place. It takes me a while to adjust from the spiritual plane to the physical. Now I was coming down to earth with a bump.

Elsie undid her belt, unbuttoned her greatcoat, took off her nursing hat and washed her hands in the bucket: she took far longer than she usually did. I had a strange feeling that, for once, even she didn't know how to act. She grabbed Shot and stroked his back firmly.

'Poor little doggy,' she said. I wasn't sure why.

'You won't have the pleasure of nursing me again, ladies,' Harold said later. *Ladies* – but he was speaking principally to Elsie now. 'Can you contain your disappointment?'

'We'll find a way to deal with the heartache, won't we, Mairi?'

Elsie noticed Harold was still having some problems standing. She hastily offered him our lone chair.

'You saved my life.'

'We know.' Elsie never did self-effacing. I had grown used to it by now, but Harold looked mildly surprised before a grin took over his face.

'I have a little something for you. A thank-you gift.'

'It was thanks enough that you removed that ferret from your chin!'

He ignored Elsie's jibe, and instead held out a box. 'These are for you, the English nurses… From me, but also from all of us in Belgium.'

I smiled at him: 'There is neither Jew nor Gentile, neither slave nor free, nor is there male and female, for we are all one in Christ Jesus.'

Harold looked at me gently. 'Please—'

'Mairi, your favourites!' interrupted Elsie. 'Don't eat them all at once.'

It was a tray of sweets, exquisitely wrapped.

'Oh, you remembered! Thank you.'

'You won't try one, Elsie?'

'May I be so rude… for whom is the rabbit?' Elsie noticed everything.

'Oh? This?' Harold looked doubtfully at his supplies. 'You can have this.'

'Thank you.'

There was a pause before Harold asked. 'Can you skin a rabbit, Elsie?'

'Of course.'

I could tell Harold was impressed even if he didn't say anything. I wanted to tell him that I had shot five sparrows once *and* helped prepare them. They were disgusting to eat but I had done it. Elsie wasn't the only one.

Elsie flopped down in the straw, looking exhausted. It wasn't like her.

'Bad out there?' Harold asked gently.

'Every day is bad out there. It wasn't terrible though – so that's good.'

She so rarely talked to *me* like this. I suddenly saw that there was a vulnerable side to her that I barely knew. I felt like I had when Uilleam had explained to me that the moon didn't disappear on those nights we couldn't see it: it was still there, always there, but without the light from the sun it was hidden. Elsie had concealed her distress from me, perhaps to protect me, I wasn't sure.

'The soldiers have started shooting themselves. Quite thoughtless really. Some are more accurate than others.'

'I'm sorry,' Harold said quietly.

'One chap…' Elsie started, then changed her mind – 'well, let's say I was glad I was there.'

Harold offered Elsie his handkerchief. A white silk square. I hadn't seen anything so refined as this in some time. 'I'm *sure* he was glad you were there.'

Elsie blew her nose loudly. She didn't care to disguise it at all.

'He would have preferred his girlfriend or his mother.'

'He would have preferred not to be here at all.'

Harold didn't brush the agony away; he didn't offer platitudes. He faced sadness as you would hope to face anything. Head-on.

Elsie offered him back his handkerchief complete with the contents of her nose. He didn't look disgusted, but shook his head. 'Keep it.'

Elsie smiled helplessly at me.

Harold rose awkwardly, then started. 'Um, I have a ticket for a party in the Officers' Mess. Would one of you lovely ladies…?' His voice trailed away.

Neither Elsie nor I responded.

'… care to accompany me?' he asked finally.

'Mairi?' Elsie said in a softer voice than usual.

'The officers have managed to acquire some fine wines.'

'No Elsie, you go.' There, I had said it. 'I'm no good at parties.' I looked apologetically at Harold. 'Elsie says that I'm too quiet.'

'No one can ever be too quiet,' he said cordially.

'You go, Mairi… please,' Elsie said weakly.

'There will be cake,' Harold added, as though either of us needed enticing.

I remembered what she had said about her bad day. *Every day is bad out there.*

'You've had a tough time,' I said lightly. 'It would be good to let your hair down.'

'What hair?' she said, ruffling hers up adorably.

Harold beamed at her.

'*Alors.*' She grinned. 'I hope you are not *too* disappointed, Harold. *C'est moi!*'

Elsie had wanted me to go. She had wanted me to go more than she usually did. Perhaps she understood that it was as if we were on a collision course at that moment, and everything depended on the decisions we would make in those next few seconds? At the time though, I thought we were only talking about a party. Only talking about cake. It was only later that I realised I had declined a lot more.

As I lay in the straw next to her that night, I tried to work out why I had given up so easily. I was so used to deferring to Elsie, I suppose. It was always Elsie Knocker and what's-her-name her friend. Arthur said I was like the get-away driver and she was the cat-thief. Docility versus glamour. *Not much of a choice there.* Or, as my mother might have said, I was the crust, she was the whole sandwich. All I had needed to say was, *I'd like that invitation please*, but I was afraid. Living with death every day made me love less. It only made her love more.

*

I hoped Elsie had forgotten about Harold's party but of course she hadn't. A few days later, she asked if I would be able to manage on my own that evening, and I said over-brightly, 'Oh, you're going out tonight!'

And she said, as though *I* had forgotten, 'With the Baron, yes.'

I was struggling to fix a flat tyre that morning; they happened more when Elsie had been driving the Fiat, although she wouldn't hear of it, and I was so annoyed that I kicked it, hurting my foot. Paul saw and laughed. We did our trench-runs as normal, Elsie commenting that if there was a badly injured boy she would stay in that evening. I was a hateful person, because all I wanted was a boy to suffer terrible injuries – or rather injuries that *appeared* terrible but actually weren't – to keep Elsie home. I pictured a shell landing in a ditch right next to some innocent boy, and only Elsie having the skills to bring him back to life. She would simply have to stay! But luck was on her side – on every boy's side – that evening.

We dispensed Martin's meat broth (a 'meat broth untainted by meat' as Elsie called it) and reassured men who were growing increasingly frantic at the prospective push over the top.

'My mum is alone now – my dad is dead, my brother is dead… I mustn't die, Missus.'

'No, you mustn't.'

Elsie swore that the more confident the soldiers were, the more chance they had of surviving. I didn't quite see how that worked. Nevertheless, she insisted it was our duty to instill self-belief.

'And you won't.' I patted the young soldier's hand and whereas once I might have recoiled at its filthy clamminess, now I just held tighter. 'You will be fine.'

'If I'm not—'

'You will be.'

'You'll tell my mum?'

'Yes.'

Two lads needed new dressings but that was no problem. No one needed to be urgently escorted to our *Poste de Secours*.

What was there for Elsie to wear to a party? I wanted to give her something – a brooch or some rouge – to share the occasion, or perhaps remind her of my existence back in the cellar. I didn't have anything to share though. After some consideration, I offered her Madeleine's red ribbon – my *lucky* ribbon – but she said, 'I don't think so,' then, looking closely at me, she added, 'You're sweet to think of it.'

She looked marvellous anyway, despite the absence of dressing-up clothes: she was so strong and fine, trembling with excitement. She bit her lips to make them redder and she rubbed her cheeks to get some colour into them, and when I tersely pointed out what she was doing, she shrugged. 'I'm not going to lie, I want to look nice for once.'

'You always look nice,' I said meekly and she cackled. 'Oh, I wish everyone thought the same way as you.'

I thought to myself, *there is something different about this date*, but I hoped that was just in my mind.

We shared a cigarette, then promptly at six she mounted the stairs, leaving me behind. Paul grunted that there was poker at the engineers' house but I declined. After they left, I stared at the jigsaw pieces for a while, but could make no progress. I didn't know what I wanted to do – I didn't *feel* like doing anything – so I went to lie down on the straw. Shot was heavy on my legs. He alone seemed indifferent to Elsie's absence.

Of course, I couldn't sleep. My mind was inundated with thoughts of Elsie, with boys with pleading eyes who cried out for their mothers. I tried to conquer my runaway thoughts with imaginings of Madeleine, or memories of Uilleam, or motorcycles… but it didn't work. Even prayers couldn't hold my heart back from its fearful panic.

I imagined Elsie and Harold dancing in a field, him pressing a flower to her breast, telling her he loved her. I saw her singing to him and him telling her she was an angel. I imagined them riding a horse together, galloping through the cornfields. I imagined the horse lifting them up and down, sprouting massive white wings, deliriously flying them away from here.

What if the Germans broke though tonight while she was out? I would be trapped here. Would I submit or fight? What if they tried to violate me? I would endure, I would pray, and then, with any luck, they would kill me straight after. *Perhaps*, I decided, *it would be better if they came tonight, because then at least Elsie would have escaped.*

I was still wrestling with my dark thoughts after midnight, when Elsie bounded down the stairs. It sounded as though she was falling from the sky.

'Good time?'

'Oh yes. Have you plumped up the pillows, Mairi?'

I laughed despite myself.

'*Anchoise d'Ecosse, asperges Irlandasies, haricots verts, poulet, petits pois, saucisson* and the wine!' she added deliriously, although most of the menu meant nothing to me. '*Chateau Grand Puech* and *Haut Medoc* and champagne!'

While Elsie obsessed over the food, she didn't say anything about Harold, neither that night nor the following day. She didn't mention dancing or cake, never mind cornfields or winged horses. When eventually I asked if Harold was good company, which seemed a reasonable request for information, she smiled and said, 'You know he is, Mairi.' I don't think she referred to him once after that, so it suited me to hope he had disappeared off the face of the earth like all her other Gilberts.

*

I was so anxious over the following days that Elsie asked what I was fretting about. I couldn't say that I feared that she and Harold would fall in love and abandon me, and she was fed up with hearing my worries about money running out (even with the bike-sale and donations we were short of what we needed). So I told her my fears of being murdered in the cellar.

'That's not going to happen, Mairi,' she said, but she wasn't mocking for once. 'Our cellar house is perfectly safe. Please don't give it a second thought.'

But then, exactly one week after the party, while we were driving back from a Furnes-run, the cellar house *was* hit by a shell. Downstairs – Elsie was right – the cellar was virtually untouched, although the blankets around the WC collapsed and my half-done Eiffel Tower jigsaw parted by itself. The two men recuperating in cot beds upstairs were miraculously safe too, though one poor man with an arm injury – who could run, so took shelter by the wall – was killed.

CHAPTER FIFTEEN

Dr Munro said it was a sign that we needed a break. For someone who didn't believe in signs, he could sound quite superstitious. He insisted we would be no good to anyone unless we took care of ourselves. This was an important rule of nursing (albeit one he had neglected to tell me before).

'Just a week or two away,' he said. 'You owe it to your patients to be strong.'

'We are strong!' I argued. We had lifted the bricks from the fallen walls in a matter of hours: hard, hot, back-breaking work. No one could say we weren't strong.

'Not *just* in physical health,' he responded somewhat incomprehensibly.

'Isn't it pointless going now?' I argued. 'It's only a few months 'til Christmas and surely it'll all be done by then.'

'*This* Christmas?' He raised his eyebrows. 'Who told you that? Christmas 1916, more like!'

I resisted until Dr Munro said, 'Mairi, think of King Solomon, and the baby.' I didn't see how the cellar was our baby or which of us was King Solomon, but I understood we had to go otherwise Dr Munro might do something drastic, so I too suggested to Elsie, 'Maybe it's time.'

We were exhausted. We hadn't had a proper rest since we'd arrived at the cellar – nine months ago now. The hum of shells was so pervasive that I almost missed it when, for a short time, it stopped. Sometimes the dust was unbearable in your eyes and throat, and every word came out with a cough. Sometimes it felt like we had been caged. And our cage was clearly not the safe place we had imagined it was.

It would be good to get out.

Still, Elsie was unconvinced: she couldn't bear to be away from the injured or needy.

'What about Shot?' she eventually said, which was when I knew she'd given in. Martin would be more than delighted to receive the extra doggy cuddles. I wondered if Harold figured in her calculations to stay – perhaps she couldn't stand to be away from him too? – but she didn't mention him, so I wasn't going to call him back into her mind.

*

Throughout the journey to England, Elsie kept stewing. She said we had taken the wind out of Dr Munro's sails, that he was sending us away to spite us! It was disconcerting that she still nursed such resentment against him.

As I listened to her, I realised her bravado sprang from the same well as mine: fear. Elsie still believed that we might be forced out – not by the Hun, but by our own side. She was sure a reason would be found to get us out: lack of money, lack of safety or lack of something else we had failed to foresee. The exception they made in our names wouldn't – couldn't – last forever.

'But I won't let it happen,' she said ominously, gripping my hand. 'We're staying put, little sister. Whatever Munro thinks.'

Arriving at Dover, we saw shiny-booted new recruits heading in the other direction. Wonderfully clean, every button firmly affixed. Warm, lice-free socks. Combed hair. Eyes that were alive. Blister-free hands. All eager-cheeked and full of raw enthusiasm.

We sat on our suitcases amid the smoke and whistles, waving.

Elsie yelled excitedly, 'Let's cheer the boys… for King and Country!'

And the people who were in that station did just that. Their cries rang out and the new soldiers grinned excitedly. We clapped until I was sure my hands would fall off.

After they had left, Elsie's demeanour changed. She transformed into an image of despondency, flopping over her suitcase like a puppet without a string. The energy faded from her voice.

'God help them. They know not what lies ahead.'

I remembered what Dr Gus had said: '*As long as both sides believe they can win this by killing each other, it's never going to end.*'

'I'm glad Kenneth is too young to be called up,' Elsie continued, still slumped. 'I couldn't stand it.'

Father was the opposite. He was too old to fight, but still chomping at the bit for his piece of the action. 'My father wants to visit,' I told Elsie.

She sat up straight. 'Visit what?!'

'Us,' I said uncertainly. It had been at the end of a recent letter from my mother. '*When can Father come to see you?*' Just like that. Out of the blue. We'd never discussed it before.

'What an idea!'

'He'll stay out the way, Elsie.'

On our train, we stuffed away our luggage and sat opposite each other next to the window. It didn't smell of struggle, sweat and death here but polish and upholstery. Elsie morosely lit a cigarette. Dragging her away from the cellar had been a mistake. It was like she'd run out of fuel.

'I can't see why your father should come. It's pointless.'

'Dr Munro would be delighted. I expect the pair of them would reminisce about the grand old days of the Boer War.'

Elsie shook her head at me. 'How peculiar.'

But the more I thought about it, the more I wanted my father to come and admire our mission. Lately, he sometimes added a postscript to my mother's gossipy letters admonishing me to *'Dig deep'*. That was pleasing, if brief. How stupidly I yearned for an 'I'm-proud-of-you'. I told Elsie, 'It'll be good for him to see what we do. We can show how important it is.'

Elsie wrote 'As a box of frogs' on the steamed-up window. I wasn't sure if she meant me, my father or Dr Munro, but I didn't ask. She had begun smiling again.

I thought of Madeleine and her family travelling to England, sitting anxiously on the train. Maybe she had been fretting about the things she had left behind.

Perhaps they had sat in these very carriages, on these wooden benches, listening to the clunking rhythm of the train, on their way to a different life.

Now the house had virtually been flattened, I changed my picture of our union. I would meet the family *before* they came back to Belgium. I would explain sensitively that almost everything had disappeared. There would be a ceremonial handing over of the toys.

'Madeleine, the house may have gone, but we have preserved the cellar and your things the best we could.'

Watching the English countryside fly past our window, I considered how affected England had been over the past year. I had heard there had been Zeppelin attacks in London. It must have brought the war horribly home. I wondered if everyone back here was changing as fast as I was changing.

As we walked up to the buffet car, a couple of soldiers nodded at us. Elsie responded with her broad smile and I heard one of them say, 'She's a cracker!' and the other replied, 'A sight for sore eyes.'

Times like these, I was glad to be the less visible one.

Elsie was still absorbed by Munro. 'I am so fed up with him,' she muttered.

'He just wants us to be safe.'

'What kind of ambition is that?'

There was no food left, but the lady at the bar offered to make us tea. The tea wasn't half as good as Lady D's but Elsie and I took a sip and, at the same time, both said, 'Lovely!'

After we returned to our seats, I said, 'You've been having such bad dreams lately, Elsie. Calling out in your sleep. It's getting worse.'

'I'm fine.'

'Sometimes you say things about your late husband—'

'Goodness. What do I say?'

'I can't make it out.'

'Well, that's something!' She gazed out the window at the galloping fields. Fields that were green and yellow, flourishing with life, not brown and impotent-grey like in Belgium. 'What about you, Mairi? Are you in tip-top condition?'

At first, I was too amazed to reply. *What could she mean?*

'There's nothing wrong with me.' I was fit as a fiddle!

'You've not got a boil that needs treating?'

This was so *typically* Elsie that I was momentarily lost for words. I did have a boil on my back, but I had never told *her* about it.

'Do you know *everything* about me?'

'Not *everything*. You want me to lance it for you when we've arrived?'

'I'll never tell you anything again,' I said. *We both knew that wasn't true!*

'I still remember the maid who ran off with your mother's cousin. The scandal! And your brother's best friend? Percy, wasn't it? Percy peahead who chased you around the garden with his pants on his head.'

'He was six!' She was incorrigible. 'Elsie Knocker! Don't you ever forget anything?'

'I *never* forget a secret. They are *much* too powerful.'

I shook my head incredulously. 'I'm surprised you agreed to take this holiday.'

'Holiday? We're not going on holiday! We're going fundraising, Mairi.'

CHAPTER SIXTEEN

Elsie had been invited to speak at the Glasgow Assembly Rooms! I had never been there before, but I knew – everyone knew – that it was a large and impressive venue. I couldn't believe it.

'To speak about what?'

'About our work at the cellar, everything,' Elsie said vaguely. 'Think about it, Mairi. What an opportunity to get the word out there.'

'And the money in here,' I said pointing at the purse she was clutching in her lap. 'Why didn't you tell me before?'

'I only got the telegram this morning,' she replied. 'But it's perfect timing. We'll take the overnighter from London to Scotland – they've offered to reimburse us – and in the morning, we'll pop out to get hats,' Elsie went on, as though hats were my biggest worry. 'The actual meeting isn't until midday, so we'll have time.'

I gaped at her. I wondered if she had sprung it on me at the last minute so there was less chance I could wriggle out of it. I could have refused to go. I could have insisted that I had to see my family, but actually I wasn't keen to go home to Dorset. The less time spent dissecting Uilleam's latest infraction, the better. At home, I was even less visible than sitting on a train with Elsie! Even the thought of Cook's venison, steak pies and gravy could not lure me back. (Besides, Cook had joined the war effort and, considering the shortages, I doubted even my well-to-do parents could source quality meat.) Glasgow sounded quite the adventure. Plus, as I wearily admitted to Elsie, 'I haven't had a new hat in a long time.'

'You'll look sweet in a nice hat.'

'A massive bonnet with full netting to hide my flaws…'

'Silly girl,' Elsie said. 'I wish you knew how lovely you are.'

I smiled, but I was thinking, *why are we discussing the hats?*

The next morning we went directly from the station to the guesthouse where we would stay that night. We enjoyed toast with (*oh my word!*) thick, sweet marmalade. Then the guesthouse manager, a kindly older lady, directed us to 'Scotland's Top Hat Shop', where we would be able to select the finest bonnets – with netting or not – for the afternoon. As we walked, the scenes that passed in front of me were so diametrically opposed to my life on the Western Front that it almost took my breath away. How could I reconcile the fact that one moment I was stumbling across the hand of the man buried by our cellar wall and the next I was shopping for pretty headwear?

Still.

I was torn between a hat topped with decorative cherries (shades of Lady D) and a fat green one with a thick band of ribbon. Elsie said the green 'set off my features'. She made it sound like setting off my features was a desirable thing, so I bought it. She didn't hesitate in choosing a flamboyant bonnet the crimson shade of her lips. The pretty sales-girl was wary of us, but she finally approached Elsie with an urgent question.

'Why is your hair so short?'

'It's the new fashion!' Elsie gave her a broad wink.

I imagine the girl might have stared into the mirror that evening wondering if she too could carry off the new look.

I asked Elsie if she had prepared anything for the talk but she said not.

'Shouldn't you practise?' I would rather have died than got on stage without notes.

'Some things are better off the cuff,' she said casually. She meant, *I don't want to discuss this with you.*

I reminded her that whatever happened in the meeting – and I was thinking that she might run out of things to say – I was not going to speak. Definitely not.

The last time I had spoken in public was reading Shakespeare in front of my class at school – '*Oh woe, O woeful, woeful, woeful day! Most lamentable day, most woeful day…*' It had not gone down well.

Elsie laughed. 'Fine, little piggy,' she said, then nudged me playfully: 'Who'd want to hear you speak anyway?'

Elsie had arranged to meet a friend – she *did* have friends everywhere – so we agreed that we would meet at the hall just before midday.

At half past eleven, I went to the door of the Assembly Rooms. I felt like a gooseberry. It was raining. I should have bought an umbrella, but after the expense of the bonnets I had been reluctant to purchase anything else for myself. Finally, someone came over asking for my ticket. Of course, I didn't have a ticket. I hadn't even seen any tickets! The woman apologised but said she couldn't let me in: 'Rules are rules, duckie.'

As I was about to turn out into the downpour again, I told her, by the by, that I was here with Elsie Knocker – but she wasn't here yet – so…

Confused, the woman looked at her notes, then smiled at me. She had shiny cheeks like a picture-book farmer's wife and perspiration on her forehead like she'd been out in the fields digging.

'It *isn't* Miss Chisholm, is it?'

'Yes?' I didn't understand how she would have heard of me.

'Why! You're just a young thing!'

'Nineteen,' I said to prove her wrong as she pulled me into an embrace. I felt stiff as a board in her warmth, but she didn't seem to mind.

She was Mrs Grange, the organiser of the event. She bustled around, helping me to remove my wet coat, taking my damp bag, offering me hot drinks. I was too nervous for anything.

I asked which other speakers were on the bill today. She didn't seem to understand what I was saying, then she shook her head fast like a cornered gerbil.

'Oh no, dear. It's just you and Mrs Knocker!'

'Really?'

'And it's a sell-out!'

'But—'

'But nothing,' she said, incredulous at my reaction. '*Everyone's* heard of the Madonnas. You just wait.'

More and more chairs were brought in. I counted: fifteen in each row going at least thirty back. Surely, they didn't expect to fill them all! And in this wet weather too? Who'd come out in this, to see *us*?

Mrs Grange went to greet a group of finely dressed people. I heard her say, 'That's Mairi Chisholm, one of the Madonnas of Pervyse,' and they looked over and nodded. The men tipped their caps at me. I was glad of my great bonnet; I could pretend to be the kind of person who always wears an elaborate green hat on a Friday afternoon in Scotland.

I tried to assist with the laying out of the chairs but was told firmly I must sit down. I was an honoured guest.

I smelled wet. It was my habitual smell in Pervyse, but here it felt different. Here, everyone seemed tidy and immune to the elements.

Then people began pouring through the doors. Soldiers, mothers, fathers, everyone, and I felt even more of a fraud. I was afraid that the star of the show was going to be late: *where, in heaven's name, had Elsie disappeared to now?* I kept my eyes fixed on the door, watching out for her elaborate hat. Plenty of people arrived, some in elaborate hats too, but none of them were her.

She couldn't be with another Gilbert, could she? She couldn't be kissing, not now, of all times?

Elsie arrived bang on twelve. Not only was she wearing her brand-new bonnet but when she took off her coat, I saw she had changed into the most wonderful frock I had ever seen. I wondered if she had been rained on, and if she had, how she could look so refined. It was a mystery to me. Elsie didn't ever need window dressing, but as she clattered in from the back of the room and onto the stage, I could hardly believe this glorious vision was my nit-infested, constantly smoking, cave-dwelling, tomato-gorging sister. Never had the word 'Madonna' seemed more appropriate!

Mrs Grange introduced us to the crowd. I was too anxious to take it all in, but Elsie gave me an encouraging look. Then it was her turn.

She began in her low husky voice. 'Good afternoon everybody!' but the crowd could hardly see her and a couple of men heckled, 'Can't hear ya!' and 'Speak up, love!' before she'd even had a chance.

A young boy shot out from nowhere with a wooden crate. He held Elsie's hand while she stepped up onto it. She ascended graciously, like a queen. Now she was two or three feet taller than anyone there. Everyone, and I mean everyone, gazed at her like she was Moses on the mountaintop promising to free the children of Israel.

I should have known Elsie would prove to be the most splendid raconteur.

She spoke about the formation of our flying ambulance corps, her enormous affection for its founder – 'the indomitable Dr Munro' (*since when!?*) – and our move from Furnes to the cellar house at Pervyse. It was while explaining our work in Pervyse that she became most impassioned.

'We call it the golden hour. The quicker we treat the men, the more likely they are to survive. Since we have moved closer to the battlefield, into the cellar, the results are… impressive. I have testimonies here.'

Elsie reached in her bag, then waved sheets of paper at the transfixed crowd. I didn't know she had collected them. I gazed at her incredulously. She *had* prepared.

'However, it *does* not come cheap, and that is why we come to you, with our caps – or rather our bonnets – in our hands.'

She took off her hat, and the audience gave a collective sigh at her cropped hair.

A handsome man yelled out from the audience. He had curly hair and shaking hands. I knew he was just back from some terrible place. You come to recognise it. It's not just the eyes, it's the mouth, it's the colour of the skin, it's their gait, it's everything.

'Why don't the Belgians pay?' His voice was vicious. 'You're in *their* country after all.'

Elsie put down her papers, collected herself and then beamed at the speaker, as though that was the very question she had been waiting all her life to answer.

'But then I'd be under Belgian bureaucracy, and if there is one thing I have always liked to keep clear of, it's that appalling red tape. Being independent means we have more freedom to save lives: *British* and Belgian lives.'

A man in the front row, in about his late sixties, said: 'Is it very lonely, Elsie, out there on the Western Front?' The plump woman next to him nudged him firmly in the ribs and squealed half to Elsie, half to the crowd, 'Mrs Knocker, I declare he's volunteering to come out and give you a cuddle!'

So what did Elsie do? She only clambered off her soapbox and marched over to him, arms outstretched. He got up and they shook hands enthusiastically. I had never seen anyone work a crowd like she did.

Elsie got herself up on the box again, and when the clapping had died down, she recommenced her speech.

'But everyone, you are mistaken if you think I work in solitude. I am certainly *not* alone! You see… Mairi, my sweet, step forward.'

She had *promised* me I wouldn't have to speak. I shook my head at her feverishly.

'Let me tell you about Miss Mairi Chisholm here!'

I lowered the brim of my hat, bowed my head and wished a huge catastrophic shell would detonate on top of me.

'This… quiet, humble woman is devoted to her work. She has a calm and courageous spirit, she is my backbone, my conscience, keeper of my secrets, my moral compass and my sister.'

I had never heard Elsie say such generous words and, despite my fury, tears sprang to my eyes. Some of the audience, the older women mostly, went 'aww', and the others clapped while I broke into a stupid sob.

Elsie grabbed and then squeezed my hand. I cringed because my palms were so damp.

'Mairi, darling, they'd love you to speak.'

I looked around fearfully. All these faces were peering up at me from the three hundred or so chairs, waiting for more pearls of wisdom to come their way. Playing nurse, either on the battlefields or in *Romeo and Juliet,* was nothing on this.

'I c-can't.'

'You can.' Elsie smiled like it was the easiest thing in the world. She didn't let go of my hand.

'You promised.'

Her face fell. 'Trust me, Mairi, you're a very impressive person.'

There was no getting out of this.

'What should I say?'

'Just be yourself,' she said. Her eyes may have been kindly, but it was her fault I was in this predicament. 'And…' she hesitated. 'Play up the Scottish bit.'

'Wha-at?'

'Just… you know… Do the "Och aye the noo…"'

I hated her then. I staggered up on the box, holding my silly hat. My heart was beating so loudly that I was sure the people in the front rows would hear it.

I took a deep breath.

'Thank you for your warm welcome, Glasgow!'

I was astonished that they cheered. The crowd actually cheered back at me.

Three hundred seats, all occupied, and there were also people standing at the back.

'I just want to support everything Elsie has told you,' I began. My hands were trembling so much I was glad to be holding the hat. 'It's a hard life, on the Western Front, but we do our best to ease the suffering around us…' I continued. Elsie was nodding encouragingly.

'As a widow, Elsie knows what it is to lose a loved one.'

The room was hushed again. I could see how pale Elsie was out the corner of my eye. 'Elsie knows how important the boys are to you, their wives, their mothers and fathers, their sisters and brothers.' I thought of Uilleam for a moment. If only he were grinning at me now. 'We do our best to keep them safe.'

The crowd was nodding. I searched around for something to add but my mind was blank.

'Does anyone have a question?'

They *all* had a question.

Mrs Grange pointed at one of the many hands raised.

'How would you change things, if you had the power?' It was a journalist I think, in the front row. Pen poised for an answer. Only I couldn't think of a single answer. How ridiculous was I!

Elsie jumped in. 'The war needs to stop, that's all.'

The same questioner said, 'Mairi? How about you?'

'Oh yes, absolutely, sir. What Elsie said.' I wiped my brow.

'Who should we vote for?' asked someone else. I knew Elsie wouldn't like that so much. Politics was all talk to her. She preferred action.

'I don't know who *you* should vote for,' Elsie said.

I thought she failed to conceal her impatience but the questioner didn't seem to mind and added, 'Who would *you* vote for, though?'

This time, I *did* have something to say. My hands had stopped shaking and I felt a sudden sense of opportunity. I knew the leaflets by heart. I took to the box.

'That's an interesting question, thank you – because as you know, in the antiquated parliamentary system we have, we women don't even have the vote!'

A man yelled out from the audience. 'A woman's place is in the home!'

I countered furiously, 'Whether it's home, hospital or cellar… a woman's place, sir, is *wherever* she makes good.'

It felt like the place erupted. I mean, everyone started laughing and clapping. A good few of them were cheering too.

'God won't like that!' another called.

'There is *nothing* in the Bible that says women are inferior to men, sir.' I gazed around the room, thinking, *somebody needs to say this.* 'The suffrage must be widened. We are entitled to nothing less than a voice. The vote is our voice.'

There was some more cheering. I thought, *Lady D would be so proud of me!*

Elsie was whispering alongside me. 'Good, Mairi, but let's keep emancipation out of it.'

I shook her off. The audience were in the palm of my hand and I had never experienced that before. What a revelation it was! 'But it's ridiculous, isn't it?' I continued to the crowd, feeling elated. 'We women contribute. We work as hard as the men, but unlike the men, we can't cast a vo—'

Elsie stepped up again. 'The big question today is: how can we continue to support our boys? And the answer is: we can only help them if you dig into your pockets, dig deep. Please.' Her voice was desperate, but she was soon smiling again as she shook a tin bucket at the crowd, then dropped down to pass it to the front row. The audience were putting in not just coins but notes too. This could secure our post for months.

'Is there anything else we, back home, can do to support you?' Mrs Grange asked as she walked over to us.

'Send blankets. Oh and… we want you to visit us,' Elsie said firmly.

'What?' I exclaimed.

'Why not?' Elsie shrugged, then raised her voice to the crowd. 'Come, see what we face, every night and day. You will be impressed by the resilience of the soldiers—'

'There's one other thing,' I interrupted.

Elsie didn't think she had forgotten anything. She gazed at me quizzically. I knew she would be running through her mind what I might be about to say.

'Mairi?'

'If you could send loving prayers, we—' I smiled at Elsie, who shook her head mutinously, 'I mean, *I* would be grateful.'

As we walked off the stage, Elsie was still shaking her head, but now she was laughing.

'Oh, Mairi. I thought the war would have knocked the religious stuffing out of you by now.'

I could barely find the words to retort. 'My faith is stronger than ever, Elsie! We need God more now, not less.'

Elsie smirked.

'Don't make that face, Elsie! Anyway, where are all those testimonies?'

'Why?'

'I want to see them.'

'Mairi—'

'Please.'

They were in her bag; I knew *exactly* where they were. Naturally, Elsie didn't want me to open it, but she didn't resist when I grabbed it and pulled out the pages. I scanned through each sheet. On every one, by hand, was written:

I'm Gilbert the Filbert the Knut with a K
The pride of Piccadilly the blasé roué
Oh Hades, the ladies, who leave their wooden huts
For Gilbert the Filbert the Colonel of the Knuts…

I couldn't believe it. Elsie's bare-faced lies! *How dare she?* Hauling me up on stage when she had promised me she wouldn't, telling me to act more Scottish! Her testimony of untruths, then cutting me off when I was talking of women's suffrage. I felt suddenly enraged, properly enraged. *What did she think she was doing?*

'Why wouldn't you talk about the suffrage with them?'

'I had no idea you were such a Pankhurst fan, Mairi!'

'Of course I am!' I said. 'Aren't you?' I had just assumed, naturally, that with the life Elsie led, she would be one hundred percent behind it. I stared at her incredulously. I felt like I had never seen her before. 'Don't you believe in a woman's right to vote?'

Even my mother, even her circle, had been making murmurs about women's right to vote. When Father suggested that 'perhaps women didn't have the intellectual capacity', my mother did her bit for the cause by not speaking to him for a week. I found it inconceivable that Elsie, my dearest, my most brilliant *sister*, might have reservations about suffrage.

'Oh, I don't *mind* it,' Elsie said casually, as though she were talking about spam or gooseberry jam. She rearranged her hat, smiling to herself. She knew she looked a picture.

'You don't mind it? What does that mean?'

'I mean it's not my decision to make.'

I didn't understand this either. I knew she loathed political 'chattering' but this was something else.

She sighed wearily as though dealing with a small child. 'Thing is, we don't want to put off any potential donors.'

I stared at her aghast. 'How would women's suffrage put anyone off?'

'Oh Mairi, Mairi, Mairi,' she said, the way she had that first night at the hotel, the way she had on the SS *Clementine*. My anger grew at each 'Mairi'. '*I* know what people are like. They're… simple.'

'No, they're not.'

'We came here to talk about the boys out there, not to make a political stand.'

'People can cope with more than one thing at a time.'

'I'm not sure they can.' She laughed hollowly. 'All right, I'm not sure *I* can!'

'What about *principles*?'

'Sometimes, you have to pick your principles,' Elsie said.

'*You* may do, but I don't.'

Elsie laughed and said 'I understand' in a way that suggested that I was the one who didn't. I had noticed before that whenever Elsie was fed up with a conversation, she simply changed it. She did that now.

'Mairi, you were grand up there after all.' She grinned delightedly. 'I knew you would be.' She had flagrantly ignored my wishes, yet, because I hadn't crumbled on stage, she thought it meant nothing. 'I don't know why you were so worried.'

CHAPTER SEVENTEEN

I helped pack away a few of the three hundred chairs while Elsie went off in her fine dress and pretty hat, with the curly-haired man from the audience maybe. I didn't know or care. Mrs Grange and a few others were collecting empty glasses and plates.

A young fella came over to assist with the stacking. I preferred to keep the chairs to three high, but he made extravagant towers of six or seven. I thought it was a mistake but I didn't like to tell him.

'She's quite the gal, isn't she?'

I was still bruised by my exchange with Elsie and full of the things I should have said, but I looked over to him. His smile was clearly an effort, for it dropped away within seconds. His shiny black hair was slicked way back, while his prominent ears came forward. He looked young, but close-up not *that* young – twenty-two, twenty-three maybe. He was losing his hair, that was certain. Never mind; aside from that, and the ears, he had a nice, serious face, red with exertion. It wasn't a handsome face but it wasn't plain, as Elsie might say, 'for an Englishman'.

'She sure is.'

'So are you. I liked what you said.'

I didn't know how to respond to that. We carried on lifting our way through the hall. Although it wasn't my job, I felt committed to this mission of returning chairs to their proper place.

I felt his glances on me. They may have been admiring, but I didn't know. I'm not sure how anyone can be certain with that most foreign of languages – the one between men and women (although Elsie never had a problem translating).

We were almost finished when suddenly there was a tremendous crash: a tower of his chairs had come down. I looked up and caught his eye. The colour had drained from him – his cheeks, even his lips were white. I recognised the fear on his features, as familiar as an old friend. *He* knew.

His name was Jack. Jack from Ingatestone, he said as though it was his title. After we had finished reorganising the fallen chairs, he invited me to a tearoom across the way and I surprised myself by accepting. He said he was visiting the family of a friend, but he didn't know them well, so—

'I don't know anyone here either!' I said reassuringly. It was still raining a drizzle, making the streets slippery. When I tottered on a cobblestone, he offered me his arm, but I waved it away. 'I'm fine.'

He smiled, more to himself than at me. 'Course you are.'

The door made a dreadful ringing noise when we pushed it open. Apart from us, the only customers were two old ladies who nodded at our arrival. I felt they didn't approve of Jack but I imagined they liked my bonnet. The yawning waitress could hardly be bothered to cover her mouth. I chose a macaroon from the menu but regretted it when Jack said he wasn't hungry. I wondered if it was because he didn't have enough money, but didn't know how to broach the subject. He had warm eyes that dropped away quickly when I tried to meet them with mine, which made me think of my reaction to Harold. While the waitress made the drinks, Jack and I sat silently and I wondered what on earth had possessed me to come here with him.

The waitress returned and, with minimum enthusiasm, announced, 'No macaroons left.'

Jack looked concerned but I said, 'Jolly good, I didn't want anything anyway.'

Perhaps because the place was so empty, the conversation on the next table reverberated around the room more than it normally might. Or maybe those two ladies had particularly booming voices. We weren't listening but we couldn't help but hear:

'If they only had any gumption it would be over by now.'

'They're too soft,' agreed the other. 'They just let it go on.'

'A captain I know says he's never seen such weak, lily-livered, feeble young soldiers.'

'They should be ashamed to call themselves British.'

This time Jack met my eyes. His jaw was set quite differently now.

'The war will be lost because of men like them.'

Jack couldn't control himself any longer. He swept away his napkin and rose from his chair. Half of me was petrified he would make a scene, but the other half couldn't help but admire his dignity.

He stood in front of them. Even the backs of his ears looked furious.

'You have… *no* idea what it's like,' he interrupted. 'You have NO idea how t-t-terrible it is.'

They didn't argue with him, thank goodness. One of the women wiped her thin lips slowly with her napkin. The other looked at him as though he were something crawling across her empty plate. He looked like he would say some more, but then he backed away from them, still shaking his head incredulously.

They called for the bill and the waitress came out still yawning, as though nothing had taken place, which, I suppose as far as anyone except us was concerned, it hadn't.

Jack's arm was wobbling as he tried to pour more tea. It came out of the spout orange and then turned yellow as it spilled onto the tablecloth. It created a shape like Africa on a map.

'Dash it,' he said crossly. 'I've w-wound myself up.'

I smiled and without thinking much about it, reached across the table and grabbed his hand to soothe him. Compared to Elsie's, his fingers were solid and grainy but his hands were clean, unlike the boys in the trenches, whose fingernails were always black with mud.

'People don't appreciate what's going on.'

'I'm not good at speaking about it,' he said regretfully, 'but… how can I tell them?'

'It's okay.'

It was a strange bond we had, I realised, but it was a bond.

*

Jack said he didn't receive any letters when he was on duty. I tried to imagine how it must feel to have the post-boy pass you by every single day.

'Not from your parents?' I asked hesitantly, wondering if his, like Elsie's, were dead.

'They can't—' he mimed writing, 'you know.'

'Oh.'

I knew some boys went letterless. It had never occurred to me *that* could be the reason. I don't know why I said it, it was just one of those things that came out, but I offered to write to him, 'If you would like me to?'

Jack's gloomy eyes lit up. He managed to hold his smile for a few seconds longer than before. And then he looked anxious again.

'B-but I'm not on the front, Mairi. I'm at Stow Maries'. He looked at my quizzical face. 'It's an airfield. Back in Essex.'

'That's fine.'

'That doesn't change your mind?'

'Course not.'

'Then I would treasure that.'

'It's nothing,' I said. 'I write to people most days.'

As I went back to the guesthouse, I couldn't stop thinking of Elsie and replaying her views on suffragettes, principles and phoney testimonies. She wasn't back yet, of course. How nice it would have been to be the last one home! I got into bed far earlier than usual, determined to be asleep before she came in. I wondered if Harold had heard of the collapse of the cellar house and if he would try to see us? I didn't give Jack of Ingatestone or his letters another thought.

CHAPTER EIGHTEEN

Although I was still unimpressed with Elsie's behaviour at the Assembly Rooms and the position she had put me in, my grievances had to wait. She woke the morning after the meeting uncharacteristically anxious.

She needed to buy Kenneth a present and she didn't have the faintest idea where to begin.

'Help me,' she pleaded, gnawing at her knuckles. 'What am I going to do?' There was no way I could turn her down in her moment of need.

Out in the market, stallholders were calling out fast and incomprehensibly. We browsed stalls of combs, pins, biscuits and sheet music. There were shouting tramps, shameless beggars and women sitting on the cold ground with two babies apiece. There were mothers with raggedy children and grandmothers pushing perambulators, and filthy workers in caps with pipes. As we walked between them, I realised, curiously, that I felt more at home here than I had in the tearoom the evening before.

Fumbling with her bag, Elsie muttered, 'The truth is, I don't know the first thing about what Kenneth likes.' She couldn't undo the clasp of her purse. It was like she had lost the ability to function. Tears filled her eyes, and I had to hold her hand to steady her. Kenneth was seven now, nearly eight. I tried to think of Uilleam at the same age. What kind of things had he liked? According to Mother, we had mostly spent our time punching each other or destroying her furniture. I remembered he didn't like learning his scales. We used to play 'Ring-a-Ring-a-Roses', 'Duck, Duck, Goose' and 'What's the

Time, Mr Wolf?' I remembered a rare occasion when we played that with my father in the garden, Uilleam and me creeping up to him: '*Two o'clock,*' '*Four o'clock…*' And then his wonderful anticipated roar – '*Dinner time!*' –causing us to scatter across to the rose bushes. *How could it be that I once adored being frightened?*

We came across a stall selling tops, horses, cars, dolls, soldiers and guns made from tin. I told Elsie the little soldiers would be just the thing.

'Really?' she looked doubtful.

'Yes!' I thought of Dr Munro lining up his coins for battle on the Ypres Salient – '*The living conditions for our men will be far worse…*'

'I don't want Kenneth to think—'

'Think what?'

'Nothing.'

She counted the soldiers into a tin box and they made a clitter-clatter noise as they fell in. Clitter clatter. The sound stayed in my head.

How strange it was to be out and about, in the open, wearing bonnets on our heads instead of helmets. I was alert, still looking for the sniper, still listening out for the shell. Working out the best exit through the crowds, feeling around for my emergency kit. But the cries were the market traders calling out their wares, and the holes in the ground were made by rain and wagon wheels. That sudden boom was the slamming of a front door. That rat-a-tat was an old man's cough.

Further along, there was a stall displaying board games and Elsie became animated as she looked at the chess sets. The old stallholder had an ear trumpet, and Elsie was soon shouting into it, 'Which is best for a starter? Is seven a good age to learn?' Without even asking, she got the price knocked down too.

The stallholder carefully wrapped a set in crisp brown paper, wishing Elsie the best of times. 'Chess will help your young man learn war strategies!' he added encouragingly as we walked away.

Elsie looked tearful again.

'You've got two lovely presents there, Elsie,' I reassured her. 'Kenneth will be thrilled.'

Ducking shells, driving through the blackness, she never looked so worried as she did now. She was almost quaking with fear. I squeezed her fingers. They had grown thinner over the last year, and they must have been *a lot* thinner otherwise I wouldn't have noticed. Kenneth would be delighted with his mother, I was sure. Who wouldn't be dazzled by this extraordinary woman blowing in from the east?

We had tried to arrange to journey back to Pervyse together, but marrying our train and boat timetables proved too convoluted, so we agreed to travel separately. I said I might be back in three days. She might be there in four or five. 'It depends,' she said vaguely. She didn't say what it depended on.

I knew I'd miss her. She was my right hand; she said I was her left foot. We didn't have to speak to know what the other was thinking. It was only after she'd got on her train to Exeter via Birmingham, after she'd tearfully waved her grubby handkerchief at me, only once I was outside of the bubble that surrounded me whenever I was with her, that I grew annoyed at her again about the meeting the day before. Hoisting me up onto the stage! Laughing at my principles! 'Gilbert the Filbert' testimonies indeed!

*

I didn't go to Dorset. I had sent a telegram to my mother asking if she wanted to meet me in the city. I didn't particularly want her to accept, but unfortunately she did. She had medicines, a tailored coat and new shoes to collect in Knightsbridge (Dorset was too provincial for her shopping tastes).

We arranged to meet by the Eros fountain at Piccadilly Circus. I had heard people talk of the statue – even some of the Belgian boys had asked me if it was as fine as people said. Gazing skyward,

I saw the chubby naked cherub, his arrow pointing towards me. I tried to feel a rapport with this great work of art, but couldn't. In any case, it was rapidly becoming apparent that meeting here wasn't my brightest idea. The area was jammed with horses, carriages and swerving buses. There were dozens of women, who I think may have been prostitutes, milling about, perhaps attracted by Eros and the promise of love. The women were wearing lots of make-up – which only served to enhance their unhappy expressions – and they were calling out 'Special offers for our boys!' and other such indelicate things. Sometimes I would see servicemen who looked, from behind, like Harold. Each time they turned around it was a disappointment. Plenty of soldiers appeared half-cut: one man, a lanky streak in naval uniform, put his face close to mine and yelled 'Raaaa!'

I thought, *here he is, 'The pride of Piccadilly, the* blasé roue', and suddenly I laughed… I probably looked as nutty as the '*Knut with a K*'!

I wondered if Mother and I would even recognise each other in the crowds. But then I saw her, waving, from across the way, and I could breathe again. My mother was wearing a wonderful black fur and shiny high heels, still more polished, more groomed, than most women half her age. I crossed over to her, carefully dodging the buses and the horse manure, and as I did, one of the made-up women hissed at me, 'Ooh, Miss Hoity Toity…' and another said, 'You'll get yours!'

'Mairi, look at your hat!'

Mother seemed relieved at my appearance. I think she was expecting worse. Putting her arm through mine, she brushed my cheek with her lips. 'Let's get away from here.' She confidently led me down a crowded side alley, which was a relief because, in truth, I could never find my way around London.

'We'd hoped you'd bring her.'

'Who?' *And who was 'we'?*

'Mrs Knocker, of course.'

'I didn't say that I would.'

'Oh well,' she said. 'I suppose she was occupied. Come and meet Mrs Godfrey.'

My mother had brought a friend along to meet the daughter she hadn't seen for a year! I was hurt, but also relieved. Had we been alone, I'm not sure that – apart from dissecting Uilleam's life – we would have found a great deal to talk about. Perhaps Mrs Godfrey might make a pleasant diversion.

Mrs Godfrey was large and imposing. She said she was a member of my mother's discussion circle. I didn't know how much discussion would have happened with her in the group. She was as dominant in conversation as she was physically. My hopes of a pleasant afternoon began to fade.

'I'm taking you to The Ritz, child,' she said, looking me up and down as though I might have scurvy. 'Aren't they feeding you over in France?'

'Belgium.'

She and my mother marched off and I trailed after them.

I heard my mother say, 'I don't know what she's done with her hair underneath that dreadful bonnet… Whatever possessed her to wear green?!'

Mrs Godfrey replied, 'There, dear, she doesn't look half as bad as she did in the newspaper.'

The Palm Court at The Ritz was like nowhere I had ever been. Opulent and ostentatious, with panelled mirrors and glamorous pictures in glamorous frames. Chandeliers dripped half the height of the room. The dining tables had shapely carved legs and were covered by tablecloths so dazzling white you almost wanted to shade your eyes. There were people milling everywhere, although much to the chagrin of my mother and Mrs Godfrey, they looked neither opulent nor ostentatious. On one table, two soldiers, one with a dirty bandage around his head, were talking excitedly. They had Australian accents, I think. Their mouths and forks were full of food. They couldn't eat quickly enough. I knew that feeling.

'It wasn't like this last time we were here!'

'It seems the whole world dines here now!' said Mrs Godfrey disapprovingly.

My mother whispered her greatest insult: 'They have gone too cheap.'

On the next table, there were six girls. I would guess they were celebrating a birthday or an engagement, for they were making a big fuss of one of their number. Three of them had yellow skin, which meant they were munitionettes. Their red lipstick clashed terribly with the colour of their cheeks. I could hardly take my eyes off them. I had read about these so-called 'canary girls', but it was the first time I'd seen them. The celebrated girl was the most yellow of them all: as she opened her present, I saw even her fingers and her fingernails were discoloured. If you didn't know about the war and the factories, you would think they were a different race. You might think she was from space, just visiting Planet Earth.

'I'm glad you're not doing *that* work, Mairi,' my mother said loudly.

'How do they bear it?' agreed Mrs Godfrey.

'It's not flattering,' my mother added.

I don't think the girls heard. Even so, I smiled apologetically at them. They didn't smile back, not even after I took off my expansive bonnet so they could see my utilitarian hair. Hopefully they understood that I wasn't a privileged loudmouth like my mother and her friend. I too knew about dangerous, rough work.

Mrs Godfrey leaned forwards. She was wearing a white lace top with a high collar and tiny delicate buttons that didn't suit her. She was an affront to tiny, delicate buttons.

'So, Mairi, won't you tell us all about the indefatigable Mrs Knocker?'

Our barn-storming speech at the Glasgow Assembly Rooms was already in the London papers. I found it incredible the speed words could fly – if only action were half so quick.

'What do you want to know?'

'Well, for a start—' they looked conspiratorially at each other as though they had planned this, 'whatever happened to Mr Knocker?'

I told them what Elsie had told me, about his death in Java. I guessed it was from a tropical disease, very painful. I even borrowed her phrase, 'Slow, slow, quick,' as my mother wiped tears of compassion from her eyes.

'Such a love story. Such a tragedy.'

'Elsie's strong,' I reminded them. 'She has channelled her loss into the war effort.'

'Oh yes,' they agreed but they were nearly inconsolable.

I added, as Elsie had told me, that it was only thanks to the incredible efforts of everyone back home that we could carry on. My mother and Mrs Godfrey loved this – they preened and puffed up so much that I thought Mrs Godfrey's buttons would burst off her blouse.

Even The Ritz was not exempt from rations on food. There was corned-beef pie or corned-beef pasty on the menu. If Elsie were here, she would have said, '*Hmm, do you have any corned beef?*' And I would have been in fits of giggles. My mother explained it was a job to get meat now. They were meat-free most days. Cheese was a poor substitute.

'Have you started eating vegetables, Mother?'

She didn't like that. She blinked at me. 'I always have, Mairi.'

When Mrs Godfrey went to use the facilities, my mother leaned in and patted my hand. My instinct was to draw back my fingers but I let them stay. This felt unfamiliar but perhaps it was progress. I thought briefly of how Jack might have felt when I grabbed his hand. I wanted to ask about Uilleam then, but Mother got in first with another pressing question –

'Any *amour* on the Continent?' My mother refused to say 'Pervyse' and Belgium did not sound nearly glamorous enough for her.

I quickly dispelled thoughts of Harold from my mind. I had tried to convince myself that the entire episode was a childish error: not unlike the daft rumours that kept circulating that the war was over. Only an inexperienced idiot would fall for those.

My mother was staring at me.

'*Amour*? Not really, no.'

She wasn't the type to throw random French words into a conversation. 'It means "love"—' she added, looking annoyed.

'I know what it means,' I cut in. 'The answer is still no.'

I felt exasperated by her. It was true that of *that* kind of love – the romantic kind – I had nothing to report… but what love I *had* seen! I'd seen men cradle their friends in their arms the way mothers caress their newborn babies. I'd seen people risk their lives for the wounded of the 'other side'. I'd seen men run through gunfire to pull a trapped comrade free. I'd seen men write last letters for other men too weak to sit up and form the words themselves. I'd seen what Elsie did in our tiny cellar and I knew how the Belgians suffered and fought for their country. Plenty of acts of love every hour of every day that I knew my mother wouldn't be interested in because they wouldn't result in an impressive society marriage.

'There must be some suitable… *officers*?'

'No.' *Not regular soldiers of course. My mother. The snob.*

'Or doctors?'

'I'm not interested, Mother.'

'I always thought Dr Munro was quite the gentleman.'

'He is.'

'Then, wouldn't it—'

'Wouldn't it what?'

Mrs Godfrey came back, also scowling. 'Frightful lavs,' she said. 'Appalling lighting. Could hardly see beyond the end of my nose.'

Yet another thing that had gone downhill. Those poor visitors to The Ritz!

However, the thought of Mrs Godfrey enduring our commode, or even squatting in the woods, cheered me up and got me through my corned-beef pasty.

*

I stopped at Furnes on the way back from England.

Helen and Arthur were leaving Belgium. If they had hoped to go out on a high, they were to be disappointed. Helen's round glasses were now held together with sticky tape in the middle *and* on both sides. It gave her the look of a lunatic. They made me think not of Charlotte Brontë and Mr Héger but of Mr Rochester's wife in the attic. Arthur had visibly shaky hands. They had been in a car accident just the day before. Arthur had come off that damn slippery road from Menin and partly wrapped the Daimler around a tree. Untypically of him, he seemed determined to make light of it.

'It just jumped out at me!'

But when Arthur left the room, Helen whispered that it had been pitch-dark, and an explosion had gone off right in front of them. They had careened off the road, smack, and it wasn't Arthur's fault… The two soldiers they were transporting in the back were killed, one instantly, the other lingering on for a desperate hour. Helen said despondently, 'They were half-dead anyway.' She continued, 'Before he… went, the boy called out for his grandad.' She looked at me incredulously through those wonky lenses as if it were an amazing thing. 'I never heard *anyone* do that before.'

We played pontoon, then Newmarket. We used some nuts I'd bought at Ostend as gambling chips. I won three games in a row. They all seemed so downhearted that I grew fearful I'd win the fourth. I didn't want to be the one who was lucky in cards.

'Shall we play snap instead?' I suggested.

'For God's sake, Mairi, not snap!' Arthur said so fiercely that we looked up in surprise.

Later, when he left the room again, Helen whispered, 'It's not you, Mairi, he just can't stand a sudden noise.'

Dr Munro said he wanted to speak to me. As we walked into the kitchen, I noticed his limp was more pronounced than before. He said he'd had a brush with a bullet the other day. In the candlelight, he looked like a goblin or a wizard about to perform magical spells.

He said the collapse of the cellar house last week was 'the final straw'. It made me remember the three little piggies and I thought, *no, the final straw will be if the Germans blow our house down.*

'It's no longer secure.'

'The cellar itself is fine. We won't build upwards again, that's all.'

'Why don't you come back here? Our work is invaluable too.'

I knew it was, and I felt bad that Dr Munro could think that I would ever look down on him. I fully understood that his contribution at Furnes was as important as any.

'You could achieve as much here as you do in Pervyse,' he continued.

Did he really think I could leave our first-aid post behind? I felt like I was being tempted. *Is this how Moses felt?*

'Elsie would never agree to it,' I said.

'Then come alone. She might have to follow then.' I didn't say anything. Dr Munro must have known Elsie did not follow anyone.

'What if the Germans breach the line?' he said, voicing my greatest fear.

I thought of Elsie's love for the boys, her love for *me*. We were still sisters after all. 'That won't happen.'

'You'd only have minutes to get out.'

'I know,' I said weakly.

He didn't press me further.

*

I decided to stay two nights in Furnes – It would be my last time in a comfortable bed for a long time and, for once, I wanted to savour it. The meeting with my mother was still much on my mind. I had tried not to have high hopes about seeing her, but I must have had, otherwise I wouldn't feel this downhearted. I wondered if that was because of the war and her failing to understand, or if there were something else too. While my grandmother – her mother – was alive, they had never been close, so maybe the emotional distance between us was normal for her? I reminded myself what Elsie had said –the best thing to do was to make your own beloved family. Maybe that's what growing up is – realising your family can't always be what you want them to be.

Before I left I tried to persuade Mother to explain clearly what was going on with Uilleam. I explained that I learned so little about the situation from their letters. She usually loved to discuss how misunderstood Uilleam was, but instead she mouthed, 'Not in front of Mrs Godfrey!', and there wasn't another moment during the rest of our meeting when we weren't in front of Mrs Godfrey; my mother made sure of that.

On my final morning in Furnes, after the usual porridge breakfast (which tasted so much the worse after my having been spoiled by the luxury of thick-cut marmalade in Scotland), I got my things ready. Helen hugged me, her glasses wavering. She whispered conspiratorially, 'Look out for a copy of my book!'

And I whispered back, 'Can't wait!' though I doubted she'd ever finish it. She was joining some 'Stop the War' campaign group in America and Arthur didn't look too healthy to me. He would need some looking after, no doubt. Helen didn't have time to write more limericks; how would she find the time to write an entire book?

Arthur walked me out. 'No need to leave your newspapers, Arthur!' I told him, but he insisted I needed help. My bags were weighed down with as much food for the boys as I could manage to carry, but still I ended up helping *him* – I didn't trust Arthur not to drop everything.

'How *is* Elsie?' Arthur asked after we had loaded up the car. He put his hands in his pockets. I supposed it was to disguise the trembling.

'Fine.'

'Why didn't she come back with you?'

I was surprised he didn't know. 'She's gone to see her little boy.'

Arthur chewed his tongue. 'You believe that?'

'Of course,' I said uncertainly. *Why wouldn't I?*

'You'd never know Elsie was a mother, would you? Or a widow even.'

I didn't know what he was trying to say, but I didn't care. Arthur was odd, and now he seemed even odder. His accident had probably made it worse. We noticed that sometimes – how the proximity of death exaggerated a personality. An easy-going person might become lazy, a coper might become efficient, or an angry person might become aggressive.

'I hope we meet again, Mairi,' he continued.

Even that sounded strange – I realised it was because he hadn't called me 'young Mairi' for once. I was glad he had finally stopped patronising me and I doubted we would meet again anyway, so I could afford to smile warmly at him.

I bounced into the driving seat, excited to get back to the cellar. To see my best friend again. It had been the longest time Elsie and I had been apart in nearly a year. Nothing else mattered.

Arthur leaned in. He was so close to me that when he spoke, spit landed on my arm and on the steering wheel. 'Mairi – a bit of advice. Don't be a cock-tease like her. It's not nice.'

*

I knew the cellar needed a tidy-up, and after that I wanted to sift through Madeleine's things for a while. I always found that soothing. As I drove back, planning everything I would do, I decided that Elsie and my conversation about the suffragettes must have been a misunderstanding. No woman, especially one of Elsie's capabilities, could *possibly* be against the women's vote. It was simply that Elsie didn't feel a fundraising speech at the Glasgow Assembly Rooms was the appropriate place to discuss it. She was probably right.

I drove past vehicles carrying ammunitions and trucks carrying new soldiers. If they hooted, I waved back. The routes to and from the Western Front were growing busier. Was that a good sign?

The first thing I saw when I pulled up in Pervyse was darling Shot. He ran over, barking wildly, his ears flapping madly, letting me know that I was home. Was there ever a friendlier, more heart-warming sight than that? Here was innocence, here was loyalty! Shot didn't care if I had too many freckles and not enough bosom! He didn't worry about the future or regret the past. I grabbed him, stroked him and he gazed in my eyes so lovingly it almost brought tears to mine. *This is* amour *too, Mother*. Martin followed Shot out, wiping his hands. He nodded curtly, then strode off.

Opening the trapdoor of the cellar, I pulled myself and Shot down.

'Wait 'til you see what I've got for you,' I told my good boy.

Everything was as quiet as I expected it to be but as I reached the bottom of the stairs, I suddenly spotted four shiny boots in the straw. *Had the Germans invaded?* Shot didn't seem alarmed. The boots were attached to legs. The legs were attached to two people, both fast asleep.

'Hellooo?' I called uncertainly, doubt coursing through me.

Elsie and Harold jumped up to greet me, delighted. Shot wriggled out of my arms and made his way into the straw too, tail wagging.

Elsie hugged me fiercely. 'Mairi, Mairi, Mairi. I *hate* it when we're apart!'

Harold hugged me too, which was unusual. I blushed. It was easier to pick up Shot again and to direct my attention to him. 'You just wait, little fella…'

I was discombobulated. Not that Harold was here – no reason to think he wouldn't visit – but why was he asleep in the straw? I wondered if maybe he had been hurt again, but there was no sign of an injury.

'You have straw in your hair, Elsie.'

She smoothed it out.

I wished I had returned sooner. I had wasted precious time at Furnes, and with Mrs Godfrey and my mother at The Ritz. Elsie wasn't supposed to be back yet. Had I known she was coming back early, I would have made sure I did too. Elsie hated being alone above anything else. It was her weak spot. She'd do anything to avoid it.

*

Elsie had bought me a jigsaw puzzle: a picture of Bruges with canals and a bell tower. I don't know why she had got me a present or why she had chosen this. Bruges was under German Occupation now and I'd never shown any interest in it anyway.

'Ladies, when all this is over, I'll take you there.' Harold was being unusually effusive.

'When all this is over' was one of our favourite phrases. We prefaced many of our sentences with it. What we would eat, what we would do, what lives we would live 'when all this is over'.

But although we said it more than ever, I had begun to believe it less. The war would never be over. It was nearly one year old now. What they couldn't resolve in one year, they probably wouldn't resolve in ten.

'Not *just* Bruges,' declared Elsie, who seemed unusually bright-eyed too. If she had had a tail, she would have been wagging it. 'We'll visit all the European cities, won't we, Mairi?'

I kept looking between her and him. *What had happened? Was I missing something?* If they were together now, they didn't say it outright.

'Maybe.'

'Do you like your present?'

'I… love it. Thank you.' They shared a look. More body language I couldn't read. 'So how was Kenneth?' I asked wildly.

Elsie declared he had been utterly brilliant. He loved the chess set. 'He loved *everything*,' she enthused, which I guessed meant that contrary to her fears, Kenneth had adored her too.

Later, as we sat having tea, she said in a high voice most unlike her usual measured tones, 'The toy soldiers ended up in the mud.' She turned with lowered eyes to Harold.

'*La plus ça change…*' Harold said. I nodded knowledgeably although I wasn't sure I understood.

Shot gnawed with satisfaction on his bone.

CHAPTER NINETEEN

I tried a different strategy with the Bruges jigsaw. Usually, I took the traditional 'edges first' approach. This time I started in the middle with the clock but I was making scant progress. What was it about beginning with the edges that meant success?

Harold continued to drop in to see us, and sometimes he would sit with me while I did my puzzles. Sometimes, he would go off with Elsie. I looked forward to our stove-side discussions on morals or ethics and I always wished he could stay longer.

*

After our Glasgow trip, the appetite for stories about Elsie and me had grown. Every week that autumn, there were articles about us in the papers. Journalists and photographers visited us in the cellar and not just British ones; people came from all over the world to tell our story.

There was a lot of censorship and even though we were asked to paint a picture of our lives, it had to be the right kind of picture. I already knew from experience that the British had very strict rules about what could be sent back home in letters. But if we thought the censorship in the letters was tight, the censorship of the newspapers was astonishing.

The message we had to convey was not our men's desperation, not a fight for survival, but patriotism, nationalism, honour and duty.

We had to be the kind of women that people back home would warm to: we couldn't be too fierce, too strong, too agitating or too trailblazing, we mustn't be those dreaded suffragettes or women's liberators, for then people might lose all sympathy for us. We certainly mustn't get above our station.

We had to be consistent in our sweetness, our *maternal* love for the boys. We had to be gentle nurses, and pleasant women *above all else*. As long as we kept to this image, I gathered, people would still be interested. If they were interested, we could continue our work helping the boys. And that, after all, was what we were there for.

The photographers liked us arranged in front of the Chater-Lea and the sidecar. They were quick at setting up their tripods and their cameras and we stared where we were told to stare. Usually Elsie stood upright with a reassuring arm around me or a parental hand on my shoulder.

One time, I suggested we tell the man from the *Liverpool Echo* about Madeleine's family and the things I collected. 'He could take a photo of the bear!'

But Elsie wrinkled her nose. 'Stick to the script,' she said emphatically. 'The readers don't want to hear about that.'

Another time, as we posed awkwardly, an acned photographer in a cap told us that we were the most photographed women of the time.

'What? Us?'

'Don't look so surprised!' he said.

'Look devoted,' Elsie said out of the corner of her mouth, smirking.

This unsettled me. It was all right for Elsie with her natural charm and confidence – hers was a face that could launch a thousand ships, but my face wasn't going to convince anybody of anything. In fact, mine was a face that could well put people off forever.

Flash, the bulb went off.

When I told Elsie my concerns, she couldn't understand what I was blathering about.

'Why, you're lovely to look at, Mairi!'

Sometimes, I tried to get Shot in the frame, but he would jump away. He could be most uncooperative. Once he did a wee right where the photographer wanted us to sit. 'Shot understands,' Elsie said, laughing. She was unfazed. 'He doesn't want to be involved!'

I hardly recognised myself in the photos. I looked hearty and out-doorsy. (My mother would have said I looked like a peasant.) Here I stood in my headdress and uniform – Elsie wasn't wrong – like a warrior woman. Like a Native American Indian but without the feathers or face paint. I wondered if Harold ever got the newspapers? He never said. Or Jack from Ingatestone? Did he recognise me?

The newspapers had curious headlines too:

CRINOLINE NURSES!

'Have we ever worn crinoline? Which century do they think this is?'

DORSET GIRLS ON THE FRONT!

'Since when was I a "Dorset girl"?' I complained. 'I'm not a Dorset *girl,* either,' replied Elsie indignantly. 'I'm thirty-two!'

As for ELSIE SAVES THE DAY, well, of course I didn't want or expect to be headline news but to be absented was painful too. I was just an addendum, a paragraph at the end: *'Mrs Knocker is joined in the cellar house by Miss Mairi Chisholm, daughter of Mr and Mrs Roderick Chisholm of Chedington, Dorset.'*

Then there was: THE COMPASSION OF THE WIDOWED MRS KNOCKER. I joked that it sounded like a terrible folk song but I did wonder, what about the compassion of the young Mairi Chisholm? Wasn't that worth a line or two?

'Take it all with a pinch of salt,' advised Elsie.

'Why do they write about what we do, anyway, and not the boys out there? Why us?' I asked.

'The boys are all in there, darling. Ninety-nine percent of the time. Why shouldn't they shine a light on us ladies? Just once in a darned while?'

'B-b-but…'

'This press is our bread and butter, Mairi,' she warned.

She was right. The press was bringing in money, and increasingly, I was striking off things from our wanted list. We had more bandages, painkillers and antiseptics than you could shake a stick at. I began a new page in the logbook: '*Buckets, spades, towels.*'

Elsie leaned over me, laughing: 'Anyone would think we were going for a trip to the seaside!'

One time, I asked Elsie which she preferred dealing with – 'Chilblains and syphilis or photographers and fan mail?'

She said, 'Chilblains and syphilis, any day!'

I'm not sure if that was *completely* true, but what was true was that despite her love of the press, her smile was never more satisfied than when she'd sewn someone up or when she'd brought someone back to life. I recalled Arthur and Helen saying that she *hadn't* brought a man back to life in Furnes, but I'd certainly watched her bring men back to life in the cellar at Pervyes.

*

A few weeks later, in October 1915, a modern ambulance I hadn't seen before rolled up the road and parked noisily. Elsie and I were coming back from the trenches with a poor chap showing signs of shell shock. With any luck, we'd got him early enough and a few days in the cellar might just about sort him out.

'Who on earth is that?' Elsie asked indignantly. She was fiercely protective of our patch. Arthur once joked that he wouldn't put it past Elsie to piss up the cellar-house walls to mark her territory. Elsie had countered with 'What do you think Shot is for?'

We ignored the new arrivals with their show-off vehicle, carried our fella in and warmed him up. Shortly afterwards, there was a tentative knock on the door. Shot growled, making his typically poor attempt at being menacing.

They were two doctors from the English town of Sutton Coldfield. They looked similar: smart men with neat moustaches; and they had similar smart names: Cyril and Cecil. They were probably in their forties, certainly of my mother's generation rather than my father's, and both were grey before their time: grey hair, grey suits, grey faces. One of them explained that they had come to donate to us their purpose-built ambulance.

'Is this a joke?' Elsie asked abruptly.

They both looked bewildered at her response. 'No.'

'That… that vehicle out there?'

'Yes.'

'It can't be! No.' Elsie stared at them fiercely, as though she was about to throw them out. Shot barked, sensing trouble.

'Elsie?' I said, trying to calm Shot.

'It's yours,' continued one of the doctors, Cyril I think, nervously. 'Mrs Knocker, we are giving it to you. If you don't mind, that is?'

For one terrible moment, I thought that Elsie was going to refuse it.

'No, no.'

I don't think this was the reception they had expected.

'Yes, yes?' the same doctor said, only now with an anxious chuckle. 'It's all yours.'

Finally, it dawned on Elsie that it was true. She threw her arms first around the speaker and then around his colleague. I was afraid she was going to kiss both of them on the mouth. They were too old, I thought, to enjoy *that*!

We went out to explore our new vehicle and found it was as perfectly fitted inside as it looked from the outside. A proper ambulance, not a converted car! It had everything we would need. Elsie's expression was as delighted as my own. This was an ambulance that dreams were made of. After we had given it a thorough, joyful inspection, Elsie invited the grey doctors for tea and oat biscuits in the cellar. We couldn't stop smiling and it was, after all, nearly four o'clock. Time for a celebration.

'You don't *still* actually live down there?'

'We do!' I always felt stupidly proud when I told people that.

'What? Sleep and eat and—?'

'And all, yes.'

'Isn't there shelling?'

'Not much at present.'

But right then, as though proving a nasty point, a shell did whizz overhead, and we all had to flee downstairs, pulling the cellar door fast behind us. As I did so, its wood cracked, which meant yet another ruddy thing I'd have to see to.

Down in the cellar, the poor chap we'd brought in was being cheered up by Shot. From barely being able to speak, now he pulled himself up to tell us, 'I've got a spaniel at home. His name is Joey. Boy, can that dog eat!'

The two doctors looked around in astonishment, taking in the straw, the commode, the cans of Maconochie, the soaps, the buckets, the unwritten postcards, the smell: everything. I hoped they could see that while we were unorthodox, we were still careful and capable. What we did worked, or at least it worked better than anything else did.

We spent a happy hour talking about our experiences. Cyril, the more talkative one, was especially taken with Elsie. He wasn't handsome, but as he spoke I saw he had a certain charm. Elsie didn't seem in the mood for flirting though; she was unusually serious with them both.

'Being a widow must have given you a greater understanding of death and grief,' he ventured, and we all nodded.

'It was some time ago,' Elsie said.

'Only a few years, Elsie,' I said sympathetically. Elsie was always humble about what she had endured. She looked up at our concerned faces. 'I suppose,' she said, then added, 'Life can be hard.'

'I lost my wife three years ago,' said Cecil. He and Elsie looked at each other and it was as though they shared a secret communion.

Elsie stood up sharply and announced it was time we went back to the trenches. She would often cut meetings short like this. Journalists, photographers, army officers… all dismissed like children. It seemed to reveal a lack of manners and the doctors looked put out. Elsie added that the soldiers would be wanting their hot soup and they seemed to be mollified. *Ah, it was for a good reason.* It was decided that Paul would drive them to the train station, then back to Sutton Coldfield they would go. We all shook hands warmly and Elsie and I thanked them once again.

'We will write,' Elsie said, which of course meant *I* would write.

Before he left, Cyril whispered into my ear, 'A word of advice.' He was so close that I could feel the bushiness of his protruding moustache.

I was going to say: *I don't need your advice, thank you.* What was it about men who didn't know what we did telling us what we ought and oughtn't do?

But Cyril was just being silly – he pointed at the puzzle. 'You should do the edges first. Don't you know? You're making it so much harder on yourself!'

I laughed and kissed his cheek goodbye, the Continental way.

Down in the trenches, the soldiers weren't even ready for their tea.

'They came such a long way,' I said to Elsie.

'We all come a long way.'

'We could have given them another hour of our time, surely?'

Elsie grinned at me, stirring sugar into cups as we waited for the water to boil. 'Always leave them wanting more, Mairi.'

*

Shortly after the doctors' visit, I came back from the trenches to find Elsie deep in conversation with a broad Frenchman in a too-tight, grubby shirt. His sleeves were rolled up and his chest hairs were on display. She looked up at me but didn't introduce us; she just carried on talking, earnestly. *A new Gilbert? Surely not!*

'One hundred francs for each one you bring here or to the hospital… *Cent francs.*'

'*D'accord.*' He spat when he spoke. 'It's a deal.' And then he stomped off without saying goodbye to either of us. This was rare. We might have been at war, but there was no need to drop the social niceties.

'What *is* going on?' I asked after he slammed the cracked door shut. 'What deal?'

'This way the bodies get returned. Since I put up the bounty they are bringing them in like a… good harvest.'

'But…' I couldn't believe this, 'we shouldn't have to pay people to return lost men.'

'Can you imagine the hell those families are going through? I only have to contemplate Kenneth going missing and I think: just bring them home.'

'But they should give us the bodies without the bribery.'

'Well they don't, do they, darling?' she said shortly. 'It's hard work fishing them out and not everyone does as they should. I thought even you'd have grasped that by now.'

'Where's the money coming from?'

'Five thousand pounds from our Scottish jaunt – thanks to you, wee bonny lass.' I pulled away from her embrace. 'And the photos go out. The reports go out. The headlines sing our praises. The money pours in,' she added in a faux-dramatic voice. 'Mairi, publicity is a devil and my soul has been truly sold.'

I stared at her.

Something was changing. I couldn't put my finger on it. I couldn't express it because it was so silly, so small, but it seemed like I wasn't the first to know our plans any more. In fact, I wasn't even getting to know the plans at all.

*

A few miles away, there was a town, Poperinghe – 'Pop' the British called it – that hadn't been taken by the Germans. Harold said he had some officer friends in Poperinghe who wanted to meet us.

The first time Elsie went was in the middle of November 1915. I remember it especially because it was our one-year anniversary of being in the cellar.

Harold did ask if I wanted to join, but I was looking after another poor chap in the cellar – trench foot – and I was reluctant to leave him alone. At least, that was my excuse. I didn't want to go. If it were just the two of them, maybe I would have, but what conversations could I possibly have with Harold's officer friends? *How is the war progressing? How much do you pay to have dead bodies brought in? Are we going to win?* It made my head ache.

Elsie dashed around the cellar getting things in order before she left. She was full of zingy enthusiasm. Even the sick man in the corner roused himself sufficiently to stare admiringly at her. Elsie tugged firmly at the belt on her big leather coat before giving me a hug.

'Don't do anything I wouldn't do, Mairi.'

I laughed bitterly, thinking there was no danger of that. She ran out after Harold, calling happily, 'Just me today, Hal!'

When did he become Hal? I wondered. Why did we have to diminish everything? We turned everything Belgian into something small and fluffy, something easy when it wasn't. It really wasn't.

The next morning, dipping biscuits into watery, cold chocolate, Elsie was still full of enthusiasm. 'What a place!' she said dreamily. 'It was like being back in Britain. Tommies everywhere.'

'Really?'

This didn't sound like the sort of thing that would appeal to Elsie. I knew there must have been something more to it.

There was.

'There is this one Belgian bar, *La Poupée* – fantastic atmosphere. A guy on the piano thumping out all the old tunes and there were three sisters; one of them is called Ginger,' she said dreamily, 'and she was wonderful. I don't think I've met anyone like her.'

I felt inexplicably jealous. It was one thing to spend hours with Harold – I noted she didn't cut *his* time short or leave *him* wanting more – another to spend her time with another woman. Nevertheless, I tried to look as unconcerned as I could.

'Why do they call her that?'

'Her hair is the colour of yours,' said Elsie, wiping the chocolate stain off her cheek. I couldn't help feeling she meant, *that's where the resemblance ends!*

'And what does she do?'

'She's the daughter of the bar owner.'

'So?'

'She talks. She talks to the officers, gets them to buy drinks. She drinks too, she could drink us under the table. Hal' – she looked at me meaningfully – '*Harold* likes her.'

I didn't say anything. What was I meant to say? I was thinking, *Is she a prostitute, this 'Ginger' woman?* Surely Harold wouldn't be so daft as to get involved in that kind of thing. He once told me that his parents expected him to marry a titled woman 'at the very least'. I doubted whether 'she could drink us under the table' constituted a title. Harold wasn't a man to go against his parents' wishes. He had a strong sense of familial duty. That was one of the reasons he and I got on well.

'How good it was to have female company again!'

'Do you lack female company?' I asked pointedly.

'*Other* than you, darling.'

'I see.'

'No, you don't see, silly.' Elsie put down her cup and tickled me. I hated it when she did that. 'It was fun. That's all.'

Fun, I thought grimly. *More of the stuff I didn't do.*

*

I didn't see Harold again for several months. Elsie didn't mention his absence, so I didn't bring it up either. We had plenty to keep ourselves busy but I missed his visits and prayed that he was well. When he next came by the cellar in the spring of 1916, Elsie nudged me. 'It's your turn to go to Pop, Mairi.' She got into the new ambulance and drove off without a single word or even a wave to Harold.

I thought they may have had an argument, but I didn't know when they might have done so. Harold didn't seem to mind or notice Elsie's behaviour though, which I found reassuring.

'Shall we go then?' he asked, smiling affectionately at me, or at Shot, who was nuzzled in my arms. I had been going to pretend I'd never heard of Pop, but he must have known Elsie would have told me all about it.

I remembered Ginger and thought, *Wow, he is keen.*

'I don't feel like going anywhere far away today,' I said hesitantly, 'if you don't mind?' I was afraid Harold would shrug and head off without me, but instead, he said he understood my feelings – which was probably more than I did.

'Do you want to be left alone?' he asked uncertainly.

I shook my head. 'I'd like to go somewhere quiet.'

'I know just the place.' His voice was soft. He asked if he could have a cuddle with Shot before we left. Awkwardly, I handed Shot to him and watched our dear fella cleave himself to Harold's broad chest.

'He does the spirit good,' Harold said, stroking Shot's head and around his ears. Shot was delighted. I couldn't speak for a moment.

'He does,' I agreed.

It had been a while since I'd last ridden a horse and at first, I clung on to Harold's back like a beginner. He smelled of cigarettes – Elsie's probably – and leather and… man, I suppose. Within seconds, it came back to me and I relaxed, loosened my grip on Harold and just felt that wonderful ache of freedom. *If only I could re-live all those times Uilleam and I used to take out the bikes… This time I would ride with the knowledge of how precious and precarious everything was.*

If Harold preferred gallivanting with Elsie to being with me he didn't show it. And if Harold preferred to be with the party girl Ginger, instead of the quiet ginger nurse, he didn't show that either. He was a gentleman. He made you feel like the most important person in the world. He was the opposite of Arthur. I had thought long and hard about Arthur's nasty 'cock-tease' comment. Although I had never heard that phrase before, it was easy to work out what it meant. It meant he had tried yet hadn't got anywhere with her: Arthur never worked out that *nobody* got anywhere with Elsie, not even Hal… not properly anyway. And for reasons *not* to his credit, Arthur was sore about that.

We sat down amid a pretty copse of trees. Doris, the horse, stood nearby chewing grass. Sunlight dappled the leaves. The birds chirruped a welcome. I had to admit, Harold had chosen well. We passed a splendid hour or so making jokes and easy talk about politics, horses, families and cars. He let me blather on about my schooldays. He didn't make me feel small for having little of consequence to talk about, but seemed genuinely engaged in Mrs Ford's unfair uniform regulations and Miss Howard's stutter.

Harold produced a bar of chocolate, which we shared, and then he lay down, a blade of grass between his lips. He had turned melancholy, which wasn't like him.

'What is it?' I asked and my heart started racing fervently. *Was he going to make a declaration? Had he found his true ginger?*

Harold sighed, hesitated and then said, 'I want my country back, Mairi.'

'You'll get it back,' I said more confidently than I felt. I ran the chocolate from my teeth with my tongue.

'So much suffering.'

I quoted Psalm 28:7 to him. '*The Lord is my strength and my shield: my heart trusts in him, and I am helped. My heart leaps for joy.*'

Harold looked at me. I had forgotten how deep his eyes were. He sat up suddenly, and from his overcoat pulled out a New Testament.

I realised with surprise it was one of the copies my mother's group had sent. Goodness knows how he had got hold of it!

'Read me something.'

'What… what would you like?'

He sighed deeply. 'Something for one who is sick and tired of the pain his people go through.'

I rifled through the pages and found my beloved Luke:

Suppose one of you have a hundred sheep and loses one of them. Doesn't he leave the ninety-nine in the open country and go after the lost sheep until he finds it? And when he finds it, he joyfully puts it on his shoulders and goes home. Then he calls his friends and neighbours together and says, "Rejoice with me: I have found my lost sheep."

Harold smiled at me. 'Such a beautiful voice, Mairi. It is made for reading the Bible.'

You said that about my singing voice when we first met, I thought. *And more…*

'Thank you.' I smiled, never more conscious of my poor teeth, my lopsided face, my unflattering hair.

He lay back on the grass. I stayed seated until pins and needles forced a change in position, then I lowered myself on to my back beside him. *Why was this so awkward for me?* I stared up at the clouds moving insouciantly across the sky. I had planned at some stage to bounce up with a '*It's time to go Harold, the boys need their soup!*', but I couldn't bring myself to cut short our time, whatever Elsie might advise.

I didn't realise he had fallen asleep at first, but when I caught on that his breath had changed pace, I let myself doze off too. If only our days were always this peaceful…

Harold woke me up some time later. It *was* time to go; he had to get back. He pulled me up by the hand. I lost my balance and he steadied me. I couldn't stop smiling. How soft his palm was against mine.

'Do you ever pray with Elsie?' I don't know why I asked. I should have known the answer.

'One day.' He winked at me. 'I'll get her in the end.'

Oh no, you won't, I thought, but I said nothing.

*

Back in Glasgow, I had planned to write to Jack only once or twice a year – a Christmas card perhaps or a cheery birthday message – but I found it difficult to hold back. We got into such a habit – he was like cigarettes! Each time I poured out my grief or anger in letters to him, I felt stronger. It was a curious thing. And he seemed to welcome hearing from me – even my darkest thoughts of barbarian invasions or my accounts of witnessing atrocities.

All of his letters began: '*It's so marvellous of you to write!*' or '*How wonderful to receive your letters.*' And they came two or three times a month! I looked forward to them even though he wasn't the greatest wordsmith and his tone was invariably flatter than I'd have liked. But when he described his life at Stow Maries, his writing virtually flew off the page:

> *They say planes will take over everything soon. Can you imagine, the sky teeming with great big mechanical birds?*

He didn't make any rash declarations of love, which was a relief. I didn't want to lose what we had with that nonsense. I enjoyed having a correspondent who seemed *genuinely* interested in what was happening. All the things I shielded from Mother and Uilleam I let out on the page to Jack:

> *How much longer can we keep going? What choice do we have? If the boys are here, we have to be here too. It's so strange but it feels*

*as though we are linked to these soldiers by a fine invisible line, a
line like the trench itself – zig-zaggy – so you can't attack it so easily.*

*We can't abandon them. We can't give up. And even stranger,
I feel this way about all the men: the Belgian, the British, the
French, yes, but also the Germans and the Austrians. I have
met them, I have nursed them, and they are good people, Jack,
normal boys.*

By the summer of 1916, my letters were crammed with the
heat, the insects and the oppressive wheeze of shells overhead. My
constant fear was that the line would be broken and we would
be forced to submit to the Hun. Yes, I knew they were good and
normal men, but I also knew what good and normal men did in a
war. I had no illusions any more. Would they kill us there and then
or take us as prisoners of war? I don't know how he must have felt
reading all this.

I described how Elsie didn't fret about all that, how her only
concern was that the authorities would send us away. I told him
about the wounded boys, and the sicknesses we couldn't treat, and
the ones we could, the terrible vicious sniping. I wrote *'the numbers
are just overwhelming, Jack, I've lost count of how many I've seen die.'*
I mentioned our nickname, 'the Madonnas', and explained how
the fan mail made me feel like an imposter. I told him how we
always joked that little Shot was our secret weapon: he disarmed all
who met him. I even told him how I couldn't stand ox tongue but,
really, corned beef was no better. For some reason, I didn't mention
Harold once. Not my trip out to ride Doris that precious day back
in March, or that Harold came by the cellar now at least once every
month. We continued our silly plans for 'when all this is over.' He
promised us Paris. We would drink absinthe – well, Elsie would – at
the Moulin Rouge. We would climb to the top of Notre Dame – at
least I would, and take a boat trip along the River Seine. Harold
told us his life stories too: about growing up a 'pampered child' in

a strict Catholic family, about his successes and losses. And when Elsie wasn't about, he told me about his love for the Church and his hopes to be part of a congregation again.

There was no need to tell Jack all of this.

I did however tell Jack that my scalped sister, Elsie, seemed more preoccupied than ever and I didn't understand why.

Jack understood.

I felt better after each letter. *There is something healthy in honesty*, I decided. Nothing changed, but I was lighter and brighter each time I shared my struggles.

*

In August 1916, we tried to organise recreation tents. Boxing and beer, and other things for the boys to do when they were on a break from the front line. All the loitering was tough. A football tournament was Harold's idea, though because of his leg he couldn't play; he was stuck being the referee. He seemed inordinately proud of the whistle he wore on a string around his neck.

'To tell you the truth, Mairi,' he told me before kick-off, 'I was never good at the game even when my leg was *not* gammy. This suits me,' he said, blowing his whistle, then winking at me. 'Keeping everyone in line.'

He had never winked at me before, and although it was delightful, I couldn't help wondering where it had come from. It was distinctly un-Harold.

I watched him stride out onto the mudflat: the outline of his T-shirt with its braces reminded me briefly of Tommy. Harold was even taller and broader than Tommy had been. His trousers fitted tighter at the back. The players were already racing around. It was Britain vs Belgium. Nine-a-side – although it looked as though there were more Belgians than British. For goals, there were jumpers or coats: it wasn't cold but then no one ever seemed to get cold when they were playing sports.

Gazing at the men as they passed the ball, I felt like I was watching a metronome – hypnotised by the back-and-forth. They played as though this was what they were born for. A football at their feet, not a gun in their hands. The ball gliding between them like a bird soaring up in the air, then swooping down like a diving fish. Then the whistle blew – Harold – a foul committed, a minor altercation, laughter, a free kick. An attempt at a goal: England 1, Belgium 0. Back to the centre, back to the beginning. *If only life were always like this, if only there was no war.* But there was –just one hundred yards away.

I imagined a massive shell falling now. The squeal and the smash. I imagined Harold ricocheting into the air. Me finding him. Holding him; his head nestling in my lap, dust in his hair and on his lips, bending my head to kiss him. Our lips meeting. Not too dry – moist, smooth. His hand on the back of my neck, fingers on my throat. Time disappears…

'Mairi, Mairi!'

I looked up with a start.

'BALL!' The men were shouting and pointing and may have been for some time. I squelched my way over to the ball, and whacked it back with my left foot. Flashback of discovering a head without its body. *Swallow down the sickness, think of good things.*

The ball arched up, landing at a Belgian boy's feet. Unlike Harold, I used to be quite the talent at football. Uilleam would let me join in with the village matches if they were short of men. I was best in midfield. I set up goals, then the striker would come along, firmly placing the ball in the net as easily as putting a baby in its cradle, and get all the glory.

Harold waved gratefully at me and, shyly, I raised a hand back. I wouldn't mention the football to Jack. Honesty was one thing; this was another. I heard one of the boys, a buck-toothed lad from the Midlands who was very fond of Shot, say to his mate, 'What the hell is the matter with old Mairi today?'

*

When I got back to the cellar that afternoon, Elsie was writing a letter for Bernard, a patient who was too weak to hold a pen. Elsie would be the first to confess she wasn't great at writing the mens' letters. She would always prefer to tweezer out bullets from a man's chest, or saw off a gangrenous finger. Still, she liked Bernard, with his dark eyes and olive skin, and he liked her, so she had settled next to him with paper on her lap.

'You've got five minutes,' she announced. If I had said this, it would have seemed rude, but the men liked it when Elsie was bossy.

'Dear Ma,' he began. Smiling, Elsie dutifully wrote.

'I hope you got the money I sent and that you and Pa are in good health. Don't worry about me. Things are going fine.'

Elsie raised her eyes, putting down her pen. 'You want me to put "Things are going fine"?' I looked at her. I'd never dream of telling the boys what they should write. This wasn't our role.

Bernard wasn't annoyed. He laughed until he spluttered. 'So you want me to tell them about my predicament?'

Elsie considered coyly. 'All right, go on then.'

'The good news, Ma, is that I have met a wonderful girl—'

'Ah,' teased Elsie. 'Wonderful, was she?'

'And I am thinking of asking her to marry me.'

Elsie's eyes were raised to the heavens, yet she continued to write.

'She's a nurse from England and her name is Elsie Knocker!' He laughed like a drain.

Elsie slapped her thigh, bursting out, 'You rotter, Bernard!'

He spluttered again. I stood on alert in case he choked.

Elsie continued tsking. 'You had me there.'

'Wish I did!'

'What?'

'Have you.'

I gazed at the two of them in amazement. The other men were smiling as they listened to the exchange.

'Don't you have a fella, Elsie?'

'You are *all* my fellas.' Elsie looked over at me. 'Isn't that right, Mairi?'

'Oh yes,' I said hesitantly. I wanted to join in but couldn't capture the tone.

'You don't have a special one?'

Is she going to say Harold? I held my breath.

'I don't *want* a special one,' Elsie said with one eyebrow exquisitely arched. 'Why should I select just one?'

'Good point,' Bernard said longingly.

Elsie scrunched up the paper, muttering about wasted ink, while Bernard fell asleep, a smile still playing on his lips.

CHAPTER TWENTY

Autumn was fast rolling into winter when my father arrived in Pervyse. He strode around the Western Front like he owned the place *and* was considering the financial impact of improvements. I was afraid a sniper would take his head off, but part of me was also thinking, *It would teach him a lesson.*

He greeted me by shoving a note from my mother in my face: once again, her correspondence was full of questions about Mrs Knocker. Last year's meeting in London had not satisfied her lust for information but fed her desire instead. Even Uilleam barely got a mention.

My father had brought nothing else with him: no food, no soap, no supplies for us or the boys. He *must* have known we were in dire need – even the most single-minded journalists who visited brought something!

There wasn't much to show him, I realised belatedly. I took him into the cellar and indicated the straw where we piggies slept. He couldn't work up much interest in my puzzles. I introduced him to a disinterested Paul and, later, to Martin, who managed a 'Hey'.

Three young men were resting by the stove. My father nodded at the one who was awake. The boy was snuggled up under a blanket. You couldn't see at first but Shot was cosied up there too, his damp nose on the boy's chest.

'How is it out there?'

'Purgatory…' the soldier squeaked. Shot let out a contented sigh.

My father didn't like that. 'What's the matter with him?' he whispered to me.

'Syphilis,' I said, knowing he wouldn't like the answer. 'It's rife. We are treating that and gonorrhoea every few days now.'

Father looked away in disgust. They never put *that* in the papers, I thought scornfully.

It wasn't just my mother who was obsessed with Mrs Knocker. My father wanted to talk of nothing but Elsie too.

'I hear this friend of yours is a madwoman.'

'She is,' I agreed. 'A very wonderful madwoman.'

Father lit a cigarette. It was foolishly pleasurable to take one and smoke with him. I was one of the grown-ups now.

'We call it the golden hour. If we can get to them within that time, we have a chance of saving them... A few I mean, some are too far gone—'

'She's a Jewess?' my father interrupted.

'What?'

'Elsie – a Jew?'

'No. Gosh! She has no faith whatsoever.' I laughed. 'She actually *prides* herself on believing in nothing.'

'In her photographs... she's got that way about her,' my father declared.

'Umm.' I didn't know what to say. 'I believe she's from a long line of doctors.' *Surely this would win him over?*

'Like that Dr Freud fellow Munro goes on about?'

No. 'Dr Freud? Was he from Dorset?' I asked.

Elsie appeared, as if on cue. She had been clearing out the ambulance after last night's tragedies. I could see my father looking her up and down. Taking in her short hair – he wouldn't like that – and her good looks – he would like those, under normal circumstances.

'You must be Roderick,' she said coolly. 'Come to observe the great war effort up close?'

'Elsie.'

She looked at me. 'We have another flat tyre.'

'I'll do it.'

She looked at my father. 'Please tell everyone what we are doing here.' Then she strode away. Little dust clouds rose from her feet. *Well that was quick*, I thought.

My father's eyes were bulging. He could hardly bring himself to speak, he was so outraged at her bad manners.

'I am astonished that the world is calling *her* an angel. I don't know why they let her stay here. They'll change their minds soon enough.'

I couldn't believe he would dismiss Elsie – and by implication, me – in that way. Despite being here, it seemed he *still* had no idea what we went through each day. He must have thought I agreed with him. 'Her only genius is charming the Belgian authorities.'

'*And* taking care of the wounded. And the dead,' I said furiously.

'And the wounded and the dead,' my father admitted as though *they* didn't count.

'Well, that's the only genius we need out here.'

We walked down to the trenches, squelched through the muddy water. Squeezed along the terrible zig-zags that were so murderous to get into or out of. Men greeted me with 'Hello Mairi,' 'Morning Madonna' or 'Where's Elsie?' They were preparing for another offensive soon: you could feel the tension in the air. These soldiers were rattled and rightly so; soon they would be standing up and running towards their deaths.

Rumour had it that there was a French troop further down the line who made sheep noises – 'baa-baa-baa' – as they rose out of their trenches to be slaughtered.

My father saluted the soldiers. 'Excellent work, men.' They stared at him, blankly.

'And this Baron…' Father said out of the blue, when we were back in the cellar later that afternoon. 'Is he in love with Elsie then?'

This made me uneasy. I had mentioned Harold in my letters to my mother, but we never bothered with his title here. And why was my father saying this about Harold anyway? Harold, who was a good friend to both of us?

Harold? In love with Elsie?

The possibility had, of course, occurred to me afer the Glasgow trip, but I had decided that Harold was no more in love with Elsie than he was with his horse Doris! (That said, Harold did adore Doris.) I wondered where my father was getting his information from.

'*Everyone* who's met Elsie is in love with her!' I said.

'*I'm* not,' my father said defiantly. 'Nor is Munro by all accounts.'

'She has *something…*' I said. 'People are attracted to her.' I was about to say, *like moths to a flame*, but he snorted, and I knew he was thinking, *like flies to shit.*

Father wouldn't let it drop. I took our poorly boys to Paul and they climbed into the ambulance. They were going to a recuperation centre further up the line. If they were lucky – or unlucky, I was never sure – we might see them again in six months. I waved them goodbye, then returned to my father, who was staring at my puzzle with his habitual sneer on his face.

'So, is Elsie in love with the Baron then?'

I laughed at the idea of Elsie in love. That *was* funny. 'No! Elsie loves romancing *all* the men. It's her hobby. Like those,' I pointed to the jigsaw, 'are mine. She says, "do whatever it takes to get you through."' My father scowled.

I suppose I liked talking about Elsie too. I added conspiratorially something Lady D and I had discussed. 'It sounds odd but I think Elsie may still be in love with her late husband. He died… prematurely.'

'She's a gadabout.' Father's voice was full of contempt. But I still thought I could get him to understand.

'She calls the men she sees "Gilbert the Filberts", after the song.' I thought for a moment. 'Do you know it?'

I started to sing: *'I'm Gilbert the Filbert the Knut with a K. The pride of Piccadilly the* blasé roué—'

I breathed in for the next part of the verse, but Father interrupted.

'I know it,' he said. 'Your voice hasn't improved much, has it? I'm surprised.'

I fell silent.

I had told Elsie and Dr Munro that my father would sleep in the cellar with us – *why not?* – but they laughed. It was unthinkable. Arthur and Helen's room at Furnes was still vacant, so he was given permission to stay there and I would go with him.

I begged Elsie to come and spend the night with us at Furnes. It was painful being with my father. I shouldn't have expected him to warm to me or to be impressed with what we did, but I had. Just an ounce of respect would have been enough but he couldn't do it. Elsie said she would be fine in the cellar – 'it's only one night after all' – but she hated being alone and I couldn't help feeling anxious about her. Who would hold her hand when she shouted in her sleep?

As I drove away from the cellar, the sense of impending doom that had arrived with my father increased. I wished I were driving in the opposite direction. I was tempted to turn the car around! Just as I was telling myself that I was being ridiculous – *just concentrate on the road* – Father cleared his throat importantly. He needed to tell me something about Uilleam. I felt ten times worse. *Surely Uilleam can't be dead? Wouldn't Father have told me sooner?*

'What's he done now?'

Father stared out at the ravaged landscape. He didn't speak.

'Father? What is it?'

'It's complicated.'

I wasn't sure how to proceed so I thought, *What would Elsie say now?*

'Mother told me about the complication with his engagement. He didn't get some native girl in trouble, did he?' I suggested brightly.

I thought, *My brother is definitely what we'd call a Gilbert. Or what my father would call a gadabout.*

The expression on my father's face was twisted. 'Not exactly.'

'Then what?'

My darling brother. I always looked up to him. There is a photo of us with me as a baby in his arms; he is looking at the camera with a mixture of thrill and horror on his face. That's Uilleam!

'He's disappeared.'

Disappeared? My hands flew to my chest and the car slid on the road; my heart was beating fast. Despite my dark premonition, I hadn't expected this.

'What—'

'He's left the house, no one there has seen him.'

'For how long?'

'A few weeks.'

'You're only just telling me now?'

My father scratched at the dashboard, moodily.

'So… what are you saying?'

'The police are looking for him… there's an investigation.'

'A police investigation? Why? What's he done? Is Uilleam on the run?'

When the men go AWOL here, they get shot, but Uilleam wasn't in the services; he was the owner's son on a sugar plantation. It didn't add up.

'It appears that way.'

'What did he do?'

'I don't know.'

'I don't understand.'

'Put it this way – you know Major General Sir Hector Mac-donald?' Father asked scathingly. 'At least *he* did the decent thing in the end.'

I didn't know what on earth he was talking about.

'Um… is Uilleam hurt, do you think?'

'Hurt?' My father's chuckle was bitter. 'He managed to pack my car with all his things and make his getaway. Damn deserves to get hurt. Disgusting fool.'

I still didn't know what he was trying to say. I hadn't heard from Uilleam for a few months, but unlike Jack, my brother had always been sporadic with his letters. I resolved to write to him as soon as I could. My father's face had grown tight. He was lined and whiskered. *You're an old man*, I realised and it didn't make me feel compassionate; in fact, the more I looked at him, the crueller I felt. *So many boys won't get the chance to be an old man like you – and yet you don't seem to understand your privilege.*

'Don't send him any money, Mairi. Whatever he says.'

'I don't have any money,' I replied as we took the tight turn at the iron gates of Furnes.

'Good.'

CHAPTER TWENTY-ONE

The following morning, I had only just ferried us back to Pervyse when Harold rode up on Doris. I was, as always, delighted to see them. Doris neighed and my father, who loved a horse more than he loved most animals (and probably most humans), walked over and patted her long snowy nose affectionately.

'Oh Harold! You haven't met yet. This is my father… this is the Baron.'

Harold and Father shook hands. Father complimented him on Doris, then commenced to educate Harold about all the wonderful horses he had ever owned and how he should look after her. Harold listened politely but I could tell his mind was elsewhere.

'Coffee, Harold?'

Usually, Harold would accept and come down straight away but he didn't today. I wondered if Father's equine tales were putting him off. He fiddled with the leather straps of his bag, before asking, 'Actually, Mairi, is Elsie here?'

'She's not in the cellar?'

'No.'

She might have stayed up with the engineers. She was probably gadding about with another Gilbert, but I couldn't say that even if my glaring father was unlikely to hear.

'Is it… important, Harold?'

He looked over at my father and me, screwing up his face in the sunlight.

'Rather. I have news.'

*

I found Elsie in the trenches, comforting a poor young lad with the most terrible nerves. She had already got in an argument with his commanding officer about him once before, but she daren't push it too much.

'Sixteen,' she mouthed at me. I winced. The pain of the younger boys was most dreadful to bear. Over his jerking blond head, I whispered that Harold had been to see us. Cautiously, I added that he had news. She made a face that told me that she had not been expecting him.

'Is it good or bad?' she asked. I said I couldn't tell. I didn't *think* it was bad, but who knew?

Had they finally ejected us out of the Western Front? A new rule or regulation they wouldn't bend for us? Would we stop being the exceptions? It made me despair to imagine the boys without us. *Sixteen.* I couldn't bear to think of Elsie and me without the cellar. It was all so unfair.

That afternoon, Elsie and I had tea and stilted conversation with my father in the cellar. We were on tenterhooks until Harold eventually knocked and we both raced to be first to let him in. By contrast, Harold was ludicrously slow and ridiculously formal. Even I wanted to shout, *Hurry up, for goodness' sake, Harold!* Then he rummaged into his bag as though he was performing a magic trick: *was he going to pull out another rabbit?* It *had* to be the dreaded papers telling us to leave. We were the only women left on the Western Front and perhaps we didn't sit well on their consciences.

Harold stood dramatically. You wouldn't notice his gammy leg unless you already knew about it. Elsie once said that he was the most handsome soldier in active service, although she jokingly retracted that after a squadron of Canadians arrived further down the line. ('*By Jove, they're a good-looking bunch of Gilberts, aren't they? So well fed! Must be all that corn!*')

He placed two boxes on my jigsaw, then slowly opened them up. Each contained a velvety base and on that velvety base sat a medal: pink ribbon attached to a silver metal crown, leading to two crossed swords, then a heavy circle with a lion within it, surrounded by inverted triangles and a green wreath background. I had never seen anything like it.

'I have here… *Chevaliers de l'ordre de Leopold*,' Harold said with gravitas.

'Wha-at?'

'The King of Belgium wishes to give you the highest honour in the land for your bravery and support.'

For once, we were *both* speechless. I was gawping like a goldfish; tears were welling up in Elsie's eyes.

Elsie spoke in a trembling voice. 'What an *enormous* honour. Thank you for bringing them to us, Harold!'

I couldn't believe it. And to be told in front of my father (which maybe Harold had intended) made it all the more special.

Elsie grabbed me. 'Mairi, my sister, I couldn't have done it without you.'

'Well, I couldn't have done *anything* without you.'

We fell into each other's arms. Elsie's scratchy head was next to my cheek. I had never felt so emotional. *We didn't have to go. On the contrary, they liked us!*

Then Elsie went to hug Harold, and, for the first time in maybe fifteen years, I received an awkward hug from my father.

'The apple doesn't fall far from the tree,' Father said, which irritated, but I wouldn't let anything take away the joy of the moment. He must have been proud, *he must have been*, even if he could hardly show it.

Elsie said, with delight, 'Every man in the trenches will know about us now!'

Harold responded, 'It's nothing more than you deserve after two years here.'

'Two years,' she said, shaking her head. 'I can't believe it.'

Just then, Dr Munro arrived to see my father. Shot was especially delighted to see him, which was funny because Dr Munro never bothered with him. Still, Shot worked around his ankles lovingly. Elsie didn't waste any time in showing Dr Munro our medals. He turned them over, like a jeweller asked to give a valuation and not sure whether his price would disappoint.

'Congratulations,' he said, although he couldn't have sounded less congratulatory. 'Honours from the King of Belgium, no less! It's a shame more of us couldn't be recognised.'

'You weren't here, were you?' Elsie said coolly.

'We are only a few miles away.'

'Might as well be two hundred miles for a dying man. '

Ignoring her, Dr Munro said, 'I will see if Helen and Arthur will be eligible for an award too.'

'Helen and Arthur *in America*? Good luck to you.' Elsie grinned. 'Helen never even cut off her hair!'

Dr Munro looked embarrassed. But still Elsie wouldn't leave it.

'What about Lady D? Oh, but you always forget *her* contribution, don't you?' Elsie was euphoric and couldn't resist the chance to crow. 'Perhaps a nude yoga session is in order?'

I didn't like her then.

'Elsie!' Harold said, as Dr Munro stomped off.

'Oh, I can't help it. Let me be triumphant, just this once. This is the best thing ever. And… is that champagne I spy, Harold?'

'With a tin of peaches!'

Elsie looked at my father, who was looking uneasy at her exchange with Dr Munro. 'Harold has the most excellent contacts.'

We drank Harold's champagne from the chipped cups we had scavenged from abandoned homes. The bubbles fizzed up my nose. I had never understood the fuss about champagne.

'*Chevaliers de l'ordre de Leopold*!' Elsie repeated gleefully.

'What a title,' Harold said. When he drank, his eyes went sleepy and content. I wondered if Elsie found them as sweet as I did.

'Elsie… as we are gathered together on such a momentous day, I have something to ask.' Harold was unnaturally coy.

I thought he was going to ask for a recommendation for a good restaurant where we could celebrate in style. That was the gallows humour he had. That was how we always got along. But he didn't say that. He was watching Elsie intently.

'I'm listening,' Elsie responded.

Harold paused. I was still smiling. 'Would you consider converting?'

'Umm, under what circumstances?'

There was a strange, pregnant silence in the room. Harold ducked his head. He took Elsie's cup from her hands, placing it on the table. She crossed her hands demurely in her lap. I had never seen her sit like that before and I wanted to giggle but I also couldn't work out what was going on.

'Harold?' she asked softly.

'Marriage?'

'Ah. Under *those* circumstances… I might consider it.'

She looked from me to my father, then back to Harold.

'Is this a proposal, Harold? Because you're not down on one knee.'

'You know my knees, Elsie. Besides it's a wartime proposal, the usual rules don't apply.'

I heard myself laugh. *Was this Harold's idea of a joke?*

Elsie was biting her lip. She had been proposed to a million times and managed to bat away the boys like she was swatting flies from the loo, but kindly, so they never knew they were being swatted. It was an art I could never master. *How would she let down Harold now?*

'The answer is… yes.'

'Yes to…?'

My throat had constricted. I felt like I was underwater. I made a strangled gasp. *She never even prays!*

'Yes to everything, of course!'

Elsie and Harold hugged, then kissed, lips pressed together, before pulling back and laughing. I looked away from them and found myself staring at my father: his startled expression probably mirrored my own.

My father said, 'Congratulations, Elsie. You'll be a baroness.'

'Really?' Elsie twirled around to look at us with her bright sunflower eyes. 'That hadn't occurred to me!'

CHAPTER TWENTY-TWO

Over the next few days and nights, there wasn't time for any deep conversations. There wasn't time for anything. Our sports-day plans were put on hold. We didn't even have a moment to savour the tinned peaches. With great, or perhaps ironic, timing, as soon as my father left for home, the action on the Western Front heated up again. The Germans were throwing everything they had at us.

We were sending men over the top and they were dying. Their friends pulled them into the ditches. We pulled them out of the ditches and into the cellar. I sometimes worried my back was going to break with the hard work of it, but it didn't, although I think my heart may have.

Old friends – our darling post-boy, two of the Belgian football team, one of the engineers and our facilitator and friend Dr Gus – were killed. Some took their last gasps in our arms. Others we frantically gave a temporary fix, and then tore off to Furnes or Ghent where the staff were so well-drilled that the men were in the operating rooms within moments of us parking. On day three, when we pulled up at Furnes, a French doctor was squatting at the gate, smoking a cigarette. He wearily got to his feet, then stared, shaking his head incredulously at our load: 'But we've nowhere to put them any more. *Mon Dieu.* There's *no space…*!'

The ambulance from Sutton Coldfield was a dream to drive but as Elsie said, 'It can't perform miracles.' She looked at me snidely. 'Only *your* God can do that.'

It was like some terrible, disgusting game of 'Duck, Duck, Goose', only our role was to go along the trenches, *dead, dead – run for it, let's try to save this poor fella.*

I was in the trench with a young boy, somewhere between duck and goose. No way had he seen his eighteenth birthday. Paul and Martin were nearby, searching among the bodies for anyone they could help. Elsie let me stay with the boy and I hauled his dying body over my knees. There was blood everywhere, but I focused on his pale face as he was slipping away from Earth, it was the least I could do. I gave him a mother's kiss on his white, strangely unblemished forehead. But he raised his index finger to touch his lower lip.

'You want me to kiss you?' I asked.

The smallest sign of a worn smile.

I bent, meeting his lips with mine. I closed my eyes and I think he closed his. I could hear the clatter of death around us but I stayed, sharing my first sweet kiss with this unknown lad, until I felt sure he had gone.

*

After six consecutive days of bombardment, Dr Munro and Lady D drove to Pervyse and said we must take some time out or we would drop dead from exhaustion. They were going to take care of the trench-run with Paul and Martin. Dr Munro had no jurisdiction over us, but we were both so tired we didn't know whether we were coming or going. 'I'm not going to Furnes,' Elsie declared wearily.

Dr Munro and Lady D looked at each other. 'We thought you'd say that,' said Dr Munro.

'So I packed you a hamper,' continued Lady D. 'Even if it's just a few hours – it will do you the world of good.'

'Take care of Shot,' Elsie said tearfully. 'We can't afford to lose him too.'

Dr Munro put his hand on Elsie's shoulder. 'I know.'

We drove west for forty minutes. The sounds of the war receded a little behind us but not completely. There were flowers. We found a spot for a picnic and settled down on a blanket. Where Lady D had found the food was anyone's guess. She had filled the hamper with fresh tomatoes, celery and meat of unknown provenance.

'Don't imagine it's Doris,' Elsie warned.

'That's something else I'll never get used to.' I sighed.

For the finale: a raisin biscuit each. I didn't like to think when it had been baked – and if they were raisins, and not flies, as Elsie teased – but whatever it was, it went down a treat. There was also an extra surprise: two mints in wrappers. Elsie said I should take both and after some resistance, I accepted.

We walked, our boots flattening the long grass. We clambered through a field and passed through a kissing gate. I shut out an image of the dying boy. *How tender he was*. Then we continued through another field, where a lonely bull sat.

'There's supper, Mairi.'

We were almost far enough away to pretend the war wasn't happening.

After trekking a little further, we rested again. An insect crawled along my leg. It was too small to be a spider, too big for an ant. I let it walk up my thigh before brushing it away. Elsie had snuggled down on the blanket as if to sleep. I decided if we were ever going to have 'the talk' then it had to be now. I took a deep breath and proceeded, in the sympathetic way I had been rehearsing to myself in the cellar.

'Elsie, as you know, it's a… huge commitment to be a Roman Catholic.'

'Yes,' she said, gazing up at the overcast sky.

'So…' This threw me. I didn't know how much more it needed spelling out. 'It's a wonderful commitment, to take on a religion and all the beliefs and rituals associated with it, but it is… hard, Elsie. Not everyone is up to it.'

She looked straight at me. 'What *are* you trying to say, my darling?'

'Just—' I flipped. I couldn't contain it any more. 'You are the biggest non-believer I have ever met in my entire life! Only yesterday you said that God was a rotten egg and even if he did exist, which you insisted he didn't, you'd take a gun to him yourself.' I shook my head furiously. The cheek of the woman! She just didn't know – or didn't *want* to know – what she was letting herself in for.

Elsie sank back in the long grass. She looked like a woman from another age: a courtier in the palace of King Louis XVIII or a model for Vermeer. But beneath those cheekbones, those symmetrical teeth, I suspected that steel, not blood, ran through her veins, and in place of her heart was a calculator. She didn't reply and instead concentrated on the sun on her face. I was all puffed up with my arguments but with nowhere to go.

Finally, she looked at me with her green, godless eyes, which in this light were as grey as the German uniform.

'Mairi, you are so transparent.'

'What?'

'You are letting hanky-panky come between us.'

'What… how do you mean?' I asked incredulously. Sometimes, I could have slapped her around those pretty cheeks. Really.

'Don't you remember what Munro said?'

I stared closely at her, not understanding.

'At the start? The three reasons that a team will break: hanky-panky, money and ego?'

'I don't—'

'I think you're jealous.'

'I'm not jealous,' I said helplessly. *Was this what it was?* 'I'm not jealous of you! How dare you!'

She stared back, then relented. 'I'm sorry, Mairi.' But she didn't sound at all sorry.

And of course, although I was determined to say it first, she had to get in there quicker –

'Let's get back.'

CHAPTER TWENTY-THREE

A card finally came from Uilleam in December 1916. *'The heat, the rum, the cars, the herbs…'* – no hint of anything untoward. In fact, it was like all his correspondence and except for a couple of hints at the end – *'Send Mummy my love'* and *'How's my award-honoured sister?'* – it could have been the same letter as he sent last year. Still, those clues suggested he must somehow have been receiving my notes, and – small consolation – he must have been alive to write to me. He didn't ask for money and I was glad, because I didn't see how I could defy my father on this one.

When I told Elsie that Uilleam might be on the run, she screwed up her face. 'Poor Uilleam,' she said, surprising me.

What about me? I thought. *What about my poor parents*? It was Uilleam who seemed to be attracting trouble: first fooling around with some poor girl from a good family, then letting her down somehow and finally running away! But Elsie didn't like my father, so I supposed it was natural all her sympathies would flow towards my brother.

*

Since Jack was in Stow Maries, over three hundred miles away, I was sure that our correspondence, although frequent, was purposeless – 'pointless', as Elsie would say – but in the new year of 1917, a telegram arrived: Jack was doing a training exercise on the Continent. Work permitting, he would like to see me again. I found I didn't have an excuse.

It will be agreeable to get away, I thought. Elsie's engagement continued to disturb me. I had prayed about it, yet I couldn't even admit to my Lord the extent of my confusion. *Was it jealousy?* I didn't know. I had never experienced this emotion before. Elsie and Harold were possibly my two favourite people – this side of the Atlantic anyway – why shouldn't they marry? After all, hadn't I once contemplated the same fate for Elsie and Uilleam?

I set off to see Jack with Shot galloping at my heels. I explained he couldn't come and promised a treat on my return. And then I drove away apprehensively. I wasn't quite sure what I was doing.

The seaside town of Dunkirk is one of those sleepy French resorts that I imagined that history would bypass. Here you could almost forget what was going on down the road. Although it was in another country – always a thrill to cross a border! – it only took about two hours to travel from Pervyse to the steps of the City Hall where Jack and I had arranged to meet. I waited in the car, wishing I had some distraction, until I spotted him sloping hesitantly towards me. It wasn't fair, but when I saw him, I wished he could have bounded. *Why couldn't men be more like dogs?*

Jack and I discussed our respective journeys. Like me, Jack could talk at length about cars and mechanics. I think we both surprised ourselves with how easily our conversation flowed.

We found a bench facing the dark-grey sea. Seagulls nestled on the crests of the waves. There was no one else around. Jack kept saying he couldn't believe I'd come to meet him. I couldn't believe I'd come to meet him either! Sometimes the birds called and made me think there were people nearby, but we remained alone.

Jack said he hadn't known what to bring for me. In Calais, he'd found one tiny shop still open and had managed to acquire antiseptic foot powder and some Lifebuoy soap. He looked doubtfully at them in his lap.

'Perhaps I'll take them back?'

'No, no,' I said. 'They're thoughtful gifts.' *Who said romance was dead?*

He'd out-done my father, that was for sure.

I hadn't realised at first, because he hadn't made a song and dance of it, but Jack from Ingatestone was quite the hero. He had rescued men from burning planes and he had the medals to prove it. He didn't seem pleased about this though, not like my father. He didn't want to go into details but he intimated that it was horrid. He called his awards his 'ribbons' and whenever he said that I thought of Madeleine's little ribbon around my wrist.

I eventually learned that he had saved three different men over a period of a few weeks. One hadn't survived – a young man from Glasgow. It was his family Jack had been visiting when we met that day at the Assembly Rooms.

This hadn't put him off flying. Quite the reverse. When he described his experiences in the air, his face gave me a sweet indication of what ten-year-old Jack must have looked like. 'Up, up among the clouds!'

If it weren't for the war, I doubt we would have met. Ingatestone, he said, was a leafy village in mid-Essex where everyone knew everyone's business. Jack's father, like his grandfather before him, worked the land. Jack grew up working in the stables.

'Do you ride?' he asked.

I told him that I preferred motorcycles. 'I suppose they're a bit like aeroplanes.'

He laughed. 'A plane is basically a motorbike with wings attached.'

I couldn't tell if he was joking or not.

We didn't have a huge amount in common – perhaps only the war and our eagerness to talk about it when few others would. Still, at that point in our lives, the war *was* everything.

Like me, Jack was more forthcoming in his letters than he was in real life. In real life, he was reserved, often struggling to find the right words and stuttering to get them out. He wasn't well educated, that was clear, but he had a sharp intelligence. If I yawned, he yawned too (Dr Munro said this was a sign of an emotionally mature person!) However, sometimes, when he talked, I couldn't help but compare him to Harold. I knew this was wrong – you *can't* compare people, any more than I could compare Shot to Doris – but Harold was more elegant, more adept at conversation than Jack. And English was Harold's third language!

Still, Harold was not mine to compare anyway.

I asked Jack if he had ever heard of a British general called Macdonald. Had Arthur still been in Belgium, I would have asked him (I had asked Elsie but she was rubbish with names).

'Ramsay Macdonald?'

'No, Major General Sir Hector Macdonald?'

He laughed. Oh yes, Jack knew *all* about him. 'Son of a crofter. He rose to the top of the ranks but they didn't like him because he was an outsider.'

It didn't make sense.

'What happened to him?' I asked.

'They killed him – no, he killed himself – they were out to get him, see, because he was from the lower class.'

How this could relate to my Uilleam was anybody's guess.

'They accused him of being a homosexual,' Jack added. I spun around to look at him. Suffice to say, I had never heard that word spoken aloud before. He shrugged. 'They'll say anything.'

It was too cold to stay still. We walked along the beach and then into town, where we found a café. They made us coffee and *galettes des rois*, and I declared I hadn't ever tasted anything so delicious. Jack was even less at ease indoors than he was outside, so when he started pulling on his coat, I did too.

'Do you mind walking again?' he asked. He was sweating.

I said I would be delighted.

Down the road we went. We must have walked about five miles and then we found another bench where we could sit. The sun had burned off the January frost.

When Jack talked about the war, his eyes blazed with fury.

'And why the bloody hell are we fighting in the first place?'

'What would you do, Jack? Leave Belgium to the mercy of the Hun?'

Jack didn't know the answers but he was full of angry questions. He also said that whereas other friends seemed to be able to zip it away, pack up their troubles, he couldn't.

'I go over it in my head all the time,' he said, 'pathetic, isn't it?'

'No,' I said. Although I found his struggle painful to hear – in some ways, it mirrored my own.

'That's why I like *you* so much,' he said. 'I can't imagine myself with a *normal* girl!'

I laughed at the word 'normal'. He added quickly, 'I mean someone who didn't know.'

'I know what you meant!'

Jack said the only time he felt any sustained relief from the horrible images in his head was when he got in a plane.

'Up there,' he said, not realising how wonderful it was for me to see him so vibrant, 'it's like you're above everything bad, everything foolish, every human mistake, you're almost like God.' He looked uncomfortable. 'Sorry.'

'Don't be, it's interesting,' I said and meant it. 'So, they sent you to France to train?'

His face turned scarlet. 'Not exactly,' he admitted. 'I had a few days off and… I wanted to see you. I didn't think you'd accept unless I said I was working nearby.'

I was flattered but didn't understand. Why did he want to see *me*?

Jack looked at me like he was trying to read my face. 'The training is hard, damn hard, but I'm glad I'm not in the trenches. I'm out in the open, I don't have to dodge bullets and shells.'

'I'm glad you're not there too,' I said spontaneously, feeling a burst of affection for this gloomy lad who'd gone through so much. And that's when Jack kissed me. My lips were dry from the wind and chapped too, but so were his. My mind went to the dying boy, and I wondered if this was my first kiss or if that one was? His lips had moved once and then stilled. Both times were sweet and soft and made me wonder what was to happen next.

When Jack was done, he smiled his uneasy smile at me, and I smiled back, pretending that this was what I had been waiting for. A seagull cried overhead. It made me jump and Jack put his hand on me protectively.

I thought again of the boy who'd slipped away, dead in my arms. I had a painful feeling that I would never be able to kiss anyone again without remembering him.

*

When I came back to the cellar that evening with three slices of *galette*, Martin grunted that Elsie was in the trenches. One man was asleep in the cot, another warming up by the stove. Shot ignored me; he was part-playing with, part-eating an old newspaper. There was another postcard on Elsie's blanket. Again, I wondered if she had left it out for me deliberately.

Dear Kenneth,

I have a very special friend for you to meet, darling. His name is Harold. I know you will like him very much. He wears a fine uniform and he speaks four languages. I have told him all about you and he can't wait to meet you.

Love Mama! (and Shot and Harold and Mairi)

Xxx

After I read it, I decided she had not.

CHAPTER TWENTY-FOUR

The conflict ran on like a runaway train. Boys kept arriving and boys kept dying. And small cogs though we were in this giant and terrible machine, together Elsie and I did our best as the war did its worst.

The continued publicity we were getting in England was still paying off. Towards the end of January, we reinforced our cellar with concrete. A few days after that, Elsie came in cock-a-hoop. 'Guess which British luxury department store has sent us a door?'

I didn't understand the question. 'Which what?'

'HARRODS!' she shouted excitedly. 'They heard what we're doing and they're sending us a door made of the best-quality steel! Can you believe it?'

It arrived the next day. Robin and some of the other engineers helped us to fit it. It was far superior to our cracked wooden one. Elsie joked that the best thing was that a little corner of this foreign field was now 'forever Harrods'.

I wondered what Madeleine and her family would say about it. I hadn't forgotten them, although it was a long time since I had found any more of their belongings, and Madeleine's box of precious things now had medical equipment stacked on top of it. I liked to think Madeleine's English was improving quickly across the Channel. I hoped she was concentrating in class. '*Education is important, Madeleine,*' I imagined myself explaining. '*The more people know about each other and the more things we value, the more hope there is that we can stop killing each other. One day, we will all be sane again.*'

*

An increasing number of men tried not to fight. The horrors here might have been concealed from those back home, but what they were facing would have been evident as soon as they arrived. Elsie would speak at length to the desperate ones. She always made the time. I don't know what she said. She couldn't offer them the comforting prospect of heaven like I could. She couldn't paint pictures of paradise. What consolation was there from her lips? She spoke about their wives' pensions, maybe. Or the suffocating shame for generations and generations. Some still tried to run away. She had heated debates with their officers when they came to us. Sheltering was an offence. 'We are not sheltering!' she shouted, enraged at the suggestion. 'I will not accept this accusation!' And they backed off. Our medals probably helped.

I told her better the men died honourably on the battlefield than cowering in front of a firing squad. Everybody knew that.

She said, 'What a stinking choice.'

Once, I saw her whispering with one of the youngest, newest recruits, but she refused to tell me what she had said. I went on at her until finally she admitted that she had suggested that next time they were ordered out, he 'sneak down into a shell hole and wait.'

'You can't tell him that!'

'For God's sake, he's a dead man, Mairi,' she actually hissed like a wild animal. 'I will say what I bloody well like.'

I didn't know what was changing between us or how to stop it. Since her engagement, I had felt a divide go up, like barbed wire and sandbags. There were things we weren't to discuss any more. She was shutting me out.

*

The following month, Elsie was underneath the ambulance, refitting its wheel, when our first female guest came to have a look around.

I was very excited to welcome a woman to Pervyse. Apart from Lady D and Elsie, of course – oh and the infamous Ginger, who I still hadn't met – the four hundred or so miles of the Western Front were almost exclusively a male zone. Rumour had it that not long after we received our medals, the Queen of Belgium had cycled from her hiding place to see us, but neither Elsie nor I had been at home. Elsie was convinced it was more than trench-gossip: 'Of course she was here – why *wouldn't* she come to see us?!'

But I wasn't so sure – perhaps I found the idea of missing the queen's visit, maybe by just a few minutes, too painful to contemplate.

I led our guest, Madame Curie, over to Elsie.

'This is Mrs Elsie Knocker…'

Elsie muttered a 'hello' but she didn't get up. We stood patiently at the side of the car as though waiting for a recalcitrant toddler, but still Elsie was not forthcoming. We were there for a further three or four minutes but still she wouldn't come out. I felt my face grow hot. Recently, Elsie made me feel like a little girl again.

'Elsie, Madame would like to—'

But she snapped, 'I'm busy, Mairi, can you not see that?'

Embarrassed, I took our visitor away. Elsie wanted visitors but when they came, her behaviour was obnoxious. This wasn't the first time she had treated guests with disdain.

Down in the cellar, I served tea and biscuits. Madame Curie had brought packets of French cocoa and peculiar cheese-flavoured biscuits, which I tucked into greedily. *Well, if Elsie was too stubborn…*

'And these?' She held up some warm underwear.

'Is that for us?'

'I thought you ladies might be missing some comforts.'

I nodded, touched as ever by the kindness of strangers.

'They are not beautiful, but they are useful.' She had a strange, mangled accent. Slightly French, slightly English, but also with a touch of somewhere else.

As always with our visitors, she expressed incredulity that we managed to live in the cellar house.

'What hardships you endure,' she said and I replied, mechanically, 'This is nothing compared to what the boys go through.'

'But still,' she said, 'just you and Elsie too. That must have its challenges.'

This woman had a warm intellect, and I felt I could confide in her. Powerlessness was something I was used to wearing like a second skin – yet that day, that moment, with Elsie having been so rude outside, I had never felt more powerless. But I couldn't tell her how difficult I was finding Elsie so I focused on the boys.

As I talked, I found tears pouring down my cheeks. 'They are fired on, living with the threat of death – and not just the threat, the smell, the sight, the taste of death. You mustn't ever feel sorry for us. It makes me ashamed to sleep here, in relative safety, while the boys are outside.'

There was nothing Madame Curie could have said to cheer me up, and I was glad she didn't try. Instead, she walked over to me, pulled me to my feet and folded me into a womanly hug while I wept.

After our guest left, I stormed out to Elsie. She wasn't going to get away with humiliating me like that! Even Shot must have sensed I was in foul temper, for he scooted away from me. That dog, so casual when it came to bombs, couldn't stand cross words.

'Why were you so impolite?' I felt utterly ashamed of Elsie. To be so rude to someone so nice was awful. And our guest was far more than just nice.

'I am fed up with all these joyriders.'

'You invite them, yet I end up looking after them! Just be civil. That's all that's required.'

'Easy to say be civil if you're not in the middle of a breakdown.' She looked at me, annoyed. 'A *mechanical* breakdown.'

'*I'll* sort that out.'

'*I* want to do it.'

I thought Elsie was going to engage, but she went and washed her hands in a bucket. I wondered if she had had another row with Dr Munro or something, she was in such a bad mood.

'They're tourists. They want to brush against the war so they can tell stories over their grand dinners. "Lady Ascot, when you hear what I have seen: you will want to take me to bed…"'

'The campaigners and the colonels don't come for that. And the journalist who brought you tins of caviar – you didn't complain then.'

'There's so many though. They interfere with our work. That one before last even needed our petrol to get away. We're becoming a circus. Mairi, you are the strongman – no, the moustached lady.'

I felt so hurt. *Having visitors was all her blasted idea anyway!* She invited them then ignored them, and I was left to deal with it. She got the glory, I got the paperwork. Elsie always did what she liked, and I had to put up and shut up. I wasn't going to obey her any more. I had opinions of my own.

'Ha ha. And what are you, Elsie? Chief clown?'

'They are *envious* of the work we are doing. That vacuous woman! What has she ever done?'

'Do you know who that vacuous woman was?'

'I don't care if she's the wife of the Tsar with Rasputin hiding in her drawers.'

'Madame Curie is a renowned scientist who has developed mobile X-ray machines that will greatly aid our work.'

Elsie still looked furious, then suddenly she softened. She said in her low voice, 'Mairi, I *am* sorry. I will try to be a better person in future.'

I felt choked with tears again. 'You don't have to—'

'I do, I do.'

'We can cancel the next one,' I offered. He was in my logbook. An MP from Britain.

'It's fine.' She gave me a weak smile. 'If I can cope with running a field hospital, then I can manage a few well-intentioned sightseers.'

'Of course.'

'We'll manage like we manage everything: together,' she said embracing me.

I breathed in the sheer brave, energetic loveliness of her. How did she always win me around?

'You're still my sister, right?'

I nodded. She could be so brilliant. Why couldn't she *always* be like this?

I found Shot hiding under the ambulance. A cheese-flavoured biscuit soon worked him free.

CHAPTER TWENTY-FIVE

A few days after Madame Curie's visit, Lady D organised another get-together in Furnes. I was nervous about socialising with Dr Munro again after the hoo-ha over the medals, but he didn't seem to be holding a grudge.

Lady D thumped us on the backs as we arrived. 'Such news, ladies!' She didn't seem perturbed not to have got an award, but Lady D was too considerate to let you know what she was thinking.

'And the other news?' she asked, eagerly.

Elsie shrugged non-committally.

'You and Harold?' Lady D paused, but when Elsie still didn't respond, she continued. 'I would *never* have had you down as the sort to marry again, Elsie. I thought you were one of our proud spinsters' club.'

I had never heard of the proud spinsters' club. For a moment, I thought it was an actual organisation, another thing I had been excluded from. Then I realised this was a joke between them.

Lady D's cheeks were tinged with red. For the first time, I noticed the new thread-veins and the wrinkles at the corners of her eyes. Lady D was soft, she'd always been soft, but now she looked angular and drawn.

'Oh.' Elsie waved her hands around. 'We'll see, Lady D. Maybe when all this is over.'

Lady D persisted. 'You plan to convert, Elsie? How exciting!'

Elsie didn't *look* excited. 'It *is* a huge commitment and right now, we have too much on our minds, don't we Mairi?' She smiled elegantly at me. 'Do you have a light?'

Relief flooded through me. Elsie was still my Elsie and Harold was still our Harold and nothing had to change. Engagement meant nothing. How many times had I met engaged boys who never got around to getting married?

I sprang forward with the matches and lit her cigarette. I liked doing it. I suddenly felt in better spirits than I had for some time.

'And how is my favourite doggy?' Lady D had a soft spot for Shot.

'Currently cuddled up on a man with pneumonia,' said Elsie proudly. 'Shot deserves an order from the King of Belgium too.'

Furnes wasn't the same without Helen and Arthur, but we passed a pleasant evening playing Newmarket, learning a new game called 'Crazy Eights' and speculating about politics: Gallipoli and the Eastern Front, The Tsar and the scoundrel Rasputin.

Supper was bread and plum jam. Food always tasted better when Lady D had prepared it.

'How've you been keeping, young Mairi?' Lady D asked.

'Not too bad,' I said. *Would it always make me want to cry when people asked directly how I was?* When Arthur called me young, I hated it, but when Lady D did, I wanted to melt.

'Tell her about Jack,' Elsie prompted.

'There's nothing to tell.'

'You write to him all the time—'

'So?'

'When the post-boy comes, you go like this.' She imitated Shot begging for food. 'And if there is a letter from him, you're all—' She pressed her hand against her heart and swooned.

'Don't be ridiculous,' I said coolly. 'I do nothing of the sort.' I was more furious with her than I wanted to let on.

'Not *another* cellar-house engagement?' Lady D jumped in, beaming and looking from Elsie to me for information.

'No!' I hissed. 'I don't know what she's talking about.'

'A romance though? I'm so pleased for you.'

'It's nothing,' I persisted. I thought of Jack's dry lips on mine and of Peter denying Jesus three times just as Jesus had predicted he would.

'The lady doth protest too much,' said Elsie, winking at the others.

As I washed up the cups and plates, I used the opportunity to ask Dr Munro if he had heard of the mysterious Major General Sir Hector Macdonald. The plates didn't need much scrubbing – we might as well have licked them clean.

'Where's this come from, Mairi?' Dr Munro looked at me suspiciously.

'Just some talk I heard.'

Dr Munro's expression was awkward but he always tried to be clear with me. 'We-ll, Macdonald committed suicide following some lurid accusations.'

Lurid? I didn't know what he meant but it made me think, unfairly perhaps, of Ginger at the Pop bar. 'How do you mean?'

'There was gossip.'

'There is always gossip,' I said, smiling. This much I knew. They said that women gossiped, but ten men together in the trenches would come up with forty stories, and the stories they came up with would make your ears bleed!

'Involving… other men.'

'Oh? Oh.' *So Jack was right. Was that what my father meant? Was my brother a homosexual?* I could only guess that such people were as outlawed in the Caribbean as they were back home.

Dr Munro looked at me with narrowed eyes. 'Why are you *really* asking?'

My father said that my brother should do '*the decent thing*'. What did he mean? Come clean about being with other men? I couldn't bring myself to say it so explicitly to Dr Munro. I had a feeling it wouldn't show either my father or Uilleam in a good light, and I wasn't ready for that.

Finally, I said, 'My father struggles with my brother… and I don't know really.'

Dr Munro looked relieved. 'In psychoanalysis, we often observe that fathers feel disappointed that their sons have wasted their opportunities… in much the same way mothers and daughters can often clash.'

I thought of my mother and thought, *a clash would be a fine thing. A clash would mean she'd noticed me.*

'It can often work the other way around too. Children can be disappointed with their parents' shortcomings.'

I wiped the dishes dry as Dr Munro lovingly prepared his pipe. I could hear Lady D and Elsie in the other room. Whatever had been said was so funny that they were both slapping their thighs. Lady D said, 'Oh that's hysterical, Elsie, stop!'

Elsie continued in a low voice, and Lady D shrieked. 'No, no, you mustn't!'

It made me more despondent. It had been a while since we had laughed like that. Quietly, I said to Dr Munro, 'Elsie mocks God sometimes.'

'That must be hard,' he said sympathetically.

'I just… want her to understand how God loves us all.'

'That might never happen.' He hesitated. 'Elsie has different gods.'

That's a generous way of putting it, I thought.

*

Lady D wanted to play her old favourite: 'Truth or Consequence'. I suspected she had already planned the questions and her answers.

'Where is the place you love the most?'

Lady D began by talking of the lanes, the views, the dazzling light on the Cornish coast at St Ives. She spoke of lazy days spent on the beach eating pickle sandwiches. We smiled because she always mentioned food.

Dr Munro couldn't decide between Berlin and Vienna. As he extolled the virtues of the cities he loved, I realised how painful the constant references to 'dirty Bosch' and 'vicious Hun' must be when he knew the cities and the people there so intimately.

'Mairi's turn,' said Lady D firmly.

'Scotland, perhaps,' I mumbled, 'or in the woods with…' I cleared my throat. I missed my brother. 'Or, I know, Saunton Sands beach.'

Suddenly, the jellyfish came back in my mind, then Father's spanking of Uilleam in the library. *My poor Uilleam.* What a struggle. Why had all my good memories turned rotten?

'Elsie,' I said. 'Your go.'

I thought she was going to take a consequence. Or perhaps she might say Java. That mysterious, exotic place that I still knew nothing about.

Elsie looked up from her rum as if she had forgotten she was playing.

'How can you even ask this?'

I had never seen Dr Munro smile so tenderly at Elsie before. I realised suddenly there was real friendship or, if not friendship, an *understanding* between these two. All her huffing and puffing about him, all his raging about her, concealed a deep mutual admiration.

'*I* know it,' said Dr Munro.

Elsie smiled, but she had tears in her eyes. She turned her toes towards me.

'*You* don't know?'

'No.' I laughed. 'How could I possibly know?!'

'The cellar house in Pervyse,' she said slowly. '*That's* my beautiful place.'

CHAPTER TWENTY-SIX

Elsie jumped at the chance to go on a special assignment to England. It was an opportunity to spend some time with Kenneth. The chess wasn't going well; he didn't have the aptitude. He was good at wrestling though and had a bent for mathematics.

But two days before she was due to go, Elsie was struck down with a bug and she was very sick indeed. Her skin went greenish and her eyes were bloodshot. She shivered under the blankets I piled on top of her. I had never seen her so poorly. Even Shot was reluctant to sit with her. It took a while before Elsie admitted to herself how impossible her travelling to England was. Then she begged me to go in her place.

I didn't want to, not least because I was loath to leave her like this, but Elsie insisted. 'We have a duty. Mairi. Think of the boys.'

After Paul, Martin and even Dr Munro and Lady D had promised that they would look after Elsie, I reluctantly agreed.

I don't know what prompted me to do it, but I wired across to Jack that I was coming over. He replied immediately that by God's grace he was free. He would show me 'a fine time'. My first reaction was *Oh I didn't mean for that to happen*, but perhaps I did?

I didn't want to tell Elsie I was meeting Jack, but my story about heading to the Essex coast alone for rest and recuperation rang hollow, so I caved. She didn't tease me as much as I thought she would – she really was exceedingly sick – but between coughs, she said: 'I *knew* you liked this fella! Enjoy Mairi, but whatever you do, don't get in the family way.'

Did she have to be so coarse?

*

The assignment was to bring five injured British men safely home from further down the line. There were supposed to be six but at the last moment it was decided that one mightn't make the journey. Two couldn't walk, two had problems with their arms and I didn't know what was wrong with the fifth but he was groaning with pain and wasn't in a good way.

The harbour in Ostend had lost the limited appeal it once had. It was ugly and utilitarian now it was stuck transporting soliders and military supplies. Dr Munro, Lady D and I stretchered the men out of the ambulance and loaded them onto HMS *Asturias*. Dr Munro reassured me that an ambulance would meet us on the other side.

'And if it's not there?'

'You'll think of something, Mairi!'

All very well to say.

There were other nurses doing the same thing as I was, and after I looked at their injured freight, I decided I didn't have it too bad. I nodded at them politely, but not too warmly. We all had enough on our hands; no one wanted to get lumbered with anyone else's patient.

One kind-faced nurse with a strange accent did try to strike up conversation, but I didn't feel like chatting so I cut her off. Later, I saw her talking merrily in a group and wished I had stuck around.

One of the boys, who'd lost both legs below the knees, kept calling me Kate. 'Kiss me, Kate!' he went on. I let him continue until he pulled me down to his face. If I hadn't had muscular arms, I would have been forced into a kiss.

'I'm *not* Kate!' I snarled.

When I next went to check on him, he was weeping. His chest had a nasty rattle too.

The other man with a wounded leg, Lenny, was chatty. I told him what Elsie and I did in Pervyse and he said, 'God bless, we could have done with you where we were.'

He told me he had been based south of us and there was nothing good there, just a living nightmare – you didn't know whether you were awake or asleep or dead. He wanted to hold my hand, and I didn't mind. He was looking forward to getting back to his son, Peter – 'home for Easter,' he said. I had completely forgotten it was nearly Easter: in the cellar and in the trenches, days and weeks got lost.

When I said that I was sorry about his leg, Lenny replied, 'Small price to pay for getting out. I'd have given the other one as well.' Then he blushed. 'Don't tell anyone that.'

I was fascinated by the ink drawings Lenny had on his arm. He told me Kaiser jokes that I did my best to memorise – planning to make Jack laugh with them – but they slipped out of my head almost as soon as they arrived. Uilleam always declared I was no good at telling funnies.

It wasn't easy making the groaning man comfortable, but one of the others, Howard, helped me reposition him whenever he asked. (It felt like he asked every two minutes.)

Howard – who had only lost one arm and seemed quite adept without it – and I built up a rapport over this dismal task, and eventually Harold asked me if I was single. I could see what was coming, so to avoid awkwardness I said that I was engaged. He looked downcast.

'No ring?'

'Not while I'm working.'

'What's his name?'

I wanted to say 'Harold' but I knew I couldn't. *I mustn't.*

'Uilleam,' I said, flatly. 'Uilleam Chisholm.' As soon as I'd said it, I felt bad – *Jack* was the obvious answer.

'He a soldier?'

I paused. 'A pilot.'

'That's a job and a half,' he said.

'Isn't it!'

'You know they don't give them parachutes.'

'They don't need them,' I told him confidently, which is what Jack had told me. 'They don't go high enough, see.'

Howard looked at me doubtfully.

'I'm just glad he's not in the trenches.'

'Yeah,' he said, patting where his arm used to be. 'No one wants to be in the trenches. Lucky fella!'

Duty dispatched and boys safely delivered, I met Jack at Southend station. He looked almost handsome when he smiled; it drew attention away from his ears. We decided to go to the end of the pleasure pier. It became our day's mission and it gave us something to do and talk about. I don't know what we had been expecting to find at the end, a mile and a half's walk away from the shore, but truly there was nothing remarkable. It was colder than we'd imagined too, although we should have anticipated that out on the Thames Estuary where the full murk of the river met the sea. Such a mist and a wind, you could hardly tell where grey sea ended and grey sky began. It was certainly no Saunton Sands. By the sea wall, there was just mud and more mud, like where our boys lived in Belgium, but this mud was only home to crabs and sandworms.

Back on the prom, we ate vinegary cockles and winkles from yesterday's newspaper: the headline SMALL GROUP OF PACIFISTS ROUTED IN SOUTH WALES revealed itself the more we ate. Apparently, the pacifists had marched down the high street before they were apprehended by the local constabulary.

Jack worried that some of the cockles were off.

'We've paid for them now,' I said.

He examined them cautiously, like a man who'd never met with hunger. It made me full of bravado. I grabbed the cockle he was doubtful of and popped it triumphantly in my mouth.

'I've a cast-iron stomach.'

Jack shook his head. 'Being with you is like being with my men,' he said before looking up, horrified with himself. 'I didn't mean…' He went scarlet. 'I meant it in a good way.'

'It's all right, Jack.' I offered him an arm-wrestle, which is something I used to do with Uilleam. I don't know what foolishness made me suggest it, but he declined, saying, 'I'd feel an idiot if I lost.'

'Have you ever been in love?' Jack asked after I had thrown the cockle newspapers away.

'I don't know,' I said truthfully. 'Have you?'

'Not until now,' he said quietly. The impact of *that* didn't hit me until much later.

I don't know how he did it, but as we were sat there, contemplating mud, Jack worked his arm around me. And somehow, he managed to slide his hand lower so that it was over my breast. I didn't know if it was a mistake, but he didn't move it, so I think it was intentional. His fingers smelled of vinegar. We sat there with his hand sort of *living* there, like when an insect lands on you.

I thought of all the boys I had been with at the moment they died, counting them like you do sheep to try to sleep: *18, 19…*

Elsie would have said '*No, Mairi, think of all the men who you helped,*' so I tried counting them instead, starting with Dixmude and going upwards, until I got to Harold. And then my heart felt just as heavy as my breast.

I suggested a stroll, and Jack seemed even more relieved than I was to finally stand up.

There was a small funicular to the clifftop, but Jack said he would prefer to take the steps. I'd noticed he didn't like confined spaces, but he didn't make a thing of it. We walked up slowly – it was steeper than it looked – and Jack had to let go of my hand. He said enviously, 'I'm out of puff yet you're absolutely dandy!'

At the top, there was a grey statue of Queen Victoria sitting on her throne, staring out to the not-quite sea. *What would she think of what was happening in Europe?* I didn't suppose they ever told kings or queens the truth. How glorious it must be to think that everything around and beneath you was clean and harmonious.

Queen Victoria and Prince Albert. *That* was a love affair, they said.

Jack took me by the hand again as we walked back to our guesthouse – a pretty building overlooking a rose garden. I couldn't help thinking it would make a perfect hospital. Access to the sea and to the station. Nice, large windows. *What more could Elsie and I want?*

'What you thinking?' asked Jack, smiling his nervous grimace.

'Nothing.'

'See that building?' he said, pointing at the larger building that I hadn't noticed on the other side of the road. 'That's a naval hospital. Nice, isn't it?'

Inside the guesthouse, the reception area was all dark-wood panelling and there was one of those snooty, suited men at the desk, the kind of man who's never seen or done anything in his life. I could tell he thought Jack and I were just an average couple. He said, 'Mr and Mrs Petrie?'

I turned my splutter into a cough.

The snooty man pressed his bell and an ancient porter, bent double, arrived to take up our bags. We had minimal luggage between us, but still, I hated to think of the old fella struggling, so I insisted on taking my own bag. Snooty man and bent-double man were both aghast.

Jack grinned. 'I'll take it, Mrs Petrie,' he said, pulling the bag off my shoulder and onto his without looking at me.

This, they didn't mind.

As we walked along the corridors, I was reminded of my first time in a hotel, in Harwich, with Elsie. I was such a *child* back then; it was almost painful to remember my naivety. *Why on earth had I wandered off to get her that night? How had I drunk so much I was sick?* I tried to concentrate on the here and now, with Jack, but discomfitures from the past kept coming to haunt me.

The room number three dangled precariously from a broken nail on the door, which didn't create a good impression, but inside the room was elegant and pale, the sort of room you'd dream about if you were a person who dreamed about luxury hotel rooms. All the furniture matched and fitted just-so. It must have been expensive. I didn't know how Jack could afford it on his wage.

There was only one bed. A double bed, larger than the straw mattresses Elsie and I and any number of visitors shared, but still... I hadn't expected us to share.

Jack stared at it too. 'It was cheaper than the twin,' he said apologetically. 'I can ask them to change.'

'It's no bother,' I said.

'I can go on the floor.'

'Or I can,' I offered.

He shook his head at me. I was beginning to think his embarrassed look was permanent. I didn't have the will to argue so we left it unresolved.

*

We had dinner in the Royal Hotel Ballroom. I didn't have a special outfit, but Jack said I looked a treat. He wasn't much of a charmer but there was something about the way he looked at me that made me feel beautiful. I felt underdressed as we walked through the frosted-glass double doors, but once we were inside, I realised that fashions had changed while I was underground. Things were more casual now. I wasn't the only woman with short hair, though none had hair quite as short as mine. There were no top hats any more and far fewer bonnets. I gazed around. It felt nice not to stand out. Jack had wet down his hair, which made his ears look even more prominent. He was newly shaved and smelled fine.

He wanted to tell me about some of the people he'd met in Stow Maries.

'I'm all ears,' I said, before blushing furiously. *Why did I have to bring them up?*

I imagined my mother deliberating over Jack, doing her calculations. *Was I worth more than him? Could I aim higher?* Probably not with the whole brother-on-the-run business and my situation, living underground in a Belgian cellar with rats for years. Being an uncivilised cave-dweller was unlikely to increase eligibility in a woman, although it might be a bonus in a man.

Also, Jack was not just any fella, he was a decorated man – although whether that was sufficient for my mother was anyone's guess. It was unlikely to make up for his humble roots… *or was it?* I had rarely been able to predict her views on anything.

Jack told me about his life at the airbase, before saying softly, 'You don't mind? I… gave them your details.'

'What for?'

He shrugged. 'You'll hear any news direct, that's all. My parents don't—' he pretended to scribble on the napkin, reminding me that they didn't write.

I thought, *I am actually pretty sure what my mother would think.*

I laughed gaily. 'But Jack, you're in England!' and he laughed too: 'Thank bloody goodness for that!'

Mother wouldn't like his swearing, but then I swore now as well.

Jack said, 'Your letters make me happy.'

I was about to reply but the waitress came over with our cherry pies and we lost the thread. Never mind. We tucked in with great enthusiasm. When we had finished, I wiped my mouth with the napkin, looked up at him doing the same, then we both burst out laughing.

*

Our room was so posh that it had an adjoining bathroom, which was where I undressed. In the absence of anything else to wear, I came out wrapped in my overcoat and slipped into bed. I hoped Jack had checked the mattress and the pillow for fleas as I felt too shy to do a thorough inspection myself. Jack was already lying on the floor.

I felt terrible that he was paying to sleep there and said so. Even so, I was surprised when he suddenly got up, pulled back the cover and climbed in next to me.

'Of course, I won't… touch you…' he said, his voice trembling.

'Thank you.' Despite Elsie's insinuation, it hadn't occurred to me that he would try.

'Nothing to worry about.' His voice was muffled by the pillow and I could hardly hear him.

'I know.'

'Unless you want me to?' he added neutrally. 'Touch you, that is?'

I couldn't think of anything to say to that so I pretended to be asleep and I believe he did the same.

With my eyes closed, I thought about Germans breaching the line, invading our cellar right at that moment. I pictured Elsie trying to run away, desperately fighting them off. I knew she would be thinking, *Thank goodness, Mairi was spared.*

In the morning, I woke up with a hand on my thigh. I thought at first that I was lying next to Elsie. I was so used to sleeping by her side on the straw. The hand very slowly, speculatively, stroked my leg over my nightdress. It felt nice.

Then I remembered where I was. I swung out of bed fearfully.

I thought of my father's disapproving face. My mother would probably expect nothing better.

'Shall we go sightseeing before I leave, Mr Petrie?'

*

Jack insisted on accompanying me to the train. A bulky woman with a hat as large as a toddler was at the station entrance pushing her white feathers of cowardice on to passers-by. I scowled at her. I had heard of this kind of agitator before, but never had the misfortune to come across one. People tried to ignore her, but she persisted in thrusting feathers at men who weren't in uniform, hissing words like 'duty' and 'patriotism', and saying 'Whatever will your children say when they know you did nothing during the war?'

I thought of the men I knew who were waiting to be ordered to go over the top to their deaths. They had no choice.

I imagined this woman sitting in her warm living room, preparing her batch of feathers, brushing down her skirt, selecting her shawl, full of self-righteousness.

I thought she might set off Jack again, but he ignored her and shook off the feather so it fell on the ground and was trodden on by passing muddy feet within seconds. He raised his eyebrows at me.

'I'm getting better at keeping my temper, Mairi. No more shouting in public for me.'

'You were fine,' I said, thinking that woman deserves to be shouted at.

We sat on a metal bench with swirly armrests waiting for the 3.30 p.m. to Harwich. Nearby, I watched a group of children excitedly going on a trip. They formed a sweet crocodile behind their teacher.

I wished Jack would just head off. I hated a long goodbye.

'I didn't mean to be so forward.'

'It's okay,' I said. I knew he was kind.

'Back in the hotel room, I mean.'

'I know!' I said again. This was excruciating. *Why wouldn't he drop it?*

'I'm glad you didn't let me,' he whispered, and his pimply skin was quite pink. 'It's one of the reasons I love you, Mairi.'

'What is?'

He looked embarrassed. 'That the rules are still important to you, despite everything.'

I didn't know what he meant by this, but I knew he was trying, in his awkward way, to pay me a compliment.

Jack paused and the red came back to his cheeks. He hugged me and I stayed in his arms like that. If we had been there much longer, perhaps I would have relaxed into it, but I was keeping one eye on the time. I could hear the whistle of the trains, sense the incoming steam in the air. It was Jack who pulled away first. I wondered if I was too rigid for him.

He looked me in the eyes and, at least as far as I was concerned from out of nowhere, he asked, 'Will you marry me?' in a rushed and quite-unlike-Jack voice.

Oddly enough, my first thought was *What would Elsie say?*

'I don't know,' I said as honestly as I could. He deserved the truth. I felt bad, because Elsie had been so robust and positive in her response to Harold's proposal and my reply to Jack couldn't have been more tepid. I was as lukewarm as the coffee in the trenches.

Jack said, 'I thought you'd say that.' But he seemed pleased. It occurred to me that he liked me because I wasn't spontaneous: because he knew what to expect with plodding old me.

'Let me know what you decide,' he added softly. A grimy white feather had stuck itself to the underside of his shoe. 'I'll be a good husband to you, Mairi.'

CHAPTER TWENTY-SEVEN

On Easter Sunday, Elsie greeted me at Ostend with a squeal and a hug. She had made a hearty recovery, although I couldn't help noticing she was even thinner in the cheeks. Her eyes looked larger than ever and the skin around them was taking on permanent purple shadows – like the men in the trenches. I knew immediately something was on her mind.

She hadn't been looking after the car. The exhaust was puffing out a trail of thick black smoke and you could barely see through the windscreen, it was that grimy.

Once we were on the road, I asked, 'What's been happening?'

Elsie paused. I knew that look. She wasn't sure how to frame it. My first thought was Harold. *Something must have happened to him.*

'No!' She looked at me strangely. 'Hal is fine. He's in Lyon.'

'Are we finally being sent away?' Our ribbons couldn't protect us forever; but as long there were men in the trenches, we had work to do.

'They can't get rid of us that easily,' Elsie said quietly.

'Something's wrong though,' I said.

'You didn't hear?'

The newspapers in England were spectacularly useless. The pride they seemed to have in printing anything *but* a detailed account of the situation in Europe was astounding. I remembered the paper on the pier: Small Group of Pacifists Routed in South Wales

She hesitated. 'Things are getting worse, Mairi.'

'How *on earth* could things be getting worse?'

'Gas.'

CHAPTER TWENTY-EIGHT

We needed to have gas masks with us at all times.

'At all times,' insisted Elsie sternly, although we both knew she was more forgetful than me with equipment.

It felt as though a new dread had come in and sat uninvited on the bench next to all the old dreads: shells, snipers, starvation and the rest.

'How do you reconcile your God with this?' Elsie asked acidly.

I shook my head. *I'm not doing this now.*

Gas was the very worst news to come back to. Even a cellar door from Harrods was no defence. And of course, however bad it was for us down below in the cellar, it was hundreds of times worse for the boys out there.

There was something so revolting, so crude about it. I thought of David and Goliath, but I realised it wasn't that clear: this was some ugly struggle between Goliaths, and there were thousands – no, millions – of Davids on each side.

If I thought I had seen it all last year – and I *had* thought that – I was proved wrong over the next weeks.

How apologetically those poor dear boys dragged into the cellar departed from us.

'I'm sorry,' one sweet lad panted as his throat closed up. 'I'm scared.'

Elsie was ready to go out to the trenches again. *Duck, Duck, Goose.* There were more injured boys to rescue there today. We couldn't comfort everyone. These days there was little time to hold a boy's hand as he slipped away. There were too many of them.

'It's all right, love.' I couldn't stop crying.

'Mairi?' Elsie called, which got Shot up and running. 'We have to go.'

His hand was in mine. He didn't even have the strength to squeeze my fingers. 'Will God forgive me for my sins?' he whispered, or something like it. He had a strong accent – Irish, I think – but his family lived in Bristol. The damp half-written letter in his pocket informed me of this and the fact that he was only recently nineteen: he thanked his mother for the birthday socks. They kept his feet warm and cosy and reminded him of home. He asked about his grandmother, his great-aunt, his little brother and even his tortoise. '*Don't give it too much carrot or it will get bad guts.*' He wrote that he prayed his little brother would never have to go through any of this.

'Hurry, Mairi! They need us!' Elsie sounded exasperated.

'Everything will be better in heaven.' I couldn't stop the loud sob that came out. 'Dear boy, I promise.'

Elsie had impatiently thrown open the cellar door. I untangled my fingers from his. I would not cry again. 'You are loved.'

'For God's sake!' hissed Elsie.

The boy let out a croak and I changed my mind. 'You go,' I said.

Elsie looked at me furiously. Her mind was on the living, not the dead. But I couldn't leave him. Imagine if it were Hal or me… Would she go then?

Yes, she probably would have.

'Come now, Mairi,' she said in her quietest, most threatening voice. She wasn't used to me being defiant. No one was.

'I'm staying,' I said, keeping my focus on my poor lad. When I looked up, Elsie was still there, staring at me as though she couldn't believe her eyes. Then she thundered off, dragging our first-aid boxes – they might have been from medieval times for all the good they did – up the stairs.

He only took six or seven minutes more and I was glad I stayed with him, no matter what she thought.

*

We did six-hour shifts at a time, slept for two hours, then started up again. Elsie and I didn't need to speak much; we knew what had to be done. It was my idea to put vinegar on cloths and hold them over the boys' noses and mouths to numb the sting of the gas. When we ran out of towels, then cloths, then socks, it was Elsie's idea to use our sanitary protection. We did what we had to do, side by side, clearing the trenches, mending those who might make it, abandoning the ones who hadn't and muddling through with those who were neither here nor there.

To the trenches Elsie and I marched, masks over our faces, unrecognisable to even our oldest friends. Trying and failing to give the boys hope.

And then as abruptly as it had started up, the gas stopped. An international agreement? An international sense of shame? Or maybe just an unexpected wind pushing the gas back towards their own men.

We could just about breathe again. For a while.

*

The new post-boy cycled towards us with his great mail bags of messages. 'Hey ho, Madonnas!' he said, laughing. He liked to ring his bell despite the effort causing him to wobble more than usual.

Letters still came from Jack:

Sometimes, it's easier to think of myself not as an individual person, but just as one part of a great swathe of millions of people born and living around now. Just a segment, a cog in the wheel. Do you know what I mean?

I didn't know and I didn't care. Maybe it was meant to encourage me, but I felt far away from Jack now, far away from anything human or earthly.

At the bottom of his note, after his signature and heralded by a deliberate postscript, he had written:

Have you a response to my proposal yet? Here are twenty kisses for your age, and twenty-four for me, a total of forty-four kisses. Let me know before we reach forty-five!

I didn't want kisses – everything was foul and gas-filled now – and even if I did, I didn't want them from Jack. I rushed off a reply:

Did you think to ask my father for my hand, Jack? My family are old-fashioned and it would be a sign that you respected and understood our values if you did.

How annoyed my father would be if we skipped even that small step. I would hate to have Father's icy disappointment directed at me. To have both his children let him down would be too much. I thought of Uilleam – *what would he think of Jack?*

And then, because everything I had written seemed too curt and too dismissive to send to a suitor, I added, *'It is horrific here. I can't even bring myself to tell you of the suffering around us.'*

*

As soon as everything quietened down, Elsie disappeared up the road to socialise with the engineers. Then when Harold came back in the middle of May, they rode out together to drink beer and to see 'Ginger' and their officer friends in Pop where they could pretend this had never happened. Nineteen-year-old boys from Bristol hadn't been gassed and crying nurses hadn't had to fight to stay with them because there were other people out there who might actually make it.

Neither Elsie nor Harold asked if I wanted to go with them any more. *Just as well. I didn't want to.*

*

Fan mail still came for the Madonnas. The more we got, the less worthy I felt of it. *What did they know?* When I admitted this to

Elsie, she said 'Don't read them, just take the money,' but I couldn't
do that. It felt disrespectful.

Our admiration knows no bounds. May God be with you.

*Word of your kindness has reached us, even in Australia. I wonder
if you could send your autograph?*

Amid the post, I found a brief note from Uilleam:

*We don't hear much about the war out here, Mairi. But reading
between the lines, it sounds horrendous. I wish we were back in
our garden, dreaming of cars that could float and motorcycles that
could fly. Dig deep, dear Mairi.*

'Dig deep' was the phrase my father used. It didn't suit Uilleam.
He was more of a 'dig shallow, then wander off to do something
else' kind of person.

Fondly, your beloved brother.
PS. Has Gypsy got hitched yet? I'm still available.

'Where are you?' I wrote back to his old address. I wanted to shake
him. *'I need to know you're safe.'*

A sour note came from my mother. I had long stopped being excited
by her correspondence. She had heard that I had been in England, from
a newspaper article in the *Express*, no less: MADONNA'S WHIRLWIND
UK VISIT. *Why had I not arranged a meeting? How would Mrs Godfrey
and the circle feel if they found out I had been and gone without seeing
them?* In other news, Mrs Godfrey's daughter, Alice, was expecting her
second child in September. *Would I be able to send souvenirs?*

*

It wasn't until the middle of June that I realised there had been no letters from Jack for several weeks. No '*how wonderful to hear from you*'s or stirring stories of flying adventures. At first I wondered if he had dispensed with writing and simply taken the train to Dorset to meet my father face-to-face. This seemed unlikely because he would surely have had to find out the address first through me. As time went on, and I still heard nothing, I grew scared that I'd repelled him with my last letter. I had gone too far. But he hadn't known what I had been dealing with when I wrote to him. The gas had sucked any thoughts of the future away from me.

Anyway, Jack wouldn't mind, I hoped. Jack *knew* I was an old-fashioned girl. Didn't he say he liked that about me?

But then why didn't he ruddy well reply?

*

Lady D visited with a tin of biscuits and her typical good spirits. If she saw that things were strained between Elsie and me, she did not mention it. Indeed, she kept saying 'You two this' and 'you two that' so after a while, Elsie and I forgot we were at loggerheads and smiled at each other.

Over tea, with Shot contentedly curled in her lap, Lady D explained that she was finishing at Furnes at the end of the month. Elsie and I both misunderstood at first. We thought she was going back to England.

'Oh no!' She seemed shocked that we would have considered her capable of such a thing, 'I'm not going 'til this damn thing is over. We're seeing the war through, right, girls?'

'Right!' we chorused, chinking our cups.

'Careful!' Lady D laughed, as usual.

I was glad Lady D was staying in Belgium. The soldiers loved her unrelenting cheerfulness. She was like the hearty matron of a boarding school. She could mend anything she put her mind to as well.

Elsie teased her, saying that the posh boys – the officers – wanted her to thrash them. Even that didn't make her frown.

She was going to a hospital further down the line near Passchendaele. Had I heard of it? I didn't say that I had heard the British soldiers called it 'Hell' for short.

Later that evening, after the door had been bolted and the candles blown out, and Elsie had decided it was too late to visit the engineers, I asked 'Why *is* Lady D leaving Furnes?' I couldn't understand it. Furnes was as good a place to work as any. Better than most probably. They had four ambulances now and their organisation was infamously impeccable. Everyone said that hospital ran as smoothly as anything the Germans could run and Lady D had never seemed anything but happy working there.

Elsie, already in the hay, rolled onto her side. Although it was dark, I could still make out her expression. Chewing straw like some cowboy in the *National Geographic*, she was looking at me incredulously.

I stared back at her. 'What?'

'Mairi, I thought you were good at puzzles.'

'How do you mean?'

'Work it out, dear girl.'

But I couldn't.

Next morning, I asked again. 'So why *is* Lady D going?'

'Isn't it obvious?' Elsie was pulling on her boots. She wore three layers of military socks and still the boots were too big for her. Our calves had shrunk.

'Clearly not.'

Elsie enunciated her words very slowly. 'Munro wouldn't marry her.'

'Dr Munro and Lady D?!'

'Oh Mairi, Mairi, Mairi,' Elsie said, pulling her laces ever tighter. 'You really are the most oblivious thing.'

*

It wasn't until the end of July that I heard from Jack again. The post-boy enquired, 'Love letter?' as he held out the envelope.

I gave him an irritated half-smile back. 'Not telling!'

This amused him. I heard him muttering, 'Not telling, not telling!' as he wobbled away, ringing his bell.

How I had missed Jack's dull letter-writing! It had been two months! How sweet it was to hold his letter in my hands. I raced through the sentences. First, he apologised for the delay. He explained he had been thinking hard about what to write and he dearly hoped I didn't get the wrong idea. I must remember that he was not good with words:

You're the only one whose permission I want. Not your father, you. You have been living on the Western Front for a long time, Mairi. Surely you know your own mind by now?

I couldn't decide if this was an insult or not. I knew my father wouldn't like it. I felt a thrill at Jack's bravado though.

We will be good together. I know you mightn't love me yet – not the way I love you.

At that, my hand flew to my heart. It was like Jack was inside my head, knowing my doubts and confusions.

But, Mairi, I am going to be a better person. I am going to improve myself and I WILL make you happy, if you will only let me! I want nothing more than for the war to be over and for us to set up a happy life together. Is that too much to ask?
I await your decision.
Yours fondly, Jack.

But even though I was relieved to hear from Jack, in fact I was delighted, I couldn't decide on the question of marriage. I still *didn't* know my own mind. *How do you get to know your own mind?* I wasn't sure my mind and I had ever been properly introduced.

I could have asked for a long engagement, but Jack deserved better than that.

'*I need to be sure,*' I wrote back. '*I'm sorry.*' And then I finished with a postscript of my own:

I understand this probably isn't what you want to hear, Jack. If that is the case, please don't wait for me.

I was going to add that there were plenty of lovely young women who would be delighted to be with him but I left it there. There was no point in spelling it out.

We weren't exactly Victoria and Albert, were we? Or even Charlotte Brontë and Mr Héger.

I was nervous of my father's reaction to Jack. But that wasn't all. I suppose I still needed to be convinced that I had no better alternatives available to me. I still had hope.

CHAPTER TWENTY-NINE

Our work in the cellar continued throughout the summer of 1917. Some men were saved, others weren't. Our hopes that the war would one day end had left us. We stopped talking about the things we would do 'when all this is over'. It was beginning to look like this was our forever.

Things were tough. The men's pleading eyes dominated my dreams. Elsie's nightmares affected me as well. In the past I had ignored them or at least distanced myself from them. Now she called out what I was thinking too. There was no respite from horror even when we were bedded down in the straw. Certain words disturbed me. Some innocous words made me feel nauseous or even faint: *Masks. Bristol.* Even the word 'Mother' could sometimes give me palpitations.

Elsie and my relationship was taut as a game of cat's cradle. An outsider probably wouldn't see it but *I* knew it and I didn't doubt that she knew it too. A tension among all our other tensions. We still managed occasional jokes, we still played pontoon and snap, we still fussed over Shot, but Elsie was increasingly quick-tempered with me.

One time, we were carrying some poor soul on a stretcher when I tripped over some rubble. I squealed – I couldn't help it, I could barely see through the dust clouds from the explosions. However, I was relieved I hadn't fallen all the way down.

'What do you think you are doing, Mairi?' Elsie snapped. She knew – *she knew* – I hadn't done it on purpose so why did she ask?

'Nothing!'

'You nearly dropped him.'

She had never spoken to me like that before.

'I'm trying, Elsie.'

'Oh, you're very good at *trying*.'

'What is that supposed to mean?'

'Oh, forget it.'

Another time, she said my singing gave her a headache.

'You've never said that before,' I responded mutinously.

'Well, I'm saying it now,' she said.

She still went over to see the engineers, but only once every two or three weeks. That she went socialising less should have given me some cheer, but it didn't. Perhaps I was uneasy with yet another change.

*

If the war did ever end, what would happen to Pervyse, Ypres and Dixmude, I wondered? Belgium's houses and churches, cathedrals and cloth halls, museums, libraries and schools had been razed to the ground. *Would they ever be rebuilt or should this devastation be left as a reminder of what happened here?*

I imagined workers rebuilding the old cellar house exactly as it was. Madeleine and Felix hauling their suitcases home. In my thoughts, the war is a distant memory. The family sit around the breakfast table eating toast with marmalade. It's the weekend but Felix and Madeleine are learning tennis and have to get out quite early. Their mother is telling them a story she heard from a neighbour about a fairground. Their father walks in cheerily, having collected the letters that thumped on the mat.

'Darlings, we have news from Mairi. She is planning on visiting us this Christmas!'

The sound of a distant whistle. 'Let's go.' Elsie was shaking me awake.

*

Jack didn't reply again for what felt like ages. I wondered if he was eking out his responses on purpose, rationing his letters so that I would miss them more. If so, it was working.

I considered a life with Jack. Maybe we would have children: perhaps a boy and a girl? Jack would be a good father, I was sure of it, and I mightn't be such a bad mother. I would learn from my own parents' mistakes. Jack might get work with horses, I might find a place at the local hospital or school. Perhaps I might join the women's movement – smash a few windows! We women rarely committed acts of violence. Perhaps it was something to consider. I wondered what my mother and Mrs Godfrey would say if I were arrested!

Jack would support me in whatever I did, I knew he would. There weren't many men you could say that for.

Elsie probably wouldn't think much of him. In the cold, his ears went so transparent that you could almost see right through them. He wasn't a looker. He wasn't a talker. But he did think – he thought and felt things deeply.

If we were to have two children then we would have to make love at least twice. Obviously. Uilleam had made sure I had some education in 'the birds and the bees'. We were both incredulous about the whole thing, but it was all there in some magazine his friends had got him.

'*Our* parents did that?' I remember asking suspiciously.

'I can't believe anyone does *that*!' he had shrieked.

It occurred to me now that Uilleam's distaste about sexual intercourse may have stemmed from somewhere different than mine.

We wouldn't *have* to have sex, I thought, if Jack had suffered an injury to his penis. Jack had never mentioned that he had (*how* would one mention it?). I had only seen such a disability a few times, but still, with war veterans, one needed to prepare for every eventuality, which meant one needed to prepare for the worst.

I had seen a few real-life penises over the years – *how else does a man with no arms pee?* – and I understood that when engaged in congress they might look different from the way they looked in their floppy state. So although the thought wasn't exactly appealing,

I was confident there was nothing to be *too* perturbed about. *If it was God's will…*

Just when I was about to give up on ever hearing from Jack again, in the middle of August, the post-boy cycled up with several letters for Elsie and a parcel for me with Jack's laboured handwriting on the front. For once, the post-boy's bell didn't seem inappropriately jolly. For once, giving a tip of silver pennies felt entirely justified. I belted down to the cellar, dropping the rest of the post on to the table. Elsie was clearing out the stove. She smiled at me but said nothing and I was glad she stayed silent. I had been hurt by her melodramatic imitation of me at Furnes. I was no sillier about Jack's letters than any other correspondence I received.

Pulling at the strings of the package, I tried to imagine what could be inside. *Food? Underpants? Soap? Was Jack returning some item I had left at the Southend hotel?* I peeled off the brown wrapping.

No.

This was something home-made and scrappy, not manufactured in a factory or sold in a shop. I realised quickly it was a cardboard jigsaw puzzle – at a guess, there were over a hundred pieces but I couldn't work out why Jack would have sent it. I scanned the note for clues. I hardly dared breathe.

And there it was:

To Mairi,

I know you love jigsaw puzzles. So here, pick up a piece of this puzzle. I am in pieces but I will put us back together. Pick up a piece, let me lock into you. Let us be like a puzzle to the outside world, or rather, I'll puzzle, and you, Mairi, will continue to dazzle…

Your flying Jigsaw Jack xxx

PS How about here for a wedding?

Elsie took a letter from her pile, read it, then screwed up the paper and threw it into the stove.

'Stupid, stupid war.'

Putting down Jack's strange love note, I turned to her.

'Oh, what's happened, Elsie?' I had seen her letters were postmarked England, so I knew it couldn't be Harold. 'It's not Kenneth?'

'It's my brother.'

'Who?'

'My brother Sam. He's dead.'

'Oh no, Elsie!' There were so many things I wanted to say. About faith. About heaven. But I knew Elsie would want nothing of that. So I simply added, 'These are terrible times.'

'He went like a hero.' Her mouth curved into a sneer. 'Don't they say that every single time?'

We always said hot black tea was good for shock. I made some and we drank it slowly. We were out of sugar. Elsie was always so good at cheering me up, yet it felt unfamiliar or forced the other way around. I wished she could lean on me the way I leaned on her. I didn't know how she could stand it. I couldn't bear it if Uilleam were killed.

'I didn't even know you had a brother, Elsie. I talk so often of mine but…'

Elsie blinked her tears away. 'I'm being foolish.'

'Not foolish. Won't you tell me about him?'

'There were five of us. Now there are only three.'

'I'm so sorry.'

'After our parents died, we were separated. No one could take on all of us. I was the only one to stay in Dorset while he was sent to London. We saw each other once or twice a year at first, and then less often.'

'What was he like?'

'Sam was a real boy's boy, he loved charging around the garden. He studied physics at Cambridge. He wanted to work in industry.'

I bet he was wonderful. Elsie's brother would be. He was probably the kind of person our country most needed.

'I hardly knew him,' she continued, 'but… I always felt something was missing, and now there is.'

Somehow everything about Elsie suddenly made marvellous sense to me.

'Oh Elsie.' I pressed her hand to my cheek. I tried to think how Dr Munro might put it – or his favourite, Dr Freud. 'This explains why you married so young and want to marry again. You are trying to recreate the family life you had never had.'

Elsie shot up. She looked horrified.

'Make your own family, that's what you once told me,' I continued. I realised I had overstepped one of her lines straight away but it was too late.

'Enough, Mairi!' she said furiously, pulling on her coat. 'Sometimes, I think you're obsessed with my past.'

Elsie didn't come back for supper. I didn't know where she had gone. There was gunfire and every so often the earth would tremble like it was in the throes of death. I visited the trenches, dealing with an injury in the thigh and a case of the shakes. I delivered some tasteless soup. I had a few refusals, which wasn't good. Sometimes the men were too wound up to eat.

What if Elsie were killed? There would be nothing left for me here without her. There would be nothing left for me *anywhere* without Elsie. It seemed too peculiar to contemplate her death. Not Elsie, she was far too alive for that.

The sky was streaked pink, the colour of the water coming off your hands after a busy afternoon in the cellar hospital. Then it was royal purple, then dark navy (the colour of my school uniform, only we had gold piping around the collar).

Elsie still hadn't returned by ten. The bombardments still hadn't stopped. She hated being alone at night yet she'd left me to that very fate.

What if the Germans broke through tonight and I had to run for it? What if they captured me? How would Elsie find me?

Putting on my helmet, I crept outside. I didn't take my gas mask because the gas attacks hadn't happened for a while now.

Apart from the occasional flashes of distant shells, the dark was pretty much all-consuming. I was used to it now. I walked quickly down the road to the ruin where the engineers lived. That too was in darkness. I let myself in, pulled off my helmet so I could hear better and whispered a 'Hello?' It echoed back at me. Pushing through to the area they'd made 'home', I glimpsed a tin roof and sandbags, a room like the one we had before, our 'upstairs' before it was bombed.

They didn't need a fire – it was a warm summer's night but there was one in the middle of the room anyway. Some men were on chairs, some were lying on the floor. There was no glass in any of the windows and usually they were boarded up, but they'd taken the boards down – because of the smoke, I supposed. The smoke was overwhelming. It reminded me of mustard gas.

I saw open first-aid boxes, laudanum packets, pain-relief and pills: our supplies. Robin – mild-mannered engineer Robin – was prostrate on the floor with his mouth hung wide open; he was babbling like a baby.

'Look who's here! All the colours!' he said to me, opening his arms like he was greeting a long-lost friend. I stared at him, not quite believing my eyes. *What was going on?*

One of the men got up, murmuring, 'Her hair is like flames.' He walked towards me like a ghost in amateur dramatics, arms outstretched. He reached to touch the top of my head, I pushed him away and he half collapsed.

'Wow, she burns—'

'Don't touch me!'

'Can I call you Ginger?'

'NO!' I said furiously. *How dare they?*

'All right,' he said. 'Just asking!' He laughed. His pupils were huge.

And there was Elsie on an old sack, waving at me as if she were waving from the edge of a distant world. She felt like a stranger.

'What are you doing, Elsie?'

'I don't know,' she began feebly.

'What *is* going on?' I realised, unfortunately, how like my mother I sounded.

She held up her hands. 'It takes away the hard edges, Mairi.'

'Come home with me,' I ordered. I knew then with an absolute certainty that if anything were ever to be the same between us again, I had to get her out of here.

'Everything is blurry and warm,' she continued, a soppy smile on her face. I thought she was staring at me but she wasn't – she was just staring at anything. I had never seen her like this.

I felt sick. Robin was at the window, peering out in awe at the night sky: 'Look at the stars, quick!' I went over, convinced something was happening outside. It looked like any other brutally oblivious night sky to me. I felt then that I couldn't trust Robin. I certainly couldn't trust Elsie.

'I thought you said she was a God-botherer?' said Robin, apropos of nothing.

'I didn't say that.' Elsie turned her bleary eyes guiltily on me. 'I never said that, Mairi.' I thought she was about to cry.

Suddenly there were sounds of a scuffle outside. Robin excitedly grabbed his gun. It was like he'd been waiting for the chance. I got the idea this was something he did often because the others didn't even bother to look up. 'Fox for supper, anyone?'

He aimed, then fired outside.

I recognised that yelp and ran to the empty window. It was Shot. Shot must have been so worried about our absence that he had followed me here.

'That's my dog!' I shrieked. I ran outside, nearly tumbling over the rubble as I went.

Elsie was right behind me and Robin was behind her, breathing fast and moaning frantically.

'I would never hurt that dog. Tell her, Elsie!'

I found Shot almost immediately. He was cowering behind some scrawny bushes: a poor shelter to choose. He was trembling as much as I was. Trembling more than I'd known he was capable of. I picked him up, petrified of what I'd find. I checked his little ears, his shaky legs. There was no blood, no sign of a wound. *Thank God.* Robin had missed.

'Is he okay?' Elsie, Robin and a couple of the other men crowded around me. They were panting. Their relief at the sight of Shot made me even angrier. If he was unharmed it was no thanks to them, the disgusting lot of them.

'Mairi?' Elsie's voice was high and far away. 'My sister.'

'Go away!' I said and when she didn't move, I shouted. 'Go back to your… friends. Stay away from me!'

Running back to the cellar with Shot struggling in my arms, I hated her, I hated everyone and everything. Except for Shot. The Germans might as well come and savage me now for all I cared.

Pulling at the trapdoor like Alice or the white rabbit, I slipped down cradling Shot.

The next day, I got up as usual for the trench-run. Elsie was already there. She must have come straight from the engineers' place. Her eyes were red and there was something slightly off about her, but she greeted me as if nothing had happened. She floated about in her great leather coat, moving from soldier to soldier, handing out drinks. After that was finished, she still managed to sew up a boy's leg in a trench full of water. When a fat rat ran over the both of them, she didn't even tense.

By the time Harold came over that afternoon, Elsie was flat out in the straw with Shot protectively nestling at her feet. I had called Shot away, but he wouldn't come. He still loved her.

'Let her rest,' Harold said indulgently. He had heard about her brother's death and he must have thought she was sleeping off her grief or something. 'Do you want a ride out, Mairi?'

It felt too much for me. I thought of Robin's aborted aim, the way Elsie had been sitting, dizzily waving like she was sunbathing on a cruise liner, for goodness' sake. I burst into hot tears.

'Oh Mairi,' Harold said gently, 'what times are these?' Since that was another thing Elsie said it didn't make me feel much better.

We mounted Doris and rode to the copse of trees where we had rested the time before. I tried to breathe in fresh air, but the smell of acrid shells and gunpowder lingered even this far from the line.

'You're young to have seen the terrible things you have.'

'You think it is better to be older?'

'Not better,' Harold considered, 'but unlike you, I had more time to acquire some good memories to look back on fondly.'

I wondered which good memories Harold was most fond of looking back on. I knew that one of mine was his arrival at the cellar house. I could admit it now – the time he told me he loved me in his sleep was deeply precious. I knew another of my happiest moments was coming out here. This was 'our place' and being here made everything else disappear.

Harold pulled some condensed milk from his bag. He stabbed open the tin with his penknife and we drank from the tiny gap, like we were sucking nectar from a flower. I wanted to tell him about what had happened last night, the wasted laudanum and poor Shot, but I couldn't even do that.

We stayed there silently observing dragonflies, peonies, stalks, ants, blades of grass, flies. All the living things doing their living things, while we humans were battering ourselves to death two miles away.

Harold said, 'When all this is over, will anyone remember?'

'We'll make sure we tell everyone.'

Madeleine will know. Madeleine and Felix are the last beautiful hopes for the future, I thought.

'I don't know if I'll ever talk about it again,' he said.

My head was a confused knot on his shoulder. *Let's not talk then.* I suddenly wished he would just kiss me. *Get it over with!*

I wondered if maybe things had just gone too far with Elsie and he couldn't find a way back from his vows to her, but he said, 'We are so lucky to have Elsie in our lives, aren't we?'

'Yes,' I whispered. My longing for him just wouldn't go away, however much I wanted it to.

'She is the most incredible woman I've ever met.'

'She is.'

'I can't believe she has agreed to be my wife.'

I listened with an aching heart. *What is this ugliness lodged inside of me that means I can't countenance Harold being in love with my best friend?*

'You are getting married then?'

'Yes!' he said like it was obvious. 'As soon as we can organise something. I want all my family there. And I have a large family!'

He smiled at me, yet his eyes were far away. And that was the moment I understood that all my hopes were nothing but childish silliness. Harold was not mine. He really was Elsie's. She had won again. Effortlessly. And there were no prizes for second place.

'You won't wait for her to convert?' I asked, trying to pretend I hadn't given this any thought.

'Oh,' he said breezily, like it was nothing, the big obstacle had just been overcome. 'In her own time perhaps.'

'I see.'

'If I hadn't been injured and come to the cellar that day, who knows how life might have turned out? Every time my wound aches I feel blessed to have Elsie, and you, in my life. The pain reminds me not of what I have lost but of the people I have gained. I can't wait to meet Kenneth.' He looked at me, almost shyly, like that first time in the cellar when anything could have happened. I should have walked him out to the car, not Elsie. 'I want to introduce him to the Church and bring him up as a Catholic. Elsie doesn't mind. The funny thing is I've always wanted a son.'

I could see them, when all this was over, walking around their European cities, swinging hands, dark-eyed Kenneth in the middle,

Harold beaming. Everyone speaking a different language; everyone united together. Harold loved her. He would never love me in that way. But even as I torturously admitted that to myself, I knew that there *was* someone who might.

I just had to wait it out, accept these feelings and one day they would disappear and we would all be best friends again.

'I am happy for you, Harold,' I managed to say, meaning *I will be happy for you, I just need some time.* 'And Elsie.'

I imagined him rising up, calling out to her, 'Love you forever.'

'Thank you, Mairi,' he said. 'That means so much.'

The birds were still singing. Doris was still beautiful. The sky was still blue.

'Thank you for bringing me here, Harold.'

'Oh, isn't it wonderful? Elsie loves it here too.'

I nodded, painfully, but with a resignation that was somehow sweet too. I had my answer. I had my clarity. For the first time, I said it before he did: 'We'd better head off.'

When we got back, Elsie was making tea, the stove was lit and Shot was curled up happily on a blanket. All was normal. We could have been anywhere.

CHAPTER THIRTY

'I have the best news!' Elsie burst in, delightedly flapping a newspaper at me. It was a few days after my ride out with Harold. Elsie and I had been working hard and there was a semblance of peace between us.

'Shackleton is alive!'

For months, Shackleton and his crew had been missing in Antarctica, surviving on lumps of sugar, dog food and the English stiff upper lip.

'Most of his crew made it too. What a man!'

His unexpected survival represented something magical to Elsie. Perhaps she saw us all as lost explorers and this was a sign of hope. Anyway, we so rarely had good news, we would take any there was. We danced around in excitement. Elsie broke into song, then pulled away from me. 'I am so pleased!' Darting about the cellar, she reminded me of the old Elsie, the Elsie before the engagement, when she was mine.

'When all this is over, shall we go to the South Pole, Mairi?'

What about Harold? I wondered.

I didn't say that, of course. I remembered Ecclesiastes suddenly.

'A time to kill and a time to heal;
A time to tear down and a time to build up.
A time to weep and a time to laugh.'

This was a time to laugh.

'Hmm, can you promise me penguins?'

'Yes, little piggy,' she said, hugging me again. 'Whatever your heart desires.' She read the article once more, looking closely at the perilous route Shackleton and his men had charted, going over their suffering and their deprivations. I swear, there were tears in her eyes.

It may have only been September, but I was already working on my Christmas presents. For Shot, I was threading a pretty collar. It was time we let the world know that this was no commonplace stray, but a dog who belonged: a dog with not one but two mistresses. And for Elsie, two gifts: firstly I was secretly training Shot to lift a paw for thank you. Elsie had seen a dog do it once. I thought Shot could be taught it, but Elsie didn't believe me. I was right though – Shot was picking it up, if slowly. He would surely master it by Christmas and I had no doubts that Elsie – with her love of all entertainment – would adore it.

Her second gift was a new pocket watch. Elsie did not usually crave material things but I had seen her admire the watch of a staff nurse at Furnes. I hoped to get her an engraved one. Unfortunately you had to pay by the letter (I'd already enquired), so I was looking for something with brevity but gravitas. *Sisters*, maybe? Seven letters was affordable. For Harold, I was considering a lighter. It seemed appropriate for the man who had brightened our time out here.

Elsie and I didn't talk about what had happened at the engineers' house but she hadn't gone back. I decided to put the memory of that night in the box of 'grief makes you behave in crazy ways'. When I had seen Robin, he was subdued with me yet overly affectionate with Shot. Shot didn't hold a grudge, and I remembered how Dr Munro had treated us with compassion even when he disagreed with us – *especially* when he disagreed with us.

I prayed a lot. I knew God would probably be too occupied to hear my humble prayers but I felt my heart lighten when I thought of the grand plan he had for us all.

I cleaned the cellar and the ambulance. Elsie went picking turnips in a newly discovered field. She promised to watch out for unexploded shells. We had turnip salad for lunch. She drove two cases of VD and one of shell shock to Furnes. A man was brought in from the trenches and I bandaged his arm and accompanied him back. Shot practised his raised paw trick and was rewarded with some spam for his efforts.

We had turnip salad for dinner.

That evening, while Elsie slept fitfully on the straw, I finally replied to Jack. I wrote my longest letter to him yet, signing it '*from the future Mrs Petrie*'. *Mairi Petrie*, I thought to myself. *Mrs.* For the first time, I told Jack that I loved him. It was my first time telling *anyone* that, although once done, I realised it was not as difficult as I had anticipated. I found myself thanking the Lord that Jack was in England. I couldn't bear it if he were out here. In my prayers, I even dared call him *my* Jack.

And I wrote that although we must one day go to Saunton Sands – the picture on the jigsaw – I had always dreamed of marrying in the Highlands, if that wasn't too much to ask, and, if he'd still have me, of course?

My father would be in his kilt, my mother would cry into his handkerchief and Uilleam would tease us. The thought made me smile. I had an inkling Jack and Uilleam might get on. They both had something of the outsider about them.

Our children might not inherit my freckles or Jack's ears. These things often skip a generation. You never know, they might actually look like my mother (I wasn't sure if that was good or bad). I wrote that things between Elsie and me had been strained these past few months, but all was resolved now. I paused, played with my pen, then wrote honestly.

I have accepted some things, and maybe so has she.

It was surprisingly easy to be honest with Jack. My flaws felt safe with him and I knew I *had* to be honest, otherwise what chance did we have?

As I thought of what else I could tell him, I realised that I hadn't thought about Harold for an entire three days. I smiled; I had only gone and spoiled it by thinking about him then, but still. This was progress. Elsie and Harold deserved to be happy. I wondered how Elsie's first husband had proposed and I felt, once again, what a huge thing it was for Elsie to have lost him overseas, with a young child. I should remember that, be more compassionate. After all, I had been blessed and hadn't lost anyone close to me.

It was a time to mourn and a time to dance.

I wrote that *it was a time to embrace.*

I wondered if Jack might get the wrong idea. I doubted he had read Ecclesiastes; he was only a quarter-way through *Das Kapital*. He was no Arthur. Even so, I was too tired to write the letter over again, or even to explain the reference, so I kept it in. Besides, when we married Jack and I *would* have to embrace. In the dark, I was confident, his ears mightn't look so red.

Jack with his strong arms and grainy hard-working hands. I remembered the way he'd stayed to volunteer to stack chairs too high. The way he spoke to ignorant old ladies with that quiver in his voice. The way he was passionate about his men. The way he could talk about aeroplanes how I could talk about motorcycles. The way he dared to dream again.

Jack knew me. He knew what I saw. He understood how you could grow to hate Maconochi*e and* corned beef. I would never need to be anything but my authentic self with him. Jack, *my Jack.*

We *would* be good together.

CHAPTER THIRTY-ONE

The following morning, before I had time to tell my news to Elsie, the post-boy came shooting over. He was wearing flowers in his hair. I hoped he was not being bullied by the boys in the trenches, but he seemed perky enough. He had brought a package. At first I thought it was another jigsaw from Jack but he hopped excitedly, unaware of how ludicrous he looked, saying, 'America, America! Not telling!'

I hesitantly took the parcel. As I opened the note, I was racking my brains over who might have sent me something from America. It said:

Dearest Mairi,

I hope this finds you and Elsie well.

Arthur is living back home with his parents; I am in New York with mine. Things have been difficult between us, but I am optimistic that in the future, we may be able to put the past behind us.

So here is the book – you and Elsie were, as you will see, such a special inspiration.

From your ever-loving American friend,

Helen

(Please excuse the pseudonym – I couldn't risk the notoriety!)

Helen had only gone and written it! Hastily, I pulled at the strings and unwrapped the paper. The book was called *Young Elizabeth at the Wars!* by Eleanora Mountford, which was unexpected. Helen had never told me a title but I didn't think it would be that. I thought

Eleanora Mountford sounded glamorous and quite unlike Helen, which was probably the point.

Down in the cellar, I devoured her book. Shot was snuggled under one of my arms, pressed to my chin; he didn't mind when I turned the pages. Helen wrote how she spoke. It was like listening to her tell a story back at Furnes at Christmas. I could imagine her owl eyes flickering over the pages, picture her pushing back her glasses, glancing at Arthur. *How much will be exaggerated?* I wondered as I hared through the first chapter. *How much will be true?* Shot's breathing slowed and he fell asleep.

I got up to page 54 before I had to set the book down in shock. *No. It couldn't be. She couldn't have.*

And then I picked it up again. It was irresistible. I was shaking like a leaf; it was as though the book was too dangerous to hold but I had to read on. My hands were trembling like I had shell shock. Page 55, page 56… The day disappeared as I lost myself in Helen's words. I couldn't believe it.

'What *are* you doing there?' Elsie surprised me later that afternoon. I was hidden in the straw and blankets. This wasn't a time for relaxing, but the book had pulled me away from chores. 'What are you hiding?'

'Nothing.'

'Not chocolate, surely, you wouldn't keep that from me?'

'I'm not—'

'Penguins?' Elsie made a teasing grab for me but I tucked the book beneath me so she couldn't get to it. Shot woke up and looked around, befuddled.

'Oh, I know!'

'What?'

'It's more love letters!'

'No!'

'Why are you such a cold fish?' *That was rich! Coming from her!*

'I'm not!'

Suddenly, Elsie lunged on top of me – she had the advantage of surprise, and other advantages beside – and we struggled. The full weight of her was on me. I felt buried by her. I kicked out with my untrapped leg, sure that it must hurt, but she carried on pinning me down. I was strong but she was taller and more powerful than I was and I didn't stand a chance. She undid my fingers, grinning at me, her white teeth flashing. I felt weaker than I'd ever been. Shot began whining piteously. He didn't know what to make of us. When Elsie finally had the book in her hands, she examined it incredulously.

'It's a book?'

'It's *Helen's* book,' I said, defeated.

'Helen's?' she repeated slowly. I could almost see the information sink in. 'Helen from America? Eleanora Mountford?'

'She used a pretend name,' I added. I felt hot and damp. Adrenaline released, then retreated. Elsie looked at her prize. I don't know what she had been expecting. Her face fell.

'What a *ghastly* title.'

'It's not so bad.' I picked the straw out of my hair.

'Who would have thought Helen to be so… lowbrow?'

I felt hurt on Helen's behalf – and mine – for I had been more than captivated by it. Anyway, it wasn't *dear Helen* who was lowbrow, that was clear. I pulled myself upright, trying to think how to phrase what I wanted to say.

'The review says it's a triumph. A "tour de force".'

'Whose review?'

'Um…' I looked at the blurb. 'The *New York Times*.'

Elsie looked at me as if to say, 'You idiot'. I flushed. Arthur's paper.

'Oh. Yes. Anyway, I thought it was… fun.'

'It looks *utterly* unbelievable. Still, romantic fantasy is *opium*.' She said the word lightly, as though she had never come across the stuff, 'for the people. Keeps them quiet.'

Elsie picked up her coat and started up the stairs.

I could contain myself no longer. I got to my feet angrily. 'It seems Helen based one of her characters on you!'

Elsie laughed hollowly.

I opened the book and read, my voice shaking:

The group stared into the night sky. 'I see the Plough, and the Square of Pegasus.'
She swooned. 'What could it all mean?
Mrs Elizabeth Blackall was the first of the group to come down with 'khaki fever'.

'Elizabeth Blackall?' Elsie whispered.

'That's your maiden name.'

Elsie stood stock-still. I had got her.

Elizabeth Blackall was an experienced woman, who, despite having a young son, paid only scant attention to the moral codes of the time.

'Helen always displayed a rather pitiful lack of imagination.' I fought to get my voice steady.

However, Mrs Elizabeth Blackall had a terrible secret—

Elsie's foot was still frozen on the fourth step. Not fleeing, not fighting now.

And her terrible secret was this. Elizabeth Blackall pretended she was a widow, when in fact she was a divorcee! How would the young soldier, a man of impeccable and distinguished background, who had fallen passionately in love with her, feel about that?

'Helen actually wrote that?' Elsie paused. 'Balderdash, like the whole book. Like her war effort, in fact. She didn't even cut her hair.'

'Your husband *didn't* have a funeral, did he, Elsie, or should I say, *Elizabeth*?' I continued doggedly.

'I have called myself Elsie since I was six years old,' she snapped.

'What about your husband?'

'I have no idea what he called himself—'

She was infuriating. 'There never *was* a funeral, was there?'

'And?' Elsie was half-sneering, half-smiling.

Everything I had ever been angry about was right here, right now. 'There was no funeral because he is not dead!'

'Mairi, just… why are you so interested in this?'

'Because.… you deceived me. About something significant.'

'It's not significant.'

'It is.'

'After all we've done… to dwell on trivialities such as this is madness.'

'Trivialities?' I echoed, my voice raised. 'You've been *lying* about yourself all along.'

'I have never lied, not directly.' Elsie was enraged. She huffed and puffed. *My goodness, you are not a piggy, you're actually a lying, greedy wolf,* I thought wildly.

She was an excellent actress though, one of the best. She deserved awards.

'You lied to me!' I persisted. 'When I have been nothing but honest.'

'I don't understand why you are so.… *affected* by this.'

'If we don't hold on to ourselves and be true to each other, what do we have? It is more important than ever to be decent and good human beings. Otherwise, this rotten war wins.'

'I *have* been decent. I *have* been good.'

Elsie's indignation was absolute. But mine was equal to hers. I was not her silly little sister any more. I was not the sidekick, not the crust. And I still had principles.

'You are a *divorced* woman. Not widowed. Divorced. It's all been a performance.'

Elsie stood close to me, staring me angrily in the face. I remembered the time she shouted and even punched me, when Shot had run off. I remembered her demanding I left a dying boy.

'Believing our press would be a mistake, Mairi. I'm not an angel. I'm not a Madonna.'

'I never thought you were—'

She continued as though she hadn't heard. 'I'm not a hero. I'm one of the hardest-working nurses on the Western Front. Doing my best in this place where God has forsaken us.'

'Don't say that!' I covered my ears. Shot started barking at my distress. I grabbed him and cuddled him. I couldn't bear for him to hear this.

'Godforsaken place. *Godforsaken place!* Yes it is. Oh Mairi, I'm only human. Simple. Hot-blooded.' She spat the words out. 'I have ego, I like money AND hanky-panky.'

Elsie didn't get it and she never would.

Defeatedly, I asked her, 'Why didn't you tell me the truth?'

'Do you think it is easy to go against the grain? Do you think I *wanted* to split from the father of my child?'

'Best friends don't lie. Sisters don't lie. Good people don't lie. His death was "slow, slow, quick" – you said that to my face. You said, "He waited until I was out of the room to die."'

'Because, I knew you'd react like this—'

'Because you weren't *honest.* After I was so honest with you… You know all my secrets. Every one of them. There is nothing about me that you do not know. Yet, you didn't trust me. I was your *sister.*'

'You *are* my sister.'

'You *were* my sister. But you would not let me be yours.'

The whistles were blowing again. We put aside our argument and ran with our stretcher, ran as bullets ricocheted around us. We had to crouch down low for this one. He was a gunner and he'd been shelled. He was over forty, I reckon. It wasn't only the young fellas who lied about their age to fight. It looked worse than it was for once. We bandaged him up. Gave him pain relief, got him on the stretcher as though he was as light as a feather.

'Let me die,' he said. 'Don't want to frighten my kids.'

'How many little 'uns do you have?' Elsie asked.

'Four.'

'Four?!' Elsie teased him, 'No wireless, eh!' Then more seriously, 'Picture their little faces.'

Tears ran down his cheeks. 'I can't.'

'You can.'

We began to tear back.

'We'll have you cuddled up by the stove in less than two minutes,' Elsie told him. 'Blankets, morphine… Hang on. They'll be wanting their daddy.'

She gazed over the length of his bloodied uniform.

'I know why you're so het up, Mairi. It's because you want Harold.'

'It is not.'

'It is.'

I felt exasperated. Anger at how she lied to me was one thing. This was something else. 'Elsie, you need to tell Harold. As a Catholic, as a believer, in his eyes, you will still be married.'

'He has to *see* it for it to be in his eyes.'

I almost dropped the stretcher and the poor man on it in my horror. 'Elsie! For goodness' sake, you *must* tell Harold the truth!'

We had reached the cellar. I opened up the trapdoor, and down the steps we slid. We were efficient – hadn't we done this hundreds of times?

'Do you know how many women divorced in 1910, Mairi? Fewer than twenty. Do you know how scandalous it was and still is? The shame we are made to feel? No one understands.'

'He might.'

'He *won't*. I *know* Hal' – she meant, *I know him better than you* – 'and he won't.'

The gunner looked between us incredulously. He was less frightened now. He coughed and muttered, 'Don't mind me, ladies.'

Elsie was a fraud. Worse than a fraud. All those stories – that night in the hotel, on the SS *Princess Clementine*, to the English doctors, even at the bloody Glasgow Assembly Rooms – weren't true. She had been divorced. Not widowed. Elsie had deliberately lied to me, over and over again. Without any shame.

She mustn't do it to Harold.

*

Late the next morning there was a loud knock at the cellar door. Shot yelped in surprise. Elsie and I were both napping in the straw. At sunrise, Elsie had silently driven the gunner to Furnes while I sat with him in the back. Then we'd done a trench-run. Although we saw the soldiers together, we hadn't exchanged a word. I didn't want to. I couldn't imagine confiding in her ever again.

I wasn't expecting any callers and nor, from her expression, was Elsie.

I thought, *Don't let it be Harold*. I didn't see how I could ever face him.

Elsie got up, threw on her coat and swung open the door.

'Beautiful door, ladies. Harrods, is it?'

This wasn't Harold.

'Who *are* you?' Elsie snapped.

'Here for the story. *Evening Standard*. London.'

Elsie looked weary, but she wouldn't say no to a reporter. Newspapers were fame. Fame meant money, money meant we could look after the sick.

She looked at me as though asking, *Did you know about this*? I shrugged back. I couldn't remember if this one was in the logbook or not. Frankly, I didn't care.

The journalist looked well fed. I hadn't seen someone as plump as him for a while. I had a sudden understanding of those tribal peoples who eat their visitors. And we call *them* the savages!

He pulled at his woollen waistcoat. A waistcoat! What sort of man wears a waistcoat to visit the trenches? Then rummaged through his bag for a pencil.

'This *is* where inquisitions take place, right, Mairi? The Belgian inquisition!' Elsie laughed to herself.

I wished Elsie could see it from my point of view, just once. I wished she could have been the friend, *the sister*, she had promised she would be. What had Dr Munro said about mothers disappointing? Did he mean it about sisters too?

We told him to wait and we gathered ourselves quickly in the gloom. I splashed my face with water, took a comb to my short useless hair, then called him back in. Elsie lit a cigarette.

'Ready, now, ladies. Do you get lonely out here?'

It was going to be *that* kind of interview.

'Fifty yards away, you can see the might of the Western industrial complex. Belgians, British, French and even some of the German boys are perfectly friendly when you take them a hot chocolate.'

The journalist wasn't sure if Elsie was telling the truth or not. He stared at her, his flabby mouth open, drool on his lips. His pencil did not touch the paper.

'Only two days ago, I held a nineteen-year-old in my arms as he cried about the cricket runs he will never score and the girls he will never get to kiss. So, you see, this place is the opposite of lonely.'

At that, the journalist started writing fast. You wouldn't believe this slug-like fellow could do *anything* fast and yet he did it. Strange squiggles like hieroglyphics appeared on the paper. Finally, he looked up again. I counted three, no four, chins.

'Fantastic. Everyone wants to know about your love lives, ladies, so can I ask, is there any romance in Pervyse?'

Neither of us spoke.

Finally, Elsie said in her huskiest voice, 'We may as well let people back home know. I *am* engaged. To a Belgian. A baron actually. From a wonderful family.'

Sometimes, Elsie could sound like a frightful snob. I couldn't tell if she was teasing or not.

'A baron?' Of course, this slug of a journalist would be impressed.

'Related to the Queen. Of Belgium,' Elsie added.

'Was he a patient of yours, Elsie?' he asked gleefully, scribbling like a man possessed.

'Yes, he was.' She looked at me coldly, then added needlessly, 'Leg wound.'

The journalist scrawled his strange stick figures, then finally fixed his privileged piggy eyes on me.

'How about you, Mairi? No one caught your fancy?'

I hesitated. Elsie looked away, a sneer on her lips.

'I too am engaged.'

'Was he a patient as well?'

'No.' I felt I had to say something more. 'He is a pilot… in England.'

Elsie looked at me incredulously. 'Congratulations, Mairi. It seems *you* are capable of surprises too.'

'Surprises and secrets are a very different species,' I retorted.

I knew Elsie thought my anger was disproportionate, but the idea that she would continue in her own sweet way, making a mockery of all around her, made me furious.

The journalist gazed at us, pencil poised for further information, then when he realised none was forthcoming, he put it back in his bag. He thanked us and left.

'You never even went to Java, did you?'

The journalist was still eavesdropping from the top of the stairs. Elsie dismissed him, calling: 'Don't you have everything you need?'

Then she stood up, scratched her head vigorously and followed him out.

*

After years of working and living together, our peace was broken. I hadn't known it was so fragile and I didn't see it coming.

The *Evening Standard* ran a fantastic spread on us: HANDBAGS FOR SANDBAGS! was on the front page, followed by 'EXCLUSIVE! *Read all about the engagements of the Madonnas! Pages 4 and 5.'* There was a close-up of Elsie looking marvellous wearing a helmet and a photo of me looking, well, like I always look. Page six was devoted to '*Shot, Probably the Bravest Mutt in Belgium*'. There was a charming photo of him sat upright, waiting for attention.

I didn't have the heart to read it all because not long after the newspapers arrived that morning, a telegram came. Jack had been killed in a tragic aeroplane incident. Heroically (of course) and doing what he loved best.

I told myself maybe they'd got the wrong man. Yes, that was it. Wasn't it possible that someone else might be wearing Jack's uniform, Jack's boots? Wasn't it possible that Jack had lent his clothes – or worse, had them stolen? And the real Jack, *my Jack*, was desperately trying to let me know he was safe. Or maybe my Jack hadn't even heard about the dead clothes-thief… and was carrying on as normal, inventing tired jokes about the Kaiser and the Tsar, making scant progress reading the *Communist Manifesto* and swooning over new plane designs? I couldn't contact his family in Ingatestone to clarify – *would they want to hear from me anyway*? Did they even know anything about his sweetheart in a cellar house in Belgium? Did they know that he had asked for my hand in marriage and that eventually, I had agreed?

The truth was, I was utterly shocked. I had seen so many men in their prime taken down, obliterated, yet I hadn't seen this coming. I thought that so long as he was in England, Jack would be safe. I should have known 'safe' had been wiped out like the rest of the good words in the world: honesty, truth, respect.

On my knees in the straw, I prayed all evening. When Elsie came back, she gave me tea and attempted to hug me but I shrugged her off. She wanted to talk but I had nothing to say. I would take nothing from her ever again. She had not given me the one thing

I deserved: the truth. I carried on praying throughout the night. Eventually, Elsie stopped trying and climbed into the straw and fell into a typically disturbed sleep.

By morning, as the guns and the shelling started up again on the Western Front, I surrendered once again to my faith. I knew with a great and unfamiliar certainty that Jack had been spared from suffering, and that his suffering – my suffering – was nothing to the suffering of our Lord. Maybe Jack and I would meet again? Our bond of suffering was deep, I knew that.

God was the one thing I had left. The one thing that had never gone away. And I knew beyond all doubt or reason that He was good and He loved me. And this was why I bothered.

> *God grant me the serenity*
> *To accept the things I cannot change;*
> *Courage to change the things I can;*
> *And wisdom to know the difference.*

*

One week after, almost three years to the day since we arrived in Belgium, there was a bombing raid that left the cellar with more holes than a colander. The Harrods door that we were so proud of remained beautifully intact, but almost everything else came down: half the ceiling, the banister, even the commode.

While we were regrouping and rebuilding the cellar – bricks had been ordered, sandbags were on their way – the Germans didn't break through the line, but they did manage to launch a gas attack. It seemed they still believed they would win this.

I remember Shot's desperate barking that night, how I had dismissed it – 'Quiet, Shot, naughty boy!' I remember everyone waking and the spread of the sleepy, contaminated panic.

I remember the arrival of the green stench – airborne, the uninvited guest. I staggered upright, slammed against the side, then fell bang, slap, wallop, delirious on the low table. I could hear the terrible crunch of my own bones as I fell face-first onto my jigsaw. Goodness only knows where my hands were, but they didn't save my fall.

This is bad. Don't go down, less chance of making it. Gas is heavier, get up, get up, get up! Where's Shot? Where's Elsie? Where is everyone?

I'll never know how Elsie got us up those steep stairs and out. Some people described it as a miracle.

Sick herself, she managed to drag us to the ambulance, then to hurl us in the back. I came to lying down inside, gulping, desperately struggling to breathe, my throat on fire, blood from the fall all over my face and clothes. Suddenly, I was sitting up and looking around, not sure where I was. The roar of the ambulance was incredible and I could feel every bump, every shell hole, in the road. I opened one eye and there was Martin opposite, mask still on, vomit on his shirt, clutching a fur hat on his lap. No, it wasn't a fur hat, it was Shot draped across his thighs. Unlike Martin, Shot looked fine.

'Shot,' I whispered, but the dog didn't flicker.

'No,' I said. 'NO!'

Martin couldn't even look at me.

By one of those wartime coincidences that don't seem to happen half so often in peacetime, Dr Munro had that very moment turned up for duty at Furnes and, according to Elsie, he hauled us out the ambulance 'so fast our feet never touched the ground'. Credit also to the nurses and doctors who saw to us as quickly as they could.

But it was Elsie who had saved my life. Of course it was.

CHAPTER THIRTY-TWO

I was put in a small sunlit room with two English boys. The nurses apologised that I was in with men but they had never had a female patient before. They said that if I insisted they might find me my own room, but these young fellas were miles from their homes and their families… If I stayed here, not only would it be better for me (that was questionable!), it would be helpful for them.

That swung it, of course.

I asked a nurse what was wrong with me. She examined the chart at the end of my bed.

'Broken ribs and a sprained ankle. Gas. And nervous exhaustion.'

'I'm not nervous or exhausted,' I argued.

'Well then, just the other stuff.' She shrugged.

At first, blisters in my throat and weakened lungs made it difficult to breathe, but I had escaped without any real damage. Humiliatingly enough, it was my stupid fall that had done the most injury, landing on our table face-first. My nose was also broken, my eyes were black, my cheek was yellow and purple. I felt as though my face was ruined, yet if Elsie hadn't been there, I would have been exposed to the gas for so much longer – and my bloodied and bruised face wouldn't have seen daylight again.

My Bible had been lost, but one of the nurses hunted out a New Testament for me. I believed, like Harold's, it may have been another of those that my mother's circle had so optimistically circulated. There were tiny holes in its cover, made by a needle or a protractor perhaps. Certain sections had been underlined, which was a distraction. I tried to ignore it, but somehow my predecessor's choice of passages always drew me in. My predecessor was interested in Mary Magdalene.

It was strange to be back here where I had been a nurse three years before. It would have been better if Lady D was still nursing here – but she was hard at work in the mud-hell of Passchendaele. I never could bring myself to ask Dr Munro about her.

To my right was a boy so injured that virtually his entire body had been bandaged up. They gave him drinks through a tiny horizontal gap in his wrappings. He didn't speak and no one knew his name. He was in terrible pain and couldn't sleep: every time he finally nodded off, they woke him to administer more painkillers.

'He's so stoic,' everyone said, or 'Look what he endures!'

It felt like they were telling me to shut up. *You think you've got problems, Mairi!*

One of the nurses, Clara, read to him from the book he had when he was brought in. Clara was from the West Country. She had spent only six months in Furnes – she was just a newborn in war terms. She came out after she got the telegram that her fiancé, Patrick, had been killed in Gallipoli. 'What was the point of staying at home?' she asked philosophically. 'I wanted to find out what war was like.'

I didn't ask her what she had found. She had a pretty accent, so whenever she read, I would listen to her too.

To the other side of me was Edward, or 'poor Edward', as the nurses called him. He was in fine physical condition; you probably couldn't imagine a stronger, more classically masculine specimen than him. If the boy on my right was like a mummy in the British Museum, then poor Edward was like a statue by an Italian master. Six foot tall, with a well-developed jaw, healthy blond hair and a very long golden beard.

Before I arrived, apparently one nurse had tried to shave poor Edward but he went wild at her, so they let him grow his beard even though they were uncomfortable with it. He mostly roamed around in baggy pyjama bottoms. He didn't wear a top, so you were confronted with that fine, rippled chest all day long. Mentally, Edward was in a terrible place. He was in the foetal position when I woke and he was in the foetal position when I went to sleep. 'Clitter-clatter,' he often repeated, 'clitter-clatter.' It took me a while to work out what that reminded me of: the sound of toy soldiers falling in a tin box. He made a biting motion, like a rabid dog. It put everyone off him. He didn't respond well to Munro, Clara or the other bustling nurses – especially the one who came at him with the razor. Fortunately, he mostly ignored me.

For most of the day, he scampered around the room, cowered in the corner or darted to the window to try to break out. The nurses said he was making a nuisance of himself, and he was.

Meanwhile Clara read *The Jungle Book* to the bandaged boy:

> *For the strength of the Pack is the Wolf, and the strength of the Wolf is the Pack… The reason the beasts live among themselves is that Man is the weakest and most defenceless of all living things, and it is unsportsmanlike to touch him.*

Clara looked over to me. I was pleased she had stopped wincing at the sight of me. I wasn't sure if it was my bruises healing or if she'd got used to my appearance.

'I'll have finished it by the weekend at this rate. Do you have anything I could read to him?'

'This?'

I waved my Bible at her. Clara wrinkled up her pert nose.

'I don't think he'll like that.'

I felt pathetically offended. 'How do you know he likes that one then?'

'His bandages move so I think he's smiling, and sometimes, tears come out here,' she pointed to the corners of her eyes, then added haughtily. 'It's *his* book anyway. Why wouldn't he like it?'

Feeling foolish, I wanted to make amends. 'I like listening to it too.'

'It's the best thing I've ever read!' Clara said enthusiastically. She was still enthusiastic about everything though, so it meant less from her than if it had come from a more cynical person. 'A real escape.'

In the hospital, days crept past abominably slowly. If they didn't let me back to Pervyse, I decided, I would go to the Caribbean. Yes, it was hard to cross the Atlantic since the sinking of the *Lusitania*, but I could do it. Look at the things I had survived! Oceans were nothing to a girl who had been gassed.

Uilleam and I would reunite on a beach, hot sand under the soles of our feet. A hammock between two trees. A coconut drink.

I found it hard to believe that Uilleam could be a genuine *homosexual*. And in any case, why shouldn't he marry the girlfriend anyway? Uilleam was from a good family: he could be a little *undisciplined*, but he was a darling, everyone knew that.

Now that Jack was gone, I had decided that I was not meant to become a parent in this life, but there was no reason I couldn't be a special aunty. Imagine Uilleam having a baby! A tiny baby I would carry about and let rest on my stomach in the sun. I would feed it little lumps of our family sugar.

I didn't need to become a parent anyway, because I had my Madeleine. Madeleine, such a good-natured, sunny girl; she wouldn't be jealous of my niece or nephew, and she would visit us in the Carribean when she was old enough. An international education for her – I would show her the world. I pictured Madeleine's father and mother proudly waving her off from Ostend. Of course they would trust me after I had fought for their house. Madeleine would arrive, wearing one of those sailor dresses she liked so much. Hair neat but not prissy in a plait. Knee-high socks. 'How did you grow so tall?' I would ask. And 'Where did those freckles come from?' All those ludicrous phrases that kindly aunts come out with. We would take care of Uilleam's baby together, and I would teach Madeleine everything I had ever learned.

She would be a kind of daughter to me.

Once Elsie had been a kind of sister.

Shot was buried outside. Shot, who gave up his life so we could live, suffered no more. They did it pretty much as soon as they reached the hospital. I was too ill, and so was Paul, but Elsie and Martin gave him a good send-off. I promised myself that when I was better, I'd pay my respects to our lovely boy.

*

They'd put the window pole under the bandaged boy's bed (an ill-thought-out hiding place) and it had caught Edward's ever-roving eye. He grabbed it and swung it around the room like he was in a jousting tournament. Clara ran away or for help, I couldn't be sure, leaving just me and the bandaged boy behind.

'Edward,' I warned. 'Enough is enough.'

He advanced. I could picture the pole clattering down on my head, splitting it open (I have seen a head split in two several times before).

'Put it down.'

He started jabbing it towards me like it was a bayonet and I was a German. He shoved it until it was only five inches or so from my stomach. He pointed it directly at me, taunting me; we were like children, trying to make each other blink.

'I don't want it,' I said.

I just felt so tired with it all. I didn't care about anything, so I just pushed that stupid pole away, turned my back to it and sat heavily on my bed. I began to cry. Proper gulping, snotty tears. He stared at me for a moment, twisting the pole uselessly. Then he walked over and stood over me, before dropping the pole on the floor. It made a terrific boom. He sat on my bed next to me.

I put out my hand and his fingers locked onto mine. 'Clitter-clatter, clitter-clatter,' he repeated.

I began to sing softly.

> *I'm Gilbert the Filbert the Knut with a K,*
> *The pride of Piccadilly the blasé roué,*
> *Oh Hades, the ladies, who leave their wooden huts,*
> *For Gilbert the Filbert the Colonel of the Knuts.*

Poor Edward curled up on my bed next to me and I stroked his hair, like I had stroked the hair of so many boys. Not long after that, both he and I were asleep.

*

After that day, Edward tried constantly to get in my bed. He liked to grip my thumb. He liked me to sing to him (*so there, Father.* I didn't have such a bad voice after all).

Dr Munro asked, 'Does he bother you?' and 'Do you want me to do something about him?' but I said it was all right. Dr Munro said Edward had the 'two-thousand-yard stare', which meant he looked at everything but didn't see anything. Dr Munro said he was getting more cases like him but who could be surprised?

He was trying to get the long-term boys to try meditation or yoga stretches but they were never able to focus long enough on anything to do that.

'When he feels better, I'll get him to do some basket-weaving upstairs,' he said, as though basket-weaving would make any difference.

I let Edward cuddle up to me in the day, but thought it best to persuade him back to his own bed at night. He would only stay there if we could stretch out and touch palms. I thought of the hands in

Michelangelo's *Creation of Adam*. Was this something the Italian painter could ever have envisaged?

'Clitter-clatter.'

I prayed for poor Edward to recover, for the unnamed bandaged boy to get better and I thanked God that Jack was dead and didn't have to suffer like these two.

Edward went to sleep in his own bed, but somehow, silent as gas, in the early hours of the morning I would wake to find he had moved across into mine.

The autumn moon was visible from my bed, the same moon Helen had admired as she wrote her stories. The moon that was the last thing the boys in the trenches saw. And when I saw the moon, I was reminded once again of God – he was here, this was his presence. We needed to remember him and draw back into his arms. He could save us – if we only would follow his designated path, we would find peace and love and comfort.

That wasn't so difficult, was it?

One morning, about three weeks after we'd arrived, I woke up with Edward in my bed, and even though my eyes were still closed, I realised someone else was in the room.

'Morning, Clara,' I muttered, half asleep.

But it wasn't Clara, it was Elsie. She was sitting at my bedside, looking grave.

She had a new satchel on her knees. I just knew it must have been a present, for it was Harold's taste not hers.

'Are you awake, Mairi?'

Too late to pretend.

'Umm, just.'

'Good.'

I sat up. Edward snoozed on, Adonis on the pillow.

Elsie's face was contorted with concern. 'And who's your… friend?'

'Um, Edward.'

'Good-looking fella…' she said awkwardly, but just then poor Edward jumped up and started his biting and his gibberish, swiftly disabusing Elsie of any notion of a love story. Elsie's expression lightened. It seemed odd that she would be worried about *me* fraternising with men, but there we were. It had occurred to me lately that all this talk of her Gilberts had disguised the fact that *she* was the world-weary Gilbert, the one for whom nothing was important any more.

'You're looking better.'

'Really?' I didn't believe her.

'Mm. You had me worried back there.'

'Did I?'

'Yes, when you went crashing down. Oh, I didn't worry for long. I know my pig-headed Mairi is a trooper.'

I nodded at her.

'Cool as a cucumber, eh?'

It was like our argument had never happened. Perhaps this was how you made peace. You swallowed down all the hurt. But I wasn't sure I could do it. She said she had been staying with the engineers, just for the duration. And she wasn't sure what was going to happen next.

'Have *you* no ill-effects, Elsie?'

'I still have the nightmare of all headaches,' Elsie admitted. She poured me some water from the jug.

Edward embraced me then. It's silly, but I was proud that he liked me more than anyone else. He gazed at Elsie like she was an animal in London Zoo.

'He's English?'

'Yes.'

'Do you want a smoke?' Elsie asked him. I was surprised when he nodded keenly, cliter-clattered and bit and then smiled at her. I should have known by then that Mrs Knocker was irresistible to the male of the species. Even the mad ones. I suppose I should have rejoiced that she never got to get her claws into Jack.

Elsie gave Edward a cigarette, then threw him her pocket lighter. He was a surprisingly deft catch. I bet he was a cricketer once, back in the day. He had the right frame for bowling. I imagine he spent long Sunday afternoons on the green.

'What times are these,' Elsie said, which reminded me with a jolt of Harold. 'What times we are living through.' She nodded at Edward. 'Where's he from?'

'England. I told you.'

She sighed. 'Where *exactly*?'

'Oh. They say Home Counties.'

The bandaged boy on the next bed made whimpering noises as though disagreeing with me on Home Counties. *Was he perhaps from somewhere else? Had anyone ever asked?*

There was a creeping smell of burning. Smoke. Flames.

Edward had set his beard on fire.

Elsie leapt up and threw water from the jug over him. He stood there, furiously howling at us like a werewolf. Clara and Dr Munro raced in at the noise, and stood in the doorway looking at us, open-mouthed.

'Well…' Elsie said, pragmatic as ever and dusting herself down. 'My fault. I should have anticipated that.'

That night, I fell asleep thinking of the fruit Madeleine and I would eat with Uilleam in the Caribbean. Pineapples as big as pigs' heads. Melons and coconuts from silver platters. We would picnic by the sea and watch the men on the fishing boats draw in their nets. And perhaps, one day, we would get ourselves a dog, a dog like Shot, a real-life dog. For what young girl doesn't love a dog? We could call him Shot Two. No, we would call him whatever Madeleine wanted him to be called. That would be the kindest thing to do.

CHAPTER THIRTY-THREE

Dr Munro told me he'd done a bit of digging about what had happened to Uilleam.

'Well, they don't think he's dead.'

'Thank goodness.'

'But…' – he paused, then without lowering his voice said – 'he *is* a homosexual.'

Looking around the room, I decided neither the bandaged boy nor poor Edward would likely care too much about my brother's predilections.

'That is one explanation,' I replied neutrally.

Dr Munro looked sympathetically at me. 'They are even less enlightened on the subject in the Caribbean than they are here. Which is saying something. And of course, he seems to have got involved with the wrong people out there, which has ruffled a few feathers.'

Dr Munro continued, 'If he's got any sense, he will have gone to America.'

'America?' I was shocked.

'He could have taken a boat, wouldn't take long, even with little money.'

I imagined my brother jumping onto boats and trains, sneaking rides, living like an outlaw. *Was America where he was? Was that where he wanted to be?*

'He might be freer there.'

'I suppose.'

'I'm sorry I don't have any more encouraging news to tell you,' said Dr Munro.

'It's all right,' I said. 'I understand.' Although I didn't. I just wanted to see my brother again.

He would always be sixteen years old to my fourteen. In my mind we would always be racing our bikes, sailing down the open road, stretching ahead, like our bright futures. I could beat him in an arm-wrestle. He could beat me at draughts. He once made me a tiny chain of daisies. Even after the flowers themselves died, their stems clung together for days on my wrist.

*

Elsie came back exactly one week after her first visit. It was October 1917. I imagined her fitting me into her busy schedule.

'You're looking better!'

'You said that last time,' I pointed out.

'Well, it must have been true then, too,' she said.

I laughed bitterly.

She had brought me an apple that had come all the way from Hampshire: fat and round, shaped like a pair of buttocks and with shiny glowing skin. It was far too beautiful to eat.

'Special delivery for the bravest girl in town,' she said.

She expected me to be grateful. And I was. But I hated being grateful to her because I didn't like her any more. She wasn't who I thought she was. She had inveigled her way into my heart with untruths. I might have forgiven her for her divorce if she hadn't lied to me about it over and over again.

Edward was jumping about being his usual nuisance. His latest thing was to leap across between our beds, making the entire room shake. Clara was nearby, reading to the bandaged boy:

And it is I, Raksha [The Demon], who answers. The man's cub is mine, Lungri – mine to me! He shall not be killed. He shall live to run with the Pack and to hunt with the Pack; and in the end, look you, hunter of little naked cubs – frog-eater – fish-killer – he shall hunt thee!

Elsie aked if she could open a window. Like all enclosed spaces, the room was too hot for her.

'The boys like it warm,' I said disgruntledly. Just like Elsie to think she could come in here and change everything. I could tell there was something on her mind, and wished she'd just get on with it, forget the blasted temperature. You could only open the windows a little since one of the nurses, suffering 'temporary insanity', had thrown herself out head-first.

Eventually Elsie worked around to telling me what she had come here to say.

'The cellar had to go, Mairi. I mean, permanently go. We *can't* go back there.'

I felt sick.

'It served us well though,' she said. 'We helped hundreds, maybe thousands of men, Mairi.'

All those bandaged boys. All those dead boys. She looked at me as though I should join in the self-congratulations. But I couldn't. Something had been on my mind since I had arrived in hospital but it was now more important than ever before.

'What will happen when they come back?'

Elsie looked at me uncomprehendingly. 'The… soldiers?'

'No. The family who used to live there.'

They could send canaries down, I had heard. Or, if they didn't have any birds – for they were in high demand – you could lower a goldfish in a bowl full of water: if it comes up dead, it's gassed. If not, it's all right. We could at least make the cellar gas-free for them to return to. *Madeleine, we aren't going to let you down.*

'The family are not coming back.'

'Clitter-clatter!' cried Edward, jamming his hands over his ears.

'They *might*.'

Elsie didn't say anything else. She rummaged in her bag, pulled out a cigarette. 'Ed-ward!' She called to him in the same way she had called Shot. She smiled conspiratorially at me. '*I'll* light it for him this time.'

'They might, Elsie, they might,' I said hotly. She wasn't going to distract me. 'A lot of people went to England or Holland; they *will* come back.'

She nodded but it wasn't a proper nod.

'Some went to France.'

She *knew* something and she wasn't saying it.

'Or… Germany. Maybe they were taken there?'

The bandaged boy had fallen asleep at last. Clara quietly closed the book and tiptoed away, fluttering a wave at me and Elsie. She still had the elaborate delicacy of a newborn nurse.

'*Please*,' I begged. 'Please, Elsie, no more secrets.'

So Elsie told me.

The father had been away working. Not a doctor – *good guess, Mairi* – but another engineer. He ran his own business, successful by all accounts, in Ghent. It must have been a pleasant life before the war. At first the search party didn't think Madeleine or her brother were there – there was no sign of them – but a day later, once it was safe to go in, they found the body of the mother, and then, eventually, when they managed to lift her up, they found them, the boy and the girl, buried underneath her, her arms still wrapped around them both.

'No, no,' I whispered to Edward. 'Not my little girl.' I poured out all the obscenities I knew, and there were more than a few. You don't live a few yards from the Western Front without picking up some filthy phrases. There was something cathartic about it.

Edward didn't mind. In fact, he relished it. He responded 'Clitter-clatter!' back into my face excitedly. His grins, his gibberish and his sudden movements frightened Clara and the other nurses, but he didn't worry me any more. This handsome man who was in such agony. Maybe it *was* a good thing he was so far from home. *Who could bear to see him like this?*

I clutched him close as Elsie looked on impassively. He held me as I wept. I don't know how long we stayed like that, but when I next glanced up, Elsie had gone.

All the time I had been at the cellar house in Pervysye, dreams of that hard-working, loving, normal Belgian family had kept me going. I had never known that my sweet Madeleine – my not-so-good-at-English, bear-collecting, red-ribbon-wearing girl – was gone.

It was another thing Elsie had kept from me. She knew how it had sustained me, and yet she had me go on believing like a child. More lies. What a fool I was to have expected better from her.

*

They found Edward a place at a new psychiatric hospital in the south of England. 'Some big names have gone there,' Dr Munro said meaninglessly, or perhaps he was trying to reassure me. 'It's a centre of modern medicine,' he added. Dr Munro would never lose his enthusiasm for technological advancement. 'They might even give him electric shocks!'

He also said that there was no point in long-drawn-out goodbyes, so for Edward's sake – and for mine – I left the room when it was his time to go.

Through force of habit, I went through Edward's overcoat before he left. In his pocket I found a sepia photo – cut into an oval shape – of a little girl. She was maybe two or three years old, with white-blond curly hair. A beauty. Poor Edward's sister, or even his daughter? Perhaps he was older than he looked. The child had those tiny milk teeth that are so fresh to the world. Maybe this was how a young Madeleine had looked once.

Poor Edward. Poor everyone.

They had to strait-jacket him out, and he clitter-clattered and did his bitey thing all the way down the stairs. He struggled and railed all the way from the building to the car.

Clara decided to call the bandaged boy Mowgli: 'Because, he no longer lives with humans…' She looked embarrassed when she said it, like she thought I would think it was a stupid idea.

I said it was fine.

*

'You look far less purple now,' Elsie said when she came to visit the following week. She was trying to be agreeable.

'Thank you.'

'Healing up nicely then?'

'Yes.'

She looked over to the next bed. Edward had been swiftly replaced by another poor boy, Georgie, who had no legs. They were getting him home soon but he had some infection that was holding everything up. I'd heard the whisper of sepsis. He was awake all night and slept all day. He liked poetry and often read aloud from a notebook – violent lines about what he'd seen or would like to do, I was never quite sure. By his bedside, he had a large selection of Raphael Kirchner prints. I looked through them when he was asleep. They weren't all as saucy as I'd expected, but some were.

'The— Edward has gone?'

'Yes.'

'They'll take care of him, Mairi.'

'Yes.'

'He's not the only one suffering in that way.'

I didn't know how *that* could possibly cheer anyone up. How much better it would have been if Edward was just an anomaly, instead of one of thousands of traumatised humans locked out of society and into the terrible world of their own despair.

Elsie didn't sit this time, but swayed self-consciously at the end of my bed. I wondered if she had been drinking, or even been at the opium again, but it was unlikely. There were *some* things she was disciplined about. You had to give her that.

She had let her hair grow longer, or perhaps she couldn't find anyone who would cut it for her. Somehow, by hazard, it had turned into a short yet supremely fashionable bob.

'You heard that Harold and I will marry tomorrow?'

I gulped. I *hadn't* heard. I hadn't seen Dr Munro for a few days and he was the only one who would have told me. Perhaps he had been avoiding me?

I shook my head. 'You risk so much.'

'You think *this* is a risk? It's the least risky thing I have done in years!'

I couldn't help myself. 'It's a ridiculous idea.'

Elsie didn't rise to it at first. She stared at her hands, twisting her fingers around each other. I wondered if in some strange way she was waiting for my permission. Well, I wouldn't give it to her. 'You shouldn't do it, Elsie. It's not *fair.*'

Elsie would never let anyone get away with speaking to her like that. She raised her lip contemptuously.

'I'm sorry about Jack, my dear, but don't let what happened make you bitter.' She paused, her camouflage eyes locked on to mine. 'Bitter women make very poor company.'

Clara came in with my lunch on a plate on a tray. It was rabbit and mash. I had eaten better as a hospital patient than I had done in the last three years, but I couldn't eat with Elsie hovering at the end of my bed. Suddenly, I remembered the sparrows I'd caught, the sparrows I never told Harold about. Perhaps if I had, he might have looked at me differently.

When I had finished moving the food around, Elsie took the tray away and then tucked herself on to the bed, waiting for me to say something.

'So, tell me the plans?' I asked finally. It felt like she wasn't going anywhere until we had this out.

'What do you want to know?'

'Everything.'

'I have the most beautiful dress. Made by the Women's Institute in Dorset. It arrived in a lovely box in crepe paper. I feel as though the wings of excitement will fly me away!'

I didn't know what she meant. 'Harold found a church, then?'

'There are still a few that haven't been destroyed. Unbelievable, isn't it?'

I nodded.

'Hal is delighted.'

I knew she used the nickname to annoy me. She must have. He was Harold, not *Hal*.

'His family are sending a priest. They have their own priest, imagine!'

'They must be *very* religious people, Elsie.'

'Oh, they are. There are none so religious as the Belgian aristocracy.'

'You need to understand the implications of that,' I advised with some urgency. *How could I get across how important this was?*

Elsie got up. 'I do. Do you know, much as I hate this place, all of the… suffering… at least it *is* an exciting life. And when all of this is over, with Hal by my side, I will still have an exciting life. I am not going back to normality, Mairi. The humdrum English existence is not for me.'

I knew I must speak up for him. I must stand up for Harold. There was only me to do it after all. Everything we build, everything we have, is so, so precarious. Couldn't she see that? Only by keeping to the rules can we maintain the standards that we hold dear.

'What about love?'

Elsie tossed a look backwards. She paused. 'What exactly are you insinuating, Mairi?'

I wasn't even sure myself. 'Do you really love Harold?'

'Mairi! I am marrying the poor fellow! What on earth do you think?'

'Then you should tell him you're divorced. To him it will mean you are still married to someone else!'

'No!'

She walked away, slamming the door behind her. The bandaged boy groaned. Georgie let out a troubled snore. I heard Elsie's steps echo down the corridor. I felt sick so I drank some water and tried to get more sleep.

CHAPTER THIRTY-FOUR

Some nights later, I dreamed Uilleam and I were running: we were at our beloved Saunton and he was chasing me along the cliffs, only I think someone was chasing him too but I couldn't see them. I kept telling him to stop. I was shouting, I was near the edge, it was dangerous, but it was like we didn't speak the same language any more. And then he fell and he grabbed me but I jumped to the side, and he went over the cliff. I watched him fall all the way. He was flailing and flailing, his great overcoat flapping behind him, his pockets emptying into the wind, and there was nothing I could do.

When I woke up, I realised someone was standing over me. Opening one cautious eye, I saw who it was. Harold was here. Finally, he had come. He was in his uniform with its nipped-in waist, which somehow always seemed slightly girlish, and his trousers puffed up around his thighs. His eyes were bright and his chin was smooth – he always made sure it was now. I couldn't savour the moment for long – I was already scared he would leave.

'Harold?' I whispered.

'Mairi,' he said tenderly. 'Forgive me. I didn't mean to disturb your sleep.'

'You haven't,' I lied. 'I was just… thinking.' I pulled myself up and tried to look bright.

'No, the patient must not rise.'

'I'm not the patient,' I said, even though it must have been clear to both of us that I was.

I sat up as straight as I could. When I last looked in the mirror two days earlier, I wasn't half so frightful as I had been. But still. 'I look terrible—'

'Not at all.'

'But I've nearly recovered. I'll be out of here in no time.'

'Of course,' he agreed politely. 'And may I reassure you, they won't have to amputate.'

I smiled.

'See how our roles are reversed, Mairi!' he said. 'You remember the time we first met in the cellar house?'

How could he ever think otherwise?

'You reassured me that my leg would heal. And it did.'

I gave him a crooked smile. 'I remember. You won't try to sing to me though?'

It seems I learned something from Elsie after all.

'The Tipperary song? I cannot get the words right. And where is this Tipperary anyway? I will add it to the list of things about the English that I will never understand.'

Rummaging in his bag, Harold produced a bag of sweets. 'Your favourites.'

Marrons glacés. My mouth watered stupidly at the sight of them. Harold seemed pleased with himself. He wandered, restless, around the ward. He winced at the sight of sleeping Georgie – his leg-nubs on the sheets – and the bandaged boy.

'Are these sweets from the wedding breakfast?'

'Indeed. From the wedding *breakfast,* which we had at supper time. You see, the English *are* strange.'

'So… you did it? Congratulations.'

'Thank you!'

I had to ask more. 'How was it?'

'Magical. Truly the happiest day of my life. So many people came. Officers, engineers, old friends and new.'

All the survivors, I thought, *the lucky ones.*

I was about to ask if his old friend Ginger had showed up when he said: 'We were honoured that the queen was our witness.'

'The Queen of Belgium?'

This threw me. I thought of how we had narrowly missed her visit (if the rumour was true). And now Elsie had made her marriage vows in her presence!

Harold's skin was tinged with pink. 'She is a distant member of my family.' I vaguely remembered Elsie saying so, but I had thought it was for effect. He shook his head, embarrassed. 'Even Munro sent a telegram. I always told Elsie he was a marvellous fellow. Such a shame you couldn't be there, my friend.'

I wasn't sure if I'd been invited. I thought, *imagine if these fine people knew about my runaway homosexual brother.* That would have given them something to talk about.

The nurses were still clearing away the breakfast trays when Harold and I went for a walk. I leaned against him as he put his arm around me. It was almost perfect. It was only along the hospital corridor, yet we could have been walking down the Champs-Élysées in springtime. We could have been on our way to one of the many destinations we had sworn to visit 'after all of this is over'. Brussels, Bruges, the Tower of London. Harold staggered once, just slightly, and I remembered his leg. I don't think anyone would have been able to tell.

One of the nurses gave me a new look of respect and whispered, 'Nice one, Mairi.'

I wondered if Elsie knew Harold had come to see me. There wasn't a way I could find to ask.

We stopped at the end of the corridor since, to my shame, I was already tired. Harold politely pretended that he was tired too. We looked out the window. There were a few flowers in the distant fields. They hadn't been there, or at least I hadn't noticed them, three years ago.

Amazing how resilient nature can be. They were bright-red poppies – I had never really liked their bold, gaudy ways. I would have preferred a less pushy flower, a paler flower with a stronger scent perhaps. But still, it seemed to me at that moment that I was looking at something astonishingly beautiful. Something I might remember for a long time. Had they not each, in their own way, crawled out from darkness?

'How is Elsie, Harold?' I couldn't say 'your wife'.

'Back on the front. She sends her love, naturally.'

'Naturally,' I repeated. *She did know he was coming here then?*

'She is not at the cellar?'

I wanted to check that this, at least, was true.

'No, it's completely destroyed. The war shows no sign of abating – so she carries on. You know Elsie.'

Do I?

'She always wanted to protect you, Mairi,' he said. *You don't know the half of it,* I thought.

I imagined him introducing Elsie to his large family. 'The Madonna of Pervyse.' Did he tell them there were two of us? Tears came to my eyes. I couldn't help myself. 'I feel as though the war will never end.'

Harold took hold of my hand. I thought of all the time I had spent thinking about him and felt as though I should die of shame.

A couple of nurses clipped towards us, smart in freshly pressed uniforms, talking and smiling, trusting each other. Elsie and I probably used to look like that.

Clearing his throat importantly, Harold said. 'I was so sad to hear about your fiancé. What terrible luck. And in England too! He was flying?'

'Yes.'

'Knowing you loved him would have been a great comfort.'

Did he know I loved him? I didn't even know if he received my answer to his proposal.

'He was a Christian?'

I nodded, although I wasn't certain. That's how little I knew Jack, really. That's how little I knew anyone.

'Then Mairi, he is with the good Lord now.' Harold knew *me* though. 'The Kingdom of Heaven awaits. Bless you.'

We had run out of things to say. After a while, Harold got ready to leave and as he put on his coat, I saw nurses looking at him again the way soldiers looked at Elsie. They must make such a handsome couple. At the door, he turned back, shyly. It's silly, but for one stupid fleeting moment, I imagined he was going to declare that it was me he would love, forever.

'Everyone says you were amazing with the disturbed boy here.'

'I wasn't amazing,' I said truthfully. 'He deserved so much more.'

He nodded. 'There is so much suffering.'

It seemed to me that he wanted to say something else. I waited for it, whatever it was – biting my lower lip hard enough to draw blood, aching for him to continue.

I thought of Jack's letter: '*Sometimes, it's easier to think of myself not as an individual person, but just as one part of a great swathe of millions of people born and living around now. Just a segment, a cog in the wheel.*' Suddenly I understood what he meant.

Harold stood, wringing his hands. And then, here it came: 'You know, Elsie has such terrible dreams.'

'Yes.'

'I don't believe in ghosts.'

'No.'

'And yet—'

'It is *not* ghosts,' I said.

Maybe Elsie *wanted* me to tell him?

'But you have heard her terror, Mairi? Every night.'

'Yes.'

'It may sound far-fetched but… it sounds, it sounds like her late husband is haunting her from the grave!'

From that point, it couldn't have been much easier. He walked into it. Lord – for once, *I* was going to save everyone.

I had never felt so strongly about anything.

'That couldn't be further from the truth, Harold.'

CHAPTER THIRTY-FIVE

The November morning I was discharged was cool and grey-skied with barely a breeze in the air. I was lucky that (barring a torpedo hit) my crossing of the Channel was, once again, likely to be smooth. Clara, who had been copiously sick on her tumultuous journey over, was relieved on my behalf. 'Looks like you'll have untroubled waters today. You're so lucky, Mairi.'

When Dr Munro came to the ward, he looked smarter than usual: he had brushed down his thinning hair. I thought back to his visit to our house in Dorset, all that time ago, when I had thought he was after my hand. That hadn't been the only time I'd imagined innocent men were about to declare their love for me.

I wondered what life would be like if I had never joined the flying ambulance corps. Never come to help the war effort in Belgium. Never seen the things I had seen. Not lost my innocence in this way.

No, when all was said and done, I was glad I had made my contribution.

'Still such a young thing,' he said. I realised for the first time that Dr Munro had been like a father to me, and as soon as I realised this, I felt a pain that it had taken me so long to understand. *Who had taught me, who had guided me, who had believed in me?* It wasn't only Elsie.

'I'm twenty-one now,' I responded wearily. 'I certainly don't *feel* young.'

'Your whole life is ahead of you,' he said. I noticed how much he had aged these past few years. His moustache was completely silver now and he walked with a limp more marked even than Harold's.

'Well done, Mairi Chisholm. Order of the Belgian Empire. You and Elsie have done much to be admired—'

'No—' I began.

'You have taught me about teamwork! You two, living like that. So brave. So selfless. An inspiration. People must know what you achieved here. You saved thousands of lives.'

I think we both had tears in our eyes.

Clara looked between us, fascinated at such an emotional display from the reputedly unemotional doctor, then she gave me a cool kiss on the cheek. She had the address for poor Edward at his 'special' hospital.

'I bet he'd love to see you,' she said, pushing a folded piece of paper into my palm.

I said goodbye to the bandaged boy. A faint voice whispered back, 'Bye.'

Clara looked up at me with shining eyes. She whispered. 'That's the first time he's spoken since he was brought in.'

Dr Munro walked me from the room, carrying my few bits of luggage. Outside, we stood before the gates, the gates that were so difficult to enter on that dark, rainy night with injured men in the back of the car. Dr Munro was lending us his Wolseley ambulance to drive to the coast. It was a beast of a machine, a new design that was long and heavy, with a large screen and fat twin headlamps. Ten people could fit in the back.

'It drinks petrol like...' he said, shaking his head.

'Like Lady D drinks tea?'

'More like how Arthur drank rum.'

We laughed. He thanked me again and saluted me. His heels clicked together as he did.

Elsie was waiting by the ambulance. I hobbled over to her. I hadn't known how to use the walking stick at first. When to lean, when not to. Fancy having to be taught how to use a stick! It occurred to me that when I had sent off injured boys from the cellar, I had had absolutely no idea what struggles lay ahead of them.

I would have loved to have got behind the wheel of this vehicle, but Elsie said, 'Absolutely not!'

I hesitated.

'Come along, Mairi,' Elsie said kindly. 'Be a good patient.'

'That front wheel will need checking.'

'I know darling. Stop fretting.'

'Is there a spare?'

'Mairi. Everything is under control.'

I had just climbed in when I remembered. 'Oh, Shot!'

'Do you want me to come?' offered Elsie.

I told her there was no need.

During this time, hundreds of men had slipped through my fingers yet, incredibly, Shot's was the first proper grave with a headstone that I'd seen. They'd laid out a nice space marked with a small white-marble slab. Someone had laid a posy of flowers there. Dr Munro had said he'd try to get the stone engraved. I stared at it, thinking of my infinite list: *Nazareth, the German boy, the falling house, hundreds of boys in the trenches, the post-boy, Dr Gus, Elsie's brother Sam, my Jack… Sweet Madeleine.*

Our brave dog didn't deserve this. We should have protected him.

I never got to show Elsie how he could shake paws.

I prayed to God. I prayed for Him to forgive us all for our sins and I reminded Him that I was ready – as ever – to do his work.

I walked back to where Elsie was leaning against the car. She really was the picture of newly married health. One leg straight, one leg bent, she looked like she was posing for a photograph. I remembered one of the soldiers describing her as 'radiant'. One man told me that she was a reminder that there was life in the world. Another said that when Elsie came into the trenches, he thought of his mother, his wife and his baby daughter all rolled into one and he would do anything to make her proud of him.

'I'll come back soon,' I choked out. I felt overcome with emotion. Washed up and wrung out. I couldn't leave now; there was so much to attend to, so much to finish.

'You're not in good enough condition to even think about it yet,'
Elsie countered.

'I feel absolutely fi—'

'You really *have* been in the wars.' This was another of her
sayings.

'What times these are,' I replied coolly and she stared at me
uncertainly, as though she wasn't sure I wasn't laughing at her. We
started up and Clara and Dr Munro waved us off and then went
back into the hospital. That was the last I ever saw of them.

As she drove, Elsie told me she had salvaged some things from the
cellar.

'I didn't think—'

'It's not everything,' she cautioned, nodding to the drawstring
bag by my toes. 'But I did my best, Mairi.' And it seemed to me that
she was saying, *I always did.*

Holding the bag on my knees, I dug through its contents. The first
thing I found was a photo of us. You may have seen it – there we are,
side by side, in the middle of one joke or another. I look young and
determined – nothing like I did now. I could hardly reconcile that
simple face with how I felt inside. Elsie looks fierce and proud. No
photo that I know of has ever managed to capture Elsie's exceptional
beauty. It was like a secret only those who were there would ever know.

There was a second photo, one of Kenneth and his classmates.
There were about ten of them in the picture, but I could easily pick
out Master Kenneth Knocker from the other children. It was his dark,
alert, Elsie eyes and his shock of dark hair that gave him away. He
was the kind of child who old ladies would stop in shops to pinch his
cheeks and sigh, 'This one will break a few hearts!' or 'Why does the
boy always get the good looks?' That's what they always said to Uilleam.

Here were my letters from Jack, wrapped in Madeleine's red
ribbon. At the sight of these, I wanted to sob. Jack's love letters: *not*

telling, not telling. Full of his promises to be a better man for me. *Well, as it happens, Jack, you were the better one all along.*

'He loved you, Mairi.' Elsie looked over, her face wreathed in compassion. I wondered if she'd read them. Probably not. She wasn't the prying type.

I doubted I would be able to read Jack's letters for a long time.

There was Madeleine's bear – if it ever *was* her bear. There were Helen's limericks. She never did write one for Dr Munro, did she?

There were also a few articles from newspapers. I didn't know anyone had been cutting them out. There was the one that read HANDBAGS FOR SANDBAGS!, and another that I didn't recall ever seeing from March 1915: BEST FRIENDS ARE MORE LIKE SISTERS. There was an article with a photo that – God help me – made me look exactly like my father. There was also a scrap of paper, grimy and creased, which had the faded words '*Votes for Women*' on it.

I reached into the bottom of the bag, feeling that there was still something there. It felt like a book and for a moment I thought *it might be Madeleine's homework book and I won't be able to bear that.* Pulling it into the light, I realised it was just Helen's silly old romance. How I wished I hadn't read it. *Truly.*

Some puzzles don't need to be put together.

Along the road back to Ostend, there were burnt-out cottages, burnt-out villages, still more sandbags, barbed wire and troops coming in. We drove towards the coast, towards the arms factories, the chimney stacks and the man-made clouds. *It has to be over soon, doesn't it?*

I thought of those 250,000 Belgian refugees back in England. *I hope you are safe. I hope we looked after you.*

Down more country lanes – if you listened closely, there was the repetitive hum of the war. And you could still hear the birds. Why didn't the birds stop singing? I suppose they just carried on, like us.

Elsie and I were mostly silent, although she would occasionally comment on how the car was a dream to drive. 'Modern cars just keep getting better,' she said, sounding like Dr Munro.

As we drew nearer to our destination, I managed to find my voice. I said, 'Please send my love to… your husband.'

'You have no idea what pleasure it is to hear the word "husband".' Elsie smiled dreamily. Her hands moved on the wheel from nine to three to eleven to five. 'I will. I know how fond you are of Harold, Mairi. As he is of you.'

I stayed silent.

'And Mairi,' Elsie lowered her voice as though these modern cars had ears. 'You know I *will* tell him eventually.'

I just managed to get the words out. 'What do you mean?'

'Everything. About my… past.' She paused, pushing the car up a gear. 'Not now though. In my own time. When we are out of this hellhole. They sent him to northern France for two weeks. So, this is our honeymoon. Hal alone in Arras. Me here in Pervyse. Haven't heard a peep from him for ten days now. Ah, the romance! Not *quite* what the *New York Times* reported!'

She took her eyes off the road to aim a smile at me.

He already knows. I already told him. And you were right when you said that he wouldn't ever forgive you.

Elsie patted my thigh. 'I've been called a lot of things in my days, Mairi, but I have to say: *Baroness t'Serclaes* is my favourite.'

*

Here was Ostend. Here was the SS *Wandilla*. The floating hospital originally from Australia, now commissioned to transport the dead and nearly dead of Europe. No hustle and bustle today. Just a few ambulances pulling up as close to the side as they could and ambulance men dispatching the wounded like cargo. Today I was one of the cargo.

I knew Elsie would be itching to get back to the front to save more lives. I didn't want her to go yet. I didn't want it all to be over.

I was still drawn to her like soldiers to our cellar. I doubted I could live without her by my side. What did I have back in Dorset? Just two bewildered parents who wanted me to mend everything that was broken. It would be a poor substitute.

'I had better be off.'

'Please,' I said weakly, 'a few more minutes.'

Elsie looked surprised, as though it hadn't occurred to her that I might want more time.

'Oh, of course,' she said, touching her throat. 'I didn't think—'

Staring at the steering wheel, she admitted she was sorry that things between us weren't like they used to be. She said the stress, the strain, the number and the manner of the deaths had finally got to her. Her voice cracked as she said, 'You know that I'll always love you, Mairi.'

We sat on a bench overlooking some bathing machines. How had I not noticed them last time I was here? One day people would come back here and get changed again for family days out and picnics in the sand. I had a sudden memory of Uilleam and me running into the sea in stripy bathing suits, Uilleam insisting he didn't want to get his hair wet and me splashing and splashing.

A couple walked by. Him a soldier, her in civilian clothes, holding a baby. I couldn't tell if it was a boy or a girl. They were a tidy family of three.

'We'll come back again,' I heard the soldier tell the woman, 'After all this is over.'

I knew Elsie probably wanted to go but I clung on some more. Maybe it was a last chance for me to exert control. Anyway, Elsie looked relaxed and happy with the breeze caressing her face, but I would have bet anything that she was acting. Deep down she wanted to get away from me.

'Elsie, why *did* you get divorced?'

'What?'

'You did, didn't you? Your first husband – you divorced *him*? Not the other way around?'

'I divorced him, that's true.'

Another couple walked past us. These two were not bathers, nor holiday makers. They were both thin, painfully thin. They looked like bedraggled people from biblical times.

'Why?'

'Why do you think?' Elsie turned to face me. It was hard to speak with her looking directly at me like that; it was like looking into sunlight.

'What did Dr Munro used to say breaks a team – money? Hanky-panky? Or was it ego with you?'

'Ego?'

I was smiling as if it were a joke, but it wasn't. All my hurt, all my fury was welling up. She was a liar. Always had been. 'The great Elsie Knocker can't bear to be second to anyone.'

Yes, I was judgemental. That's who I was. I couldn't hide it any more. I felt I had to draw a line somewhere. A line in the sand. A line in the mud. I wasn't looking for revenge, I was looking for order. Standards had to be kept.

She was looking at her boots now. They were scuffed and mud-stained. Elsie never really cared for polish.

Finally, she spoke in her low, husky voice. 'I'll tell you why, if you really want to know.'

'Oh I do,' I said in my new, mocking tone.

She hesitated. I was still exasperated that she was pretending there was a good reason. Then she took a deep breath. 'He beat me in Java, Mairi. He tortured me.'

Her words didn't sink in straight away. They couldn't. The violent images they made just floated in front of my eyes.

'The sixth time he beat me, I left. Six times! I don't know what I was waiting for. He would have killed me in the end.'

My lips moved, but nothing came out. *My Elsie. My sister.* Who would dare to do that to her?

'Not every bad thing that ever happened is because of this dreadful war. Terrible things happened long before, Mairi, you just didn't know about them.'

The ship let out a nasty belching foghorn.

Elsie! I thought I'd said her name aloud but I hadn't. She had suffered so and what had I done? As my realisation grew, my face turned scarlet, giving me away. *Dear God*, I thought desperately. *Help me.*

Elsie could usually read me like a book, but for once she wasn't looking at me. She was just gazing at her hands.

'But with Harold, things will be different. I always wanted to give Kenneth a good father. The father he deserves. A life free of brutality and violence. A life of love.'

I was so drenched with horror and confusion that I could barely breathe. Everything felt upside down. All my certainties had been smashed. *I need time to digest*, I told myself, *I just need to work out the implications*, but deep down, I knew it was too late for that. No excuses. I had betrayed her.

Finally, I managed to mumble, 'I'm sorry,' but I don't think she even heard me, so intent was she in getting her story across. 'But I'm a survivor, Mairi. And so are you, my darling. Your war is over now. Safe journey.'

She leaned forward before I could say any more and whispered, 'Where would I be without my Mairi?' Then she strutted over to the Wolseley and ostentatiously sounded the horn so that everyone looked at the car and at her. A few men whistled admiringly as Elsie drove away.

CHAPTER THIRTY-SEVEN

I didn't last long in Dorset. A few months' recuperation was more than enough. In February 1918, I found work in a London hospital for demobbed soldiers and lodged in quarters nearby. I met a Belgian girl there, Martha, who by coincidence was from Poperinghe. She had sad grey eyes, which I suspect hid sadder tales than mine. Whereas Elsie and I were opposites, Martha and I were alike in many ways. We were both private, quiet and industrious. She seemed to understand me without my needing to say much.

I didn't stop thinking about Elsie and what I had done. I wrote to her care of Dr Munro, but my cards and letters were returned, unopened, I think. The pocket watch I had engraved came back and it had lost its time. Martha told me to 'forgive myself', and even said 'there's nothing to forgive', but I knew I would never feel quite at peace again.

I had made a most terrible mistake.

I joined a small church with an understanding vicar who had served in Vimy. When I prayed, I felt the Lord's forgiveness, but alas, the relief was only temporary. Back in the real world, my darkness never seemed to lift.

*

The war staggered on until November 1918. When the armistice came, I stayed put in London. I was trying to work out what to do or where to go. I felt a pull to Scotland, yet I was hesitant to cut the cord with my parents. I didn't make them happy, but the thought that I might move north made them unhappier.

I gained a reputation for being a good nurse. I was not the most educated or most innovative, but I was reliable and caring. I *was* a good nurse, but I felt like such a worthless person that it didn't mean much to me.

In December, I was put on a ward for the mentally disturbed. There were twelve patients. A few of the men slept day and night and some refused to speak. Loud noises triggered one man, Henry, who would jump under his bed at any bang or clatter. But mostly, we were surprisingly jolly, doing crafts and playing games. The post suited me. It was most uncomfortable when the patients' bewildered mothers or wives came in. They all said the same thing, 'He wasn't like this before, you know, before the war.'

'The war changed everything,' I'd reply, not only because it was the stock phrase that Matron used, but also because I knew it to be true.

I had a letter from poor Edward's young wife, who wrote that Edward was doing as well as could be expected. They planned to take him to watch the cricket next summer. I felt too fragile to visit him but I hoped I would find the strength one day. At night, I'd return to my lodging house, where I sometimes ate with Martha; but more often, because of our shifts, I ate alone and then went to bed.

I had so many terrible memories that there weren't enough good ones in the world to replace them. The one I couldn't wipe out – the one I thought of last thing at night, and first thing in the morning – was not of the boys in the trenches or even my poor shy Jack trapped in a burning plane. It was the look on Harold's face in that hospital room when I told him that Elsie was already married. A house without windows, like a face without a soul. All hope, passion and love flew out of Harold at that moment.

*

It was the first New Year's Eve at peace in five years and London was celebrating with fireworks and street parties. I had offered to do the night shift until 6.00 a.m., sleep for a few hours and then come in for a shorter shift at midday. I didn't need much sleep and it meant that the nurses who had families could spend time with them.

Late afternoon, on the first day of January 1919, I was counting out tablets during craft time when I heard a roaring sound outside, the unmistakeable noise of a large motorcycle. I watched Henry carefully, but this sound, thankfully, didn't trigger him and he carried on meticulously looping pieces of string around some wood.

Matron scowled. 'Dear God. Some soldiers don't know when to stop!' And I smiled to myself because no one here knew that I used to be a motorcycle girl.

The noise continued unabated.

I went downstairs to give the noisy soldier a ticking off. Also, I was curious to see what sort of bike made such a cacophony. Pushing out through the double doors into sunlight, I looked up and there she was: Elsie. I had forgotten how distinctive she was. You couldn't mistake her for anyone else. Straddling the bike, revving the engine, she was waiting for me.

'What took you so long?' she asked.

'Elsie!?'

'Not bad, is it?' She grinned down at her bike. It was a Triumph Model H, 550cc if I wasn't mistaken. A beauty. They didn't come cheap. 'Fancy a race?'

I stared. I couldn't quite believe it was her.

'I don't have anything to ride,' I said. 'Besides, you always beat me anyway.'

'Really?' she answered drily. She looked me directly in the eyes. 'I think you got me in the end, Mairi.'

I flushed. If she had read any of my letters she would have known how shame, stupidity and remorse had swallowed me up. Or perhaps she *had* somehow read my letters and had come back to shout at me, to finish me off. It was nothing more than I deserved.

'I'm so sorry,' I said, as sincerely as I had ever said anything.

'You should be,' Elsie said, but then her lips curved into a smile. 'I'm sorry too.'

*

I had two more hours of my shift. Elsie said 'fine', she had friends to see – of course she did. The next two hours couldn't pass quickly enough for me. Billy tripped over Charlie's chair, they both got agitated, then I had to see to Billy's gammy leg. I played rummy with Albert, who was a frightful cheat. At eight, I ran down the stairs, calling out goodbye to Martha, who had just arrived. I was fearful that Elsie wasn't going to be there, or even that I had imagined the whole thing. Perhaps I was going mad after all – some said it was contagious. But there Elsie was, leaning against a postbox, this time without her bike.

Elsie and I walked alongside the river, the cobbled paths wet with overflow. The sun was drawing down over the Thames and the Houses of Parliament stood serenely to our right as beautiful as any picture on a jigsaw. We stopped to buy delicious-smelling roasted chestnuts, out of sympathy for the vendor more than anything. He had only one eye, and he told Elsie that he'd left the other one in Passchendaele.

We sat crunching nuts on a wall overlooking the river, and I was waiting and waiting for Elsie to tell me what had brought her back.

'How's Kenneth?'

'An absolute darling. Still rotten at chess though. Your brother?'

'On the run, living illegally in America.' I said, thinking of his last letter, full of rich descriptions of the past and nothing of the present. 'Causing my parents no end of distress.' I paused, guiltily remembering Elsie's lost brothers. 'But he is alive so we are thankful.'

'Uilleam, isn't it? I want to meet that scoundrel again,' she said, and her 'again' reminded me of that time, many moons ago, we'd first met on that rainy day in 1914 when I had raced myself off course.

Elsie asked if I had been to visit Jack's family, and I flushed because I hadn't, *not yet*, and it was another thing I was ashamed about.

'It's hard,' Elsie sympathised. But I remembered that Jack had gone all the way to Glasgow to meet the family of a lost pilot friend. I knew I had to go and I resolved to see the Petrie family in Ingatestone before January was out. I would tell them how 'Flying Jack' was loved. About his passion for planes, how he stacked chairs, worried about cockles and how he was a puzzlemaker extraordinaire.

For the first time, I found myself smiling at the memory of my Jack.

Elsie also told me Lady D was no longer in the (imaginary) proud spinsters' club, but had married a handsome Canadian she'd met while making tea on a hospital ship. They were leaving for Ontario in spring. I wondered if she would continue her campaign for 'Votes for Women'. Helen and Arthur were living together in New York. Helen was working on a children's book. Arthur was trying his hand at the illustrations.

'What's this book called?' I asked apprehensively.

Elsie made a face. '*Shot Wins the War*'.

My heart leapt at the thought of our floppy-eared innocent dog.

Elsie continued. 'The *New York Times* writes: "The world anticipates Eleanora Mountford's eulogy to a twentieth-century hero – her best friend".

'Shot was *Helen's* best friend?'

Elsie sniggered in response, which set me off. Despite my tension, I couldn't stop giggling and neither could she. We clutched our ribs, and then each other, howling with mirth. It was like the early days in the cellar.

'So,' I said when we had finally stopped and there were no more distractions. I had to know now. 'How *is* Harold?' My swallow seemed louder than the revving of a thousand motorbikes.

'Ah,' Elsie said. 'Harold.'

*

I half thought she might say that they were living in a Bruges town-house and the Queen of Belgium popped in for waffles every other Sunday, but my heart – and my conscience – told me otherwise.

About a week after I had left Belgium, Elsie had gone to meet him at a hotel. He told her straight away that he didn't believe in divorce. He said that his family wouldn't accept her. She insisted that she and Kenneth were his family now. He said that you had to stick to the rules. I could imagine it – Elsie throwing up her arms like she had around the kitchen table with Arthur and Helen all that time ago: *'I'm saying, look where the rules get us – this urge to have the cutlery in its place, it lands us in trenches. It lands us in No Man's Land.'*

Harold wouldn't bend.

She continued to argue – it was a matter of pride. He said he couldn't trust her and she shouted. Had she not been caring for the sick and the dying in a tiny cellar, living alongside bats and rats, with nits in her hair, for years on end? Didn't that make her a good person? But nothing had moved him.

'I love you, Harold,' she had told him.

'And I…' He put on his cap and walked out.

She had never seen nor heard from him since.

*

'So it's back to Gilberts for me,' Elsie said.

'I'm sorry,' I repeated. I couldn't think of anything else to say.

'I was furious,' she admitted. 'I hated you,' she added matter-of-factly. She lit a cigarette and inhaled deeply before looking at me. 'And then I thought… you would have made a better match for him, Mairi. I should have known that all along.'

We sat there while flocks of birds circled overhead, over the Houses of Parliament, over Big Ben, in their remarkable patterns. Each one of them travelling far from home, but each one of them knowing their place.

I was going to ask what had prompted her forgiveness – *why now?* – but I didn't have to say anything. She read my mind as usual.

'Life's too short to quarrel.' She sighed. 'You'd think I'd have learned that. Besides, Munro threatened to make me do naked yoga until I agreed to meet you.'

I laughed at the idea.

'He sends his love. He remembers the day he met you. He says you've become such a strong, independent woman. You should be proud of yourself.'

I was weeping a little by now, but these were happy tears. To be side by side with Elsie again, after all this time, was such a relief. Even if we never clapped eyes on each other again, I would always have this moment. I felt extraordinarily blessed.

'We did our best,' she said.

'We did,' I whispered.

She took my hand in hers. 'I've missed you so much Mairi.'

I was too choked up to speak.

My scalped *sister.*

Elsie Knocker – 'Gypsy', motorcyclist nurse, dare-devil mother – one of only two women on the Western Front and the best friend I ever had.

A LETTER FROM LIZZIE

A huge thank you to you for choosing to read *The War Nurses*. I do hope you enjoyed it.

If you want to keep up to date with my latest releases, just sign up at the following link. I can promise that your email address will never be shared and you can unsubscribe at any time.

www.bookouture.com/lizzie-page

It was a great pleasure to write *The War Nurses*. I am in awe of Elsie and Mairi and all the other women who served with such dedication. I hope stories such as this help to shine a light on their contributions. They will not be forgotten.

I am currently working on Book Two in the trilogy: *The War Nurses at Christmas*. Elsie's friend, May Turner, is struggling to keep her family together while she works at a field hospital in the Somme.

If you enjoyed reading *The War Nurses*, I would be very grateful if you could write a review. I'd love to hear what you thought. How did you feel about what Elsie and Mairi did in Belgium? Who were your favourite characters? Were you pleased or surprised by the ending? Your reviews also make a difference in helping new readers to discover one of my books for the first time.

It's always wonderful to hear from my readers – please feel free to get in touch directly on my Facebook page, or through Twitter, Goodreads or my website.

Thank you so much for your time,
Lizzie Page

 @LizziePagewrite

🄵 lizzie.page.75

AUTHOR'S NOTE

This is a fictionalised account of the friendship between the war heroes Elsie Knocker and Mairi Chisholm. Their immense bravery and dedication saved hundreds of lives and earned them several honours including: Knights Cross of the Order of Leopold 11 with palm, Military Medal, Officer of the Order of St John of Jerusalem, Order of Queen Elisabeth of Belgium and 1914 Star.

What Happened Next...

Elsie and Harold separated, but Elsie was allowed to keep the title Baroness as part of their settlement. She became a senior officer in the Women's Auxiliary Air Force for many years, working with RAF Fighter Command. Tragically, her son, Wing Commander Kenneth Duke Knocker, was killed when his plane was shot down in 1942.

Elsie left the RAF that same year to look after her elderly foster-father. After the Second World War, she helped raise funds for the RAF Association and the Benevolent Fund. Later, she began breeding chihuahuas and campaigned for animal welfare and the conservation of Ashtead Common, Surrey, where she walked her pets. Elsie died aged 93 of pneumonia and senile dementia in 1978.

She never remarried.

Mairi Chisholm joined the WRAF, and later took up auto racing. She was scheduled to take part in a big race at Brooklands, but had to withdraw because of a fainting episode. She would suffer from ill-health for the rest of her life.

She became a successful poultry breeder with her childhood friend, May Davidson, on the Davidsons' family estate in Nairn, Scotland. In the 1930s, they relocated to Jersey.

In 1981, Mairi Chisholm died of lung cancer, aged 85, in the home she had shared with Davidson for almost 60 years.

She never married.

ACKNOWLEDGEMENTS

I first heard about Elsie Knocker and Mairi Chisholm in a thread on Mumsnet about women who've done remarkable things but aren't well-known. All the women mentioned sounded fascinating but Elsie and Mairi appealed to me in particular. I loved their determination to make a positive difference and I wanted to share their story. I feel very grateful to them and indeed to all those who risk their lives to protect others.

If you are interested in finding out more about Elsie and Mairi, I found *The Cellar house of Pervyse: a tale of uncommon things from the journals and letters of the Baroness t'Serclaes and Mairi Chisholm* by Geraldine Edith Milton, published 1917, a fabulous online resource.

I also highly recommend *Elsie and Mairi Go to War: Two Extraordinary Women on the Western Front*, by Diane Atkinson, published 2010.

The Imperial War Museum and the National Library of Scotland have interviews and resources related to both women. There are some tremendous groups on Facebook and Twitter whose posts have been very helpful, including: Lucy London's 'Inspirational Women of WW1', Deborah Cameron's 'Remembering Women on the Home Front WW1', Sue Robinson's 'Wenches in Trenches', 'Sheroes of History' and many more.

Thanks also to the fabulous t'Binnenhuis, a beautiful place to stay in Ypres, and gratitude to the lovely guides who took me around the area and gave me more insight and stories. At the Hotel Ariane, Ypres, they have a statue of Elsie, Mairi and Shot in the garden.

Thanks also…

To Therese Coen, my agent at Hardman and Swainson, for her support and persistence in the face of this author's pessimism.

To Kathryn Taussig, a great editor with a gentle touch. Perfect ability to steer me away from the darkness and towards the light.

To Bookouture, an innovative, exciting and, most importantly, *relevant* publishing company. The perfect home for *The War Nurses*.

To Reuben, Ernie and Miranda, for making it all worthwhile

To Steve, love, forever.